The Werewolf Assassin

- Book 2 of the Divinity Stone Series -

Steven Wombell

First edition paperback and hardcovers were produced in 2023.

Edited by Emmanuel Odukogbe

Book design by Thea Magerand

9780645379334 (e-book)
9780645379341 (paperback)
9780645379358 (hardcover)

www.stevenwombell

I would like to dedicate this book to two people, Josephine Webse and Dephress Betts. Both ladies were a big part of my life. Josephine was like a second mother to me and Dephress was both a friend and the mother of my niece Dana. They were good natured, caring and provided me with love and support. Unfortunately, they have both tragically passed away. They will be sorely missed.

Map of South-Western Kalmeer

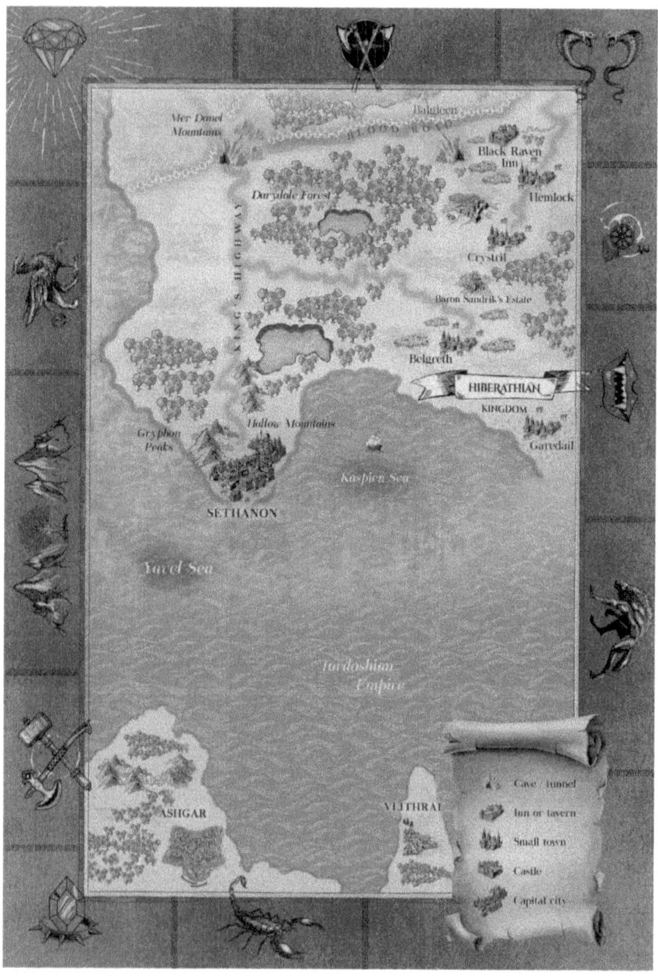

$\mathfrak{Chapter\ 1}$

The three-quarter moon illuminated the Blood Road, the dark red gravel weaving its way along like a trail of blood. The horse's hooves were padded, barely making any noise as it galloped along. Midnight was like a shadow in the night, his black coat melting into the darkness. Darla sat casually in the saddle, entirely dressed in black. Her clothes were designed for stealth and were virtually invisible.

* * *

A bedroll and a large satchel laden with food and supplies were strapped to the saddle. Two canteens and a quiver full of bolts hung from the side of the saddle while the two enchanted, long-bladed daggers and her mystical short sword were strapped securely to her belt. The heavy, bulky repeater crossbow hung strapped to her back, digging into her side and causing her to grimace. "I don't know how he manages to carry this damn thing around," she grumbled, readjusting the strap.

Darla had left early in the morning under the cover of darkness. She had snuck out of the Black Raven like a thief in the night. Unsure of how to phrase things or explain to Marek about the wyvern's presence, she had decided not to say anything and hope for the best. As it turned out the wyvern had not only left but had also cleaned up after itself. Darla had been pleasantly surprised. The hay was not neatly stacked in tightly woven bales but in a neat heap. Most of it was salvageable and could be reused. It eased her conscience. Marek wouldn't have to order more hay from overseas. He'd be able to make do until spring.

She rode silently focusing on her task and guiding Midnight with the light cast from the moon and stars. Besides the faint clip-clop of the horse's hooves, the only other sound was the wailing wind. Whether it was the wind blowing through the trees or the ghosts of the long dead fallen soldiers beckoning her, she didn't care. She wasn't afraid of the ghosts.

Monsters far worse roamed the night…and she was one of them.

A clattering noise sounded, along with a bobbing lantern light. A wagon thundered down the road, its wheels clanking as the horses galloped, spraying up gravel. Darla could see the two men at the head of the wagon looking around nervously. Merchants, no doubt, they seemed spooked and desperately trying to get to the Black Raven. Most travellers usually avoid travelling along the Blood Road at night. Darla smiled. She, on the other hand, had no qualms about it. For her, it was the best time to ride.

She heard a roar that was faint and distinct. Dawn was approaching and Darla could see a familiar shadow circling lazily in the sky through the soft light of the morning sun. It was clever, keeping to the human side, knowing full well that the elves still lurked within the forest. The wyvern let out another roar as it searched, scanning the surrounding area. It was hunting. Darla recalled reading a passage depicting how their distant dragon cousins utilised a similar tactic to flush out prey. It darted down, swooping as some deer erupted from the tree line. "Looks like our friend is about to have his breakfast."

The response was a snort and a brief flicker of Midnight's head as if saying, *'That's just fine, as long as we're not part of his breakfast menu.'* Darla merely shook her head as she guided her horse along the dirt path. Reaching into her saddlebag, she grabbed two apples and gave one to Midnight. He bit the apple in half with a crunch. "Maybe I'm fattening you up for his lunch menu," she said, giggling. Midnight snorted and shook his head. She realised what he was saying, although he couldn't talk. *'That's not even funny. You need me too much.'* Darla patted his mane affectionately. "You are right, we're partners. We need each other." A snorted chuckle was her answer, *'Do we?'* Again, Darla just shook her head and laughed. Her horse was intolerable, but she wouldn't have him any other way.

As she was about to bite her own apple, a voice resounded in her head. *'Thank you and goodbye, my friend.'* Startled, Darla nearly dropped her apple. She turned and saw the wyvern hovering nearby. "You can speak telepathically?" She realised how stupid the question must have sounded as soon as the words left her mouth. She blushed, embarrassed, as the wyvern chuckled telepathically.
'All wyverns and dragons can communicate with telepathy,' he explained.

"Why didn't you speak to me before?" Darla asked.
'Because your kind have hunted and persecuted us.'
"I may be an assassin, but I have morals. I only kill when it is required," Darla explained.

The wyvern nodded in understanding. *"It takes a lot to earn our trust. It was last night that I realised you were truly a friend.'* She patted Midnight, calming him, as the wyvern lowered itself to her level. It opened its claw and gently placed something in her hand. It was large, sharp and heavy. It was one of the wyvern's teeth. *'I am heading back to my homeland where it is colder. The tooth contains part of my magic and is linked to me. Carve it into a horn. If you ever find yourself back in the dwarven lands, blow the horn and I will come.'*

"Thank you and safe travels, my friend," Darla replied, nodding her thanks. With two mighty flaps of its wings, the wyvern lifted itself high and flew off to the north-west. Drawing her dagger, she got to work and started scraping out the tooth. While she worked, Midnight trotted quietly along the path. Darla couldn't help but wonder if she would ever see the wyvern again.

The paths were easy to navigate and enabled them to remain inconspicuous. Darla felt at home in the woods due to her lycanthropy, possibly because she knew the forest like the back of her hand. She knew where all the trails, streams, caves, camp sites and hunting spots were. The forest also helped to conceal her, especially with having a large, cumbersome crossbow strapped across her back. It was a sure way to draw unwanted attention.

Pulling on the reins, she slowed to a trot. They were nearing the Sandrik Road, the road the royal party would travel down. The road was named after the baron's family, whose lineage went back generations. She was on a gently sloping hill, with a couple of trees and bushes providing her with ample cover. "And now we wait," she said, plucking an apple out of her saddlebag and giving it to Midnight to munch on. Then, dismounting, she took a bite of her apple and patted the horse affectionately.

Darla took another bite and the sweet juice from the apple dribbled down her chin. She paused mid-crunch as a noise caught her attention. Her keen hearing alerted her to the sound, even though it was at least a mile away. It wasn't the wyvern. It had disappeared for the moment. Instead, the noise was originating down the road. Horses!

She could hear their iron-shod hooves crunching on the gravel and judging from the sound, there were at least a dozen of them. Concentrating, she counted – eighteen, nineteen, twenty horses. Plus, a slower, more methodical crunching, that of a dozen driving horses. And amid the crunching was another sound, two very distinctive clunking noises. One slow and one slightly faster. The wooden wheels of a carriage and two supply wagons. "Fuck," Darla cursed. She had allowed more than enough time, yet somehow the royal convoy had arrived early.

The convoy rounded the corner, confirming her suspicions. There were twenty guardsmen, the royal carriage and two slow supply wagons. It explained why they were early. There was a smaller retinue. But why? What had changed? What had gone wrong? Darla felt a knot in the pit of her stomach. She had a bad feeling about this. She gave a quick, brief hand signal, a silent command and with a snort, Midnight knelt next to her. To be spotted now would ruin everything. It would be better to let them pass and then follow from a distance, concealed by the shadows and the forest.

Rayze woke abruptly to the sound of fighting. The tent flapped open, revealing a silhouetted figure in the doorway. An elf! "Where is the divinity stone thief?" the elf spat, pointing his sword at Rayze's chest.

"The last time I saw it, it was sticking out of your mother's arse," he smirked, unable to help himself. Stepping into the threshold, the elf smiled wickedly as the tent flap opened further. Three of his comrades entered, each brandishing their weapons. One held a sword, while another swung a flail. The last elf had an unusual weapon, a broad short sword with a blade of unique jagged teeth. Its elvish name was *Rekaerb edalb,* a sword breaker. A master dwarven blacksmith designed it. Rayze didn't know whether magic was behind it, but the unique design enabled the weapon to snap sword blades. Reaching across his shoulder, he drew 'Nightbringer', its obsidian blade as black as midnight. The gem inserted into the pommel radiated, casting the tent in an eerie purple light. "So, who would like to die first?"

* * *

Screaming the elves charged forward, their swords raised. The other two slowly circled around him, flanking him and waiting for an opportunity. The first elf slashed downwards, a powerful, swift stroke that Rayze quickly blocked and deflected to the side. Within an instant, the second elf was there, his stroke more precise and calculated, but just as deadly. Rayze's swordsmanship was fluid and graceful though, with his feet already in the perfect position, allowing him to pivot, raise his sword and block the stroke. With a screeching of metal, the elf pulled his sword free, only for another weapon to take its place. The sword breaker!

The unique teeth had locked the blade in place, trapping the sword. A high-pitched whirring sounded and Rayze risked a quick sidelong glance. The spiked iron ball of the flail was spinning at a phenomenal speed. The leather boots that the elf wore were obviously new and not worn in. Rayze could hear the slightest creaks they made as the man walked, as he neared striking distance and prepared to attack.

Rayze had assumed that the elves were fanatical and disorganised. Instead, they had proven to be a cohesive unit. They were unified, their attack fluid and flawless. An ordinary man would have become frantic, panicked and tried to free his sword. The blade would have shattered, he would have been rendered weaponless and his skull would have been caved in by the flail. Rayze was no mere swordsman though. He was a master in his own right, well-trained, battle-hardened and disciplined. And his sword was no ordinary sword. It was the mythical and divine Nightbringer, infused with ancient, powerful magic. Rayze smiled as he waited and bided his time.

One of the swordsmen moved, positioning himself next to the elf with the sword breaker. "Now, where shall I stab you?" he said casually, waving his sword around. Even in the dim lantern light, Rayze could see that something coated the blade. It had a silver sheen to it. What was it? It was a brief and quick thought, but Rayze berated himself for the distraction. It had been reckless. The flail wielding elf stepped closer, about to make his move. It was time. Rayze had hoped the other swordsman would join the other two, but he had disappeared momentarily. He acted, twisting the blade and slashing the sword breaker.

The teeth shattered and the sword breaker snapped in half. The elf gaped, shocked and wide-eyed at the broken weapon before him. It was unheard of for a sword breaker to split in half. The swordsman was just as shocked as he stood there holding his sword in trembling hands. The whirling was close, the spiked ball swinging at velocity. Rayze pivoted, swinging Nightbringer up as he spun. He was like a dancer, his movement graceful, precise and perfect. The spiked ball grazed his cheek, scratching and drawing blood.

Using the momentum of the spin, Rayze slashed diagonally. He was like an angel of death, reaping the adversaries before him. Recovering, the elvish swordsman tried to block, but it was a futile gesture. The legendary sword sliced through the first elf like butter before connecting with the swordsman's sword. There was an explosion of shards as the sword shattered, before Nightbringer continued its deadly arc and decapitated the elvish swordsman. Wiping blood from his cheek, Rayze turned to the elf responsible. "I'm going to rip that spiked ball off and ram it down your fucking throat."

The elf continued swinging, unfazed by the threat. Readjusting his grip, Rayze tried to focus. His eyesight had become blurry and his face felt like it was burning. The flail swung and Rayze leaned back and swung his sword across his body. The spiked ball narrowly missed his face, soaring past and smashing into the obsidian blade. Spikes severed and flew like darts, embedding themselves in the walls. The chain snapped, cut cleanly in two and the chipped ball fell to the ground. Panicking, throwing the broken flail at him, the elf slowly began to back away.

The faint sound of his footfall was the only thing that gave him away. Rayze was in the middle of a turn when the sword erupted through his shoulder. Turning was the only thing that had saved him, changing his positioning and stopping the blade from piercing his heart. Nevertheless, the injury stung. The pain was excruciating, burning like the seven hells, and his arm hung by his side, dead and useless. Gritting his teeth, Rayze reversed his grip. The simple act was slow and tedious, taking every ounce of his concentration and willpower. He then plunged Nightbringer backwards, impaling the elf behind him.

Releasing his sword, the elf tried desperately to free the blade, but Rayze held Nightbringer firm. With a scream of rage, he then sliced the elf up the middle, cutting through muscle and bone as easily as paper. Blood sprayed as Rayze changed his grip and guided the blade through the elf's skull. The elf's spine was cut into two, and his torso was a bloodied mess as it flopped to each side.

Rayze looked like the walking dead, pale and covered in blood. Sheathing his sword, he looked down and noticed the sword still protruding from his shoulder. It was coated with the same silver sheen. Reaching up, he carefully touched it with his glove. It was a powder of some kind. Sniffing, he almost gagged. It was silver oak, a compound that was lethal to werewolves and poisonous to vampires. It posed the question of whether it was meant for him, or if they had intended it for Darla. As he staggered towards the remaining elf, he carefully picked up the spiked ball and examined it. It was, as he suspected, coated in the same silver powder. He held it delicately, making sure not to touch it. Then, glaring at the elf, he continued to stagger towards him. The elf was petrified. "What the fuck are you?" he stammered.

"Your worst fucking nightmare," Rayze replied, reaching behind his back and slowly pulling the sword free. The elf screamed as he backed into the tent wall. Who is this person? A creature from nightmares perhaps? If only the elf knew he wasn't far from the truth. Rayze pried his ring off his finger with his thumb and let it drop into his palm. His features automatically transformed, revealing who and what he was. The elf screamed, maniacal and insane. A high-pitched sound that resembled a screech. His eyes were tightly closed and his mouth was wide open. A puddle formed on the floor as the elf wet himself. It was precisely the reaction Rayze wanted.

Using every ounce of his supernatural strength, he rammed the spiked ball into the elf's mouth, shattering his jaw. The spiked ball was rammed with such force it got stuck in the elf's throat, causing an unnatural bulge as the remaining spikes protruded at various angles. Wheezing and gasping for breath, the elf collapsed, writhing until he died. "Promise made, promise kept," Rayze spat, slipping the ring back on his finger.

The illusion appeared as the magic took effect, and his appearance was again masked. His timing was perfect as the tent flap opened immediately and Brenan poked his head in. His lieutenant stood next to him, holding his battle-axe and covered in blood. "I'm fine," he said, smiling, noticing Rayze's look of concern. "It's mainly elf blood. I think I'll be sleeping in the barracks when we return though. The tirade I'm going to get from my wife." He shook his head. "She's going to have one hell of a job getting the blood out."

* * *

With a flicker, Brenan's eyes scanned the tent. He nodded at Rayze, acknowledging his fighting prowess and how he handled the situation. It was high praise, coming from the captain. The captain raised his eyebrows when he noticed the protruding spiked ball in the elf's throat. "The elves have declared war with this attack. Prince Zane needs to be informed. We ride now." The captain turned to go but stopped as Rayze dropped to his knees. The poison was taking effect. Rayze was sweating profusely. "What's wrong?" Brenan asked, concerned.

"Poison. Silver o..." Rayze didn't get to finish the word. He collapsed to the ground, limp and unconscious. *Silver oak!* It was rare for someone to have a reaction to silver oak. Hell, it was a common ingredient used in cooking. And Rayze had distinctly used the word poison. He would keep his mouth shut for now, but there was definitely more to Rayze than met the eye.

"Lieutenant! Help him onto his horse and tie him down to keep him secure." Brenan briefly thought of using the cart but discarded the option. Time was of the essence and there was always the possibility of the elves or humans pursuing. It had been complete and utter chaos. Their main enemy had been from within, traitors in their midst. They were the king's men, people they called their brothers. They had joked with them, shared food and drink with them, while they had secretly waited until a pre-arranged time and then attacked.

* * *

It had happened just before dawn, under the cover of darkness. It had been perfectly timed, orchestrated just before the shift change. The 'Beast' carried Rayze out delicately as though he was a child. His bulging arms were the size of small tree trunks. The lieutenant's nickname was Beast due to his size and imposing look. It was adequate, suited him and the lieutenant liked it. "Keep his horse steady, damn you," he shouted to the rookie of their squad. The horse was anxious, bucking and ready to get going. Even their well-trained horses were on edge and skittish.

Rayze's horse, Fang, saw an opening, and kicked. It was an almost-playful kick, but even shielded by his sword scabbard, the rookie was still going to sport one hell of a bruise. Rayze had named the horse Fang due to his heritage and race. With soothing words, Brenan approached and gently stroked the horse's neck, urging him to relax. The lieutenant approached and dropped Rayze unceremoniously in the saddle. "Now, someone get me some damn rope," he shouted.

He held Rayze in the saddle while the rookie limped off. The base camp was a shamble, a battlefield littered with dead bodies and destruction. The glimmer of dawn was approaching, the remnants of night slowly fading from the sky. The meadow was ablaze, lit up like a beacon, a giant bonfire. Wagons were on fire, their wooden frames cracking as they collapsed, forming a charred, burning debris pile. A horse raced past, panicked, its rider dead and ablaze from a flaming arrow. Tents were also alight, the flames dancing as their canvas flapped in the breeze. Some still had occupants inside, their screams echoing in the night as they were burnt alive.

Brenan had suspected that Prince Jerrick was behind the attack until he saw the prince engaged in his own skirmish. Either the prince was an excellent actor putting on one hell of a performance, or a large group of the elves were disobeying his direct command. The captain felt sorry for him because even though he wasn't directly responsible, he was still liable as the person accountable for the attack. Three squads of soldiers blockaded the infirmary tent, forming a barrier and allowing them time to escape, to report back to Prince Zane. He felt sorry for his friend and hoped the king returned soon because even though Zane was an adult, no prince should be burdened with such a decision as to whether to declare war on another nation, or on another race.

The rookie hobbled back with a looped coil of rope and was nearly thrown off his feet by the explosion. Wood, debris and bodies flew through the air. "Damn! That's the last of the whisky," Beast grumbled. "Where's the damn rope?" The rookie had lost the rope, discarding it when he tried to keep his balance.

"It's right here," Rayze said, grinning and holding out his

hand. The coil of rope lay idly in it. Although conscious, he was pale and sweating profusely. One could only wonder how long he would stay conscious in that position.

"Great to see you're conscious again, but you still look like shit. More so than normal," Beast said, smirking. "Now give me the rope so that I can tie you down."

"Why? So, that you can have your kinky way with me?" Rayze said smirking, raising his eyebrows dramatically. He had an evil glint in his eye. "Maybe that's the real reason you are nicknamed the Beast." He threw the coil of rope back to the rookie.

Sitting on his horse nearby, Bear roared with laughter. Shaking his head and muttering, the lieutenant returned to his horse. "Looks like you're carrying the rope, rookie. Now mount up!" he shouted, mounting his horse. The rookie looked confused.

"But what about securing Rayze, sir?" he stammered as he looped the coil over his shoulder.

The lieutenant grunted as he looked between the three of them. "Leave it. He can fall unconscious and get dragged along by his damn horse for all I care."

Brenan's horse trotted into position. "Move out!" he shouted and with a wave of his hand, his small squad kicked their horse's flanks and galloped across the meadow behind him. Rayze followed, riding just behind the lieutenant. He gripped the reins tightly, concentrating on the task at hand, on surviving long enough to reach Sethanon.

Chapter 2

The guard yawned as he escorted his prince out into the courtyard. His name was Ven and he had grown up around the prince all his life, with his mother working as one of the household servants. Even as a child, he had always wanted to be one of the king's soldiers. So, as soon as he was of age, he enlisted, becoming a rookie in Prince Zane's retinue. It was a dream job. The prince was always polite, remembering their names, bantering and even socializing with some of them. The other day he had even played cards with them. Ven had wished to be part of the game, but he had never been into gambling.

When the mercenaries arrived, their leader told the guard that Zane had requested to see him. He had introduced himself as Ecnaidar, the leader of the Bloodborn mercenaries, a notorious group with a legendary reputation who were highly sought after on the black market. It made one wonder what Zane wanted from them. He had rushed off to fetch the prince, leaving Ecnaidar with one of the sergeants. To be honest, he was glad to be doing the errand. The mercenary leader scared the heebie-jeebies out of him.

He threw the door open in his rush, almost colliding with the prince. Startled, Ven stammered an apology. He had expected that he'd have to summon him from his room, but the prince had been waiting as if he had known. He dismissed it, even though he felt suspicious and suspected something. Opening the door for his prince, he stepped back out into the cool spring night.

Instinctively he wrapped his cloak around himself to ward off the cold. The prince walked past him, humming an eerie tune. That was when Ven noticed the prince's clothes, a dark blue tunic and black pants made of light cloth and designed to keep the wearer comfortable and cool. It was summer wear, an outfit the prince wore during the warmer months.

Things didn't add up. Ven had questions but kept his mouth shut.

Instead, his gaze went to the jingling pouch that swung idly by the prince's side. He remembered the quiet evening he had been on duty with Brenan, the captain of Zane's guards and one of his closest friends. The captain had taken him under his wing and taught him how to distinguish the various coins. He had absorbed the information like a sponge, listening intently. Later, when he asked the captain how he had come to know this, the man had simply smiled, tapped his head and replied, 'It is good to know, especially when it comes to gambling with some of the guards.'

The teaching he had received enabled him to know that the large pouch consisted of gold coins. It all came down to pitch. The gold coins made a dull clinking sound due to their weight. "That is a lot of money to pay the mercenaries," he said and instantly regretted it. The prince didn't need to share any of his business dealings with him, and it wasn't his place to pry.

"Maybe," the prince replied, contemplating and then smiling. "But then again, she's one of the world's deadliest assassins and tying up loose ends can be expensive." Ven couldn't believe what he was hearing. He had heard some of the guards gossiping about the assassin, but he had automatically dismissed it as conjecture and fabricated lies. Yet here, the prince was not only confirming it, but blatantly telling him that he was also planning to eliminate her. What was happening? It was as if this was an evil doppelganger of the prince, an imposter. It was so out of character for him.

Stopping abruptly, Zane held up his hand and smiling, turned to look at the rookie. Was it a trick of the light, or did the princes eyes change colour? It was only an instant, a flicker, but he could almost swear that they altered, turned completely black. "Stay here," the prince said and continued on alone. Ven was more than happy to comply, already freaked out and wanting no part of this.

The gravel crunched as Zane continued walking towards the convoy outside the stables. Twenty mercenaries sat mounted on their horses dressed in black, high-grade, quality armour. They were also armed with expensive silver weapons of the highest quality. Ecnaidar dismounted and nodded to the prince. He gave his horse an affectionate pat before handing the reins to Ronnard, his second in command.

At the rear of the convey was a large wagon drawn by six horses. The horses were anxious, neighing and pawing at the ground. The wagoner stood by them, speaking soothingly, desperately trying to calm them. A large cage was in the back of the wagon, chained and covered with a thick canvas. The beast inside the cage growled menacingly. "Enough!" the beast master shouted, banging the cage with the hilt of his broad, curved dagger.

* * *

The wagoner glared at him, a look full of anger and hatred. "Well, he's fucking hungry," he shouted, climbing up and standing on the seat. It was a blatant lie because the creature had been fed before they reached Sethanon. The wagoner continued to glare. "Well, I guess I could always feed him one of your horses." It was a cutting comment, a stinging barb. The beast master knew precisely how the man would react. The wagoner drew his short sword and started to lunge forward. The beast master held his dagger tightly, prepared and ready. Refraining and controlling his temper, the wagoner stopped himself and whistled.

In tandem, the six horses trotted forward. Grinding, crunching on the gravel, the wagon lurched forward, knocking the beast master off balance and causing him to topple off. Pulling himself up, the beast master grumbled. He was covered with dirt and had sustained some bruises. It was difficult to tell if the physical injuries or his pride and ego hurt the most. Screaming, he charged forward. "Enough!" Ecnaidar shouted and both men halted. It was an order. A command and it was not open for discussion.

The two men climbed onto the wagon, sitting down and mumbled, bickering like scolded children. They sat, waiting impatiently, ready to get going. A small, hooded man laughed. "You think that's funny, goblin," the beast master sneered. The beast master had purposely insulted the man and goaded him. He was itching for a fight. The jibe had the intended effect as the small man began to swing his flail at lightning speed. The flail had an extended chain with a large, spiked ball attached. It was also linked to a braced stump, where his left wrist would normally be.

"I said that's ENOUGH!" Ecnaidar roared. "That includes you, Ronnard." The little man nodded. His deadly flail retracted with a winching mechanism so that the iron-spiked ball sat snugly at the end of his brace. Ronnard was a man of few words and he was not a man to be trifled with. "If I didn't need you, beast master, I'd let Ronnard rip you a new arsehole." Muttering, the beast master sat back and sulked.

His authority established, his mercenaries in order and back under control, Ecnaidar clasped Zane's forearm in a mighty grip and nodded. Unclasping the pouch, the prince handed it to the mercenary leader. The deal was done. Briskly, Ecnaidar returned to his horse, the large pouch of gold coins jingling by his side. "Okay. The prince has paid us handsomely, boys. Prepare to ride out, we have a job to do." His slick, oily long-haired ponytail flicked back and forth as he mounted his horse. The man was of medium height and could almost have been considered attractive if not for the hideous scar running across his left eye and cheek. A scar he wore proudly which added to his intimidating nature.

Ecnaidar turned, looked at Ven and then addressed the prince. "The beast apparently needs feeding. Could you spare the youngling?" Zane shook his head and laughed.

* * *

"As amusing as that may be, I have other plans for him," Zane replied. Ecnaidar mumbled as his horse began to trot forward. The leader was not happy. What was this beast that the fearsome leader seemed so afraid of? Ven didn't want to know. With a clatter of hooves, the convoy started heading for the small northern gate. The guardsmen manning the gate nodded as Zane gave the command to open it. Walking back, he slapped the young rookie on the shoulder. "Don't worry. I was joking. I had no intention of letting Ecnaidar feed you to that beast."

"Why not use the main gate, my prince?" Ven asked, walking beside him.

"Because that cumbersome beast will draw enough attention as it is. Better not to draw any unnecessary attention." It was the private gate, exclusively used by the royal family. The guards were under strict orders that only members of the Sethanon family were to use it. Ven refused to look at the prince and kept his eyes on the ground. What they were doing made no sense.

The rookie guard looked up as they neared the castle. It was eerily quiet, and the torches mounted at the southern entrance had been extinguished. "Be careful, my prince," he said as his hand went to his sword. His wrist was grabbed in an iron grip and wincing, he let go of the handle. His arm twisted and was almost yanked out of its socket. Forcibly, he was thrown against the wall with a resounding thud.

"I'm not the one that needs to be careful," Zane laughed, stepping closer and leaning in. The prince's face was so close that Ven could feel his breath. He couldn't help but stare into the prince's eyes, eyes that were soulless and as black as coal.

"Who the hell are you? You're not my prince," he spat, reaching for the dagger at his belt. His hand wrapped around the handle and drew the weapon, the steel scraping softly against the sheath. His hand came up, not by his own accord. What the hell was happening? He had no control of his body. The imposter smiled wickedly and began to walk away. He was sending a message. With a gurgling scream, Ven sliced the dagger across his own throat.

Disguised, keeping Zane's appearance, Malgorath walked towards the kennels. He had one last thing to do. Only one dog remained. Three patrolled the perimeter with the guards, while the remaining four had gone with the king's retinue. The king had taken them in case the opportunity arose to go hunting. The dog whimpered as he approached. It was the runt, the weaker dog of the pack. He was about to change that.

Opening the kennel door with a creak, he knelt and pulled something out of his pocket. A large piece of chocolate, a treat to entice the dog. Holding it out in his hand, he softly called to the dog, saying its name and beckoning to him. The cowering dog slowly crept forward. Even though the dog could sense what the imposter was, the temptation of the chocolate was too much.

As the dog gently took the chocolate from his hands, Malgorath released some of his essence. The dog would have detected the scent if he had done it earlier. But now, the dog wagged his tail as he chewed and swallowed. The result was instantaneous. The dog's body grew, its bones becoming broader and denser. His muscles lengthened, adapting, re-shaping and becoming stronger. Next was his head, which broadened, expanding into the similar shape of a dragon's head. Instead of scales though, he was covered with tough leathery skin and pitch-black fur. Coarse fur that covered his entire body. Fur that rendered him practically invisible in the darkness of the night. "Go my hellhound and terrorise the city. Show them the true meaning of fear," Malgorath said gleefully.

The hellhound almost smiled, revealing its ferocious, powerful jaw, full of razor-sharp teeth. Its ruby-red eyes stared at him intelligently. Nodding its head, accepting the command, it bounded off towards the southern wall. Malgorath smiled, watching as the hellhound phased out of existence and went through the wall. Its unique ability enabled it to phase in and out of existence at will. Its victims wouldn't see it coming until it was too late. Until now, Malgorath had only summoned illusions, manifestations to sow fear into the citizens of Sethanon. Now it was time for the real thing. Pleased with himself, he turned around and walked back towards the castle.

He entered the castle humming the same eerie tune. The entranceway was dark, but that didn't bother him. He preferred the darkness, thrived in it and his keen demonic vision could make out everything. The hallway above was still lit, the light flickering as he walked up the staircase. As he neared Zane's bedroom, he could hear the soft snoring of the two guards stationed outside. Their bodies lay in a crumpled heap. The guards had been bored from being on night duty, which made it especially easy to manipulate their minds and put them to sleep. Humming, Malgorath walked past them and continued down the hallway.

Zane stirred momentarily to the commotion outside his bedroom door. Adjusting his pillow, he moaned and moving his arm slightly, rested his hand on Millie's breast. He smiled inwardly, the last thought before falling back asleep being about the sex that they would have upon waking up. An insistent banging woke him abruptly, startling him. Still half-asleep, it took him a moment to get his bearings and realise what was happening. He had slept soundly. It had been the first good night sleep he'd had in a long while.

Millie had stayed the night, but there hadn't been any sex.

They had just slept, cuddled in each other's arms. The evening had started out very well with drinking, kissing and then some foreplay, but they had both gotten tired. Zane couldn't explain it. It was a mystery to him. "Enter," he shouted as Millie pulled the covers up to cover her naked body. It was dawn and the first slivers of sunlight were poking through the window. It was early, way too early to be waking up. Something was wrong, terribly wrong.

A bald, solidly built man entered Zane's bedroom, followed by two guards who shambled along, clanking as they were shoved forward. The two guards were shackled and hung their heads in shame as they awaited judgement. What made matters worse was that they were two of Zane's personal guards. "What is the meaning of this?" Zane roared, leaping out of bed naked. "Explain yourself, captain!" The fact that he was indecent was the furthest thing from his mind. He was furious and wanted answers. The act was an insult, a slap in the face.

The captain merely smiled at Zane. It was a smile that most men feared, a smile a predator had before devouring his meal. Reaching for his bed robe, the prince slipped it on and defiantly stood his ground. "Your guards were asleep on the job. Whether you had something to do with it or whether it was their stupidity and incompetence is yet to be proven." Zane was perplexed. Why would he put his own guardsmen to sleep? What the hell was going on?

* * *

Before Zane could ask, the captain continued. "And I strongly suggest that you address me by my proper title – General Iryss." Although smiling, it was clearly a threat. One that Zane heeded. He didn't want to make an enemy of the general, not yet anyway. Iryss was a proven fighter and an excellent tactician. He had recently been promoted to general but was also the captain of the King's guard. At least until a replacement could be found. Even Brenan, the captain of Zane's personal guard answered to him.

Zane took a deep breath, as he poured himself a drink. "And why would I put my own guardsmen to sleep general?"

"So that you could sneak out and kill Ven!" one of the general's guardsmen screamed. "He was my friend." The man was tear stricken. He was a young guard, a corporal who had been promoted, leaving his brother's guard detail and joining their father's. The outburst earned him a stern look from the general. Zane couldn't believe what he was hearing. He was dumbfounded. Ven was a rookie in his own personal guard, a nice, friendly lad, who showed initiative and promise. And he was dead?

"And you think I killed my own guardsman?" Zane replied, mortified.

"Kel and the sergeant saw you leave the castle with Ven and converse with the Bloodborn mercenaries," Iryss said matter-of-factly. Zane was baffled. The Bloodborn mercenaries were outlawed in three kingdoms. But for some reason his father tolerated them and gave them amnesty. Perhaps there was some truth in the saying, 'Keep your friends close and your enemies closer.'

"After dealing with those scum," Iryss continued, "you were escorted back to the castle by Ven. He was found dead by the castle entrance. You were the last one to see him, Prince Zane. I'm sorry to say that you are confined to your quarters until this matter is resolved. I will post four of my guards outside your door." Zane opened his mouth, ready to protest. "As you know, I have complete authority in this kind of situation. The only person who can overrule my decision is your father."

Grinding his teeth, Zane nodded, conceding to the general. He hated to admit it, but the general was right. His fate was sealed. It wasn't their fault. "It must have been Malgorath." Zane whispered to himself. To the general, he said, "There are greater forces at work here, General. What are you going to do with my guards?"

"They will spend a week in the dungeon. You're lucky you're not joining them. Your fate will be decided when your father gets back." Iryss started to walk towards the door. "And stop using this Malgorath as a fucking excuse. Just man up and take responsibility for your actions." Shaking his head, disappointed, the general walked out the door. Zane did not realize the General had heard his whisper. The man was a sceptic. He refused to believe in the supernatural. It was pointless, the general would never see reason. Zane watched helplessly as the guards took his men away. There was nothing he could do.

Things had been quiet and peaceful. He had orchestrated and put a plan into motion. He had hired an assassin to spy and possibly eliminate his mother. He had suspected her to be a demon, that one of them was even the demon prince. He had been so sure, yet now he doubted it. Could he be Malgorath? Had the demon prince been lurking in him all along?

He stood there like a statue, in a daze, contemplating what to do. "I should probably go." It was Millie. He had forgotten about her. He turned to look at her, befuddled, the cobwebs slowly clearing from his head. She stood there concerned, fully dressed. How long had he been standing there thinking? Holding his hand, she gently squeezed it. A nod was all he could manage, as letting go, she walked towards the door.

It was a fling, nothing serious. She had provided comfort and support for him in a time of need. She had been a distraction, nothing more. A tear rolled down his cheek. And yet here he was, wondering if he would ever see her again. She was scared and who could blame her? His life was in turmoil and she didn't need this drama. He was accused of murder and the worst part was that he was actually wondering whether he had done it.

As the door opened Stryxen burst in. His adopted brother was flustered and angry. "Prince Stryxen," Millie said curtseying, as she slid past and exited Zane's bedroom.

"Milady," Stryxen replied, nodding. Millie blushed and Zane smiled. Even though Millie wasn't of noble birth, Stryxen calling her this made her feel important. It was flattering and polite. He turned towards his brother as one of the guards closed the door. "This is fucked, Zane," he swore. "The general has no right to confine you. You're a prince of the realm and you're innocent. Wait until dad gets back. By the time I'm done with him, he'll be cleaning out the latrines and begging for food scraps on the street." Zane smiled and patted his little brother on the shoulder. It was nice that Stryxen was so protective of him.

"Thank you Stryxen, but there is no need to worry. I'm sure dad will sort this entire mess out." He forced a smile and tried to sound positive.

"Well, if he doesn't, I'll get a sword from the armoury. Then, I'll kill the general and break you out of the dungeon." Stryxen swung his arm back and forth, revealing to his brother the sword strokes that he would use. Zane couldn't help but laugh.

* * *

"Well, go and keep practising, little brother. You will need all the practise you can get if you plan on taking on the general." He tussled Stryxen's hair in a fond farewell. His little brother smiled and headed for the door. "And Stryxen, thank you for believing in me." It meant a lot to Zane. The guard closed the door behind Stryxen and left Zane to his isolation.

It was a master stroke by Malgorath's hand, one where his innocence was impossible to prove. He needed to prepare, to strategize, to make the most of his free time and this opportunity. It came to him like a slap in the face and he knew exactly what to do. Mumbling an incantation, he focused on the chair in front of him. Curved and cushioned with soft, padded seats, it was ideal. A swirling mixture of lights appeared, morphing, re-shaping and forming a mirage, an illusion of himself sitting comfortably in the chair reading a book.

Opening his wardrobe, he pulled out his clothes for the day and got dressed. He was focused and determined. He clasped his black cloak on, a cloak designed for stealth and walked towards his desk. His boots were padded and barely made a sound. Pulling out his chain, he unlocked the drawer with the faintest click. Quietly opening it, he reached in and grabbed a wrapped package. He quickly stuffed it into his tunic pocket. Closing and locking it, he hung the chain back over his neck and hid the key under his tunic.

Smirking, he walked over to a large two-hundred-year-old

painting. In exquisite detail, the painter had captured the war between the Allied Forces and the Jardoshian Empire. The painting was Zane's favourite. Carefully grabbing each side, he tilted the painting slightly and was rewarded with a click. Grinding smoothly on well-oiled rollers, a section of the wall slid back. *Confinement my arse,* he thought, as he stepped into the dark threshold of the secret tunnels.

Another incantation and an orb of light formed, hovering above his hand. Reaching out, Zane pulled a small lever on the dark stone wall. With slow and steady grinding, the section of the wall moved back in place. "What the hell was that?" Booted feet sounded, crunching on the gravel of the stone floor. A heavier pounding indicated that the guards had reached the steps. The tunnel started to illuminate, flickering with the torchlight. The guards were approaching, but Zane was long gone. He dimmed the orb and retreated down the hallway. "Here's the lever leading to the prince's room. He will get one hell of a surprise if he tries to leave."

"It's creepy as hell, but the General ordered us to wait here," the guard's companion said, wheezing slightly and short of breath. He was the officer in charge. He reached towards the lever. "Perhaps we should check on the prince, make sure he's still in his room?"

Zane mumbled silently and cast a spell. "Who's there?" he whispered, projecting his voice, making it sound muffled and from within his room. The officer halted, his hand stopping just before the lever.

Smiling wickedly, he slowly withdrew his hand. "On second thoughts, if he is arrogant enough to try and sneak through the tunnels, he deserves to get caught."

"I may be arrogant at times, but at least I'm not stupid," Zane said, continuing quietly down the tunnel. The tunnels were a secret, but obviously, his father had told the general about them. He cursed, feeling betrayed. The tunnels were sacred, something the Everthorn's had passed down from generation to generation. And their father had broken that trust. Zane berated himself, their father wasn't to blame, he was only trying to protect them. Or was he acting under Malgorath's influence?

He could question himself for eternity and not know the answer. He decided to forget about it. It was done and there was no point dwelling on it. To do so would lead down the road towards insanity. He had underestimated the general and not given him enough credit. He had outsmarted the guards for the moment, but getting back into his room would be a problem. He would think about it and deal with it when the time came. But first, he had work to do in his sanctuary.

He still believed the ghouls were the key to defeating Malgorath. Along with his and Jace's combined magic, they would be unstoppable. Would Jace fight with him or against him though? Was his brother Malgorath in disguise? They were questions that he dreaded. Because it also posed the question that if Jace was Malgorath in disguise, would he have the inner strength, the willpower and determination to follow through and kill his own brother?

He made his way down the spiralling stone staircase, humming a tune as he neared his destination, a large wooden door with metal strips across it. The door was ancient and covered in black runes, runes that could only be activated with dark magic and his blood. Drawing his dagger, Zane sliced open his finger and traced the rune completing the ritual before moving on to the next one. Repeating the process, he infused each rune with his blood. It seemed to take forever, but finally he traced the last rune and the entire door radiated with blue light. The metal strips spiralled outwards and the door unlocked.

Entering his magical sanctuary, he was greeted by a hulking presence. Zane nodded in greeting. A ghoul stood before him. Eight feet tall, broad and well-muscled, he towered over Zane. Although he was scary and intimidating, he was Zane's friend. Scourge. "Zane. Chocolate?" Scourge asked. Smiling, the prince reached into his tunic pocket and pulled out the package.

"First though, my friend, I need a couple of drops of your blood," Zane said. Seeing his friend had given him an idea. Nodding, the ghoul grabbed the chocolate out of his hand. Then, pulling out his dagger, he nicked the ghoul's wrist and held out a glass vial to collect the blood. "Thank you, Scourge," he said, stoppering the vial and handing the ghoul a nearby rag. The ghoul placed the rag back on the table. He didn't need it. The wound had stopped bleeding, the skin knitting itself back together. The ghoul's regenerative factor was remarkable. "You never cease to amaze me, Scourge. Now let's get to work."

Chapter 3

Zane walked up the spiral staircase deep in thought. The session had been both productive and frustrating. He was so close. His research had been fruitful, but he was still missing one element, the catalyst that would enable him to create a ghoul army. An army that he could use against Malgorath. He quickly turned right at the T-junction, skidding slightly on the gravel and almost dropping the pile of books he held.

* * *

He had brought a pile of books and journals with him to study in the confines of his room. If he had to be confined to his room, he might as well make the most of it. Juggling the books and readjusting his hold on them, he continued down the tunnel. His cat's eyes easily enabled him to navigate, providing him with night vision and freeing up his hands to carry the books. The spell was technically called Night Sight, but Zane had nicknamed it Cat's Eyes. It was more appropriate and represented what his eyes resembled at the moment.

He stepped off the last step of a steep staircase and entered the tunnel leading to his room. The guard's voices could be heard mumbling in the distance. Their torches flickered and danced off the stone walls. He crept closer, the gravel crunching softly under his feet. The torches were getting brighter and he could make out their voices now. The guards were oblivious to him, concentrating on the card game and their drinking. It was time. Crouching down, he lay the books by his side and withdrew the vial.

Tipping the blood on the ground, Zane drew an elaborate symbol. "Grrrrrr..." one of the guards said. His companion roared with laughter. "Ghouls don't make that kind of noise, you idiot. My puppy could make a more menacing growl than that."

"Fine. You think you can do a better impression? Then show

me what a ghoul sounds like." the guard replied defensively. His companion cleared his throat and they both took a drink.

"Wharrr." The guard burst into laughter, spraying whisky over his friend.

"Yeah. That's a good impersonation of a constipated ghoul." They both roared with laughter.

"So, you drunken imbeciles want to know what a ghoul sounds like?" Zane muttered, smirking as he drew the last part of the symbol. "I'm happy to oblige." Whispering the words, he said the incantation. The bloodied symbol began to radiate a glowing, bright purple. The gravel and dirt began to swirl, slowly at first and then faster and faster. Chunks of rock were ripped off the ceiling and the walls, merging with the deadly maelstrom. Then, just as quickly as it appeared, it dissipated and standing in its place was a golem, an identical clone of Scourge before the modifications.

The golem turned its head, looked at him and waited. It was perfect, obedient and completely loyal to him. Like a child though, it needed guidance and instruction. "Attack, but don't kill." The ghoul nodded.

"GARRR!" the golem roared, before charging down the tunnel. The two guards stopped laughing and looked at each other.

* * *

"Wow, that was actually a pretty good impersonation. Much better than your previous attempt," the guard's companion said, impressed and clapping loudly. He had failed to notice that his friend had gone as white as a ghost.

"That wasn't me you fucking idiot!" he shouted, dropping his cards and staggering backwards. He fumbled, trying to draw his sword as the looming golem erupted out of the darkness. The officer turned only to have the ghoulish golem grab him with its massive, clawed hands. The officer was no light weight; he was solidly built, but the golem picked him up and threw him as if he weighed nothing more than a rag doll.

The officer bounced off the wall and landed face-first in the dirt. He lay motionless with one of his arms at an obscure angle. The remaining guard screamed and his sword came free with a hiss. Thrusting his sword forward, he stabbed the golem in the chest. The blade erupted out of the golem's back. Looking down at the weapon, the golem roared in defiance. Panicking, the guard yanked and tried desperately to pull his sword free. He couldn't! Not only was it embedded, but it was stuck and refused to budge. Raising one of his massive hands, the golem smashed it on the guard's armoured head. Zane could see the huge dent in the helmet from where he stood. The guard released a moan as his sword clattered harmlessly to the ground, and wobbling on unsteady feet, he collapsed, unconscious.

Zane was mortified. He felt terrible, after all, these were his men, men loyal to his family. The General had forced his hand though, caused him to retaliate, to do what needed to be done. Kneeling, he felt their pulses and sighed with relief. They were alive. "Thank you," he said to the golem and started to do the gestures and incantation for the release spell. Blue light snaked out of his hand intertwining and enveloping the golem. Then just as abruptly, it vanished. All that remained in the golem's place was a pile of dirt and rocks.

Juggling the books, Zane pulled the lever and opened the section of the wall. He walked into his room and stopped abruptly as he came face to face with one of the guards. The guard wore dusty, blood-stained, pitch-black plate armour without any identifying insignia on his surcoat. Strapped across his back were two ornate swords, their leather-bound handles sticking above his shoulders. Zane knew how deadly the man was at fighting. Able to dual-wield both swords, he was a lethal killing machine. He was also one of Zane's closest friends. "Brenan," Zane said, putting the books on a nearby table. Smiling, he embraced his friend in a manly hug.

"I should have known that you would manage to sneak out of your confinement," Brenan smirked, laughing. Even as close as Brenan was, he hadn't informed him of the sanctuary's existence or what he hoped to achieve through his research and experimentation. It was a closely guarded secret that he didn't trust anyone with. Mumbling an incantation, Zane dispelled the mirage he had conjured earlier in a puff of coloured smoke. Brenan smirked. "I suspected that it was your magic. Either that or you had gone mute." Zane laughed. It was good to have his friend back.

"I found a dusty bookshelf a couple of weeks ago. These books were stacked neatly upon it. So, I thought I'd collect them and give them a read." He sidestepped, blocking the captain's view and leaned against the table. Smiling, Brenan merely shook his head. He knew all too well what Zane was like with his books. "Well, since I'm confined, I've got plenty of time to spare." Risking a quick glance, he made sure the titles were hidden. Zane was self-conscious and didn't want anyone to discover their content. Turning back to face his friend, he noticed the other soldiers in the room.

"Beast, Troy, Larin, Erik, Devan, Bear," Zane said, nodding to each of them. He had made it a common practice to know all his guard's names. '….and who do we have here?" Zane raised his eyebrows as he noticed the man that Devan and Larin supported. The man was half naked with his shoulder heavily bandaged. Zane wrinkled his nose. Both bandages were bloodied, having a metallic scent mixed with something else. His cheek had a dressing that was also bandaged in place. Besides these obvious wounds, the man was sweating profusely and delirious as he mumbled incoherently.

* * *

"This is Rayze. He was allied with the assassin," Brenan said. "And he comes bearing gifts." He passed Zane a satchel with a large, green, diamond-shaped emerald inside it. Zane raised his eyebrows questioningly. "It's apparently called a divinity stone," Brenan explained. "It's a magical artefact that Malgorath wants." Zane nodded, closing the satchel. Of course, it went without saying that they needed to lock it away, that they needed to keep it away from Malgorath, either that or use it as bait to lure him out.

"What's wrong with him?" Zane asked, concerned.

"He was poisoned by silver oak," Brenan replied. Again, Zane raised his eyebrows questioningly. Like Brenan, he knew how rare it was for a human to have a reaction to silver oak. There was more to this man than met the eye.

"Have you summoned Varyn Kabel?" Zane asked.

"Yes, my prince. He instructed us to bring him here. While we wait, I'll report and fill you in on current events." Zane nodded, eager to hear the news. "The contract was delivered and after some deliberation, she accepted the job." Zane sighed with relief. He felt horrible having orchestrated the contract and taken matters into his own hands, but he was glad he had. Something had to be done and his older brother Jace and their father had refused to take on the responsibility.

* * *

"Before accepting the contract, she insisted on completing the job that she was currently on." Brenan's eyes darted towards the divinity stone and Zane immediately got the meaning. The woman named Flow, had come highly recommended and had a repertoire of skills – thievery being one of them. "I don't know the complete story, but I know it involved some fanatical elves, a deranged, psychopathic elven prince and a demon."

"A lesser demon," the lieutenant, known as Beast, corrected. Brenan's eyes glanced towards him, a silent reprimand. Bear smirked, trying not to laugh. Muttering, Beast elbowed him lightly in the ribs.

"I stand corrected," Brenan continued. "A lesser demon, but a demon nonetheless and more powerful than anything that my squad has ever encountered. Flow handled herself exceptionally though. With the help of Rayze, who is an extraordinary swordsman." Brenan glanced at the mysterious warrior before continuing. "They defeated the demon, killing it and turning it into a smouldering black mess. The demon killed one of the elven princes, Prince Velander, before almost decimating the inn. It was hard Zane, challenging, almost impossible. We lucked out, nothing more. And this was a lesser demon; how the hell do we stand a chance against a demon prince?" The captain was grim, genuinely worried.

Zane put a reassuring hand on his friend's shoulder. "We can overcome anything with my magic and your squad by my side." Brenan nodded, but it was half- hearted and full of doubt. The captain sighed and Zane knew that there was more dire news. He unstrapped a satchel at his belt and reaching in, pulled out a map. Zane moved the books to the side and unfolding the parchment, Brenan placed the map on the table.

He pointed at a symbol bearing resemblance to a house. In swirling, neat writing was the label Black Raven Inn. "The fanatics were camped near the inn. One hundred and fifty elves, possibly more, camped right on our border because of this." The captain pointed accusingly at the giant emerald with his other hand. "I sent out two riders, who managed to muster about two hundred soldiers from Fort Targen. I ordered them to camp here." Moving his finger, he then pointed to a clearing. Zane nodded. Strategically, it made sense. It was an intimidating tactic, making their presence known with the intention of preventing a war.

"Just before dawn, a contingent of elves and a group of our own Hiberathian soldiers attacked. It was complete chaos. Our soldiers were killed. Prince Jerrick could be seen assisting, fighting the fanatics. What happened to him afterwards, I do not know. Rayze killed four elves, preventing them from reclaiming the divinity stone. We owe him a debt of gratitude. If it wasn't for him, the divinity stone would be in Malgorath's hands by now."

* * *

"I'll personally thank him when he recovers. How did you manage to escape?" Zane started to pace back and forth, occasionally stopping to look at the map. Brenan knew his friend well and knew that he needed time to process and analyse things. "Three squads covered our retreat, allowing us the necessary time to get away, to deliver this and report back to you." Zane nodded and once again looked at the map.

"And where was Prince Jerrick when you saw him?" Brenan sighed and pointed. He had been dreading this. "Then the elves have broken the terms and conditions of our alliance. By doing so they have dec…"

He didn't get to finish the sentence as a loud, insistent knock at the door interrupted him. "Enter," Zane said, as with a creak, the door opened and Kabel entered. The varyn was carrying a vial of dark purple liquid. Seeing the varyn, the soldiers gently eased Rayze onto the couch. Without saying a word, ignoring his prince and the captain entirely, Kabel barged in and walked towards his patient. He looked at Rayze quizzically.

"You're lucky you called me. An hour or two longer and he would have been dead. Our young man here has had a very severe reaction to silver oak." Holding the vial to Rayze's lips, he watched as his patient swallowed it in small gulps. Putting the empty vial back in his pocket, he delicately unravelled the bandages. The last part was stuck and he had to carefully peel it back. A sticky yellow coating had adhered to it. Zane almost gagged from the smell that wafted to him a few feet away.

"Infection," Kabel explained. "It doesn't surprise me. Luckily, I brought these." He reached into his pocket and pulled out two other vials and a small jar of reddish-brown paste. Placing them carefully to the side, he addressed the soldiers. "First, I will need one of you to go to my workshop. You'll find a small steel pan on one of the shelves, clean bandages and some rags. Fill the pan with warm water and bring them to me." Brenan motioned to the rookie and with a nod, he ran off.

"Sergeant! Make yourself useful by throwing some logs onto the fireplace. Zane, I'll need you to light it using your magic. Consider this a practice session in elemental magic," Kabel instructed. The sergeant immediately got to work, nobody questioned Varyn Kabel. Wiping his hands, Bear nodded that he was done. Zane walked towards the couch and the fireplace, muttering and concentrating. The wood began to crack as it heated and smoke slowly rose into the chimney. A single flame danced amongst the logs, then another joined it. Within an instant, the hearth was blazing and providing a cosy warmth to the room.

Zane turned to face his tutor, pleased with himself, but the varyn was distracted. Kabel had seen a faint sparkle out of the corner of his eye. A sparkle originating from a slight gap in the satchel. And then his attention was caught by the pile of books and journals on the table. Zane cursed silently. "Those books look old, Zane. You can tell by their binding. But they appear to be in excellent condition. What titles do you have there? And are those journals as well?" He didn't get a chance to pry further as the rookie entered clattering and knocking into the doorway, juggling the pan, rags and the bandages. Kabel cursed as he spilt some of the water.

Placing the items on the large wooden armrest of the couch, the rookie backed away to give the varyn space. Kabel muttered something that sounded like a thank you. The rookie was unsure, but instead of asking, he opted to be silent and let the varyn get to work. The rags were used one by one as if it were a production line. The varyn would wet the rag, wipe away the pus, clean the wound and dispose of it by throwing it into the blazing fireplace. He was far from gentle, but Rayze didn't even scream once, although he clenched his teeth. Zane marvelled at the warrior's pain threshold. Kabel finished by applying the paste and wrapping the clean bandages over the wounds. "The paste will help with the infection," he muttered, cleaning up his mess.

"Now, my boy, I need you to drink these, he said picking up the two vials. Before he could say anything else, Rayze snatched them from his hand and gulped them down in one go. The warrior's expression said it all. Kabel laughed. "I could have told you that taking them together would result in a foul concoction." Zane poured a whisky and handed it to Rayze.

"Don't worry. I've had to deal with Kabel's foul potions and elixirs all my life," the prince said as the varyn huffed in indignation.

"Thank you," Rayze said, downing the whisky. He collapsed onto the couch, exhausted, struggling to keep his eyes open. The empty crystal glass slipped from his fingers. Lunging, Zane caught it before it shattered on the floor.

"He'll probably be out for a while. The two vials both had cannabidiol and passionflower in them, which both act as a relaxant and sedative. Now about those…"

"Thank you for coming. As you can see this warrior was in dire need of your masterful healing practices," Zane said, interrupting Kabel. He politely escorted him to the door, before the inquisitive varyn could further enquire about the books, journals and satchel.

"Well, it looks like you have a roomie," Beast chuckled. Brenan gave him a stern look. "At least for a little while anyway," he quickly added, clamping his mouth shut before he got himself in any more trouble.

"I'm sure he'll be pleasant company. And it is the least I can do, considering all the trouble he went to to get me this."

Zane picked the satchel off the table and pulled out the large green emerald. He had a closer look at it. "So, this is one of the divinity stones." He looked at it admiringly before putting it back. Their father's divinity stone was embedded in his crown.

He wore the crown only on special occasions, opting to keep it locked away in a gnomish-designed safe. The safe was a marvel, having multiple locking mechanisms which would unlock using a code that Erithen had. The only other person to have the code was his chief advisor Varyn Kabel. For the most part, the king wore a replica. He found it more comfortable and joked that it didn't weigh him down with stress and responsibility.

The princes had been told stories of the divinity stones, about how the goddesses had given each race a divinity stone to safeguard. That each divinity stone was a magical artefact. How powerful were the divinity stones though? And why did Malgorath want them so badly? They were a mystery, one that Zane was determined to unravel. He needed to do some research and find out more about them.

"I'd be careful. Millie might have her heart set on that if she sees it. You know how women are when it comes to anything sparkly and expensive," Troy said jokingly.

"Millie is scared. I don't think she will be coming back any time soon. With the murder of Ven and everything with

Malgorath, who can blame her?" He looked at the squad. They weren't surprised or shocked by the news, but why would they? The general had already told them. Yet, they had come to visit him. They were his men, loyal to the end.

"We know you had nothing to do with it my friend," Brenan said, putting a comforting hand on his shoulder. He sighed with relief. They believed and trusted him, which was all that mattered.

"Yeah. The general needs to get his head out of his arse," Beast chipped in.

 "There's no way you could have done it, my prince," Troy added.

"Yeah!" chorused the others, nodding in support.

"Through the valley of death, we are united," Brenan said. It was an ancient saying told by warriors and brothers of war. He clasped Zane's forearm and nodded. The saying and the simple gesture were reassuring, a promise that they would be there for him no matter what. "Considering how badly Malgorath wants it, I think it's best to hide the divinity stone." Zane nodded. The stone needed to be kept safe at all costs.

Mumbling an incantation, a perfectly square section of the polished wooden floor slid away, revealing a secret compartment. He trusted his guards explicitly, knowing that they would rather die than reveal the divinity stone's location. The interior of the compartment was also inscribed with various runes, powerful magic that would protect and shield the divinity stone from prying eyes. Kneeling, he carefully placed the stone within the compartment. Mumbling the incantation, the section of the wooden floor slid shut, sealing it within. It was safe, at least for now.

"Now, my prince, we will bid you a good evening," Brenan said, nodding farewell. "We smell like the rear end of a horse, so we're going to head off to the barracks and freshen up."

With that, the squad started to depart towards the door. The prince's guards shared a barracks downstairs with a communal bathroom next to it. The bathroom had a latrine, toilets and four tubs for bathing. They would place buckets beside the tub to be filled with cold water. It made bathing convenient for them.

As the men opened Zane's door, a young red-haired girl stood before them. Surprised, she quickly pulled her hand away from the door and stood aside to let the guards exit. "My prince, my name is Brandy," she said, curtsying and introducing herself. Zane had noticed her in passing a couple of times and being the attractive red head that she was, she had caught his eye. "I am here to fill up your bath."

* * *

"Usually, Millie fills the bath for me," Zane explained, as Brandy got the tongs from next to the fireplace.

"She asked me if I could do it," she replied, smiling cheekily. Zane nodded. It confirmed his suspicions. Millie was distancing herself and avoiding him. She carefully pulled the first heat rock out of the fireplace. The heat rocks were harvested deep in the dwarven mines. Kyrene had tried to explain the concept behind the heat rocks at one stage, but admittedly Zane had only been half listening. Through the concept of the heat rocks and a gnomish designed compartment under the tub, it enabled Zane to have the luxury of a nice warm bath.

Zane watched Brandy as he poured himself a whisky. She was in the process of bending over and placing the last heat rock in the compartment under the bath. Zane didn't mind watching as her dress lifted, revealing her sexy, pale legs. It posed the question of what the rest of her body was like. Zane didn't mind the view or the titillating thoughts it gave him. Wiping some of her long, curly hair out of her face, she picked up the bucket and began filling it with water. Steam rose into the air as she poured it in.

The bath was large, usually taking about eleven buckets to fill it to the point where Zane could comfortably soak in it. Zane started to undress as she poured the seventh bucket in. As she poured the eighth bucket, he slipped into its watery depths. The water was perfect, just warm enough that it wasn't scalding hot. He sighed contently, "Would you like me to soap you down, my prince?" she said, handing him a sponge and a bar of soap. Zane shook his head. As pleasurable as it would be, he would rather wash himself. He was trying to be faithful to Millie, even though they weren't committed. He had grown accustomed to her company and genuinely missed her.

"Then perhaps you can wash me then," Brandy said, as she started to unbutton her blouse.

"Thank you for the offer, but I am committed to someone else," Zane replied. He regretted what he said and was kicking himself for it. Her legs, her breasts, her body were perfect in every way. Zane started to wash himself. Pouting, Brandy watched the prince as she slowly retied her blouse. She was hoping that he would change his mind. He didn't, so she stormed out angrily. Sighing, Zane finished bathing himself. He had come to the realization that he actually loved Millie.

Darla waited and watched, hidden by the cover of the foliage. The guards passed, bored and unalert. Darla observed keenly taking in their armour and weapons. Most of them wore heavy, plate armour and were armed with swords and axes. Half a dozen of them were spearmen. Dressed in chainmail armour, it provided them with protection and the flexibility of movement. Their long-barbed spears rose high into the sky like long skeletal arms. Two of the guards were dressed in hardened leather and were armed with heavy crossbows. Darla took special note of them. She would need to take these guardsmen out first.

These crossbowmen wore light armour and relied on picking their targets off at a distance. The longer they remained alive, the more of a hindrance they would become. As the carriage rolled by, she picked up the aroma of wine and the distinct smell of four different types of perfume. Four women in the carriage. The queen and her lady-in-waiting. But who else? Two of the perfumes were exotic, expensive brands. Then it dawned on her – the baroness. They had travelled to the estate and the baroness was travelling back with them along with her own lady in waiting. This complicated things.

Behind the carriage were the supply wagons. There were two of them, carrying the supplies and baggage. The maids and servants sat in one of them, uncomfortably squished together. Unlike the ladies-in-waiting, they weren't entitled to the luxury and privilege of travelling in the carriage. Following behind the wagons were the remaining two guardsmen.

They were hooded and dressed in hardened leather. Short swords were strapped to their hips. Elvish-designed, top-grade quality recurve bows were also strapped to their saddles. A quiver of arrows hung idly across their backs.

Rangers, the king's elite, trained by the elves. "Fuck me," Darla whispered. As they passed, both rangers turned their heads and looked in her direction. Had they heard her? She stayed silent and motionless, watching intently. Finally, the rangers passed and no alarm was sounded. Darla let out a sigh of relief. She hadn't even realised she had been holding her breath.

Squinting her eyes, Darla judged the position of the sun. It was almost lunch time. The convoy would be stopping soon to rest and have a bite to eat. Her shoulder was nudged gently by Midnight's head. A quiet whinny followed. His action screamed, *'I know it's lunchtime. I'm hungry. Feed me! Feed me! Feed me!'* The convoy was far enough away now, that Darla deemed it safe to stand. Standing up, she gave the hand signal and Midnight rose. He stamped the ground, stretching his legs.

Darla laughed. "You're getting old boy," she said, patting him affectionately. Midnight flicked his head indignantly and snorted, *'Look who's talking'.* Darla sighed. "You're right, but hopefully this is our last contract. Then we can both retire." She now had enough money to buy her friends freedom and live comfortably for the rest of her life. It was a dream come true, what she had been longing for. Let someone else fight the demons and monsters of the world.

Reaching into her saddlebag she pulled out a large wooden bowl and filled it with oats. Carefully reaching into a pouch, she plucked out a small handful of blueberries and mixed them amongst the oats. A neigh and a flick of his head said it all. "I love you too, boy," Darla laughed. The horse had developed a love for blueberries a while back, so she ensured that she always kept some on hand. It made a nice treat for Midnight, but she also enjoyed the sweet, indulgent berry.

Her lunch was bland, consisting of hard bread and some dried beef. She grimaced, washing it down with some water. She hated travelling rations, food that stayed preserved and took up little space. It was perfect for travelling, camping and situations like this, but it also tasted like shit. She had packed enough food to last for three days, hopefully it would be enough. If she needed to, she would drop by a neighbouring town and pick up some supplies.

Plucking some more blueberries from the pouch, she shoved them into her mouth. A snort and a shake of his head. "Deal with it. You have to share." Picking up the empty wooden bowl, she packed it in the saddlebag. Putting her foot in the stirrup, she mounted up. It was time to head out. Crossing the road, they entered the forest on the opposite side. Judging from their speed and factoring in their lunch break, Darla had a fairly good idea of where the travellers would be camping. She needed to make sure though. Entering the forest, she followed the convoy from a distance, making sure not to get spotted by the rangers.

Chapter 4

Clunk! Clunk! Queen Raylene cringed as she was jostled in her seat, the carriage wheels going over some larger rocks embedded into the highway. She was trying to read her favourite book and had reread the same paragraph three times now. The book was small and leather bound, the stylized gold title written boldly on the cover reflecting in the lantern light. The jostling was causing the lantern to swing, flickering the light and causing shadows to dance throughout the carriage. This was only part of her dilemma. Her main reason for cringing was the prattling woman sitting across from her. The woman's name was Baroness Adele and she was the wife of her husband's best friend.

Baron Sandrik had been the king's best friend since they had been children. He was a tall, well-muscled man who was down to earth and had a quirky sense of humour. The baron was also easy going, level-headed and completely loyal to his friend, the king. They hadn't seen each other in years, not since Gareth's wedding. Gareth and his wife now had a beautiful baby boy, an heir that would one day take over the Baron's estate and his role as Warden to the king.

She wondered if Jace and Zane would ever settle down and have children for her to fuss over. Hopefully, one day they would provide her with the chance to be a grandmother. She took a sip of her wine. It was a vintage bought at one of the wineries near Sandrik's estate and was exceptionally good. The holiday had been fantastic, a well-needed escape for the family. Perfect for everyone except the queen who despised the baron's wife.

She admired the friendship that her husband and the Baron had, and forced a pleasant smile around the Baroness, taking her rantings and gossip with a pinch of salt. Their children were also close, developing the same kind of friendship that their fathers had. Gareth was the eldest being twenty-six and married. Rylan and Jace had been inseparable since childhood and had got up to mischief like only best friends could. They were both twenty-four years old, with Rylan being a couple of months younger. Prince Zane had only recently turned twenty-one, while their youngest son Stryxen was twelve.

Technically, Stryxen was Jace and Zane's cousin, but his parents had died when he was one. Rumour had it that a window had been left open and a savage monster had brutally massacred his parents, while Stryxen had survived by hiding. They were yet to uncover the mystery of the kind of monster it had been. Their bodies had been unidentifiable, with pieces of them scattered throughout the bedroom. The walls, floor and even the ceiling had been red, covered as if painted in blood. Being his only living relatives, the king and the queen had adopted Stryxen, granting him the title of prince and treating him as one of their own.

When told about the family holiday, Stryxen had begged, pleaded desperately to visit the Jardoshian Empire. For some unknown reason he had developed an obsession with the orcs. Raylene just hoped that he'd grow out of this fascination. Even though there was currently peace, the orcs were a race bred for war. They were volatile and untrustworthy. There was a bitterness there, a feeling of resentment and because of that she would never consider them allies.

* * *

Her husband had smiled warmly at their youngest son and kneeling next to him, had rested his hand affectionately on Stryxen's shoulder. He had explained that the relationship between the two kingdoms was tentative at best, but that hopefully they could soon visit the orcs. He only briefly got to tell him about the possibility of going hunting when Stryxen angrily shrugged his father's hand off his shoulder and stormed off crying to his room.

He had locked himself in there, refusing to come out or go on the holiday. The queen had been upset but had respected her son's wishes. She organised for Kabel and his tutor to look after his education, while two of the maids took on the role of nannies for the duration of the holiday. Then Zane had been bitten by a snake and injured himself. It was a shame that they had missed out on the holiday. The queen looked at the bottle and the sheathed dagger lying next to her. The bottle of wine was a present for Zane. The wine was his favourite; exquisite, sweet and made with a combination of wild berries.

The dagger was only slightly smaller than a short sword. Ever since Stryxen had begun weapons training with his brothers, he had wanted his own sword. *They have their own sword, why can't I have one?* he would argue. *Because you're not old enough,* would be their constant reply. The dagger was a starting weapon. It was a compromise, a weapon he could call his own. It was long and forged from the highest-grade steel. The leather-bound handle was ornate with a steel pommel and embedded with a blood-red ruby. The leather handle was decorated with the emblem of a flying gryphon and a stag with its head lowered and its antlers bared. The gryphon was the Everthorn emblem and the stag represented Baron Sandrik's house. Two noble houses intertwined and loyal to the end. It was a present worthy of a prince.

She missed them so much and hoped that Zane was feeling better. Surely, the wine would help with that. Sighing, she returned her attention back to her book. Most people would have seen that the queen was trying to read and kept quiet, entertaining themselves. The baroness however refused to get the hint. She sat opposite the queen with a large crystal goblet of wine in her dainty hand and prattled on, gossiping about the lords and ladies of the court. Unfortunately, Raylene couldn't even share the burden, because the two ladies-in-waiting were already passed out and snoring softly. The worst part was, she was stuck with the baroness's company for another day, possibly two. Meanwhile, the king, the baron, Jace, Rylan and most of the household guards were enjoying a hunting expedition.

They had heard a rumour at one of the wineries they had visited on their way back. The owner had complained of a monstrous boar lurking in the forest near his vineyard. The boar had killed two of his dogs and the owner had pleaded with the king to hunt the monster down. The king and the baron's eyes had sparkled as they happily agreed to hunt down the beast. They started babbling about weapons, supplies, horses, carts, hunting dogs, food and alcohol; all the important necessities required for a hunting expedition. Orders were given and soldiers were sent riding off on errands. They had barely been able to contain their excitement, acting like little children in a candy shop.

Rumours were often fabricated or over exaggerated and there was the distinct possibility that there wasn't a monstrous boar, but that didn't matter. The opportunity for a hunting expedition was what mattered. It was something they loved, the bonding, the experience and the hunt. The queen had just smiled, whatever made her husband happy. That and the fact that her husband had promised her jewellery as compensation for having to endure the baroness.

The queen opened the curtain to the carriage, to see the sun beginning to set over the distant mountains. The men would hopefully have caught the boar and would be sitting and drinking around a campfire. They were due to rendezvous with them tomorrow afternoon, possibly tomorrow evening depending on their hungover state. The baron, baroness and their guards would then stay as guests in Sethanon with them, before booking passage and making their way to Vasering. If the hunt was successful, they would bring the boar carcass back with them and roast it back at the castle. Boar was her favourite meat and the thought of a roast boar meal with all the trimmings, made her mouth water.

* * *

The baroness tilted the wine bottle, refilling her empty goblet, before inclining the bottle towards the queen. The queen politely refused with a wave of her hand. She was still on her first drink and it was three-quarters full. "More wine for me then.", the baroness said, smirking. She placed the bottle back in the bucket and prepared to take a sip. At that precise moment, the carriage lurched to a stop. Wine splashed from the goblet, all over the bodice of the baroness's expensive, light blue dress. The queen raised her book slightly, bit her lip and stifled a giggle.

"We're stopping for the night my queen", the coach driver shouted. The four horses neighed, glad for the rest. They had stopped alongside a small clearing next to the Hallow Mountains. The area was fairly open, except for a few trees and bushes. The mountain that they were next to was smaller than the rest, with a smooth cliff face facing them. It was as if the side of the mountain had been cleaved off, leaving a sheer rock wall. A wall that stood as a barrier, protecting them from the elements.

Darla trotted into the small alcove which also acted as a Brotherhood hideaway and campsite. Being enclosed by trees and bushes and situated next to the Hydranian River, it made an ideal spot. It was rumoured that centuries ago the river had been part of the Kaspien Sea and was a popular spot for sea creatures to breed. The entrance to the river had been closed off leaving some of the sea creatures trapped and lurking within its murky depths.

An elaborate glowing symbol radiated on the surrounding trees. They had been activated by Darla only moments before. The symbols were invisible to the naked eye but had revealed themselves due to the ring she wore on her left hand. The symbol activated the mirage spell—one that completely masked any occupants, enabling them to avoid detection. To gain access all one needed was to say the password. It was an added measure of security. Being an elite Brotherhood operative, Darla had memorised every password.

She had been right about the location, but she had simply put herself in their shoes and based her decision on what she would have done. It made sense, it was practical and enabled them to travel at their leisure on the following day. From her position she could see them establishing a camp, staking the ground and picketing the horses in a semi-circle around the campsite. It was a smart tactic and provided them with a perimeter alarm. The horses would give them ample warning if anyone approached.

Some of the guards were digging latrines while others were digging a pit for a large campfire. A barrier of rocks surrounded the pit, providing both a barrier and protection. Bedrolls were then laid out in a circle around the campfire. The campfire was big enough to cook their dinner and provide the guards with sufficient warmth. Both rangers had gone off with some snares and their recurve bows. The queen had requested rabbit stew for dinner and they needed meat for it. They were happy to oblige. Hunting was second nature to them and although the task was menial and beneath them, it was also necessary and they were the best men for the job.

She needed to get into a position that enabled her to have a closer look. She waited until dusk and the first glimmer of stars could be seen lighting up the sky. The moon was still hidden behind the tall mountain range known as Gryphon Peaks. It would rise soon enough illuminating the land in its unearthly glow. Midnight neighed, saying goodbye. He was a good companion, being loyal, well-trained and protective. Mind you, he was also stubborn, cheeky and argumentative. The horse had a personality and she loved him for it, she wouldn't have it any other way.

She tossed him an apple, which he caught in his mouth, crunching it and spraying juice everywhere. She then lifted a bag off the saddle and tipped a pile of oats into a large wooden bowl. "Now don't be a pig and eat them all at once", she said stroking his mane and giving him a reassuring pat. Another neigh and a toss of the head telling her, *"I'll be fine, now go!"*. Midnight knew the routine, he would stay where he was and wait for her, knowing that she'd be back the following morning. Adjusting the quiver, she crept forward, hidden within the shadows of the Hallow

Mountains. A ghost in the night, unseen and unheard.

The last mountain before the campsite was slightly smaller than the rest and had been modified. Dwarven and human engineers had cut out a path and a platform two metres up the side of the mountain. A pile of large rocks lay below the platform at the base of the river. The platform faced the Hydranian River and was rumoured to be a great fishing spot. Hand over hand, Darla warily climbed up the rocky slope, careful not to dislodge any rocks or make any noise. Pulling herself up onto the path, she hid amongst some bushes and tall grass at the edge of the platform. The coverage provided her with an ideal viewing point and concealed her perfectly. The setting sun aided in this, casting shadows and leaving a faint orange hue in its wake. Soon she would be cloaked in the darkness of night. She would be in her element.

She noticed that the carriage was parked alongside a small crop of trees, next to the wagons. The coach driver had unstrapped the horses and driven a stake into the ground, picketing them nearby. They were now happily grazing. The campsite had been efficiently established, with everybody contributing. Even the queen pitched in, offering to fill up the canteens with fresh water. She enjoyed mingling with the soldiers and it provided her with a welcomed respite from the baroness, even if it only was for a short while.

The guards had chopped down a couple of trees, providing

themselves with some log seats to sit on. All that remained were some stumps and bushes. They lit the campfire and were now sitting idly around joking and drinking whisky. The rangers had arrived earlier, proudly holding up their catch and boasting to their comrades. They handed off two strings, each consisting of half a dozen rabbits to the coach driver who also happened to be the camp cook.

Darla recalled one of Marek's drunken stories, where he had told her about his mentor and friend Brithren who was also an expert crossbowman. The man was apparently the head cook. Marek had been one of his assistant cooks and during his spare time had taught him how to use his repeater crossbow. They'd had quite the adventures together. The last Marek had heard the man had gone on to be a coachman. Was this the same man? Darla felt a knot in the pit of her stomach. She had a niggling feeling that it was.

Prior to leaving the baron's estates, the coachman had obviously raided the household kitchen, packing an assortment of vegetables and spices into a sealed box and storing it in a compartment at the back of the carriage. It was the only explanation for the assortment of goods and the fresh produce.

He had already unpacked the box and had diced the vegetables, tossing them into two large, iron cooking pots. The pots consisted of onions, potatoes, carrots, celery, parsnip and pumpkin, providing a myriad of colour and texture to the stew. He promptly skinned and deboned the rabbits, dicing the meat and adding it to the mix. Water, wine and a mixture of herbs and spices were added and stirred into the mixture using a large wooden spoon. Flour was then added to thicken the gravy. Happy with his efforts, he nodded satisfied and left it to simmer.

With a loud whistle, he called for four burly, well-muscled soldiers, who eagerly came bounding over. They each grabbed a handle of a cooking pot and carefully carried it across, hanging it over the roaring fire. It didn't take long before the fragrant aroma of the rabbit stew began to waft around the campsite. As she waited, aching and itchy, Darla got a whiff, her heightened smell taking in the aroma and causing her stomach to grumble. Rabbit stew…and it smelled divine. She pulled some dried beef from her cloak pocket and grumbled as she took a bite and chewed vigorously.

Instead of joining the rest of the guards, the rangers isolated themselves, sitting on the steps of the carriage fletching arrows. Their hoods covered their faces, shadowing them and hiding their features. One of them hummed a tune as he worked. His partner's hand shot up, halting the tune as he scanned the surrounding area. Darla was practically invisible, concealed, but this ranger unnerved her, made her feel spooked. It was as if he could sense her. The tune started again as their heads lowered and they got back to work. Darla let out a sigh of relief.

* * *

Darla turned her attention to the queen and watched as she knelt, filling two more of the canteens. Her head down, with strands of hair cascading over her face, she concentrated on the task at hand. Out of the corner of her eye, Darla noticed a ripple in the water. A moment later a dark blue appendage emerged, skimming across the surface, before submerging once again. She had only seen it briefly, but it had her questioning herself. Was it an eel or a large water snake? Possibly, but she doubted it. The queen lifted the two full canteens, stoppered them and hung them over her shoulder.

Queen Raylene placed the last canteen in the river. Ripples in the water caught Darla's attention, closer this time. Whatever the creature was, it was moving and heading straight for the queen. Darla merely watched, intrigued and captivated. The creature was about to do her job for her, it was about to kill the queen.

"Don't worry about filling that one, your Majesty," the Sergeant called out. "It has a small crack in it and leaks water anyway." The queen nodded, pulled the canteen out and stood up. Her eyes were black, soulless and demonic. Then just like that, they changed back to their normal colour. Smiling, she turned around to face the sergeant and walked back to camp. The creature near the shore, abruptly turned and veered away. The queen had been lucky and was completely ignorant to the fact that she had nearly become its next meal.

* * *

That confirmed it for Darla. The queen was a demon. "Well, enjoy the few remaining hours that you have," she said quietly to herself. "Because come nightfall, your death is imminent."

An hour later, the soldiers were chowing down on a hearty rabbit stew. Everyone received a thick piece of bread as well. Some people ate it separately, while most used it to wipe the last remnants of gravy from their bowls. The ladies-in-waiting had already eaten and gone back to sleep. The queen had taken two bowls and retired back to the comfort of the carriage. As soon as she entered, she was greeted with the loud snoring of the baroness. She was sprawled across the couch, one leg hanging over the side, in a deep, drunken sleep. The queen smiled, she didn't mind the snoring, it was a welcome change to her endless prattling and enabled her to sit and enjoy her meal.

She placed the baroness's stew on the side table, next to her empty bottles of wine. It would be cold, but at least she would be able to have something to eat when she awoke. The queen ate the stew and drank the last of her wine, before grabbing a thick blanket and dimming the lantern. Lying down, she wrapped the blanket around herself and settled in for the night.

* * *

Darla lay there watching from her vantage point, as the flames of the campfire flickered and danced, waiting patiently for the darkness to take hold. She watched like a hawk, alert and taking in every detail, observing the shift changes, their positions and the layout of their camp. The captain of the rangers had remained with the king, so he had sent his second-in-charge with the queen. Being part of the king's elite guard, he had automatically been promoted to Captain as well, outranking the sergeant and putting him in charge of the queen's retinue. Due to this, it was his responsibility to organise a sentry duty roster.

He posted two sentries per watch for the nine shifts. Each duty lasted two hours. This enabled every guard to also receive a decent amount of sleep if they opted to. Some of them chose to stay up, sacrificing their sleep for the opportunity to drink and gamble. Much to the disgust of the sergeant, the captain's fellow ranger was excluded, apparently having done a double duty the night before. Whether it was true or purely favouritism, the sergeant didn't know, but he was seething and irate. Grinding his teeth and mumbling under his breath, he went on duty with one of his fellow guards.

As the guards finished their shift, the sergeants companion picked up his rod to try his luck at fishing. The sergeant decided to forgo it, picking up his pouch and opting to join the gambling and drinking instead. The guard stumbled up the path, juggling his rod, a whisky flask and a bucket full of bait in one hand. He had apparently dug through the rabbit carcasses, collecting some of the remains for bait. Darla had to admit, the man showed ingenuity and determination. Either that or desperation. His other arm was outstretched carrying a bobbing lantern. After grazing himself a couple of times, he finally reached the ledge and baiting the hook, threw the line into the water. Holding onto the rod with one hand, he carefully sat on the edge, wriggled the cork free and took a swig from the flask.

He took another swig and slowly reeled in some of the line. "Why are we the ones stuck here babysitting the queen while all the other guards get to go on a hunting expedition with the baron and the king?" He threw the flask for emphasis, sending it careening through the air and landing with a thud, centimetres from where Darla lay.

She silently let loose a string of curses, it confirmed her suspicions and put things into perspective. The king and the prince going hunting had been an unforeseen occurrence, a turn of events that even her benefactor hadn't foreseen. It didn't help her situation though. She hated complications, leaving her contract incomplete. She doubted her benefactor would be forgiving and understanding. She would have to kill the queen in such a fashion that it left a very distinctive message, a message stating that Prince Jace and the king would be next, that her contract would be fulfilled.

The guard was still muttering when he felt a tug on the line.

Excitedly he started to reel it in, as the fish leapt out of the water, splashing, trying to break free and escape. The fish was a descent size, about half a metre long. It was a good start and would provide good eating. Darla used the distraction to push the flask away from her, sliding it along the dirt towards the edge of the path.

Slowly, the guard reeled the fish in. It was resisting, putting up a struggle. He stopped reeling, holding the line firm and letting the fish thrash and tire itself out. Impulsively, he let go of the rod with one of his hands and reached for the flask. "Seven hells," he cursed, remembering what he'd done, how he'd thrown the flask in a stupid outburst, a fit of rage. He glanced towards the bushes and spotted it laying at the edge of the path. Keeping a firm hold of the rod, he leaned to the side and stretched his hand towards it. His fingers touched the cool metal, pawing at it, trying to slide it closer.

Darla saw a ripple in the water. The fish started acting erratically, leaping into the air and thrashing about. The rod bent with the strain. Then with a final splash, the fish disappeared into the murky depths. The line spun rapidly as the rod thrashed back and forth, before being ripped from his hand. The guard's body jolted, sliding forward. All he could do was watch as his hand brushed against the flask, knocking it and sending it tumbling over the side. "Fuck!" he swore as lowering himself over, he began to climb down to the rocks below.

* * *

Darla watched, captivated from her vantage point. It was like watching a scene from a horror show at the theatre, were the performers kept the audience in suspense. Darla had always found the entertainment amusing, knowing exactly what was about to happen. The guard stumbled down the rocks, scraping his knee and cursing in the process. Blood trickled down his leg, dripping onto the rocks and into the water below.

A ripple appeared in the water. The dark blue appendage emerged again. Darla could see it more clearly now and was able to make out the glistening scales that the appendage consisted of. She had her suspicions, but they were yet to be confirmed. The writhing appendage glided through the water and headed straight towards the guard.

Getting a foothold and holding on with one hand, the guard gingerly reached down toward his flask. His fingers brushed against the smooth metal, but he was just out of reach. He readjusted his footing and stretched, smiling as his fingers grasped hold. It was then that Darla saw the size of the appendage and knew exactly what it was. "It's a fucking hydra," she said loudly, astounded and not being able to help herself. Alerted, the guard looked straight at her and opened his mouth.

He was about to raise the alarm. Silent and deadly, the hydra's head burst out of the water. It clamped around the guard's neck, killing him instantly. Another head erupted out of the water, biting with its long, jagged, razor-sharp teeth into the guard's leg. Lifting the guard high into air, Darla heard multiple cracks as his leg and neck snapped. With a tearing squelch, the guard's head and leg were torn off and devoured. With a splash, the bloodied torso dropped down into the water. Three more heads rose from the deep and started feasting upon it.

Its powerful jaws enabled it to easily tear through the armour and bone. Slowly, the five heads sunk back into the watery depths. All that remained was a pool of blood, spreading across the water. It was indeed a hydra, one of the apex predators of the deep and judging from its size and colouring, it was a young adult. Darla made a mental note, to stick clear of the water's edge.

As the evening wore on, things began to quieten down. Soldiers stumbled away drunkenly, most grumbling about their loss of money. The shift changed with two groggy soldiers stumbling towards the fire, while their comrades climbed into their bedrolls. They wrapped thick blankets around them to keep warm and were soon sound asleep. Nobody noticed the missing soldier who had gone fishing and had failed to return.

Darla crept forward cautiously, making sure to keep low to the ground. She kept to the darkness and used the bushes and trees for cover, making sure that she remained concealed so that the sentries didn't spot her. She also ensured that she stayed away from the shore of the river. After all, she wasn't the only predator stalking and hunting the royal party.

Chapter 5

Darla looked at the sky and the stars sparking down at her. The red, ringed planet Kryton, shone brightly. Many cultures associate the planet with the warrior or the reaper, war and death. It had been nicknamed the blood planet. To Darla and every other werewolf, it resembled the hunter and the planet played a far more significant purpose.

* * *

As she gazed at Kryton, the moon passed behind a cloud, shining in all its glory. It was a full moon tonight, a perfect night to hunt and kill. Gauging from the position of the moon, it was roughly 9pm. Things would start to quieten down soon. To Darla, it didn't really matter whether it was a full moon or not. Unlike most werewolves who could only transform on a full moon, Darla could manifest her transformation on any night, regardless of the size of the moon. Although there was no doubt that a full moon had mystical properties for a werewolf. It fuelled their blood rage, manifested their bestial nature and enhanced their senses.

Most werewolves ran rampart, caught up in the blood rage, in a frenzy, massacring, killing and unable to control themselves. Darla had always been different, being able to control her lycanthropy. She was able to control the transformation and her bestial nature, harness the power and utilise it. It was a mystery she hoped to solve one day. Darla continued to gaze at the full moon, she could feel its mystical power in her blood, bones and soul. It was exhilarating!

There was only one moon more powerful than a full moon and that was a blood moon. It was a rare occurrence when the red planet Kryton aligned with the moon, eclipsing it and giving the moon a red tinge to its nightly glow. During a blood moon, every werewolf transformed, even the ones who could control the transformation. They gave in to the urge, losing all self-control. It was like a primal urge; a darkness enveloped them forcing the change.

It was also rumoured that if a werewolf bit a human during a blood moon, the human would be infused with the mystical qualities and would instantly turn into a powerful werewolf – a force of nature to be reckoned with. This rarely happened though, due to the frenzied state that the werewolves were in, most of their victims were torn apart and massacred. The blood moon was powerful for monsters and dark magic. It was when evil ran rampant throughout the world.

Things began to quieten down an hour later. Guards staggered drunkenly off to bed while others grumbled about their loss of money. Two went to bed happy, smiling and boasting as they tucked their winnings under their pillows and wrapped blankets around themselves. Darla continued to wait…and watch. She waited until it was almost the end of the shift and the sentries began to show signs of drowsiness, lethargy and inattentiveness. They were far from alert as they just wanted to go to bed.

One of them sat on a log near the campfire taking sips of liquor from his flask. His crossbow was loaded and resting on the log beside him. His companion stood near the bush Darla was hiding and gazing ahead. He had a thick, fur-lined cloak wrapped around himself and carried a broad, battle-axe held tightly in his fur-lined gloves. Darla wrapped her fur cloak around herself as she felt herself freezing from the night's bitter cold. Her muscles being stiff and sore were beginning to ache. It was an exceptionally chilly night, but she could at least rejoice that spring was approaching.

With steady hands, she raised the repeater crossbow and aimed, the razor-sharp bolt knocked and ready to fire. She gently squeezed the trigger and with a soft twang, the bolt was on its way soaring through the air. The guard had just lifted his flask, preparing to take another sip when the bolt nicked the metal rim with a soft clunk before embedding itself in the man's throat. With a look of bewilderment on his face, he gurgled up a mouthful of blood, spraying it on the ground before him. Then, he toppled backwards off the log, the flask tumbling from his dead hands. The flask landed with a thud spilling its content across the ground.

Darla cursed silently as his companion whipped his head around, alerted by the sound. She had a moment to act before the alarm would be raised. There wasn't enough time to re-cock the crossbow. It clattered to the ground as she leapt to her feet. Her long-bladed dagger was out of its sheath in an instant. Leaping forward, she took the guard by surprise. Her arm was a blur as it swung across, the blade shining as it reflected in the firelight. The dagger pierced the guard's neck, going through to the hilt and protruding through the other side. The soldier let out a startled gasp, dropping his battle-axe at his feet. As he began to topple forward, his legs giving way, Darla grabbed him around the waist and gently lowered him to the ground. It was done quietly and efficiently. She looked cautiously around and was relieved to see that everyone was still fast asleep.

She pulled her dagger free and blood gushed out, pooling around the guard's corpse. Quietly, without making a sound, she crept towards two spearmen who were wrapped in their blankets with their spears dug into the ground and propped up against a nearby tree. She knelt over the first one, clamped a hand firmly over his mouth and slashed her dagger across his throat. Crimson blood flowed rapidly pooling on the ground around his blanket. Stepping quietly over the spearman's corpse, she knelt next to his comrade and repeated the procedure.

She crept forward, keeping to the shadows. With a moan, one of the ranger's heads turned, looking directly at her. He was leaning against the carriage dressed in light armour, with his legs outstretched and his recurve bow lying next to him. Darla froze, holding her breath as she waited. The way the man was watching her silently from under his hood was unnerving. But in her shock, Darla noticed that his breathing was rhythmic, slow and steady. He was still asleep. With a sigh of relief, she continued on her way.

The next two guards had positioned themselves next to some bushes and trees in the cover of darkness, away from the campfire. One of them was snoring so loudly that Darla was surprised he hadn't woken the entire campsite. She nearly gagged as she neared the bush and was hit by a horrific smell. It reeked of faeces, urine and god knows what else.

Why the hell would they sleep next to the latrines? The guards were either drunk or had no sense of smell.

She covered her mouth and nose with her spare hand, trying desperately to mask the smell and progressed slowly forward. She felt like she was going to vomit. Suddenly, the guard before her lashed out, thumping his companion and mumbling some slurred expletives. He was drunk and obviously annoyed at his friend's snoring. The guard mumbled something again, louder this time and sat up, throwing off his blanket. Darla froze mid-step.

She was just in front of the bushes, mostly concealed by the shadows and darkness. Only a very keen eye would spot her. Luckily though, the guard was still half asleep as he stood, blurry eyed, and walked towards the trees. He stopped next to the bush and untied his pants ready to relieve himself. "I knew I shouldn't have drunk that last ale," he muttered. A trickle started as he began to urinate at the edge of the latrine. Darla crept forward along the edge of the bush. Chuckling, the man swivelled spraying the area around him. Darla took another cautious step.

With a final trickle, the man finished and began to tie up his pants. Darla leapt up behind him, clamping her hand over his mouth and plunged her dagger into the man's side, killing him instantly. The guard didn't even have time to scream. As she pulled her dagger free and let go, the guard toppled forward, landing in the latrine with a squelchy splash. Quietly, she crept back around the bush towards his snoring companion.

Darla knelt over him and placed her hand firmly over his mouth stifling his snore.

Lowering her dagger, she began to slice across his throat, stopping mid-way as she suddenly heard a slight creak. The man, fully awake now, eyes wide and panicking, reached desperately to his throat and tried to scream. His eyes stared into hers, afraid, pleading for her to stop. Blood gushed from the wound, covering his hands and pooling on the ground. Darla drove her dagger through the man's throat and into the ground beneath him. His breathing stopped and his hands dropped to his side limp and lifeless. His eyes continued to stare into hers; the last thing that he would see.

Darla pulled her dagger free just as she heard another creak. She froze, waiting and watching. Someone was trying to be covert, trying not to wake the camp. A moment of silence passed, and then a thunderous noise that could have woken the dead. It was a loud, bellowing fart, one that any guard or soldier would be proud to boast of. The person who made the monstrous noise was not a guard though and felt it was extremely unladylike as she blushed with embarrassment. "Oh my," the Baroness said, as she clambered down the last step of the carriage. She suddenly realised how desperately she needed to go to the toilet.

The latrines were a good twenty metres away. They were

directly across from her on the other side of the campsite. The baroness lifted her dress, breaking wind again and frantically started to run towards the latrines and Darla's position. Running and farting, it was almost comical. In any other situation, Darla would have laughed. With a flick of her wrist, she let her dagger fly. It spun end over end, its blade flickering in the firelight, whirling towards its target. She was an expert knife thrower and rarely missed her target which in this case was the baroness's heart.

The dagger was on target, true to its mark and then mid stride the baroness's foot hit a loose rock. Her arms flailed as she stumbled and almost lost her balance. As she righted herself, the dagger embedded itself into her shoulder, spraying blood in her face and toppling her backwards. She let out a startled, horrified scream and landed with a thud, soiling herself in the process. "Damn it," Darla cursed, leaping back into the safety of the darkness. The stumps and bushes behind her provided little cover, but the shadows and the gloom at least concealed her from the now stirring campsite.

The scream was as good as an alarm, waking the guards instantly. The guards leapt out of their bedrolls, discarding their blankets. Dressed in their bed clothes, they looked around anxiously, immediately discovering their fallen comrades. They were alert and ready for battle. Weapons were grabbed, unsheathed and at the ready. Their armour was left by their bedrolls, discarded for the moment, due to the time it took to strap it on.

The baroness lay moaning and crying, blood soaking into her dress and forming a crimson pool around her. The captain immediately stepped forward and helping her to her feet, started barking orders to his men. He quietly cursed to himself as he took note of the dead bodies. This assassin had already killed half a dozen of his men. The campsite suddenly became a buzz of activity, the guards rushing, disciplined and well-trained as they followed their captain's orders. Torches were lit and promptly stuck in the ground, illuminating the campsite. The remaining crossbowman climbed on top of the carriage, giving himself the advantage of elevation. The captain promptly escorted the distressed baroness back to the safety of the carriage. Darla looked around for the other ranger. Where the hell was he?

During the scrambling, the ranger had disappeared and it took a moment for Darla to locate him. His cloak practically camouflaged him, and she would have missed it if it were not for her keen sight. He was kneeling on a branch above the carriage, his bow partly drawn, his hood twisting ever so slightly as he scanned the area. She had heard stories about the King's Rangers, the wars, missions and feats that they had accomplished. They were renown throughout the world, having earnt themselves a formidable reputation. If left unchecked, the ranger could prove quite the hindrance. Darla would have to take care of him quickly. The crossbowman could wait, the ranger was her number one priority.

Two guards came running, juggling and clanking an array of armour components. They were newcomers and it was their job to don the sergeant's armour due to his rank. The captain stood guard, his short sword drawn, his eyes scanning, searching for any sign of movement. He and his fellow ranger slept in their light, hardened leather armour. It was part of their motto *'Always alert, always ready.'*

One of the rookies assisted the sergeant into his gousset – a light chainmail top that protected the unarmoured areas. The other placed the fauld over the sergeant's waist and hips. The fauld consisted of plate strips and provided both protection and manoeuvrability. They still had the arm, leg pieces, breastplate and helmet to go. When finished, they would help the other guards. Lastly, they would assist each other with their own armour. Armoured, alert, battle ready, Darla did not care, nothing could prepare them for the attack that was about to come.

Werewolves were a myth to most people, the information about them based on rumours and speculation. It was extremely rare for someone to encounter a werewolf, especially considering most of them resided in Lycanthaw. Lance and his family were slaves in the gorkin kingdom of Gorkinthal. Darla cringed. The gorkin were arrogant assholes. Not only had they incorporated their race, but the word 'thal' in their language meant rule or ruler. So, it translated to gorkin rule. It was complete and utter werewolf shit! Darla was an exception. She was the only werewolf roaming amongst the kingdoms.

When werewolves hunted, they stalked and attacked people, tearing them to shreds. They were vicious, feral, giving in to their urges and their nature to hunt and feed. That was what people believed, what the old stories told and what the bards sung about. It was also why werewolves were banned in all the kingdoms, except theirs. Their kingdom was a sanctuary. They were protected, weren't hunted down and killed. Darla had always been careful when she transformed, making sure she did it in a secluded, isolated location. She only killed when necessary, making sure there were no survivors and that no-one was turned.

The guards were battle ready to deal with a human enemy, but not a monster like her. Besides decapitation or amputation, steel weapons were useless against her. She had even heard a story of a werewolf who had his arm amputated and surgically reattached. It had left a horrific scar, but after a couple of months it had become fully functional, as good as new. It was a story though and not something she wanted to test the theory behind. To find out for herself. If the guards had been armed with silver weapons, it would have changed things completely. Silver was like poison to a werewolf. Wounds caused by silver weapons took a lot longer to heal, even with a werewolf's phenomenal regenerative abilities. Still, silver weapons were rarely fatal unless it was a severe wound.

The only weapons that could kill her were weapons like her short sword. It was still a mystery to her, its origin and the powers that it held. Rayze also wielded such a weapon, proving to her that there was more than one within the world. At some point she would need to investigate it and either do some research or question Rayze. Like the weapons, the swordsman was also a complex mystery and Darla suspected that he was understating and playing himself down, that he was a lot more than what he made out to be. One sure thing was that the weapons were of a divine, archaic nature. Darla could only imagine how powerful they were. But one thing she knew was that they had been made for one purpose – to kill monsters and demons.

Darla stood there in the dark and unstrapped her cloak, the short sword and her belt. Wrapping the contents and folding them neatly, she placed the bundle carefully in a nearby bush. Untying her boots, she slipped them off and placed them on top. Her tunic and pants were gnomish-designed and made from a fur-lined elastic material. She had spent a fortune on them, buying two outfits and secretly hoping that they could withstand a transformation. One of them had got ruined during her previous contract to the point that it was unsalvageable and had to be burned. She now knew that this tunic was also about to get ruined. Rumour had it that a new improved version had been designed, but that would have to wait for another day.

* * *

Concentrating, she allowed the lycanthropy to take hold and give her a complete transformation, a stage three werewolf. Using her willpower she kept the mental barriers in place, enabling her to keep her humanity and rein in the primal urges. It allowed her to retain control of the beast within, the beast she was about to unleash. The transformation was a painful process, but it was a pain Darla had grown accustomed to. She welcomed and embraced it.

Her eyes were always the first to change, becoming bestial and yellow. Her jaw then elongated, her teeth growing bigger, her canines becoming longer and sharper. Teeth ideal for biting, tearing and ripping apart her victims.

Her ears transformed next, growing long, pointy and enhancing her hearing. Her hands and feet started to grow longer and broader, reshaping and changing. The enamel in her nails strengthened, hardening as they grew longer, becoming razor-sharp claws, weapons for killing. Lastly, her body transformed along with her body hair. Her hair grew at an alarming rate, becoming thick, coarse, brown fur with bright red streaks running through part of it. Her muscles and bones became denser and sturdier, tearing apart her clothes as they reshaped themselves, making her stronger and more agile, superhuman, a monster to be feared.

A rumbling, threatening growl erupted from her throat. Her ears twitched, picking up a soft buzzing sound and she instantly moved. The arrow hit with a thud, piercing her shoulder. Her quick reflexes were the only thing that had saved her. It had been a kill shot, aimed straight at her heart. It would have killed an average person instantly. It was a testament to the ranger's ability. He had been able to distinguish her from amongst the shadows. It was no mean feat! She needed to take him out quickly.

Two spearmen approached, their spears outstretched as they walked slowly and cautiously. Gripping the shaft, Darla pulled. The arrowhead was barbed, designed to cause even more damage when it was removed. Her skin tore, spraying blood and staining her fur. The arrow was well made, sturdy and strong, with the head being made of the finest steel and honed until it was razor-sharp. The two spearmen started stabbing blindly with their spears. Enlightening their campsite had worked in Darla's favour. It had blinded them to her presence momentarily, at least until their eyes adjusted to the dark.

Snapping the arrow, she quickly threw the shaft. It was scrap; she didn't need it. It hit a rock, cracking and splintering. "She's over there," one of the spearmen said as stabbing, they thrust their spears forward. Darla stood motionless, holding the jagged, splintered end of the shaft with the arrowhead attached. It made the perfect throwing weapon. In a blur of speed, she acted, hurtling the weapon forth. Spinning through the air, it hit with perfect accuracy, stabbing the spearman through the eye and puncturing his brain.

"Holy fuck!" the other spearman screamed as his companion dropped to the ground dead. He was surprised and momentarily panicked. Her ears twitched as she heard the ranger partly stretching the bow string. He was already in the process of knocking another arrow. Darla grabbed the nearest stump firmly. Bark and wood chips sprayed as her claws sunk into the wood, gaining purchase and holding it tight. Her muscles bulged, tensing with the strain, but slowly the stump began to move. Darla's ears twitched as she picked up another buzz. Another arrow had been loosed.

Soil and tree roots erupted from the earth. Darla was on the move as the trunk came free. She pivoted into position. With a thud and a spray of wood chips and bark, the arrow embedded itself into the centre of the stump. With a fierce growl, she charged forward into the light. Recovering, the spearman brought his spear to bare, lowering it, ready for the attack. But it was too late, Darla was already past the deadly weapon. She swatted it aside as she barged past and rammed the stump into the spearman with the force of a battering ram.

The spear toppled harmlessly to the ground in front of her as the spearman was thrown off his feet. He landed with a thud a couple of metres away, his ribcage shattered and his chest turning a deep purple. He coughed up blood which dribbled down his chin. The man would die within minutes from internal bleeding. Another twang as the bow string released. Followed by a short, sharper twang. That of the heavy crossbow. Both projectiles were deadly, fired with the same velocity and from the same distance. Her timing had to be perfect.

She swung the trunk up, diagonally across her body. Her timing was immaculate as the arrow and the bolt thudded into the stump. Besides a spray of wood chips, the trunk had shielded her perfectly. With a growl, she swung it back. Her muscles tensed as she threw it, sending it hurtling towards a tree. Lightning quick, she then dived at the ground, grabbed the shaft of the discarded spear and bound back to her feet. Throwing back her arm, she threw the spear.

The stump twirled through the air with pinpoint accuracy. The ranger cursed himself. He had thought himself untouchable. Deftly he leapt into the air, landing gracefully on the neighbouring branch. The stump collided, smashing into the trunk of the tree and shattered. Swinging his cloak around himself, he shielded himself from the onslaught of wood chips and shards. "Very good, but you are going to have to do better than that," the ranger said before feeling excruciating pain.

Darla had anticipated the ranger's move and had planned for it. The large stump had not only forced him to move, but it had also limited the options of where he could go. The velocity of the impact had then caused the stump to shatter, which provided her with the perfect distraction. She had aimed the spear perfectly and the ranger hadn't even seen it coming. The spear had pierced him through the stomach, tearing through his light armour and erupting out the other side. The force threw the ranger off the branch, leaving him dangling and dying, as the spear embedded itself into the trunk of the tree.

Darla continued without stopping. Her target was the Sergeant who was in the process of having his breast plate strapped on. They were standing in front of one of the massive log seats situated near the campfire, the Sergeant having already donned his helmet and most of his armour components. He stood holding a huge, spiked mace above his head in one of his beefy, gauntleted hands. He was restless, his head turning this way and that as he urged the rookie to hurry up. The rookie was flustered as he stood behind the sergeant and fumbled with the side straps. His partner had already gone off to assist the other guards and the captain had gone to check on the queen and the baroness.

Darla ploughed into the Sergeant, knocking the two of them off their feet and sending them flying. In the process, one of her clawed hands grabbed the Sergeant's shoulder, while the other grabbed his helmet. Her razor-sharp claws screeched on the metal with an ear-piercing shriek. As they landed, Darla slammed the Sergeant's helmeted head into the log. The helmet and the Sergeant's skull caved in with a sickening crunch.

The poor rookie who had been strapping him flew back, his legs slamming into the log and somersaulting over it. He landed on his head, snapping his neck before landing in the campfire. Embers and ash sprayed into the air and a moment later. His clothes ignited and filled the air with the rancid smell of burning flesh.

Darla leapt over the log, landing before another guard. He held a flaming torch in one hand and a sword in the other. "Stay back beast," he shouted, holding the torch in front of him while swinging wildly with his sword. Darla lunged forward and in a flash the torch was discarded, spinning through the air and landing on a guard's discarded bedroll. It immediately went up in flames, igniting the bedroll next to it. To his credit, the guard stood his ground, feinting with his sword and then lunging. Darla easily dodged, leaping to the side, only to have something pierce her shoulder.

It was the crossbowman. He had fired another bolt and was now in the process of re-cocking it. Darla needed to take him out, but she was currently engaged in more pressing matters. The brief distraction nearly cost Darla her life. She leant back as the guard swung. The sword narrowly missing where her head had been only moments before. He tried to follow through with a back-handed swing, but Darla caught his wrist, immobilising it and stopping the stroke. Then, with an almighty crack, she snapped his wrist in two. His sword dropped to the ground, clattering as his hand hung limply at an unnatural angle. Clutching his wrist, he screamed in pain.

The swordsman was defenceless and exposed. Pouncing, Darla slashed, her claws raking across his chest, tearing through muscle and slicing to the bone. The guard staggered back, screaming, covered in blood. Darla growled menacingly and stepped forward. The guard was afraid, panicking, as he held his good hand over his chest trying to stem the flow of blood. He collapsed to his knees as his legs gave out. Looking up, the last thing he saw was Darla's claws descending on him once again.

The captain dutifully stood by the carriage door, guarding it while shouting for the coach driver to hurry up. He had helped one of the wagoners strap the horses. Climbing onto the seat, the wagoner cracked his whip. The horses needed no encouragement, as they galloped forward with a spray of pebbles and dust. The servants, maids and handmaidens were away, heading to safety. The other wagoner was struggling to strap his horses in, but the coachman had his own problems. He needed to strap the horses to the carriage and get the queen to safety.

He managed to strap the two rear horses on quickly. He patted them reassuringly, as they neighed nervously. Running, he led the remaining two from the picketed stake. The baroness could be heard crying hysterically within the carriage, while her lady-in-waiting's gentle voice offered words of comfort and support. The two guards stationed near the coach driver watched on anxiously as they guarded and protected him.

Darla ploughed into a nearby swordsman, knocking him off his feet and sending the sword clattering to the ground. She landed on his chest, hovering over him, baring her teeth and growling menacingly. One of his arms was pinned, her claws digging into his flesh. His breathing was rapid and his eyes were wild as the gravity of the situation dawned on him. Screaming, the soldier lashed out, clenching his fist and smashing her in the shoulder and the side of the head with his free hand.

Seeing the situation, the captain turned to the two guards. "Help him," he shouted. The guards looked at the coach driver and hesitated, unsure of what to do. He knew he had ordered them to protect the coach driver, but circumstances change and so do orders during a battle. "Both of you. NOW!" he screamed, glaring at them. It was all the encouragement the guards needed. Lowering his spear, the first guard warily stepped forward, while his companion covered him with his battle-axe. Approaching their comrade, they left the coachman undefended.

The guard's punches were relentless, thumping and pounding Darla. She waited patiently for the right timing and caught his arm mid swing. She squeezed and…CRACK! The man gritted his teeth but didn't make a sound, even when he noticed the bone protruding out of his wrist. *Fine, have it your way,* she thought as she yanked on the arm and popped the shoulder out. She continued to pull and a moment later, with a sickening, tearing sound, she tore the guard's arm off. A fountain of blood sprayed forth, covering Darla's fur and forming a crimson pool around them. The guard finally screamed, his eyes rolling up as he passed out.

She threw the arm and blood sprayed across the ground in its wake. A strange rumbling sound came out of Darla's mouth, the werewolf equivalent of a laugh or a chuckle. The arm continued its grizzly flight, spinning end over end towards the captain. It was a message that held a challenge. Seeing it coming, the captain quickly dodged to the side and the arm slammed into the carriage door, smearing blood over the window.

As she prepared herself for the approaching guards, her ears pricked as she heard the familiar twang and leapt to the side just in time. The crossbow bolt grazed the side of her head, drawing blood, before shooting past her and embedding itself in one of the log seats. She growled, not out of pain, but out of frustration. The crossbowman was now frantically loading another bolt and trying to re-cock the crossbow, providing her with a slight reprieve.

She returned her attention to the two guards still heading her way. The spearman thrust the spear tip forward, hoping to impale her, but Darla nimbly dodged out of the way. He thrust repeatedly, the spear head darting in and out, but each time Darla eluded it, dodging, ducking and leaping left and right. Every time she leapt to the other side, the battle-axe wielding guard would follow, moving behind his companion and ensuring that he remained on the same side as the werewolf. He was covering the spearman's flank. It was a dance, a deadly game of cat and mouse.

The spearman thrust high, aiming for Darla's chest, but instead of moving to the left she feigned and ducked under the spearhead. The spearman had already retreated, backstepping and allowing his companion with the battle-axe the opportunity to engage the werewolf in close quarter combat. The guard swung, the battle-axe gliding through the air in a deadly swing. Darla leapt backwards, straight into the spearman's path. The guard held his battle-axe firmly, keeping it at the ready in case she closed the distance again. The spearman jabbed, keeping her at bay and retreating backwards. Then a twang sounded as the crossbowman fired again. She was a sitting duck.

The crossbowman had predicted her movements and aimed accordingly, assuming that she would step backwards. Instead, she lunged forwards, directly into the path of the spear. She dodged to the side at the last minute as the bolt flew past her and lodged itself in the ground. Darla had timed the manoeuvre perfectly. The spearman recovered instantly, realising what had happened and quickly changed his grip. He swung the broad razor-sharp barb sideways, hoping to impale it in the side of Darla's head.

Darla caught it mid swing, grabbing the shaft just below the curved barb. She twisted her wrist and…snap! The heavy-duty oak pole cracked, the wood splintering and the metal reinforcement buckling and snapping as the spear head broke off into her hand. The spearman gasped, looking helplessly at the splintered remnants of his pole. He threw it at her and she swiped it harmlessly out of the way. Fumbling, he reached for the dagger strapped to his belt.

Growling Darla lunged, feinting as she stepped back quickly. The guard automatically retaliated, swinging his battle-axe and falling for the ruse. It swung wide as the guard overcompensated and Darla lunged forward. Her raised arm descended, ramming the spearhead through the guard's eye. Letting go, the axeman fell backwards like a toppled tree. Dead. Swinging around, she then caught the battle-axe from the guard's lifeless fingers and completing the pirouette manoeuvre, slashed it across the spearman's throat.

It was futile, but the spearman clutched at his throat and tried to stem the flow of blood. Dropping to his knees, he collapsed face first and died. Darla promptly hefted the axe and threw it at lightning speed, spinning end over end towards the crossbowman. The crossbowman was oblivious and didn't see it coming. He was too busy concentrating on re-cocking his crossbow. With a whirring sound, the axe flew towards its target. A second later a crack sounded, followed by a thud as the axe sliced through the crossbow, shattering it and implanting itself in the crossbowman's chest. The force of the impact was so great that it propelled him off the carriage.

Two guards remaining and the captain. The guards were cautious, having borne witness to the carnage that she had done. The first one held a two-handed sword; a weapon that in the right hands could prove devastating due to its power and reach. His companion was armed with a large two-handed battle-axe, the blade wickedly curved and razor-sharp. They stood together, a bastion, a last line of defence before she reached the carriage.

The swordsman swung a diagonal stroke. It was fast, deadly and forceful. The stroke would cleave her in two if it connected. She leapt deftly to the side, retreating momentarily only to find herself in the path of the axeman. Diving to the ground, she crouched on all fours as the battle-axe glided over her. She heard the swish and saw the gleam of the steel reflecting in the firelight as the two-handed sword swung down like an executioner's blade.

Darla rolled and the blade hit nothing but dirt. She waited patiently for him to raise the sword and present her with an opportunity. Dirt flicked onto her fur and her muscles tensed. As the blade rose, ready for an overhead strike, Darla pounced. Her arms outstretched, she flew under his arms and knocked the great sword from his grasp. The sword sparkled as it spun into the air.

Her clawed hands outstretched; Darla grabbed each side of his helmet. Metal screeched as her claws dug in. Growling, she twisted. She heard a loud crack as the swordsman's neck snapped and his head turned one hundred and eighty degrees. Darla let go and the corpse fell to the ground. Then, she reached up, grabbed the sword's handle and plucked it out of the air.

Darla easily held the hefty sword one-handed, a feat few mortals could accomplish due to its sheer size and weight. She was no mere mortal though. Tapping into every ounce of her supernatural strength, she threw the two-handed sword at lightning speed. It flew, twirling through the air like a spear. The axeman barely had time to react. The blade sliced his head, almost cleaving it in half and punctured through his helmet on the other side. Another corpse, another dead guard. Darla turned to face the captain, the only obstacle stopping her from assassinating the queen.

Chapter 6

The captain stood near the carriage door, protecting it. He was the last line of defence, now that all the guards were dead. He twirled two short swords menacingly, daring her to engage him. Were both swords his? Or did the second one belong to his fellow ranger? Either way Darla didn't care as she welcomed the challenge. "Come on, werewolf, if you want to kill the queen, you're going to have to go through me first," the captain spat, glancing quickly at the carriage, before focusing his attention back to her. The carriage! The captain was merely trying to distract her.

Her ears twitched as she heard a creak. She turned to the carriage, knowing exactly what had caused the sound. She had forgotten about the coachman. She let out a low growl, causing the already spooked horses, to panic. They had caught hold of her scent even though they were well-trained. "Go! Now! Get the queen to safety," the captain screamed.

"But what about you?" the coachman said, struggling to calm the panicked horses. His hesitation was all the time Darla needed. She darted sideways, as the captain ran forward with his swords. The race was on, determining who would reach the carriage first. The coachman pulled on the reins, but it was useless. As Darla neared the panicked horses, her scent became stronger. Freaked, they started to buck and kick wildly. The carriage was immobile which made her job easier, but she still needed to be careful. A panicked horse was unpredictable and dangerous.

"No!" the captain screamed, lunging and swinging one of the short swords. It missed Darla by millimetres as she leant back and skidded under the blade. Dirt sprayed into the air as her clawed hand slashed across the captain's exposed wrist. The sword clattered to the ground in a spray of blood as the captain's tendons were severed. It had been a clumsy and stupid mistake on his part. One driven by pure desperation.

The coachman frantically cracked the whip, an extreme measure, but he didn't know what else to do. The horses were still panicked, but at least they were under control. Yanking on the reins, he urged the horses forward. The wooden wheels ground against the gravel as the horses galloped forward. The carriage lurched, bumping and tilting as the wheels rolled over the large rocks. Rocks that had been positioned to stop the carriage from rolling forward. The carriage tilted and landed with a thump, cracking one of the wheels. It stopped momentarily, providing the opportunity that Darla needed.

Her arm outstretched, Darla reached and raked her claws along the shaft pole of the carriage. The thick wooden pole chipped as her claws scratched into it. The horses were beside themselves. They were wide-eyed and frightened. With flared nostrils and their necks braced upwards, they rabidly turned this way and that, looking for a direction to escape the danger near them.

As the carriage lurched forward again, the pole buckled and then snapped. Ropes and straps loosened, becoming unsecure as the horses broke free from their restraints. Stumbling forward, on broken wheels, the carriage rolled for a couple of metres and then stopped. The coachman reached behind his seat for something. "I will not let you kill the queen, monster," the captain roared defiantly, positioning himself between her and the carriage.

"Neither will I," the coachman said, pulling forth a repeater crossbow. It was the only proof that she needed as it confirmed the man's identity; that this was indeed Brithren. The man was a mentor to Marek, one of her closest friends. Killing him was out of the question. She had to incapacitate him somehow. The repeater crossbow was loaded with dazzling, white-tipped bolts. Marek had educated her on the various bolts he used and the ones that he'd come across. The one was she saw was a mystery to her and that worried her immensely. If the guy was as good as Marek made him out to be, Darla was in serious trouble.

A normal crossbow was a big enough threat, but having to dodge an expert marksman with a repeater crossbow would be a challenge, even for her and she still had the ranger to deal with. Even though he was injured, he was still a formidable foe. A slight clicking sound alerted Darla. Darla was already on the move when the coachman squeezed the trigger. The bolt hit the ground and exploded into flame. The flame was a blue blaze, dancing and radiating with an intense heat. "You are lucky, werewolf. But you cannot escape my inferno bolts forever."

The damp grass contained the fire, but Darla could only imagine what would have happened if it had been summer. The fire would have burnt everything in its path and been unstoppable. Rapidly and with expert precision, Brithren began to crank another bolt into position. "Quickly. Fire another one. I'll keep her at bay," the captain yelled, his eyes darting between her and the coachman.

The bolt in place, Brithren aimed, the white-tipped bolt pointed straight at her. Damn, he was quick. The entire process had taken him a matter of seconds. Her muscles tensed as she prepared to move. His finger began to squeeze the trigger. Growling, she bounded forward and rammed the carriage. Thrown off balance, the shot went wide. High pitched screams erupted from inside the carriage. "No!" Brithren wailed, realising what he had done.

He had discharged the inferno bolt into the interior of the carriage. The screams died down, replaced by silence. The blue flame grew, dancing and flickering throughout the carriage. He had just killed the queen and the baroness, along with their ladies-in-waiting. Brithren prepared to jump. Then with an ear-splitting crack, the coachman's seat exploded into shards. A black clawed hand shot out and grabbed the coachman by the tunic. Screaming, Brithren was yanked off his feet, disappearing into the confines of the carriage.

A scream of fear and pain sounded from inside followed by a loud thud. The impact shook the carriage, tilting it and cracking the side. "There are worse things in this world than me, captain," Darla growled.

* * *

"Maybe," the captain muttered. "But you are the one trying to kill the queen."

"You fool, can't you see that she is no longer your queen?" Something thumped against the carriage door, rocking the carriage. Blood sprayed against the window, dripping down in red streaks. An eerie silence ensued. Disregarding Darla's presence, the captain slowly approached the carriage door. The only sound that could be heard was the soft crunching of his boots on the gravel. The haunting words said a moment before resounded in his head, repeating itself '*she is no longer your* queen.' He turned his head abruptly to check on the werewolf, but she was gone, disappearing into the night.

The carriage door sprung open, thrown off its hinges. Spiralling, flipping end over end. Ducking, the captain quickly dodged out of the way. Queen Raylene casually walked down the wooden steps. The captain automatically bowed his head and went to his knees. "My queen," the captain stammered. "I fear for your safety. There is a werewolf…"

"I know, captain. Where is this troublesome beast now?"

"I do not know, my queen. I got distracted and it fled. It is stalking us and waiting for an opportunity to attack. Let me get my horse…" The queen's wicked laughter interrupted him.

* * *

"Ahh…and what captain. You will ride me to safety? I think not. This werewolf has proven to be quite the formidable adversary. I welcome the challenge it will provide."

The captain glanced up briefly and then lowered his head again. "But my queen…" Malicious and cruel laughter interrupted the captain again.

"You see, captain. The werewolf was smart to flee. It obviously realised something you did not."

"And what was that my queen?"

Resting a gentle hand under the captain's chin, she lifted his head up. Gasping, he tried to raise his sword but all the captain could do was stare, horrified at the queen's eyes. Eyes that were pitch black, soulless and demonic. "Your queen is dead, captain. She died when I possessed her body. Now there is only me, Mavelyn." The captain reacted, his willpower snapping him out of the spell as his training kicked in and he finally managed to raise his sword. He swung it around in a mighty slash, but as quick as he was, the queen was quicker.

Her other hand swung around with her nails extended into demonic claws. Razor-sharp, they sliced through his neck and cleaved his head off. The short sword dropped from lifeless fingers as with a spurt of blood, the captain's head rolled across the ground.

Darla had known exactly what was going to emerge from the carriage. She had retreated towards the latrines and her stash. She had partially transformed back, keeping the enhancements of her lycanthropy but also taking on a more human appearance. She strapped on her belt and readjusted the short sword so that it was easy to access. Lastly, she re-clasped her cloak and wrapped it around her to ward off the cold. Her tunic and pants were torn, the warmth they provided ruined, but they would have to suffice. Even though she had packed a spare tunic and pants in her travel bag, she didn't have time to change. She had a demon to kill first.

Prepared, she approached the demon. She had opted to play the side of caution and to get the short sword. It was a sure thing, a proven demon killer. Somehow, she figured getting into a clawing match with a demon just wouldn't cut it. And besides, she had no idea of the powers this demon possessed or what it was capable of. The queen laughed. "And here I was commending you on running away and yet here you are, foolish enough to return."

"I was contracted to kill a demon queen. I am not one to renege. I fulfill all my contracts," Darla replied, approaching the still blazing campfire. She blocked out the smell of burnt flesh that was still emitting from the corpse and focused on the task at hand. Another laugh, the demon was genuinely amused. She was fearless and arrogant which Darla intended to take advantage of. The gravel crunching under her feet, she casually approached, coming into the light.

The queen had transformed, taking on a more demonic appearance. Her eyes were dark, as black as obsidian. Her skin had become a pale grey and her nails were deadly weapons, claws the size of a short sword. They glistened with a dark red substance. Initially, Darla thought it was blood, then she got a whiff of it. Her nose wrinkled and she almost gagged from the smell. Poison!

"You are wise not to engage me in a clawing match, werewolf," she mocked, noticing Darla's reaction. "Mind you, I am intrigued to find out what my venom would do to one of your kind." Venom. It wasn't man-made like Darla had assumed.   The demon secreted venom? Interesting! Darla's hand slowly went to her dagger. Smiling, the demon darted in lightning quick. She closed the distance in seconds and slashed with her lethal claws.

Even the slightest scratch could prove fatal. But instead of dodging, Darla stepped in and welcomed the attack. Her fingers brushed against the dagger and then slipped further around and grasped hold of the hilt of the short sword. She drew it out in a blue blur and slashed. Her timing was perfect. The runes glowed bright blue, illuminating the blade as it sliced through the demon's wrist and sent it toppling to the floor.

* * *

The demon howled, screaming in pain as she tried to stem the flow of gushing blood. "You bitch!" she screamed, letting go and with a backhanded swing, she slashed with her other hand. Darla dived nimbly backwards and rolled out of the way, knocking into a barrel. The barrel was sturdy and solid, indicating that it was mostly full. "Wow, that's strong," she said, as she got a whiff of the whisky. Even though the thick barrel was sealed and plugged shut, her enhanced smell could easily detect it. Darla enjoyed an excellent quality whisky, but this was anything but refined. It smelled like cheaply distilled whisky mixed with moonshine and sweetened with honey; the whisky commonly known as 'soldiers brew.' It was both sweet and potent.

The campfire was to her right, the smouldering logs crackling and providing warmth. It gave Darla an idea. Her muscles tensing, she hefted the barrel into the air and swung it around just in time. The demon's deadly clawed hand swung at her again, knocking her back slightly as wood shards and whisky sprayed. The barrel made the perfect shield. She poked her head above the barrel and smiled. "Is that the best you've got?" she taunted, enraging the demon queen.

She planted her feet, bracing herself as she watched the demon's shadow and manoeuvred the barrel accordingly. The demon hit the barrel continuously, and Darla listened intently, judging and calculating. The barrel was losing whisky steadily as the liquid trickled from multiple holes. The barrel was now just over three-quarters full. Finally, a mighty crack sounded and Darla knew it was time. The barrel had almost lost its integrity. She threw the barrel, just as the demon started to pull its arm back for another swing.

The barrel smashed into the demon's torso and shattered, spraying the soldiers brew all over the queen and the surrounding area. The demon was blinded momentarily. Drawing her sword with a faint hiss she darted sideways and skidding under the demon's right arm, swung the short sword. The blade sliced cleanly through the demon's elbow, as smooth as butter, cutting through bone, muscle, ligaments and flesh. The demon's forearm dropped to the ground behind her as Darla continued skidding straight towards the fire.

Digging her boots into the ground and spraying up dirt, she screeched to a halt just before the campfire. Reaching in, she grabbed a partially charred, burning log and with a spray of embers pulled it from the fire. She could feel the heat through her glove. Ignoring the pain, she threw her arm back, aimed and halted as she heard the faintest twang. It was barely discernible. She listened and swung. The blazing log erupted into a pile of wooden shards and embers as the bolt hit it and fell harmlessly to the ground. The demon looked around. Somehow the assassin had disappeared. Loud clapping sounded, the clang of metal from gauntleted hands. Whoever the person was, they were wearing heavy plate armour. "Bravo, bravo," the person said, hidden in the darkness.

* * *

Hidden behind a log seat, Darla peeked cautiously around the edge and watched the proceedings. She counted twenty-two men. Twenty were mounted on horses and wore black, high-quality, unidentifiable armour. The remaining two were situated with the wagon. One stood calming the horses. He was unarmoured and dressed in a simple tunic, identifying him as the wagoner. The other one wore a lighter, hardened leather armour, which was also black and unidentifiable. He was busy whistling commands, leading something from a cage. A beast master. The cage was huge, sturdy and well-made. Darla could only imagine what it housed. The only explanation was that the group were mercenaries. But why had they interfered? Darla felt a knot in her stomach, this was not boding well.

"She is mine!" the demon screamed. "Do not interfere…" Her sentence was cut short by multiple thuds. Surprised, she stared at the two silver bolts sticking out of her chest. It was then that Darla noticed the growth – bones, muscles, tendons and some flesh. It was the beginnings of a hand. A spear of bone and muscle had formed on the other side as the demon regrew its forearm. Yet again, Darla marvelled at the demon's regenerative powers. They even rivalled her own. Laughing, the demon awkwardly plucked the bolts out with her regrown fingers. She needed to end this quick before the demon could fully regenerate. She needed to take advantage of the demon's distraction.

Sprinting from cover, she slid into the light. Stealth had been sacrificed. Whether she was seen or heard no longer mattered. Speed and precision were vital. And she needed to hurry. She needed to dispose of the demon before it could regenerate. Turning her head, the demon smirked. "I believe these were for you," the queen said throwing the bloodied bolts straight at her. The demon had factored in her speed and thrown with deadly accuracy. Darla was skidding right into their path. She didn't have time to manoeuvre and dodge out of the way. She only had one option – to go up!

Planting her heels firmly in the ground, she braked and kicked up a mound of dirt. The bolts thudded into the ground just before her feet as she soared upwards and catapulted into the air. As she flew forward, she twirled her body, spinning her short sword and slashing across in a deadly arc. The bright blue blade cleaved through the queen's neck, almost severing it from her head. With her malformed hand, the demon grasped at its neck. Poisoned blood spewed forth, oozing down her hand and pooling on the ground. Darla crinkled her nose at the obnoxious smell. A glitter of gold and jewels caught her eye as she landed in a crouch. The queen's tiara lying amongst the blood, the only thing symbolising who she was.

Darla twirled, spinning on the spot as she slashed again. The blue blade radiated as it glided through the air. It sliced through muscle and bone with the greatest of ease. Severed at the knees, the demon flailed for support before toppling to the ground. Another round of applause. "Well done," the mercenary leader said as he gracefully dismounted and whistled an eerie tune. He unstrapped a wicked, spiked two-handed hammer. The weapon still had blood stains on some of the spikes.

She raised her eyebrows questioningly. "And dare I ask. Who in the seven hells are you and why the fuck are you here?" She was not in the mood for idle chit-chat.

"Oh, so sorry. How rude of me," the leader said dramatically. "My name is Ecnaidar and this is my rabble, otherwise known as – the Bloodborn mercenaries." The Bloodborn mercenaries had earnt themselves a reputation of being ruthless and barbaric. Darla had seen and even committed some gruesome and horrific things, but they paled compared to the atrocities the Bloodborn mercenaries had committed. They had been exiled, banned in most of the kingdoms, including the Hiberathian Kingdom. What the hell were they doing here? Ecnaidar smirked. "We were sent here to eradicate any demons or monsters lurking about. Now finish the demon bitch off."

The queen laughed. "They are here to kill both of us. Surely you can see that." It was said softly so that only Darla could hear. "Looks like we are unlikely allies. At least for the moment." Darla nodded and lowered her short sword. She wiped her blade and slowly walked across to the other side of the campfire. A whole barrel of soldier's brew was still standing there untouched. Another almost empty barrel sat next to it. Darla had been watching the guards drinking out of it earlier.

"Well, as you can see, I have already incapacitated the demon. I have practically done the job, but why should I have to do all the dirty work? You can finish her off yourself. Surely, some demonic blood stains would add to your war hammers demeanour?" she replied smugly, watching the mercenary leader out of the corner of her eye.

Ecnaidar smiled pleasantly. He was delaying and stalling his attack. But why? Then she noticed that the beast master had disappeared. He shook his head, all humour gone and replaced by a cruel, calculating look. "I think not. We would be depriving you of your prized kill. And like the demon pointed out, this is between the two of you. We wouldn't want to interfere."

Sheathing her sword, she grabbed the top of the full barrel. "Do you mean like when you shot at both of us?" Ecnaidar whistled. His sadistic grin said it all. One after another the other mercenaries dismounted and drew their weapons. She should have known. The demon was right. "Fuck," she cursed, tasting the bitter taste of betrayal. Ecnaidar walked forward, flanked by his mercenaries.

Chapter 7

The roaring campfire made the mercenaries armour glisten as they stood there steadfast, prepared and unafraid of the threat before them. They looked like demonic shadows emerging from the night. They were death incarnate, ready to send her to the afterlife. And that was exactly the reason they were here – to kill both her and the demon. "This is going to be easy," one of the mercenaries sneered.

* * *

"I was about to say the same thing," Darla replied, grinning wickedly. Her muscles bulging, she hefted the barrel into the air. She heard multiple twangs and listened intently as the bolts soared towards her. The crossbowmen were smart, they had seen what she was capable of and had adjusted their trajectory, making it impossible for her to shield herself from both bolts. She reacted, making her decision and lowered the barrel slightly, while leaning to the side. The first bolt hit the barrel with a thud, while the second bolt soared past where her forehead had been moments before.

The bolt landed just before the campfire with the edge of the shaft being lit. "You'll have to do better than that," Darla smirked, as she readjusted the barrel. The bolt had pierced the hard oak, embedding itself into it and causing a small amount of the soldier's brew to spray across the ground.

"Oh, we plan to. We've got something special in store for you werewolf," Ecnaidar said maliciously. They knew what she was and were armed with silver weapons. This confirmed her earlier thought about being betrayed.
"You will not interrupt our fight," the queen shouted.

"Shut up demon. You'll die soon enough," Ecnaidar spat, advancing towards Darla. His mercenaries flanked him, closely grouped together. Darla planned to take advantage of it. Her muscles bulged as she heaved the barrel into the air. Clutching the ground, the demon screamed and suddenly the ground began to tremor. Gentle at first and then more violently. A bright green tendril of energy snaked across the ground. Nature magic. It was oblivious, disguised by the grass, but with Darla's keen eyesight, she could see it as plain as day. Darla threw the barrel as thick spiked branches erupted from the ground.

For a big man, Ecnaidar was quick, dodging and swinging at a branch that sprung up in front of him. The branch shattered, splintering into debris. The six mercenaries at the rear also managed to escape unharmed, but for those at the forefront and in the middle, it was a different story. They were impaled and shredded, with the magically imbued spikes easily penetrating their plate armour.

The barrel added to the chaos, hitting the spiked branches and shattering. Whisky sprayed across the surrounding area, splashing across the branches and the mercenaries. Diving backwards, Darla plucked the burning crossbow bolt from the ground and ignoring the pain it brought, threw it towards the mercenaries. The blazing bolt embedded itself in a branch, igniting it instantly. The blaze spread like wildfire, igniting the mercenaries armour, heating, scorching it and roasting them from within. Their screams echoed across the night.

"Maybe you should have brought more men," Darla said sarcastically. She heard the familiar twangs of the crossbows and reacted, heaving the almost empty barrel into the air. It was unusual, their shots were far from accurate. One of the bolts skimmed across the side of the barrel, ricocheting into the grass, while the other embedded itself in one of the spiked branches and instantly caught alight. Darla gazed into the night, her wolf-like eyes easily seeing the crossbowmen in the darkness.

Their horses had sunk into the ground and disappeared. All that remained were the two crossbowmen floundering amongst some deep, thick mud. They had discarded their crossbows, freeing up their hands. But it was useless, futile, they were slowly sinking. The top of the mud had a bright green glow, casting the crossbowmen in a ghastly illumination. From the mud another bright green tendril led to the demon. More nature magic! The demon obviously had an aptitude for magic, but she had used none during her fight with Darla.

Their arms flailing, the crossbowmen slowly sank below the surface. Their arms and hands disappeared below the mud and then they were gone. The green glow and the tendril vanished, leaving the area in darkness. The earth hardened. The long grass flapped in the night breeze. All was quiet, except for the chirping of insects. It was as if the crossbowmen had never existed.

Throwing her arms back, she aimed the barrel at Ecnaidar and the remaining mercenaries. If she threw it at the right angle and sprayed enough of the soldier's brew, it would ignite and cause an inferno. They would be as good as dead.

She threw the barrel, hurling it through the air. Twirling, it began its descent, only to have Ecnaidar leap forward. Seeing what the mercenary commander was about to do, Darla reacted and grabbed her cloak. In a heartbeat she swung it around her and used it as a shield. With a mighty two-handed swing he smashed the barrel.

The spiked hammer shattered the barrel and sprayed the potent whisky over both of them. The whisky-soaked cloak caught fire a moment later. Twirling and unclasping it, Darla threw the burning mess on the ground. Ecnaidar rolled in the dirt, extinguishing his burning armour. His cloak was still on fire, discarded and burning on the ground. The armour was ruined, the polished sheen now replaced with scorch marks. Half of Ecnaidar's face was also severely burnt. The pain would have been excruciating. But the mercenary commander ignored the pain, smiling as he stood up. Walking over, he picked up his spiked hammer.

Even with her muscles enhanced, they strained as she picked up the log seat. Holding it in front of her like a shield, she prepared for the assault. Her ears twitched as she heard a rustling in nearby bushes. It was on the other side of the carriage. It was getting louder and judging from the ruckus it was making, it was something large. The carriage shattered into a pile of burning debris as an enormous black beast leapt forth.

It had a feminine, feline face with intelligent, cunning eyes and a mane of long black hair. Opening its wide mouth, it roared, revealing a double row of sharp, pointy teeth. The mouth and teeth were covered with blood which indicated that the creature had fed recently and was a small consolation.

The beast's huge feline body moved gracefully as it slowly edged closer on padded feet. Its razor-sharp claws scraped the ground as it moved. Behind it, the creature's long, chitinous tail swished back and forth as if it had a mind of its own. The tail stopped abruptly, poised above its head, ready to strike. At the end of the tail was a large barb dripping venom so potent that it could kill almost anything, possibly even a werewolf. "Oh fuck!" Darla muttered. Standing before her, waiting and watching, with its barb poised ready to attack was a manticore.

The poison master had once told her that manticores were native to his homeland. Their poison was prized and worth a fortune. The manticore was an intelligent creature, an expert hunter that stalked its prey. They hunted in packs and were the apex predators of the desert. Even as skilled and adept as the sandrigar were at immobilising the manticores and harvesting their venom, they would often have casualties. Horrific, painful deaths caused by the manticore venom which was why it was so rare and valuable.

A man emerged, climbing over the debris of the carriage. He walked casually towards the manticore, without a care in the world and gave it a friendly pat. The man was a beast master, a person who had a unique affinity with creatures. The manticore was his pet and was completely loyal and obedient to him. With a sardonic smile, he gave a short, sharp whistle, commanding the manticore to attack.

The manticore moved fast, leaping forward. Darla adjusted her grip and swung the log as hard as she could. Claws outstretched, the huge bulk of the manticore bore down on her. Its teeth bared. Darla could smell its rancid breath as it closed in ready to rip out her neck. Then with an almighty smash, the log whacked into the side of the manticore's head. The manticore's head snapped back, as with a loud crack a piece of the log tore off and flew into the fire sending up a spray of embers.

The manticore landed awkwardly as it stood before her shaking its head in bewilderment. Its tail darted forward, and Darla leapt backwards, the deadly barb narrowly missing her. Slowly, the manticore crept forward, stalking her as its barbed tail flicked back and forth, ready to strike again. The manticore's eyes narrowed as its legs tensed, ready to pounce. Darla was ready and watching. The manticore leapt to her right and Darla flung herself to the left, the same direction that the manticore's tail whipped towards. She realised her mistake too late and quickly tucked herself into a ball before hitting the ground and rolling. The barb struck, slicing Darla across her thigh and drawing blood. Darla screamed in pain.

She flipped into a standing position and staggered as her leg wobbled, her muscles spasming. Her thigh throbbed and she could feel the venom coursing through her veins. Her blood felt like it was on fire. The wound was just a scratch but with the toxicity of the venom, the small dose was enough to kill a human. Darla just hoped that it wasn't enough to kill a werewolf. Fighting the manticore was futile and wasn't an option, especially in her injured state. She looked around desperately. The best she could hope for was to escape and survive, but even that option looked grim. Darla stepped backwards, her foot sinking in the wet sand. The manticore had herded her towards the river. She had nowhere to go. Sensing her pain and her weakness, the manticore pounced.

The sheer weight of the manticore hit her like a battering ram, bowling her over. She landed on the soft sand and water splashed over her. The manticore landed on her with one of its forepaws trapping her arm, while the other rested on her opposing shoulder. One of its rear paws pressed against the wound, pinning her to the ground. The pain was excruciating. Its barb shot forward again, lightning-quick, whipping past its head and heading straight towards Darla. In the blink of an eye, her hand was there, grabbing hold of the barb, its deadly point resting mere inches from her face. She stretched with her free hand, trying desperately to reach a weapon.

Her head was pounding and she struggled to concentrate. Her life depended on it though. Shaking her head and clearing it, she reached for the short sword. But it was pinned underneath her, pressing into her lower back. Fumbling, her hand clasped around the hilt of her dagger and with a soft hiss, drew it from its sheath. Her vision blurred, blinding her momentarily. Then the excruciating pain started as her stomach cramped. It felt like her insides were being pulled and twisted. Her hand spasmed and the dagger dropped from her shaking fingers. The wound burned, throbbing, as gritting her teeth she tried not to scream. She could feel the venom coursing through her system. Closing her eyes, she concentrated and fighting through the pain picked up the dagger. The pain eased and opening her eyes, she gripped the dagger firmly.

She was about to thrust it towards the manticore's head when her ears pricked causing her to pause. The manticore would have to wait. She heard multiple crunching sounds of grass, sticks and leaves being stepped upon. There were three mercenaries walking cautiously towards her, their footfalls distinguishing them. Two wore plate armour, their steps being heavy and distinct. The third one wore leather boots, his steps softer and more precise – the beast master.

Darla bought her dagger up to the barb and wiped the blade along the tip. The clear, fluorescent poison glistened as it coated it. She waited patiently holding the barb firmly and listened. *Crunch, crunch, crunch.* She could see the black boots. "She has hold of the manticore's barb, how about I cut her hand off and then see how she fares?" the mercenary said, laughing as he drew his sword.

"I'm going to fare better than you," she replied, slashing across with her dagger. The enchanted blade sliced through the plate armour as easily as butter. Blood trickled down his black armoured greave onto the grassy shore.

"You bitch!" the mercenary shouted, trying to stab her with his sword. The sword fell from spasming fingers and dropped harmlessly to the ground. The mercenary screamed in pain, as his leg gave out and he toppled backwards onto the sand. He immediately started convulsing and frothing at the mouth. The man would be dead within a matter of seconds. Darla heard the twirling of a flail, the spiked ball attached to the chain spinning at a phenomenal speed. A grinding sounded as the chain extended, giving the weapon more reach. The mercenary came into view. He was small for a man, only slightly bigger than a tall dwarf. Darla knew exactly who it was, the man's reputation preceded him. "Fucking seven hells," she swore.

It was not his size that distinguished him, it was his flail. Ronnard had lost half his arm in a battle and had spent a small fortune to have a gnomish designed brace. When asked what weapon he wanted attached to the brace, he had opted for a specialized flail. A flail with a winch mechanism that could extend it for greater reach or be retracted, turning the weapon into a deadly spiked mace for melee combat. Since then, Ronnard had earnt a reputation for his brutality and was known to be a psychopathic killer. He had also earnt the nickname 'The Butcher' because most of the time his victims looked like pieces of meat. He was far from stupid though. He had seen what this woman was capable of and approached cautiously, his plated boots crunching softly on the grass.

The flail gained momentum. Ronnard was playing it smart and keeping his distance. He didn't need to be within melee range to strike. Darla cursed. She refused to throw the dagger at him. She had other plans for her poisoned dagger. He swung, grazing the manticores leg. Turning its head, it let out a low growl. A warning not to interfere. Ronnard blatantly ignored it. He began twirling again, gaining speed and within moments the spiked ball was nothing but a blur. "I'm pinned to the ground and you still can't hit me," Darla jibed. "A blind dwarf could aim better than that."

Her only reply was a grunt and a sadistic smile. The flail was a blur of speed. He twisted, adjusting his aim and sent the spiked ball shooting towards her, with the chain untwirling and trailing behind it. Darla waited, watching and listening. The chain clinked as the spiked ball rotated and spun. It was nearly upon her. Her timing needed to be perfect and precise, not giving Ronnard an opportunity to alter its course. She pulled the barbed tail to the side, straining and holding tight, preventing the manticore from freeing itself. Using it as a shield.

* * *

The ball hit with a thud, embedding the iron spikes into the manticore's chitinous tail. Darla let go as it screeched in pain, raising its tail instinctively and flicking it from side to side. It was trying to free itself from the spikes, but in the process the manticore wrapped the chain around and entangled itself more. Yanked off his feet, Ronnard found himself dangling precariously in front of the manticore.

Laughter sounded as the beast master stepped forward. "Looks like Jassy is going to get a feast tonight," he snickered. Darla could not believe it. He had even named the manticore as if it was a pet. "Serves you right, you stupid little goblin." He huffed, shaking his head. "What do you expect when you attack a manticore."

A voice shouted behind him, causing the beast master to pale slightly. "Help free Ronnard from that stupid creature otherwise I will break both your legs, tenderise the fucking beast with my hammer and make you watch as me and the men enjoy a feast of manticore meat," Ecnaidar said threateningly.

"No!" the beast master screamed. "He attacked my manticore…" A momentary defiance. Darla bit back a scream. Her stomach and chest were on fire. The pain was intense. Closing her eyes, she took a deep breath, followed by another. After three more deep breaths, she opened her eyes. The pain had subsided, at least for the moment. It was coming in waves. It would subside momentarily and then come back with a vengeance. The worst thing was the unknown factor of whether her regenerative abilities would be enough, or whether she was just prolonging her death.

"I said NOW!" Ecnaidar screamed. He would not be defied, not by anyone. He ruled by fear, his authority was absolute. The manticore turned its head and growled threateningly. It was loyal and protective. The mercenary leader was either oblivious to the threat or didn't care. "Now I need to take care of the demon." He turned around, dismissing them, ready to carry out the gruesome task of pounding the demon into oblivion.

"You heard him, you fucking maggot. Help me," Ronnard sneered, smug and satisfied. Slowly he reached behind his back.

"He said that I had to help you. He didn't say that you had to be in one piece." The beast master drew his dagger, wickedly curved and razor-sharp. He gave a short, sharp whistle and the manticore growled, baring its teeth. Ronnard merely laughed. Swinging back, he then lunged forward and kicked the manticore in the side of the head. His plate mail greave connected with the manticores skull. Howling in pain, the manticore staggered sideways, concussed and off balance.

Darla pulled her arm free and arching slightly, drew the short sword. She was still pinned. The manticores rear paw was holding her down while its claws dug into her wounded thigh. It was a situation that she was about to rectify. Darla gritted her teeth as the excruciating pain reared its ugly head yet again. Her vision blurred and her stomach was in knots. Then opening her mouth wide, she vomited. She shook her head to clear it and spat out the last remnants of vomit. She needed to focus, she needed to concentrate.

The beast master's knuckles turned white from gripping the dagger so tight. His eyes were full of unbridled rage. "Now free me!" Ronnard sneered. "Otherwise, I will be tempted to kick your precious manticore in the head again. Then I'll keep kicking poor Jassy in the head, pulverising her with my boot. And once I've finished and had my fun, your manticore's head will be nothing but a pulpy, bloody mess. Then finally, once I've stopped laughing, I will fucking free myself."

"I'm going to kill you," the beast master murmured. His voice was barely audible, a deathly whisper.

"Come on then. What are you waiting for?" Ronnard was goading the beast master, tormenting him to no end, but why? Then the chain turned slightly and Darla saw the glint of silver from the dagger that he was holding behind his back. Swinging like a pendulum, his boot shot forward again, straight towards the manticores head. Manticore's were far from stupid creatures though. It had already been attacked once. This time it was prepared and turning its feminine head, opened its mouth wide. It snapped shut with a crunch, its jaw like a vice and its teeth puncturing through the metal greave.

Ronnard screamed as the manticore tossed its head, the chain rattling as he was shaken like a ragdoll, like Jassy's personal chew toy. Blood dripped from Jassy's mouth as she mangled his foot. The beast master stood there and laughed. "I'm not waiting. You were stupid to kick my manticore you ugly goblin mother..." He stopped mid-sentence and stared at the dagger sticking out of his stomach. A clear fluorescent, sticky liquid could be seen coated on the blade. Venom that was now mixed into his bloodstream. "You bitch!" he said, looking at Darla. It was all he managed to say before he collapsed to the ground and began to spasm violently. He was dead within seconds. Darla smiled at the irony of a beast master being killed by his own beast's venom.

Ronnard chuckled. "Nice throw, assassin. I will make it worth your while if you help me free myself from this beastie."

Now it was Darla's turn to laugh. "You have no morals or ethics Ronnard. So why in the seven hells should I trust you? And besides, a moment ago you tried to kill me." She tapped into her lycanthropy, enhancing her leg muscles to their full extent. Aiming for the manticores rear leg, she swung her sword.

* * *

"Don't tell me you're holding a grudge. I only did what I was ordered to do." The manticore screeched in pain as the blade sliced through muscle and bone, cleaving one of its hind legs off. Blood sprayed across her tunic and cloak. She was free of the manticore, but her thigh still throbbed with an intense, burning sensation. Gritting her teeth, she blocked out the pain. Slowly, she raised her knees to her chest.

"I don't hold grudges," she replied. "Like you, I was hired to do a job. Unlike you though, I am willing to give you a fighting chance. If you manage to free yourself from the manticore." She said it matter-of-factly, blasé as she kicked out. Her powerful leg muscles propelled the manticore, sending it hurtling through the air. The huge beast somersaulted awkwardly, before landing in the river with a splash. Ronnard followed a moment later and came up drenched and spluttering water. The manticore thrashed about, panicking, before finally finding a steady footing on the dark, sandy riverbed. The catapult manoeuvre hadn't tossed them far, but that had never been her intention.

Ronnard stood up next to the manticore, the chain running along the riverbed between them. He pressed a button and began to winch in the chain. Somehow during the manoeuvre, the chain had untangled itself and the flail had come free. The spiked ball rose out of the water and re-attached itself to the brace. "I suppose I should thank you," Ronnard smirked, lifting his modified arm. The mercenary began limping back to shore wielding it like a mace.

* * *

The manticore stood there with water dripping off its fur coat, roaring in defiance. Darla smiled as she noticed a ripple further out in the river. The water had darkened around them, a steady, spreading pool of bloodied water. It had been a gambit, a risk, but it had paid off. The blood had attracted an apex predator, one that lurked within the river. She had sought help from an unlikely ally. The hydra!

Darla wobbled on unsteady feet. Her muscles felt like they were on fire and her arm began to spasm. Her head was throbbing, she couldn't concentrate and her vision was becoming blurry. The venom was affecting her both physically and mentally. Ronnard laughed. "Damn and I was hoping for a challenge," he sneered mockingly. The manticore growled, snarling, as her tail whipped back and forth across the surface of the river.

Shooting into the air and spraying water in its wake the barb hurtled towards her. She didn't even notice. Her vision had blurred again, blinding her momentarily. Relying purely on instinct, she dived out of the way just in time. The tail whipped back, ready to strike again. Darla tried to get up, but her stomach knotted. Her muscles cramping, she collapsed back onto the sand. It was the closest to death that she had come. She wasn't ready to die, clinging desperately to life, she prayed, she hoped that her regenerative powers were enough. All she could do was watch helplessly as the barb struck forward.

* * *

With a spray of water, one of the hydra's heads erupted from the river. Like a giant, slithering snake it quickly wrapped itself around the manticores tail and bit into it, latching on. The tail halted mid descent. Growling out of frustration, Jassy desperately dug her claws in, but it was futile. The wet sand of the riverbed was too soft and she couldn't get any purchase. Scrambling and panicking, she was slowly dragged back further into the river.

Giving up and trying a different tactic Jassy spun and pounced, launching herself partially out of the water. Her mouth opened wide and clamped shut. The hydra roared in pain, releasing its grip as Jassy's powerful jaws clamped down. Her razor-sharp teeth easily cleaved through the thick appendage, tearing it in half. Dark green blood spurted forth, as her barbed tail flicked back and forth and shook off the disentangled obstruction. Free, the manticore turned back around, growling as it faced the assassin. Its tail then flicked up, poised, before lunging once again at Darla.

Darla rolled to the side moments before the barb struck and embedded itself in the sand. Reaching across, she once again grabbed onto the tail. The blurriness was gone, and her vision was returning. The cramping had also eased, for now. The bitten off stump erupted out of the water, but it wasn't a stump anymore. The appendage had grown back, along with the head. It was the unique regenerative power of the hydra. The only way to kill it was to cauterize the stump. This was the only way to stop the hydra from growing back its head. Then you needed to repeat the process with the remaining heads.

The appendage weaved towards the manticore. Patient, the manticore waited and then snapped at it, missing as it slithered out of harm's way. The appendage danced back and forth with the hydra's head darting in and out, teasing and tempting Jassy. What the manticore didn't realise and failed to notice, was the two submerged appendages that snaked there way silently under the surface. The appendages struck, enveloping the manticores hindlegs and biting into its rump. Even with its powerful jaws, the manticore's chitinous plating around its rump was barely punctured. The hydra's jaws were open wide, with its sharp teeth stuck in the chitin. Stuck, unable to free itself, the two appendages squeezed pulling the manticore off balance.

Jassy splashed in the river, thrashing and trying to bite the unseen appendages. Her head emerged with a spray of water, only for the regrown head to strike, wrapping itself around the manticores neck and clamping onto it with its powerful jaws. The hydra had a firm hold and blood was gushing from the manticore's neck. Jassy was thrashing about, panicking. It knew it was in trouble. The hydra slowly pulled the manticore further into the water and its remaining two heads emerged, ready to feast on manticore meat. The problem was, Darla was still clinging to the tail and being dragged along with it.

* * *

Embedded in the sand, her boots left a trail as she was dragged into the river. Leaning forward, the short sword flashed across her body. The runes radiated blue as she slashed, cleaving the barb from the tail. It came away in her hand, a bloodied poisonous mess. Holding the bloodied barb in one hand and the short sword in the other, she turned to face Ronnard as he limped towards her. His booted feet splashed water as he trudged through the riverbed sand. Then he stopped.

With a click he released the spiked ball and began twirling it. It made sense that he would do a ranged attack, he had seen firsthand what she was capable of. The spiked ball was a blur, whirling at a phenomenal speed. And then with deadly precision it was flung straight at her. It happened so fast that Darla barely dodged out of the way in time. It was a narrow miss. In a deadly arc the spiked ball swung back and was twirling at his side again.

Again, the deadly spiked ball was flung at her and pivoting the short sword she deflected it. Pressing a button, Ronnard retrieved the spiked ball and extending the chain he had it spinning once again. Darla was on the defensive, forced to give ground. She backstepped and wobbled, as suddenly her leg gave out. Toppling backwards, she automatically tucked her body in and rolled. It was instinct, something that had been ingrained into her from years of training. It was also the only thing that saved her.

* * *

Seeing her fall, Ronnard sent the spiked ball hurtling towards her. Using the momentum to tuck and roll, she had been lucky, escaping with the spiked ball slicing open her shoulder. It could have been a hell of a lot worse. If she had fallen at the trajectory that she had been heading, the spiked ball would have slammed into her head and caved in her skull. Darla landed in a crouch, with her weapons poised and ready. It was time to end this little dance.

Watching him like a hawk, Darla anticipated his next move by watching his body movements. Ronnard swung sending the spiked ball whipping around low. She jumped over it, letting the deadly ball and chain swing by harmlessly. With a twist of the mechanism, he had the spiked ball thundering back. This time it was it was swung high, with its trajectory in line with Darla's head. Landing in a crouch, she sprang forward and swung.

The runes along the blade radiated a bright blue as the sword sliced through the chain and sent the spiked ball careening off into the river. "You fucking bitch!" Ronnard cursed, swinging the chain and using it as a whip. Leaning back the chain swung overhead, narrowly missing her face. With a flick, the mercenary swung it back and with a clinking of metal wrapped the chain around the sword. Pulling his arm back and yanking on the taught chain, he tried to yank it from her grasp.

* * *

Darla held firm, unyielding, her feet dug in as she refused to relinquish the sword. With a click, Ronnard activated the mechanical winch. Her feet skidded along the wet sand as she gave ground. Smiling wickedly, Ronnard then drew his dagger. Wide, razor-sharp and jagged it made for a deadly weapon. It was a show of what was in store for her – a slow, agonising, torturous death. Then surprisingly, the chain slackened, as Darla suddenly propelled herself and leapt forward.

The manoeuvre was unexpected and took Ronnard completely by surprise. Recovering his arm raked across, slashing, ready to cut Darla in half. Turning slightly in mid-air, Darla blocked the blade with his own chain. The chain that was firmly wrapped around her short sword. Deflected, the dagger swung harmlessly past her. In a blur of speed, she then twisted and turned, wrapping both of his arms up in the chain. Screaming, he desperately tried to free himself, but it was futile. He was immobilised. "You bitch," he screamed, as Darla rammed the barb through the exposed bit underneath his helmet. It was driven with such force that it went through his jaw, his nose cavity and punctured his brain.

"You're lucky I decided to be merciful," she replied, as his body fell to the ground. She could have pricked him with the barb. The poison would have given him an excruciatingly painful death. It would have been justified. He would have deserved it, considering the brutality, raping and torture that he had caused. The runes on the short sword radiated intensely shattering the chain wrapped around it. "Well, that's new." The short sword never ceased to amaze her.

Darla risked a quick glance towards the river. Even though its barb had been cut off, the glands in the manticore's tail still secreted venom. With its tail free, it sprayed venom into the mouth and the eyes of the two heads attached to its rump. The appendage that was wrapped around the manticore's neck loosened, as the hydra's three remaining heads roared in pain. Jassy took advantage and snapped down on the appendage with her powerful jaws. Dark green blood spurted as the appendage was ripped in half. Even mortally wounded, the manticore was still fighting back.

Walking over to the beast master, she pulled her dagger from his corpse and wiped it clean on his tunic. As she sheathed it, her gaze fell on the five remaining mercenaries. Two of them were busy plundering weapons and valuables off the corpses, while their comrade sorted through the debris of the carriage. The wagoner was storing what they had plundered in sections of the cart in an orderly fashion.

Ecnaidar was in a world of his own though. He was busy tenderising the demon queen, a barbaric, torturous procedure developed by the orcs. It was a sadistic practice that he enjoyed. One could even go so far to say that he relished in it. He had slowly tenderised her limbs with his spiked war hammer, squashing them to a bloody, messy pulp. He was slowly doing it at his leisure, dragging it out to prolong the demon's pain. Darla smirked. What she was about to do would severely piss off the mercenary leader. She was about to make herself public enemy number one.

Grabbing hold of Ronnard's corpse, she lifted it up slightly and swung. The corpse dropped back to the ground and she was left holding his helmeted head. His face had spiderwebbed with thick black lines due to the venom and his mouth was open in a silent scream. "Ecnaidar," she shouted, throwing her arm back and lobbing the head at him.

Ecnaidar turned at the sound of his name, a moment before the helmeted head hit him in the chest plate. Blood splattered over his face, which he casually wiped off with the back of his gauntleted hand. The look he gave Darla was one of annoyance, until he glanced down and noticed the helmet. With the toes of his boot, he tipped the helmet over and screamed. The sound was of pure, undulated rage. Staring back at him was the face of his second in command, Ronnard who also happened to be one of his closest friends. His face was streaked with the black lines from the venom and the barb was still protruding from his jaw. He had died quickly, a small mercy, one that he didn't plan on giving to this troublesome assassin.

"Kill her!" he screamed. He shook the money pouch attached to his belt. "Fifty gold coins to the mercenary that brings me her head." Drawing their weapons, the three mercenaries ran over. All thoughts of what she'd done to the guardsmen, the manticore and their comrades was dispersed, replaced with the sole purpose of what they lived for. Greed! The incentive of gold, the only thing that a mercenary cared about. Ecnaidar watched with grim satisfaction, his spiked hammer resting by his side. Let the demon queen regenerate, he would just tenderise her again later. He would do it at his leisure and savour every moment.

Drawing her remaining long-bladed dagger, Darla positioned herself and made ready for the onslaught. The first mercenary to reach her was an axeman. His large double-sided battle-axe swung across in a wide arc. The blade was razor-sharp and cracked in multiple spots. It was part of being a mercenary, instead of looking after their weapons they simply replaced them with the ones they plundered. Even still, it was sharp enough to cleave her in two.

Using her short sword, she nimbly hooked the axe, deflecting it and swinging it in front of her. With her other hand, she then rammed the dagger's pommel onto the guard's elbow. Even with his plate armour, the elbow was only lightly armoured to allow for flexibility and movement of the arm. It was the perfect spot to hit, to cripple an opponent. There was a loud crack as his elbow shattered and his arm suddenly became limp, hanging at an obscure angle. Screaming in pain and unable to hold the heavy axe with his good hand, he was forced to drop it and sent it clattering to the ground.

* * *

Continuing the momentum and swinging her sword down, Darla then stabbed the axeman in the side. The divine short sword easily pierced his plate armour, cutting through it as if it were nothing more than paper. The blade sliced through his rib cage and pierced his lung. The mercenary dropped to the ground wheezing and coughing up blood. She moved on to the two swordsmen who were approaching from behind. The axeman was no longer a threat, he was disposed of and would be dead within a minute. Turning her head Darla vomited again, mostly bile but also mixed with something else. Globules of blood and some manticore venom. Her lycanthropic regenerative abilities were fighting off the venom and trying to heal her body any way that it could. Wiping her mouth, she prepared to face the swordsmen. The battle wasn't over yet, she needed to focus and concentrate.

The two swordsmen tried to flank her. One had a short sword while his companion had a broad two-handed sword. She targeted the two-handed swordsman first. He posed the greater threat. Angling in his direction, she waited until he swung, focusing on the slightest movement of his muscles. From that she could anticipate where the sword would go. He swung in a wide arc, slashing horizontally across. It was a manoeuvre normally used to dispatch multiple enemies. It was his mistake. Darla dived low and bending back slightly, slid across the ground on her knees. As the sword passed harmlessly overhead, she slashed cleaving both of his hands off at the wrist.

* * *

The two-handed weapon fell to the ground with his gauntleted hands still grasping the hilt. Darla wasn't finished though. Her arm then swung across in a wicked back handed swing, cleaving both of the swordsman's legs off at the kneecaps. Springing back to her feet, she then faced the last swordsman. The last swordsman twirled his short sword in a figure eight. It was show boating, fancy tricks, nothing more. Darla slashed as the short sword came back up. The bright blue blade sliced the short sword in half, sending the silver blade spiralling into the darkness. The blade then sliced through the mercenary's neck. Dropping the hilt, the mercenary's face paled as he clutched at his neck and tried to stem the flow of blood.

"Looks like I'm going to have to kill you myself," Ecnaidar muttered. "I've added demon blood stains as you suggested, but I've yet to add werewolf stains." He lunged forward, swinging, but Darla gracefully dived to the side and dodged the blow. She leapt back up into a standing position and almost doubled over in pain. It felt like someone was repeatedly stabbing her in the stomach. The pain was excruciating. She could feel the venom coursing through her system. She vomited again, a combination of bile, blood and venom.

Changing direction, Ecnaidar took advantage of Darla's weakness. He pivoted, following her movement and reversed the hammer into a backhanded strike. For such a big man, he was agile and quick. She had no choice but to block the swing with the short sword. The blade glowed blue, shattering some of the spikes, but in her weakened state the force of the blow was too much. The short sword flew from her hand and clattered onto the ground. Ecnaidar lunged in for the kill.

Darla was forced to dive to the side, narrowly missing the campfire. Ecnaidar smiled, as he slowly approached. She had nowhere to go. She had her dagger but unless she got a kill shot, she was defenceless. And to use her dagger in a melee fight against him, would be like fighting a bear with a toothpick. She had one option. But to do it she needed a distraction, a moment to prepare.

Darla crept closer towards the campfire, positioning herself and waiting patiently. Ecnaidar approached her position cautiously, his spiked war hammer held poised and ready. She bided her time, watching, waiting, judging his position. He edged closer, took another step and then she reacted, sliding her leg forward and swinging her foot into the edge of the campfire. Embers and ash flew up, spraying into his face and blinding him momentarily.

Unbuckling her belt, she discarded it, throwing it to the ground. She then quickly unclasped her cloak and threw it on top. She didn't have long, Ecnaidar's vision was already starting to clear. She was about to delve into the unknown, do something that she had never done before. She was about to transform twice within one night. She didn't even know whether it was humanly possible, whether it would kill her. Tapping into her lycanthropy she began to transform. The transformation was especially painful the second time around, but gritting her teeth Darla endured, welcomed and embraced it.

Her eyes were already changed, along with most of her muscle enhancements. Her jaw elongated as the muscle, skin and bone grew and reformed. Her teeth grew bigger and her canines became longer and sharper, that of a predator. Her ears grew long, pointy and wolf like. Her hands and feet grew and reformed, reshaping and becoming broader and longer. Her claws grew, elongating and becoming razor-sharp. Her body transformed, reshaping her muscles, enlarging her internal organs and making her bones denser and stronger. Lastly, it was her body hair. Growing rapidly at an alarming rate, it quickly became a coat of thick, course, brown fur with bright red streaks.

Ecnaidar swung and ducking, Darla bounded out of the way. Another back handed swing, but she had anticipated this and ducking under it, raked her claw across, aiming for the exposed, lightly padded section between the neck and the shoulder. Her vision was blurry though, her speed slower than normal and the mercenary leader easily dodged the blow. Instead, her claws raked across his shoulder plate and the lightly armoured section of his elbow. It drew blood and Ecnaidar winced, but it wasn't the fatal blow for which she was hoping. The poison wasn't out of her system yet. It was affecting her speed, judgement and her ability to fight. This was going to be a gruelling skirmish.

Ecnaidar swung a vicious overhead blow that had Darla bounding backwards. Each move was precise and calculated. Darla was constantly on the defensive and found it hard to find any opportunity or opening. He pivoted with his arms extended, going into a round house spin. Darla prepared to dodge out of the way. As he spun, he let go with one hand. His muscles bulged in protest. It was a true testament to his strength. His free hand darted behind his back and with a soft hiss, drew a short sword. Darla did not realise what he had done until it was too late. In a blur he thrust it forward. It had been aimed at her heart, but Darla had dodged just in time. Her quick reflexes had saved her life. It did not stop the cry of pain though, as the sword pierced her shoulder.

With a sadistic grin, he slowly pushed it in to the hilt. Darla screamed. The pain was excruciating, it felt like her shoulder was burning. Then with a horrifying realisation, Darla realised that the short sword was made from silver. Gritting her teeth, she growled low and menacing, ignoring the pain. Slowly, agonisingly, she reached up and grabbed Ecnaidar's gauntleted wrist. Her claws dug into the joint, the vulnerable spot that allowed for the free range of movement. She squeezed, her claws screeching along the metal. The plate mail cracked from the force and the strain. Sharply, agonisingly, she twisted and snapped it in two. Ecnaidar screamed, letting go of the short sword, his hand hanging limply at a sickening angle.

Stepping back and giving himself some room, he swung.

The war hammer whirled through the air with a whoosh, passing over where Darla's head had only been moments before. Darla had just managed to dodge the crushing blow, nimbly leaping to the side. Clenching her teeth, she grabbed the hilt of the short sword and pulled the blade free with a spray of blood. The wound would take a while to heal due to the silver. With a clatter, the short sword dropped at her feet.

Charging forward, he swung a vicious overhead blow. Darla rolled out of the way just in time, with the war hammer smashing into the ground and spraying up dirt and gravel. She leapt to her feet, just as Ecnaidar swung the war hammer in a backwards swing. Darla leaned backwards, watching as the mighty weapon swung harmlessly over her head. She landed, tucking into a ball, rolling and springing into a crouched position. She waited for the mercenary commander to swing and pressed her own attack.

The war hammer flew underneath her as she leapt over it and lashed out with her claws. Sparks flew as her claws scraped against the reinforced metal of his pauldron. Darla landed and sprung backwards. The mercenary leader swung two more times and Darla repeated the manoeuvre, darting in and raking his pauldron and vambrace with swift, precise strikes. Darla had attacked the same heavily armoured area three times, but to no avail. Ecnaidar laughed. "You stupid bitch, my armour is reinforced steel plate. You won't be so lucky this time." The pauldron and vambrace were a mass of scratches.

Ecnaidar swung, the war hammer soaring through the air. Darla sprung forward again, her claws raking the vambrace. Digging in, they scraped and sparked against the metal. She landed, springing back, but this time the mercenary leader was ready. He had already reversed the hammer into a backwards swing and caught her in mid-flight. The huge hammer connected with a meaty thud, smashing into her thigh, the spikes leaving multiple puncture wounds. The force of the blow sent Darla flying. She landed awkwardly and her leg gave way. Howling in pain, she toppled backwards and crashed to the ground. Ecnaidar didn't waste an instant. Leaping forward, he bought the spiked hammer crashing down.

It stopped mid descent as Darla's hands shot up, grabbing the handle with both clawed hands. Ecnaidar grunted and gritted his teeth, as his muscles tensed. He pushed his arm, slowly edging the deadly spikes towards Darla's head. Darla's grip held firm as she pushed back, edging the war hammer away from her. It was a titanic struggle a battle of wills. Hearing a slight crack, Darla bent her knees and snaked her legs around each side of his arm. Her plan had worked. As she tried to hook her feet, Ecnaidar laughed and raising his arm lifted her cleanly off the ground. It was a herculean effort, a tremendous feat. He then slammed her back down, jarring every bone in her body.

Darla kept a firm hold and refused to let go. She heard more cracks. "Fine, have it your way werewolf," he said, raising her once again and lifting her above his head. He had mocked her and thought her attacks futile, when in fact each scratch had been calculated and precise. She had weakened the structural integrity of the pauldron and vambrace parts of his armour. Ecnaidar had been oblivious, he hadn't even realised.

He had thought himself invincible and his arrogance was his undoing. Darla grinned wolfishly and squeezed her legs together, constricting his arm and cracking the metal sections completely. Ecnaidar screamed, as with three loud snaps, his humerus, radius and ulna bones broke in two. Unable to keep hold of it, he released his grip, relinquishing the hammer to Darla.

Darla readjusted her grip and untwining her legs, landed gracefully on the ground. Growling, she swung the hammer forward, her rage and strength powering the swing into a mighty blow. The speed and ferocity of the attack was phenomenal. Ecnaidar was defenceless, helpless, there was nothing he could do but raise his injured arm. He was completely at Darla's mercy. The blow hit his arm first, shattering it and pushing the broken gauntlet into his face. A moment later the hammer crashed into his helmet with a sickening crunch, caving the mercenary leader's helmet and half of his skull. Like a fallen tree, he toppled to the ground dead.

Silence, except for the chirping of insects, greeted her. The campsite looked like a battlefield, littered with corpses. Darla looked around for the wagoner, but he was nowhere to be seen. He had disappeared, taking the wagon and what valuables that he could. It didn't matter. He was insignificant. Releasing the war hammer, she let it clatter to the ground. Concentrating, she transformed back into her human form. Her tunic was in tatters, but that was no surprise. She had expected that.

She stumbled forward, fell to her knees and vomited. More bile, with blobs of poison and blood throughout. Her body ached and she felt exhausted. She was sweating profusely and was feverish. She slowly forced herself back up and stumbled towards the short sword. She buckled her belt and did up the clasp on her cloak. Sheathing the short sword, she stumbled towards the demon queen. "You look like shit," the demon said in way of greeting.

"Look who's talking," Darla replied, laughing. She was feeling marginally better, she had vomited most of the poison out of her system. The queen had fared a lot worse, it was a miracle that she was still alive. Her limbs had been pulverised into a mushy concoction of blood and bone, with stringy bits of muscle throughout. "How long will it take you to regenerate?" Darla had her own morals, ethics and principles. A warrior code that she abided by. She would continue the fight once the demon's limbs were restored.

"The damage is too extensive and I have used to much magic," she replied, coughing up some blood. "I am dying. And I was so looking forward to finishing our fight." The demon laughed weakly. "Could you do me a small favour assassin?" Darla nodded, dubious of what the boon would be. "Could you fetch my tiara. I would like to wear it one last time. I would like to die a queen. Queen Mavelyn." She laughed, coughing up some blood. Without a word, Darla retrieved the tiara and gently placed it on the demon queen's head. Teary eyed, the demon queen smiled. There was no need for words, it was thank you enough.

"Why didn't you use your magic before?" It was something that had puzzled Darla. It would have changed the outcome of their fight. She would have been killed and the demon would have won.

She tried to laugh and coughed up another mouthful of blood. "Because I considered you a worthy opponent. I am honourable and wanted a fair fight. You won fair and square. Well fought assassin." Darla was speechless. A demon that had morals and was honourable. It was questionable and she was dubious. She didn't know what to believe.

"You speak of honour. Yet you attacked your own people," Darla questioned.

The queen laughed weakly. The effort was obviously painful. "I am a monster, a demon. It is in my nature to kill."

"Well, if I wasn't betrayed, we could have finished what we'd started."

"Betrayed?" the queen asked confused.

"Yes. By my benefactor, the prince, the one who contracted me to kill you. He obviously considered me a loose end, hence the mercenary attack."

"You think Prince Zane did this?" the queen looked genuinely amused. She laughed and coughed up some more blood. "No, my dear. Malgorath is the one that orchestrated this attack. He is the puppet master pulling the strings."
Darla raised her eyebrows questioningly. "Aren't they one and the same?" She had suspected the prince, everything seemed to lead back to him.

"No, Prince Zane isn't a demon. Malgorath has consumed the soul and taken possession of..." The demon queen died, her voice trailing off into the night. Not of this realm, the demon's body lost all substance and disintegrated. All that was left was a pile of dust, which blew away into the night. All trace of the demon queen had dissipated. The only proof of her existence was the golden tiara lying nearby.

Darla did not know what to think. Was Malgorath the king or one of the other princes? Or was the queen lying about Prince Zane not being Malgorath? The demon queen had tried to kill her one minute though and befriend her the next. It was questionable. Why should she trust the word of a demon? She didn't know what to believe. She was determined to find out though. She looked up at the sky, it was fast approaching dawn. She needed to make her way back to the Brotherhood campsite, she needed to make herself scarce. She had no intention of being here when the king and his hunting party arrived.

Before going to the Brotherhood hideaway, she had one last thing to do. Staggering towards the bush, she went to retrieve Marek's repeater crossbow. He would never forgive her if she left it behind. It was his pride and joy. The bush was just ahead. Gritting her teeth, she fought against the pain as another wave of stomach cramps hit her. It felt as if her stomach was being ripped open from the inside out. She vomited. Her legs began to wobble and her vision became blurry. She took a step and toppled, falling to the ground face first. Looking up, she gazed upon the repeater crossbow. It was just in front of her amidst the foliage of the bush. Her arm slowly stretched out towards it and then fell limp to the ground as she lay there unconscious.

Chapter 8

The hunting party galloped along the King's Highway, the riders jostling in their saddles and the horses snorting with exhilaration as they sent a great cloud of dust and gravel bellowing behind them in their wake. They had been trotting at a steady pace for the last two hours and still hadn't caught up with the wagons. The wagoners had set off early, eating on the road, while their sturdy pack horses trotted along carrying the prized boar carcass, along with their belongings. The pack horses were bred for their strength and stamina, enabling them to carry heavy loads at a decent speed, all day.

The hunting party had spent time having breakfast and packing up their little camp. It didn't help that some of the soldiers were quite lethargic this morning. The king had ordered the gallop for three reasons. The first being to catch up to the wagons, the second was to stretch the horse's legs and the third was a more spiteful reason.

The king and the baron led the gallop, with their sons and the guards following close behind them. They hung over their saddles slightly, leaning forward, the wind whistling through their hair, whooping and laughing with joy. They were reliving their childhood, acting like immature children and enjoying it. Prince Jace, Rylan and a few of the guards were jostled awkwardly in their saddles. Moaning and grumbling, they had their heads hung down and were far from thrilled with the experience. One guard even vomited over the side of his horse, luckily there was no-one behind him. After a couple of minutes, they slowed down, bringing their horses back to a canter.

Jace brought his horse alongside his father, with Rylan cantering on the other side of him. Both had their heads down and their hoods up, leaving their faces in shadow. "That was cruel, father," Jace muttered, turning his hood to face him. The king just smiled slyly, not saying a word. He had been young once, just like his son. His father had also done the same thing to him. Now it was his turn, such was the circle of life.

"I'm sure my father was just as much to blame," Rylan said casually to his friend. They were both speaking quietly due to the throbbing headaches that they had. The headaches resulting from copious amounts of drinking the night before. It had been a celebration though, with the two men having much to drink about.

The boar was monstrous, the biggest that they had ever seen. It was only slightly smaller than their horses, but a lot heavier set, covered in muscle and thick fur. Its tusks had been bigger than their arms, a trophy they each planned to have. They would hollow them out, trim them slightly and make war horns out of them. They would roast the meat back at the castle, providing a hearty meal for everyone.

The dogs had tracked the boar to its den, provoking and flushing the beast out. The enraged beast had charged through the bushes, right into the hunting party's path. The dogs having done their job had scurried out of the way. The party were ready though, waiting in a semi-circle with weapons at hand. The crossbowmen had fired, the bolts hitting their mark, but hardly penetrating its thick hide. The boar just continued charging, heading straight towards the prince.

* * *

The King had banned him from using any magic. "Hunting is for men," his father had said. "It separates the men from the boys." And here Jace was now, readying himself and gripping his long, boar spear tightly. The spear was made of sturdy wood and had a thick, long, jagged head. A head designed to spin and saw into the boar, penetrating and killing it. Nervous, he quickly glanced towards his father and could have sworn that for the briefest of moments that his eyes turned pitch black. Rylan, his best friend, stood next to him, grinning, his own boar spear in hand. He welcomed the challenge. The boar was theirs to kill, they had been given the honour.

They threw the spears, the deadly heads spinning towards its target. Halberdiers quickly moved in front of them, kneeling and holding their lethal halberds pointed towards the boar. They were the last line of defence. Both men, having thrown their spears, now only had their swords to rely on. They were unarmed, their swords futile against the boar. The king and baron were taking every precaution.

Both spears hit the boar in the head, the first one through its jaw and the second one hitting it right between the eyes. The boar died instantly, its legs crumpling underneath it and causing it to roll into a tree and come to a sudden stop. Neither man could distinguish whose spear had dealt the killing blow, but both the king and the baron suspected it was Rylan.

* * *

The baron's son was a natural at handling most kinds of weapons. He was more experienced and had more training than Jace, who had to juggle his weapon practice, his study of magic and his royal duties. Rylan was modest and a loyal friend, denying it and giving the credit to the prince. Both knew the truth of the matter but vowed to keep it to themselves. They had celebrated, drinking ale, wine and spirits into the early hours of the morning. They were both suffering for it now though.

An hour passed with the king and the baron chatting jovially, while their sons rode in relative silence beside them. As they rounded the next bend, they saw the wagons in the distance. They were a faint silhouette against the morning sun, distinguishable by the boar carcass that they carried in the back. "Let's catch up to those wagons," the king shouted, smiling at the baron as they both kicked their heels into their horse's sides. The two horses raced off at a gallop. Jace and Rylan groaned and rolled their eyes. Nudging their horses' sides, they galloped their horses along with the rest of the guards.

Darla woke up to a wet lick across the face. A slobbering lick that she immediately recognised. "Midnight," she groaned, struggling as she slowly forced herself into a sitting position. She felt as if her muscles were on fire and her head was throbbing, pounding like a war drum. Turning her head to the side, she vomited, the bile burning her throat. "Midnight," she croaked, as she gingerly reached for the canteen strapped to the saddle. Her voice was hoarse, her throat was dry and the foul taste of the vomit was lingering in her mouth. Unstoppering it, she carefully raised it to her lips. Drinking the cool water was relieving, easing her parched throat. Her throat bobbed as she took large gulps and drained half of the canteen.

She felt like crap, as if a pack of war horses had galloped over her and then she'd gone one-on-one with a dragon. That was beside the point though, she had survived manticore poison. It was an incredible feat. The lycanthropic regenerative powers that she possessed, never ceased to amaze her. Pulling herself up with the aid of the saddle she gingerly walked over to a nearby bush. Her muscles were tight and felt like they were on fire. Each step was an effort.

In the morning light she could see the bush for what it was. It was thick, robust and covered with dark blue berries. Looking around she noticed a mass of similar looking bushes. Wild blueberries for the travellers to eat. As she knelt next to the bush, she noticed the broken branches and leaves covering the ground. She felt a knot in her stomach as she reached into the bush. She was preparing herself, deep down she already suspected what she would find. She still grimaced though, as she pulled out the quiver and the repeater crossbow. They were indented with Midnight's teeth marks. Marek was going to kill her! Midnight neighed and shook his head sheepishly *"I couldn't help it. I was hungry."*

Darla slung the crossbow over her shoulder so that it rested comfortably on her back and hung the quiver on a hook attached to her saddle. Putting her foot in the stirrup, she mounted Midnight and nudged him in the side. "Okay boy, time to get going." Midnight stood steadfast, refusing to budge. He turned his head and neighed as if to say, *"I want an apple."* Darla's ears twitched. She could hear horses, the clunking of wagon wheels and voices, faint but distinguishable. They were still travelling down the King's Road but would be at the campsite any minute. They were about to arrive and discover the carnage. Darla needed to go, and she needed to do it now.

"Stop being a pig. You've had some blueberries," she said, grinding her teeth. She didn't have time for Midnight's stubbornness. Another neigh, loud and decisive as if to say, *"I'm still hungry!"* Fuck!! "I will give you a small bag of apples once we get back to the Raven." Midnight flicked his tail as he contemplated this. The riders were getting closer. He nodded his head and snorted, thinking that this was an acceptable compromise. Darla cursed as she nudged him again and veered him to the left. Thanks to Midnight's procrastination, they had run out of time. Their only chance was a small crop of trees nearby. Galloping, they entered the tree line, just as the first horses turned the corner and entered the devastated campsite.

Hidden amongst the trees, Midnight stood like a silent sentinel, hidden in shadow. Darla pulled her cloak tightly around her and watched the proceedings through a gap in the trees. Rummaging in her saddlebag, she pulled out a juicy red apple and placed it near his mouth. "Eat it quietly," she whispered. Her only reply was a faint nicker, an acknowledgement, before he devoured the apple and began crunching. She counted twenty-eight riders. Twenty-two were mounted on horses, while six rode in the four wagons. "King Erithen, Baron Sandrik, Prince Jace and Lord Rylan," Darla whispered, rattling off their names. She could easily distinguish them by the finery that they wore.

The guards were dressed in plate armour. Their armour was similar, almost identical, but their surcoats stood out like a beacon, identifying and distinguishing them. Silver antlers on a black background, represented the loyal, honoured house of Baron Sandrik Ashburn, while the royal house of Everthorn bore a golden gryphon on a blue background. It was rumoured that the royal family even had an affinity with the gryphons that resided in the nearby mountain range. The wagons also had the house emblems painted upon them, distinguishing who they belonged to. All except one that was unmarked and stood apart from the others.

Three men sat awkwardly, upon the unmarked wagon. The wagon was designed to seat two people comfortably, allowing for the wagoner and a passenger. Two of the passengers were the king's guards, dressed in their heavy armour. The man sitting in between the guards had his wrists and feet bound tightly. His head was hung down, hiding his identity and his clothes were covered in blood. He had obviously put up a fight. He was a prisoner awaiting the king's judgement.

Upon seeing the carnage, the guards displayed a mixture of emotions. Some were distraught, while others were angry. A few of them were just shocked and speechless. Each of them was grieving in their own way. One of the guards drew his dagger, screaming in rage as he lunged at the prisoner between them. "Halt," Erithen said calmly, dismounting. The guard paused, holding the dagger inches from the other man's throat.

"Why!" he shouted, weeping openly. "He's partly responsible for the queen's death."

"It's nnnot my fffault," he stuttered in between sobs. The guard grabbed the prisoner's hair and yanked his head up. With the force that was applied, Darla was surprised that he didn't snap the man's neck. The prisoner was visibly pale and trembling uncontrollably. Deep down he knew what fate awaited him.

"Fuck!" Darla cursed quietly, recognising the man. It was the wagoner of the Bloodborn mercenaries. In his hasty retreat he'd been captured, caught red-handed with armour, weapons, jewellery and money. Most of it belonged to the queen's retinue, which condemned him without a doubt. After witnessing this carnage and knowing that he was involved, he was as good as dead. Darla had a feeling that he wouldn't even live long enough to be sentenced in the throne room of Everthorn Castle.

"I would like to confirm something from this treasonous coward," Erithen replied matter-of-factly, his voice a monotone and completely devoid of emotion. He walked over and leaning down, picked up a handful of the dust. His hand clenched into a fist. Darla gasped as she saw his pitch-black eyes. The king was a demon himself and knew exactly who the dust belonged to. Erithen picked up the golden tiara, the only thing remaining, a memory and reminder of the queen's existence.

The prince looked confused and a little worried. He had been with the king when the golden tiara was picked up and had witnessed the change in his eyes. It had been only momentary, but he had seen it. Standing back up, Erithen turned to face his eldest son, the heir to his throne. His eyes had returned to normal. He forced a smile even though tears were streaming down his face and embraced Jace, hugging him fiercely and sobbing on his shoulder.

Sandrik and Rylan stood there silent and resolute while their king mourned. They had lost someone dear to them as well.

They set their emotions aside. Dutifully, they would support the king and his family. They would grieve later, in private when they returned to their estate. Composing himself, Erithen turned to the prisoner. "And you claim that my son, Prince Zane, hired this monster, this werewolf assassin, to kill my wife, Queen Raylene?" The prisoner nodded vigorously.

"Are you seriously going to take the word of a mercenary and condemn your own son without any proof?" Jace asked, hoping his father would see reason. His father rubbed his goatee, something that he did while contemplating and thinking things through.

He came to a decision. "My son is right. You are a traitor to the Hiberathian Kingdom, your word means less than the shit on my boot." He wiped a finger across his neck, giving an order to the guardsman. The guard sliced his dagger across the prisoner's throat. As the wagoner gave a gurgled gasp, the guard threw him out of the wagon. "Let him rot with his brethren," Erithen said spitefully. "I will put a contract out on this werewolf assassin and pay handsomely to the one that brings me her head."

"That's near impossible, father," Jace questioned. "How the hell do you expect them to hunt down one particular assassin? There are hundreds out there."

Erithen clasped his son's shoulder and laughed. "True, but

there is only one who owns a dagger like this," he said holding up a dagger. Darla recognised it instantly. The dagger was hers. The blade still had the baronesses blood stained upon it. The mercenaries had obviously scavenged it from the carriage remains. It was the one thing that led back to her, the proof that they needed.

Grim and stoned faced, the king's retinue rode out. The king and the baron clasped hands in a fond farewell. The baron and his guards were heading back to their estate. The family holiday was ruined and even though Sandrik needed a break, he wanted to keep busy and distract himself in his work. Work that needed his attention and would keep him from reliving this dreadful event, from having to mourn the loss of his wife.

Lord Rylan was heading to Sethanon along with the king's retinue. Apparently, the rangers that had died had provided an opening that Rylan was eager to apply for. It had been a dream of his since childhood, to serve in the king's elite guard, to be one of the Royal Rangers. It would enable him to get away from the quiet life and enjoy the hustle and bustle of the major city of Sethanon. And even though the princes were like brothers to him, he had been adamant that he expected no special treatment. He knew that the training would be gruelling and rigorous, but to Rylan it was an honour and a privilege to serve in the rangers and he wanted to earn his place.

* * *

Darla paled. It was the story of her life, a mistake that she seemed to consistently make. Even though the contract had paid extremely well, it had turned into a complete and utter cluster fuck. "Fucking seven hells," she cursed. The king's word was lore. She had just made an immensely powerful enemy. She had planned to keep a low profile for a little while. Let things die down and not draw any unwanted attention. The king had no idea who she was, that she was the one responsible. She had thought that it would be impossible for him to track her down. That she would be safe.

To lay low was no longer an option. The king's vengeance was a motivational factor, one that drove him to seek justice for his wife's death. He also had the royal treasury and the resources available to him. She would have a couple of days at the most before someone tracked her down. But that was all she needed. A couple of days to rest and recover from the manticore venom. Then she would travel to Sethanon and kill the royal family and eliminate the Everthorn bloodline from this world.

Darla waited for a couple of minutes before giving Midnight the command. The horse neighed, trotting forward. "Home boy," she said, grimacing, as she clutched her stomach. A neigh, followed by a flicker of his head, *'Can I have another apple?'* Patting him affectionately, Darla reached into her saddlebag. They rode in relative silence along the dirt track, a commonly used hunter's trail. Darla knew this forest like the back of her hand, they both did. Midnight could get her back to the inn even without her guidance. The only sound that could be heard as they trotted along, was the crunching from Midnight as he happily ate his apple.

She felt weak and exhausted. She was still sweating profusely, even though the weather was cool. She was feverish and found it hard to concentrate. Her eyes felt heavy, but she was afraid to close them. She couldn't help it, within a matter of seconds they closed of their own volition as she fell forward in the saddle, limp and unconscious. Midnight neighed as if to say, *"Fine sleep, but I am going to hold you to that bag of apples."* He continued to trot along the path, through the forest, as he carefully carried Darla back to the inn, back towards home.

Chapter 9

Prince Jace dismounted in the courtyard of Everthorn Castle. The memory of the ride back was a blur as all he could think about was the horrific scene that had befallen them at the campsite. It was early evening; the sun was setting and torches had been lit to illuminate the castle grounds. Two stable hands ran over to help with the horses. He nodded and mumbled his thanks as he handed one of the stable hands Snow's reins.

He had named his warhorse Snow because of his pure white colour. The horse stamped in defiance, refusing to budge. "Behave," Jace said sternly, then sighed in resignation and patted Snow affectionately. "We have had a long ride and even though he is a little cranky, for the most part he has been well-behaved. Perhaps, he could have a treat." Snow neighed happily, nudging the prince and just about bowling him over. Jace laughed and the stable hand smiled in understanding.

"There are some fresh oats and some blueberries in the stables, my prince. Would you like some blueberries, Snow?" the stable hand asked, giving him a gentle pat. Snow trotted off happily, the stable hand being his new best friend. Jace sighed as he noticed the general walking towards him with six guards following in toe. He wasn't in the mood for General Iryss's report or drama. All he wanted was a nice warm bath, one of Varyn Kabel's sleeping elixirs and then to curl up in his bed. He wanted to hide away from the world and forget about the recent events, about the loss of his mother.

"This is not the time, general. Your report can wait until morning," Jace said, with a wave of his hand dismissing the general.

"I answer only to the king, Prince Jace," Iryss replied

smugly.

"I am heir to the king…." Jace was cut off as his father interrupted.

"It is alright, Jace. Let the general speak," Erithen said diplomatically, placing a hand gently on his son's shoulder. Jace was seething. His father was too lenient with the general and gave him too much authority and power. He could feel his wild magic raging like a torrent, ready to be unleashed. He closed his eyes and took a couple of deep breaths. It was a calming exercise that Varyn Kabel had taught him.

Wild magic was something Jace had been born with, it was ingrained into him. It was a part of who he was. He didn't have to incant, study, or memorise spells. The magic was natural and flowed through him. His study involved how to control the magic and his emotions. He had learnt early on that the two were linked – that when he became emotional, the magic would rage uncontrollably like the rapids in a river.

He had managed to keep his emotions in check when they rode into the devastated campsite. When questioned about his lack of emotion, he had replied with a grim smile "I will mourn later. I need to be strong for my family." The truth was that he was relieved. He missed his mother terribly, but at least she was at peace. He hadn't told anyone, but the wild magic enabled him to see an aura of the demons residing in his parents.

* * *

Was Malgorath his father? He couldn't tell, but the aura was more powerful than his mother's. Yet, if his father was Malgorath, why didn't he mask his aura? Surely, he was powerful enough to mask it. This question was racking his brain, yet he was no closer to finding out the answer. His mind was in a constant state of turmoil and it frustrated him to no end.

The general strolled forward his greaves crunching the pebbles and knelt before his king. The six guards standing in formation a step behind the general, immediately followed suit, their plate armour creaking as they paid homage. "I'm sorry to disturb you, my liege, but I…." He stopped mid-sentence as his head turned and looked expectantly around. "Where is the queen?" He was generally puzzled.

"The queen is dead," Erithen replied in a monotone, his voice devoid of all emotion.

"I'm sorry, my liege. You have our condolences. She will be sorely missed. Unfortunately, I bear grave news that cannot wait," Iryss replied. His eyes darted towards Jace, before flicking back to address the king. "It requires your urgent attention." The king nodded for the general to continue. "I have isolated the person in question, but your judgement is required because of his title."

"And who is this person in question?" Jace inquired. Iryss

looked at the prince but refused to answer.

"You will have to forgive my son's rudeness general. He is grieving. Who is this person in question?" Erithen's approach was diplomatic. Jace felt his throat tighten. Deep down, he already knew the answer.

"Your son, Prince Zane. He was seen dealing with the Bloodborn mercenaries. He was also the last person seen with Ven, one of his rookie guards."

"Ven…" Jace started to say, but stopped when his father gave him a stern look.

"Ven's body was discovered the following morning. His throat was slit and the bloodied dagger lay in his outstretched hand. Even the servant Millie agreed that Prince Zane could have slipped out after their sexual exploits."
"This is crap," Jace shouted, earning another stern look from his father. He didn't care, his brother was innocent. He knew Zane better than anyone. Someone had to be setting him up. "Surely, you don't believe this father? Zane is your flesh and blood - your son and my brother."

Erithen shook his head. "You wanted proof, son. Now you have it. Your brother has dishonoured and tarnished our name. He is no longer a prince of the realm. He can enjoy a nice, cosy cell in the dungeon and await my judgement."
Jace was speechless and shocked. His brother had just been

condemned and was about to be imprisoned. He couldn't believe it.

Jace's gauntlets creaked as he clenched his fists. He wasn't about to let his brother be thrown into the dungeon when he knew this was a setup. He felt unadulterated rage surge through him, uncontrollable, like a tidal wave. His eyes glowed bright blue, blazing with wild magic. His left hand swung across his body and with a soft hiss, drew his sword. The blade automatically flared to life, ablaze with bright blue fire. It was his wild magic, igniting the blade and preparing him for battle.

"My brother is innocent," he screamed, swinging the sword. Iryss paled and Jace could see the fear in his eyes. In a blur, the general's sword was suddenly there, held defensively, preparing to block the stroke. He had acted purely on instinct, honed from years of experience and training, but it was futile. No ordinary weapon could stop the blazing wildfire. The general's sword glowed red, burning with intense heat as the wildfire sliced through it. Jace's sword continued its deadly decent.

Only to halt inches from the general's face. "Do you want to join your brother in the dungeon?" Erithen shouted, blocking the sword. How had his father blocked the wildfire? Then he saw the long-bladed dagger his father held. It was glowing dimly. Jace didn't know whether the glow was from the dagger or the wildfire. But the assassin's dagger had blocked his sword. The only explanation was that it was enchanted. But how did the king know? The demon. It must have known the dagger was magical and was the only thing that could stop his wildfire.

Jace kept quiet and refused to answer. Reining in his magic, he extinguished the sword and sheathed it. "I'm going to talk to Zane," he said, excusing himself and walking towards the southern entrance. He could vaguely hear the general and his father talking about him, but he took no notice. His mind was preoccupied. His mother was dead, his father was demonic and one of his brothers was about to be imprisoned.

"Stop…" Iryss said, but Erithen raised his hand and halted him.

"Let him go, general. He is mourning the loss of his mother…and now his brother. Let him say his goodbyes."

"But…" Iryss started, but stopped himself mid-sentence as the king threw him a fierce look. "As you command, my liege." Erithen hmphed. He did not like to be questioned but he was willing to let the matter slide with the general this time.

Jace briefly heard the 'Your highness' from the guard who saluted, thumping his chest plate with his gauntleted fist and bowing his head in homage to his prince. Then the guard rushed to open the door as the prince hurried through. Jace had not meant to be rude. He was normally polite, but with the way he was feeling and the current circumstances, he was in no mood for pleasantries. He stormed up the staircase, taking them two at a time.

There were four guards stationed outside Zane's bedroom. They were all part of the general's squad and loyal to his father. The door was wide open and Jace could hear talking and laughter coming from within. "I would like to see my brother," he stated, addressing the corporal in charge.

The corporal was hesitant. "I need the general's authorisation," he mumbled. The other guards stared nervously at the ground.

"Who do you think sent me up?" Jace lied. The corporal sighed, his relief apparent on his face. He motioned the prince to enter.

"Jace, you're back," Stryxen screamed, racing down the corridor. Jace gasped as he was almost bowled over by the bear hug his younger brother enveloped him in. Laughing, he ruffled Stryxen's hair as he led them into Zane's bedroom. Without a word, the corporal closed the door with a soft click and gave them some privacy. Jace had missed his brothers terribly, but unfortunately, he had to be the bearer of bad news and inform them about their mother's death.

Zane was playing cards with some of his guards at the table

but upon Jace and Stryxen's entry, their laughter and banter stopped. The sound of scraping chairs filled the room as they hurriedly stood to attention and saluted the princes. All except one who sat next to Zane and idly watched the proceedings. "Bear, Matthias, Larin, Beast," Jace said, nodding and smiling to each in turn. He made it a habit to develop a rapport with the guards and knew all of them except the stranger. Before he could ask, Zane leapt up and embraced his brother in a fierce hug. "Welcome back, Jace," he said. "How was the holiday?"

"The holiday was good, but I have some dire news to share with you two." The look in Jace's eyes told Zane that something was terribly wrong. Before he could ask, someone else entered the room.

"Welcome back, Prince Jace. Good evening, Prince Stryxen." Brenan said, behind them. As Jace turned, Brenan nodded to each of them and thumping his armoured chest, saluted the princes.

"You'll have to excuse our captain. He has the bladder of a little girl and had to relieve himself," Bear sneered. Beast couldn't help it as he slammed his mug on the table and roared with laughter. The two guardsmen nicknamed Bear and Beast were monstrous men and excellent fighters who were completely loyal to Zane. They were also brothers and were inseparable.

* * *

"I'm glad you both find it amusing," Brenan snickered, a glint in his eye. "Because you two are on latrine duty tonight. The rest of you should collect your coin pouches and return to the barracks. You too, Rayze, I've got a cot assigned for you." The man had healed exceptionally fast, too fast for a mere human. Brenan knew there had to be more to the mysterious stranger, something he was determined to find out. And how better than by incorporating him as one of his own.

Rayze stood up and nodded to each of the princes. It was a show of respect and acknowledged the position that they held. He was a prince himself and usually saluted to no man. Times had changed though, and he didn't want to reveal his true identity…not yet! Not until he knew Malgorath's identity, his purpose and what his endgame entailed. Swallowing his pride, he gently thumped his fist against his chest. It wasn't a proper salute, but it was the best they were going to get out of him. The last thing that he wanted to do was arise suspicion.

"Why is the pommel of your sword wrapped?" Stryxen asked. Rayze looked confused for a moment. He'd wrapped the pommel prior to joining the bandits, protecting and hiding the divinity stone that was inserted in the pommel. He had grown accustomed to the leather straps and had completely forgotten about them. Now, the straps were worn and faded, wear and tear from the battles he had fought.

* * *

"You have a keen eye, young princeling. The leather protects the pommel and the gem inserted into it," Rayze explained.

"Can I have a look?" Stryxen held out his hands eagerly. Rayze laughed and shook his head. And just like that, the young prince's demeanour changed. He sighed dramatically. "I was trying to ask politely, but it looks like I am going to have to demand it. I am a prince of the realm and you will obey me. Show me NOW!"

"Sorry, young princeling, but I don't answer to you," Rayze stated calmly.

"That's right Stryxen. You can't order around Zane's guards," Jace said. He looked the newcomer in his bright blue eyes. "I know most of the guards, yet I don't believe I have met you?" Brenan opened his mouth, but nothing came out. He was desperate, trying to fumble for an excuse. Thinking quickly, Zane beat him to it.

"I received word of an elven army massing near our border. I sent Brenan along with a squad to investigate," Zane replied, wording his answer carefully. Brenan nodded, masking his relief.

Deep in thought, Jace processed what he'd just heard. "To invade would be an act of war. They would be forfeiting their pact, would be expelled from the alliance and feel the full might of the human and dwarven armies. Did you let the general know? Why isn't he massing the army?"

"We informed Prince Zane upon our return," Brenan said. "Unfortunately, Zane has been confined to his room.

"We briefly told the general, but I think he was too preoccupied with having his head stuck up his arse," Beast quipped. Prince Stryxen covered his mouth with his hand as he tried to stifle a giggle. Jace directed a stern look on the lieutenant.

"You shouldn't talk like that, lieutenant," he reprimanded Beast who nodded sheepishly. "Even if it is true," he added in a lighter tone. This earnt another giggle from Stryxen.

"We found out about the elves through one of Prince Zane's contacts who happened to be staying at the Blood Raven Inn," Brenan reported. The princes had various contacts throughout the realm that were used as spies and informants. "Rayze is one of the finest warriors that I've had the privilege to know," he added, looking at Rayze. The vampire smiled at the compliment and nodded at the captain in acknowledgement and gratitude. "We encountered a lesser demon that killed elves and humans alike during its rampage and destroyed half of the inn. Rayze helped us defeat the demon."

Prince Jace's eyebrows raised in surprise at the turn of

events. "A lesser demon?"

"Yes, Prince Jace. We were lucky to escape with our lives," Brenan replied. "Rayze helped in defeating the demon and also brought back an artefact called a divinity stone." Zane watched like a hawk, observing his brothers' reactions, seeing if Jace gave anything away. Jace was surprised and intrigued; an appropriate reaction while Stryxen merely seemed confused and bored. It could be understood since he was still young and probably didn't even know what a divinity stone was.

Zane was right. "What's a divinity stone?" Stryxen asked, puzzled.

"It's rumoured to be an immensely powerful magical artefact," Jace replied.

"How powerful?" Stryxen queried. He was curious, but also doubtful.

"Apparently it has the power to kill Malgorath." Jace laughed as his younger brother bounced with excitement and screamed that he wanted to see it. "Where is it?" Jace asked.

"It's hidden and protected," Zane stated matter-of-factly. Jace nodded and sighed with relief. Zane wondered if it was his brother enquiring or if it was Malgorath.

* * *

"Well, you know Stryxen will continue to screech and carry on until he sees it," Jace chuckled. Zane laughed as he looked at their younger brother, contemplating and weighing things up.

"Please, please, please Zane. Show us," Stryxen screeched, jumping up and down again.

What he was about to do was a dangerous gamble, but he needed to know. "I'll get it and show it to both of you. Sorry for the interruption, Brenan. Please continue."

"Prince Zane cast a portal, so that we could travel there in due haste. Upon arriving we were informed that a small elvish army was camped west of the inn. I sent out two riders, who managed to muster about two hundred soldiers from Fort Targen and positioned them in a nearby meadow as a deterrent. After killing the lesser demon and acquiring the divinity stone, we made our way to the meadow. We were attacked during the night by the elves and our own troops."

"Our troops?" Jace questioned, his eyebrows raised in alarm. He wondered if he'd heard correctly.

"Yes. About a third of the men from Fort Targen and a large group of elves. Even though Prince Jerrick had every intention of recovering the divinity stone, he seemed caught up in the chaos as well. I saw him fighting our soldiers, but he also seemed to be fighting his own soldiers too."

Jace huffed. "Are you sure it wasn't an act, Brenan, orchestrated to deceive you?"

Brenan laughed awkwardly. "Well, it was a pretty damn convincing act," he said defensively. Jace's jaw clenched and he had a look in his eyes that Zane recognised all too well. He had grown up with Jace and received that look often enough. It was a look that meant Jace was about to say something in the heat of the moment. Something he would later regret, so Zane quickly interceded.

"You weren't there Jace, but Brenan was. The battle was raging around him, yet he managed to observe this before retreating and relaying the information to me," Zane said, walking over with the satchel. Jace and Stryxen had been focused on Brenan's recount and he had used the distraction to retrieve the divinity stone.

Jace nodded, calming down. "I apologise, Brenan. I am tired, moody and have bad news for my brothers."

Brenan nodded slightly, accepting the apology. "No need to apologise, Prince Jace. We'll give you some privacy so that you can catch up with your brothers." As the guards walked past the three princes and Brenan, Zane heard Bear and Beast grumbling about latrine duty. He started to snicker, then quickly disguised it as a cough.

"What do you think caused the attack?" Jace asked, as Brenan turned to follow the squad out of the door. Stopping at the doorway, he turned to face the prince.

"I suspect it was Malgorath's doing. He was after the divinity stone," Brenan replied. "I think the guards and the elves that we encountered were loyal to him. They were demented and fought like fanatics."

Jace nodded in understanding. "You are lucky to be alive. Thank you for bringing us this information."

"I just hope the divinity stone helps defeat Malgorath. Otherwise, the soldiers, my brothers who sacrificed themselves would have died for naught," Brenan replied before walking out the door. Zane waited until the corporal closed the door and gave them some privacy. Then reaching into the satchel, he pulled out the fake divinity stone. Jace gasped in awe, while Stryxen huffed and then laughed.

"It's just a big emerald," he scoffed, unimpressed. Zane smiled at his younger brother. Stryxen was ignorant and didn't understand the importance of such an artefact.

"Our younger brother raises a good point," Jace said sceptically. "We don't know if it really is a divinity stone or even if it is going to be powerful enough to defeat

Malgorath."

"It must be. Why would the fanatics try so desperately to recover a fake?" Zane said, putting the divinity stone back into the satchel and returning it to the compartment. Mumbling the words once again, he activated the runes. Jace nodded, conceding the point, but Stryxen merely huffed again. Bored, he started to head towards the door. Jace gently put a hand on his shoulder, stopping him.

"Please sit, Stryxen. I have some news for you and Zane." Grumbling, Stryxen shrugged off his brother's hand and stormed over to the couch. Throwing himself onto it, he plopped onto one of the cushions.

"Don't worry, the divinity stone will be investigated. I won't go in half-cocked and put our lives at risk. I'll research and test it before we face Malgorath," Zane said, reassuring his brothers as he walked over to a small, wooden table. On the table was a crystal decanter full of an amber liquid. It was a honey flavoured whisky, strong and sweet. Zane poured three crystal goblets to the brim.

Jace raised his eyebrows questioningly. Zane shrugged. "You said that the news was dire. If it's anything going from your expression, then I think we are going to need these," he said as he carried two of the goblets back and handed one to each of his brothers.

* * *

Stryxen beamed. He had never drunk alcohol before because their parents said he was too young. "Thanks Zane." He sniffed at the contents within the goblet. "It smells good. What is it?"

"It's honeyed whisky," Zane replied, laughing as he walked back and collected his goblet.

Jace glared at Zane. "I know he's too young to drink, but if the news is as dire as you're making out then I think he's going to need it. If not, then I'll take full responsibility for my actions." Jace was not impressed, but he nodded as Zane took the seat next to their younger brother. Taking a small sip, he winked at Jace and mouthed *'He probably won't even like it.'*

Stryxen took a tentative sip. Grimacing, he sprayed some of the alcohol across the cushion. "That's foul. It's burning my mouth," he cried, handing the goblet back. Zane chortled as he accepted the goblet. He had anticipated Stryxen's reaction and had hoped the prank would lighten Jace's mood. Then he noticed his sombre expression and the inner turmoil that was raging within. Something was wrong.

Jace sighed, taking a deep breath. "Our mother is dead. She was killed by an assassin." Jace watched their expressions as the news sunk in. Stryxen's lips trembled as he struggled to put on a brave face and hold back the tears. Zane seemed dumbfounded by the news. Raising the goblet to his mouth, he downed the amber liquid in one gulp. He took the second goblet and downed that as well. Tears welled in the corner of his eyes. Jace loved Zane dearly, but the general's accusations lingered at the back of his mind and left him wondering whether the brother that he'd played with, fought, argued and bantered with, could be responsible for their mother's death. Could Zane be Malgorath in disguise?

"How did the assassin kill her?" Zane queried. Jace was taken aback. The question he would have asked was *'Who?'*. He would have enquired after the assassin's identity, but then again Zane possibly already knew that answer. He had just incriminated himself further.

"We don't know. All that was left was some black dust that littered the ground," he replied. Zane's mind seemed to tick over, processing this new information.

"Black dust?" he said, baffled as he tried to blink away the tears. Jace took a large sip of his honeyed whisky. He was trying to be brave and was barely managing to hold back his own tears. "Maybe she was a demon? It would explain why there was only black dust, instead of a bloodied corpse." Jace nodded, agreeing with his brother's theory. It made sense. As far as they knew, demons weren't of this realm. Perhaps the black dust was a result of their death? But the question was whether Zane was theorising or clutching at straws. Was he guilt ridden and trying to justify their mother's murder?

* * *

Jace sighed. He hated being the bearer of bad news. "What?" Zane asked, concerned. Was there more?

"General Iryss and a wagoner with the Bloodborn Mercenaries have also made allegations against you. They are claiming that you hired the mercenaries and are responsible for mother's death." Zane paled slightly. Stryxen looked confused. "Father has authorised for you to be sent to the dungeon and await his judgement." Stryxen burst into tears. "I wanted you to hear it from me."

Zane nodded, accepting his fate. The door burst open and their father walked into the room. Behind him strode General Iryss along with the four guards. One of the guards carried a pair of iron manacles, ready to cuff Zane's hands behind his back. The guard looked pompous as he let the chain clink as he walked. He was enjoying this, showing everyone what was in store for the prince. "NO!" Stryxen screamed. "You can't take my brother. He didn't kill the guard." He stomped on the ground and the guard snickered, amused at the young prince's theatrics. This just angered Stryxen even more. Irate, he ran forward and held his arms out. "Arrest me and throw me in the dungeon then." The guard looked at the king, not quite sure what to make of the situation.

"Your loyalty to your brother is commendable, Stryxen" King Erithen said, smiling. "But he needs to pay for his crime."

* * *

Grim and revealing no expression, Zane walked forward and confronted the king. "I am innocent, father. You are making a grave mistake."

"I am your father NO more. You forfeited the right when you chose to betray this family and our kingdom. You have tarnished the Everthorn name." The King paused to take a deep breath. "You are responsible for your mother's death, the Baroness Adele's murder and the massacre of the loyal guards who valiantly fought and died protecting them." He thrust something forcibly into Zane's chest. "Your assassin left this behind."

"If I wanted to kill anyone, I'd do it myself," Zane lied. "And if I did hire an assassin, I wouldn't hire one that was so sloppy." Zane could feel the cold metal pressed against his chest, but he refused to grab the dagger. He refused to give his father that satisfaction.

"Well, if Zane doesn't want it, can I have it?" Stryxen asked. And just like that, his mood had changed. But such as it was with him being a teenager, an adolescent with hormones. He was excited about the prospect of having his own weapon, but he was also conflicted by the whirl of emotions he felt at his mother's death and his brother's possibly incoming death.

The king removed the dagger and smiling, placed it in

Stryxen's outstretched hand. Now that the dagger wasn't being thrust at him, Zane couldn't help but admire the weapon. The blade was long and thin with intricately carved runes engraved into it. The iron pommel was of a detailed snarling wolf's head. "We got you a dagger for your birthday present…"

"A dagger? More like a short sword," Rylan said, interrupting, as he entered Jace's bedroom. He nodded and smiled. "Zane, it's good to see you."

Zane nodded in response. "I'm sorry about your mother, Rylan," he said. He was genuinely sorry about Rylan's loss.

As good as it was to see his friend, he was about to be imprisoned. Looking at his glaring father, he couldn't help but be amused. Only a handful of people could talk to the king like that and get away with it and luckily for Rylan he was one of them. His father grunted and biting his tongue, let the matter slide. "Hope you don't mind, Zane, I had one of your guards show me the way." Looking past his friend, Zane spied a shadow lurking in the doorway – eavesdropping.

"It was a large dagger, but unfortunately it got lost during the carnage," Erithen apologised. Stryxen would be turning thirteen in a couple of days. He was coming of age and becoming a man. The large dagger would have been the ideal present. Now he had to find an alternative, something that would suffice.

Stryxen looked at the dagger, taking in the runes, the exquisite detail and the blood stains. Noticing this, the king held out his hand and Stryxen reluctantly handed it back. Erithen laughed. "I need a scribe to copy this dagger so that I can send it to the Brotherhood. I want this assassin hunted down and killed. Her head will be mounted on a pike and displayed for the world to see. It will serve as a warning to anyone who wants to try and eliminate the Everthorn name. "His face softened. "You may have the dagger after the scribe has finished, Stryxen."

The young prince's face beamed, his eyes lighting up with excitement as he grinned from ear to ear. "I'll even get it polished for you. It will be as good as the day it was forged." Erithen smiled. He had solved the dilemma of Stryxen's birthday present.

"What are those markings on the blade?" Stryxen asked intrigued.

"Magical runes," Erithen answered. Jace and Zane shared a look, an unspoken question. *'How in the seven hells did their father recognise magical runes?'* It had taken them years to learn about the intricately designed runes and the more advanced runes, they still hadn't grasped yet. Yet somehow their father recognised them. It was unexplainable and left an ill-boding in both of them. Unlike the two of them, the rest of their family didn't have the gene for magic. He turned to face Zane and smiled like a wolf about to devour a sheep. "Mind you this whole process could be made quicker if Zane would give up the name of the assassin he hired. Then I wouldn't need the use of a scribe and you would be able to have the dagger now."

"Please, Zane. Can you just tell dad what he wants to know? Then I can have the dagger," Stryxen pleaded.

Zane sighed. "Sorry Stryxen, I can't tell him what I don't know," he said, putting his hand on his younger brother's shoulder. Stryxen shrugged off the hand and ran out of the room crying. He turned to the man before him. A man whom he had once called father and proudly called his king. Now he didn't know what to call him. "Hope you're happy."

Erithen glared at him and without a word waved the guard forward. Zane stared at his father. His face devoid of emotion as the guard bolted the iron manacles onto his wrists. Two of the guards drew their swords. "Is that really necessary?" Jace enquired, glowering at their father. The king refused to answer.

"It's just a precautionary measure to ensure he doesn't try any magic," Iryss explained. Tiny runes on the manacles worked in harmony with each other, nullifying any magic. To break the link was near impossible. It would take extremely powerful magic.

* * *

"Really?" Jace shouted. He couldn't believe what he was hearing. "Do you really think that Zane would attack our guards?"

"He was responsible for the queen's death. My wife, your mother is dead. Dead because of Zane!" Erithen screamed. "If he is capable of that, who knows what else he is capable of?" He waved the guards towards the door. "Take him to the dungeon." Zane stared blankly ahead. The eavesdropper had dispersed. He didn't know how much the person had seen and overheard and he wondered what he planned to do with the information.

"We have a nice cosy cell for you, princeling," the corporal sneered. The guardsmen took up their positions, surrounding Zane with two swordsmen taking the rear. One wrong move and the guards would stab him through the back, impaling him from behind. It was a small mercy, at least he wouldn't see it coming. Their plated greaves clanking on the wooden floorboards, the guards stepped forward, prodding him in the back with their swords as they escorted their latest charge.

"Don't worry, brother. I'll get you out of this. I'll make dad see reason," Jace yelled. He still couldn't believe this was happening. There was nothing he could do but watch as his world crashed around him.

* * *

"No, you won't Jace. I've already been condemned. Dad has made his judgement," Zane said, lunging forward and receiving a sharp prod for his troubles. He could feel blood trickling down his back. With his face inches from his brothers, he whispered into Jace's ear. "To unlock the compartment and disarm the runes say *Targeth Bownd Ven Fanal End Glurie*. I trust you with this brother. The responsibility now lies upon you. You need to kill Malgorath." Roughly pushed and prodded, he was led out into the corridor. "You are the only one that can stop his reign of terror." Jace stood there in silence as his brother's words echoed down the corridor. The only sound was the clanking of the manacles as he was led to the dungeon.

Rayze walked briskly, navigating the streets of Sethanon. The streets were relatively quiet due to a monster lurking the streets and killing the citizens. He had heard the guard's stories about the gruesome remains that they had discovered. Patrols had been sent out, but their results had been futile. The creature had evaded the patrols, stalking and attacking solitary people, with the exception being a young married couple. That had been the first group attack.

To make matters worse, there had even been reports of mutated animal carcasses found around Gryphon Peak. The gryphons often hunted around the area, but they completely devoured their prey. The gryphons were now hunting abroad due to food shortage. They were intelligent enough to avoid the city, opting to hunt in the forests to the north. Concerned, Brenan had asked him if he wanted an escort, but he had refused. He wasn't afraid of getting attacked. He welcomed the challenge.

The tavern was fancy, an upper-class establishment for the rich and wealthy. The drinks were expensive, but he could easily afford it. Two bruisers stood guard; silent sentinels that protected the tavern from any unsavoury customers. Even though his clothes were respectable, more than suitable for this establishment, Rayze still felt uncomfortable, like a fish out of water. He didn't want to be there and wanted to get his business done as quickly as possible. Revealing his coin pouch, he received a nod and a grunt from one of the bruisers. "Let's get this over with," he muttered, entering the establishment.

The interior was posh, decorated with plush carpet, marble tiles, chandeliers and statues. He didn't even have to look around, the man he was there to see stood out like a sore thumb. The man's name was Illian and he was the Brotherhood ambassador for Sethanon. He oversaw all the local pickpockets, thieves, spies, smugglers and ruffians. He was also the one that authorised what messages were despatched from Sethanon. As painful as it was, Illian was the one he had to deal with.

Illian was flamboyant to say the least, dressed in a blood red doublet with gold stitching and silver buttons. What distinguished him from everyone else though, was his multi-coloured hair with streaks of blue, pink, green, black, red and silver interwoven with one another. He was like a majestic bird, prancing and showing off its plumage. He was drinking a goblet of wine with one hand, while the other patted and stroked his gay lover's erect penis. People were glaring at him and whispering in hushed tones, but he didn't care. Their attention encouraged him. He thrived and lived for it.

Rayze walked forward and pulling a chair out, sat opposite Illian. Two bruisers stepped forward and stood on either side of him. They were Illian's bodyguards, his hired muscle. "Well, if it isn't my good friend Raz. No? That's right, it's Rayray," he said, clicking his fingers.

"It's Rayze," the vampire replied through clenched teeth. Illian knew exactly what his name was. It was all a game to him, his way of establishing his power and control. Rayze had been around for over a century and Illian was by far the worst of all the predecessors he had known. His lover moaned in ecstasy as he neared the point of orgasming.

Grinning like a cat who just got the cream, Illian slightly shuffled across. He licked his lips teasingly and held up his hand. "You are going to have to wait, Rayray. As they say, it's pleasure before business." He started to bend down, opening his mouth. Illian was establishing his power and control and letting Rayze know that this was his city. It probably worked with most Brotherhood operatives, but Rayze wasn't just anybody. And he wasn't in the mood for such crap.

"Don't even think about fobbing me off, Illian. I am a senior operative and you will deal with me now!" Rayze said through gritted teeth as he tried to control his anger. Eyes turned towards their table, before nervously glancing away.

"Senior operative," Illian spat. "That means nothing. This is my city. I'm in charge here!" Ignoring Rayze, he lowered himself to pleasure his lover. Quick as lightning, Rayze's arm shot across the space between them. Grabbing a handful of Illian's colourful hair, he smashed his face into the table.

His nose was broken and bloodied. Afraid, his lover drew a small dagger with a shaking hand. "Tell him to put that away, before I grab it off him, cut off his cock and shove it down your throat," Rayze threatened in an icy tone. Furious, Illian waved the two bruisers forward. They drew their weapons as they approached. He planned on making an example of Rayze. Nobody threatened him. Nobody.

Rayze stood, his chair flying backwards and crashing to the floor. His hand was a blur as he grabbed the first bruiser by the wrist and bending it at an awkward angle, snapped it in two. Screaming in pain, the bruiser released his grip on the short sword, enabling Rayze to snatch it from his grasp. He slammed it through the table to the hilt. The bruiser's companion stood pale and frozen in fear, his mace trembling slightly in his hand. "Tell your bruisers to back the fuck away before I rip out their jugulars and feed on them." Illian paled slightly and with a wave of his hand gave the order.

The bruisers obediently went back to their position. Gagging at the sight of the protruding bone and limp wrist, Illian threw the bruiser a gold coin and waved him off to see a healer. Rayze threw a sealed, tightly rolled parchment on the table. "I need this delivered to the high councillor immediately. It involves Darla."

"Why didn't you say so?" Illian replied defensively, grabbing the parchment and stuffing it in his pocket. "We could have avoided all of this embarrassment." Illian knew that if this involved Darla, it was of the highest priority. Darla was like a daughter to the high councillor.

"You didn't give me the opportunity, you righteous prick. This is on you. Now deliver the fucking message," Rayze said in an icy tone.

"Meet me in my room, lover. I need to see the rook master." It was the last thing Rayze heard as he left the tavern. He'd done all he could do. He only hoped that it was enough. The gravel crunching under his feet, he began the long trek back to Sethanon Castle.

Chapter 10

The water was crystal clear and shimmering with her reflection. She splashed a blonde-haired boy slightly older than her. Giggling, she dived under the water before he could touch her. A fish darted past and she gave chase, following it in between the reeds. She was only five and was already an excellent swimmer. Gasping for air, she surfaced to take a breath, only to be tapped on the shoulder. "You're it, little wolf," Lance said smiling, before quickly swimming away.

She stood, her feet squelching on the shallow muddy bottom of the lake and began to count. "One, two, three, four..." Her eyes roamed across the shore of the lake as she continued to count. "Five, six, seven..." Half a dozen pairs of glowing, bestial eyes stared at her, alert, watching her every move. Most of the werewolves were black, their fur coats blending into the shadows. Two of them stood out though, one with fiery red fur and the other one with fur as white as snow. She didn't feel threatened by them, but felt at ease, secure, knowing that they were there to protect and guard her. "Eight, nine, ten." She finished counting and dove under the water. She loved this game. The chase was on!

Darla moaned, her eyes flickering open. She didn't know how long she'd been asleep. she'd lost all concept of time. Had it been hours, days or even weeks? She reached for her canteen with trembling hands and grabbing it firmly, took a longing sip. Her throat was dry, parched and sore, and it hurt to swallow, but she was thirsty and needed to stay hydrated. Re-stoppering the canteen, she let it swing on her bedhead.

Every muscle ached. Slowly, straining, she forced her head up and took in her surroundings. It was dark, but she could make out the numerous baskets, sacks and wooden crates stacked throughout the room. They were all neatly labelled in red writing. She started to panic. Where in the seven hells was she? She noticed one of the labels on one of the smaller crates. *Orc Mead.* She sighed, as she realised where she was. She was home, at the Black Raven Inn.

Everything was groggy, but it started coming back to her. Midnight had got her back safely. She had lulled in out of consciousness during the trip back. She remembered Marek lifting her from the saddle and carrying her inside. Knowing that she had installed precautionary measures in her room, Marek had carried her to the spare bed in the basement.

It was peaceful and quiet down here. She wasn't exposed to the noise and the commotion of the inn. It also enabled her to keep a low profile. The human king had both money and power. He would put a contract on her and pay handsomely. The way Darla figured; she had a couple of days at the most. They would track her down and try to kill her. In her weakened state, she was vulnerable. She needed time to heal, to replenish her strength. Closing her eyes, her head lulled forward, and she fell once again into a restless sleep.

Large paws silently crept forward on the soft damp earth. She was stealthy, barely making a sound. Her yellow, bestial eyes stared at her prey, a deer grazing in the grass. Its musky scent filled her nostrils. Her claws dug into the ground and her muscles tensed. The deer looked up, scanning, knowing she was near. She could sense its fear, it was intoxicating. The deer was skittish, ready to bolt, but it was too late, its fate had been sealed. She pounced forward, her teeth bared, clamping down on the deer's throat. It let out a small, startled cry, before going limp. It had been a quick, clean kill. She sat there in the dark, tearing its flesh and feasting upon its carcass. It had been the first time she had hunted as a werewolf and it had been exhilarating.

Darla groaned as she tossed and turned in her bed. Her eyes flickered open and she moaned softly. Reaching for her canteen, she gulped down the last of the water. When Jenna or Marek came back down, she would ask them to refill it. Closing her eyes, she went back to sleep. It wasn't long before she was dreaming again.

She crept down the corridor on silent padded feet. Without a sound, she approached the sliver of light. She could see flickering candlelight, coming from the study where her target was situated. The door was ajar, the lord focused on the documents that he was signing. He had been forewarned on the contract on his life and had promptly doubled the guards. That hadn't phased Darla in the slightest, she'd looked forward to the challenge. Evading the multitude of guards had been easy, the two stationed outside the study door would be a different matter though. She would have to kill them!

Darla stirred in her sleep, moaning softly. The dream was vivid, real, a memory from her past. It was a fond memory though, her first contract as Darla. It had been a priority 'A' ranked mission and the Brotherhood had assigned it to her, testing her, seeing if she was up to the task. She had accepted eagerly, being out to prove herself, to utilise her newfound abilities and earn herself a reputation.

It had been the early years of her transformation and she'd been amazed at her new capabilities, her enhanced speed, strength and heightened senses. She had been practicing, honing them to this point, but this opportunity would enable her to put them to the test. She'd felt invincible. Moaning again, she slumped back into the depths of sleep, returning to the dream she had left behind.

She crouched and continued to creep forward, staring at the guards before her. They stood resolute, like stone statues, guarding and protecting their lord. Both held hallards; an elvish-designed weapon that was a smaller version of a halberd and was primarily used for close-quarter combat. When she was about a metre away from them, she leapt into the air and punched the first guard in the neck. Twirling her leg around, she then kicked the second guard in the head. With a clamour, both collapsed to the ground. One was dead and the other unconscious. Either way, they no longer posed a threat.

The lord leapt to his feet as Darla grabbed one of the discarded hallards and sent it hurtling through the air. Grabbing hold of the heavy wooden chair, the lord quickly raised it in front of him, protecting himself, using it as a shield. The chair shattered, the wood splintering as the curved spear slammed into the lord's shoulder. The force of the blow was so powerful that he was lifted off his feet and thrown backwards. As he propelled through the air, he crashed into the window ledge before toppling out the window. Screaming and flailing, he fell four stories to the courtyard below. Darla watched, amazed. It wasn't how she'd planned to execute the lord, but a kill was a kill and her contract was now complete.

Within moments, screams and shouts sounded from the courtyard, the alarm had been sounded. Booted feet could be heard pounding on stone steps as the guards hurried up the flights of stairs. Darla didn't have much time. She hurried down the corridor and entered a small enclave. A door swung gently before her – a door she had picked open earlier which led to the attic. The attic was dusty and full of cobwebs, paintings, chests and old furniture. In the far corner was an open window, the curtains fluttering in the cool night breeze. Climbing through the window, she scurried like a spider up the wall and onto the clay roof tiles. Quickly, without pause, she ran across the roof, escaping into the night.

Waking up, Darla slowly opened her eyes and grabbed hold of the canteen that was held in front of her. "I refilled it with some water. But take small sips, I don't want you to vomit." Marek said in a soothing voice. She lifted the canteen and trickled some water into her mouth. It was cool and refreshing, moistening her lips and easing her sore throat.

"How long?" she asked.

"You rode in three days ago and have been in and out of consciousness ever since. We've been worried, Darla. We've never seen you this sick."

Darla smiled weakly. "Silver weapons and manticore venom will do that to a girl." Marek's eyebrows rose as he gazed at her. "I'll tell you all about it." She started to rise, only to be gently pushed back by Jenna.

"Not now, dear. You can tell Marek about your adventure in due time." She smiled at her husband. "Beloved, could you please fetch her some soup and some of my elderthorn tea?" The elderthorn fruit was mixed with the tea. It was sweet and gave it a floral taste. Not only was the tea refreshing and delicious, but Jenna swore blind that it also had medicinal properties. Marek nodded and left them. Darla slowly raised herself into a sitting position. Even though her muscles still ached, she felt a lot better. "You need to get some food into you and regain your strength," Jenna stated, grabbing the pillows behind her and fluffing them up. "After you have eaten, I want you to take it easy and rest."

The inn was empty at the moment, which suited Marek just fine. A couple of the regulars had dropped in for lunch or an afternoon ale, but they had since dispersed. After doing this errand for Jenna, he would chop more firewood and prepare for the evening influx of patrons. He hummed as he entered the kitchen. The soup simmering on the stove smelled divine. Picking up the ladle, he took the iron lid off and got a waft of the aroma. The soup was hearty with chunks of chicken, corn, onion, celery and parsnip. Continuing his humming, he scooped soup into a large ceramic bowl. "One more scoop," he said to himself, as he dunked the ladle back into the pot.

He poured half of it into the bowl, almost filling it. Looking at the remaining soup on the ladle, he shrugged and poured it in his awaiting mouth. Then, putting the ladle in the sink, he quickly wiped his mouth, getting rid of any incriminating evidence. The tea was in an iron kettle and was already brewed. His wife was extremely organised, especially when it came to her kitchen. Grabbing the kettle, he poured the hot tea into a ceramic mug and added a dash of milk. Reaching for another pot, he added a teaspoon of honey, just enough to enhance the flavour and bring out the sweetness of the elderthorn fruit. Placing the soup and the steaming mug of tea onto a wooden tray, he carried it down to Darla.

Marek placed the tray on Darla's lap and gave her a hug. "I am glad you are feeling better. You had us both terribly worried. Silver weapons and manticore venom. Sounds like quite the story." He went to sit on the edge of the bed and received a clip to the side of the head from Jenna.

"A story that will have to wait for another time. You have wood to chop and Darla needs some rest," she said. Darla smiled weakly and reached up and grabbed Jenna's hand. "Thank you," she said, squeezing it gently.

Jenna hmphed. "There's no need to thank us. We're family and it is what families do." Darla smiled, letting go of Jenna's hand. She was with family, family who would protect her and nurse her back to health. Turning around and facing her husband, Jenna sighed dramatically. "Now that lunch service is over, I need to start on the preparation for dinner and in order to do that I need more firewood for the stove." Turning back to Darla, she smiled. "Rest up and I'll bring down some dinner for you later." The wood creaked as she began to make her way up the staircase.

Giving her another quick hug, he winked before scurrying off. "Okay. Coming dear," he said, as he followed his wife up the stairs. Before he reached the top, he called down to her. "I'll check on you later." And then the door slammed shut and he was gone. Darla giggled and smiled. It was good to be home.

Chapter 11

Mishka rode her horse into the quaint courtyard of the inn. A young lad ran up to her beaming. "May I take your horse, lady," he said, reaching out his hand. She dismounted, smiling as she handed him the reins.

"Thank you for the compliment, but I'm no lady, lad," she said. "The title of 'lady' refers to a woman of nobility."

* * *

The boy shrugged. "I call every woman who rides in here lady. It's a polite endearment and a compliment. Whether they are noble or not doesn't matter."

Mishka laughed and nodded, conceding the notion. "Fair enough, lad. That's a valid point. What's your name?" she asked, reaching into her coin pouch and tossing him two silver coins.

"My name's Garen," he replied, patting the horse.

"Nice to meet you, Garen. My name is Mishka," she replied.

How long are you staying for?" Garen asked. He was staring sceptically at the coins.

"One night," she replied casually. One night was all she needed to complete the job.

"You paid me too much then," the stable hand stated, handing one of the coins back.

Looking around, Mishka noticed some blueberry bushes nearby. "Keep it. Treat her to some oats and blueberries and give her a good brush down." Garen nodded enthusiastically and pocketed the coins. With a flick of her wrist, she brought out a gold coin and twirled it between her fingers. The shimmering gold sparkled in the fading sunlight. "You can also earn this if answer honestly and give me some information."

Garen contemplated the proposal. The two silver coins were a generous payment. The gold coin was a fortune, more than he would make in a year. "My dad has always told me it is better to keep your mouth shut when someone asks you for information, because it usually spells trouble." Mishka shrugged but didn't put away the coin. Biting his lip, Garen looked at it greedily. He was weighing up an internal dilemma. Temptation won out. In Mishka's experience, it always did. "What is the information you need?" he asked, cautiously.

She pulled out some parchment from an inside pocket and unfolded it so that he could see. "I have tracked down the woman who owns this. She is residing at this inn. Have you seen her and if so, where is she?" The picture on the parchment was expertly drawn, showing exquisite detail. It was of a dagger, a unique dagger that belonged to a fellow assassin. An assassin she had been contracted to kill.

"Most people tend to hide their weapons. I've noticed a few people with swords and daggers concealed under their cloaks. Nothing that looks like that though." Mishka nodded her thanks. Her hand moved in a blur of speed and sent the coin spinning through the air. Garen caught it, his reflexes as quick as a snake. She could tell when someone was lying to her as she could pick up on body language and inconsistencies. The boy had told the truth and even though the information hadn't helped her, he had earnt the payment.

She also couldn't help but feel that Garen had been hiding something. She could tell from looking into his eyes. She had dismissed it for now. Everyone had secrets, but the question was whether his was worth killing for. She watched the boy briefly as he led her horse into the stables. Turning, she started walking towards the inn. It was time to see if the information she'd received was correct. Walking up the steps, she entered the Black Raven.

"Welcome, my name is Marek and I am the proprietor of this fine establishment," he said jovially. "What may I interest you in this evening?"

Mishka smiled, as her eyes flickered and instantly took in everything in the room. As friendly as the inn keeper was being, he subtly had one of his hands concealed under the counter. She also noticed the small hole installed in the counter, allowing for a small crossbow to be fired. "Greetings Marek. My name is Mishka and I'm a bard from Garedail. I would like some food, drink, lodging and some information," she said pleasantly.

Marek tensed slightly. The woman was lying. Marek knew most of the bards within the Hiberathian Kingdom, at one point or another they had entertained at the Black Raven. He hadn't heard of this woman though, which was a cause for concern. Shrugging, he forced a smile. "If you play tonight and entertain our guests, you can have the food, drink and lodging for free." With a jingle of her pouch, she withdrew some coins.

"I'm afraid I can't play my flute. It was stolen by some bandits," she replied, with a sigh.

"I'm sorry to hear that. You are lucky that you escaped with your life. The bandits have been ruthless as of late," he replied, shaking his head. "The king's guard should patrol the roads more. Then we wouldn't have this bandit problem."

Pulling out four gold coins, she placed them in his hand. "That's okay. The king's guard can't be everywhere. As precious as my lute was to me, at least I escaped with my life." Marek nodded, conceding the point, even if her whole story was fabricated and a blatant lie. A bard's instrument was their livelihood, they would rather die than lose or break their instrument. What also made the story questionable was that the bandits had only settled with taking her lute. They hadn't raped, killed, or stolen her money pouch and her clothes were neat and nicely presented. They weren't the clothes of a woman that had just escaped a group of bandits.

Most inn keepers would have fallen for the lie, would have been suckered in and felt sorry for her. Marek wasn't any ordinary inn keeper though, he had been a mercenary prior to inheriting the inn. He was intelligent and wise to the world.

Marek had regretted speaking ill of the king's guard. He had a lot of respect for them, but it had enabled him to provide a final test. One that she had failed miserably, because the truth of the matter was that the king had increased the patrols. The number of bandit attacks had decreased dramatically.

"Unless you are requiring a merchant room, you have overpaid me?" he stated, handing the money back. The merchant rooms were expensive. They were large, elaborately decorated and furnished with multiple beds. Because of this they mainly accommodated rich merchants and nobles, along with their entourages.

Mishka laughed. "No. A single room will be sufficient. The rest is for the food, drink and most importantly the information. And information isn't cheap," she replied and gave Marek a knowing look.

Taking the money and pocketing it, he handed her a large copper key. "Have you seen the lady who owns this knife?" She watched him intently. It was his eyes that gave it away. "My informant has told me that she resides here," she said, smiling. The smile was full of malice, like that of a wolf about to devour its prey. She already knew the answer. It was nothing but a game to her. She was toying with Marek, testing him to see if he would tell the truth. Marek was about to answer, about to lie, when the inn door opened and a cloaked lady walked in.

* * *

The woman had her hood up and wore a cloth mask covering her mouth. Her long black hair had pink streaks dyed through it. Loose, wavy strands cascaded from her hood towards her breasts. Her shimmering blue eyes and her pale complexion were the attributes that distinguished her to Marek. He gasped. It had been a while since he had come across one of her race. The last time was during his mercenary days. To the day he died, he would never forget those distinguishing features. The features that depicted her as a vampire. "Welcome to the Black Raven Inn. What may I do for you?" Marek asked, nervously.

"I am here regarding the contract on the woman named Flow. I would appreciate it if you could take me to her," the vampire said, her voice intoxicating and sweet as honey. Mishka looked between them and smiled.

"I'm sorry, but we don't have anybody by that name staying here." Marek replied. He had no choice but to stick to his story. Protecting Darla was all that mattered, at any cost. She was family.

"Fine. I guess I'll go to the dining room and have a meal and a drink then. It has been an awfully long trip and I am starving," she said politely. Marek pointed towards the dining room, speechless. The vampire smiled mischievously. "Even us vampires eat meals and drink alcohol occasionally." Marek couldn't help but laugh as the vampire strolled into the dining room.

* * *

"I'm sorry I couldn't help you, Mishka. Your room is upstairs, the fourth on the left. Now if you'll excuse me, I have drinks to pour and meals to serve," he said as he walked towards the dining room.

"I'll go and freshen up first," she said sweetly, smiling as she walked up the staircase. "Could you please get your son to bring up my saddlebags?" That confirmed her lie about the bandits. If bandits had attacked, they'd steal her horse along with her belongings.

"I'll get him to bring them up in a minute," Marek lied. He had no intention of letting his son anywhere near this woman. Inserting her key into the door, she unlocked it with a soft click. A spacious single bed was situated against the side wall. A painting of a beautiful elven woman hung on the wall above the bed. It was elaborately detailed, with exquisite line work and beautiful colours. Mishka glanced at it briefly before dismissing it. She had never taken an interest in art. She thought it was boring and a waste of time. In a little hidden alcove off to the side was a bath and a toilet.

Mishka was impressed. The room was not only cosy, but it also had gnomish plumbing. The toilet had piping leading into the wall. One allowed for fresh water, while the other led to the sewers and disposed of the waste and excrement. The bath had piping and a heating system, allowing for the luxury of both hot and cold water. The gnomish plumbing was a marvel of ingenuity, one that she was about to enjoy.

Stepping into the alcove area, she undressed, unstrapping the long, slightly curved dagger from her thigh. The blade was broad and razor sharp, with jagged points at the bottom, just before the handle. The handle curved slightly in the opposite direction. The pommel was in the shape of a demonic skull. It was the signature weapon of a faceless assassin.

The faceless were an order that were contracted through the Brotherhood. They lived in isolation, in a temple on the outskirts of the Rawn Desert. Originally, they had been part of the sandrigar race, but now they were outcasts. They were humanoid in appearance with pure white featureless skin and black, soulless eyes. Being imbued with magic, they were able to morph and transform their bodies, taking on the appearance of anyone. Given time to study the person, they could take on their identity, mimicking their appearance, voice and characteristics. They were the perfect spies and assassins. Because of their mutation, they had been shunned, ridiculed and persecuted. They were feared and because of that they were hunted down and executed.

The Brotherhood had been the only ones that had accepted them for who they were. They were different and because of that they had utilised their ability. Thanks to the Brotherhood, they had protection, they didn't have to fear the world any longer. They were utilised, they had a purpose, being used as spies, with a select few being trained as assassins. Carefully lifting a section of the mattress, Mishka hid her dagger, secreting it away for the moment.

Humming a little tune, Mishka turned on the taps and climbed into the steaming hot bath. She lathered herself up and admired her body, her breasts where perky and she had curves in all the right places. She had chosen well, stealing the identity of a young woman in Belgreth, a prostitute that she had isolated by luring into her room. After garrotting the woman, she had cut out her heart and eaten it. As sacrificial as the practice was, it was also a necessity. A person's physical appearance was easy enough to take on, but the heart enabled them to take on their voice, personality and knowledge.

Mishka smiled, pleased with herself that she had infiltrated the inn. She had taken on the role of a travelling bard. Under normal circumstances it was the perfect cover and had seemed like a good idea at the time. That was until the inn keeper had asked her to play. She cursed herself for her stupidity. After all, a bard without an instrument was no bard at all. But she was tired from playing the damsel in distress, injured and distraught. She had wanted a change, something different. And then there was the vampire. That was an unforeseen occurrence. One that she would deal with if she had to. She would let nothing get between her and the target, even if it meant killing a rival assassin.

* * *

The water was hot and soapy. She lathered herself with the lavender scented soap that lay on the rim of the tub. Washing it off, she laid amongst the soapy bubbles feeling content and relaxed. Any other day, she would be there until the water turned cold, but she had work to do, a contract to fulfill. Reluctantly, she climbed out of the bath and wrapped the fluffy towel around her.

Walking back into the bedroom, she caught Marek by surprise. "Your saddlebags," he stammered, throwing them onto the bed and blushing. "Garen gave them to me to bring up." His excuse was questionable. Marek was suspicious and didn't want her around his son. It was obvious, but she didn't care. Mishka would kill the two of them if she had to. They were nothing to her, collateral damage in the scheme of things.

"Thank you," she said, undoing the towel and letting it drop to the floor. Marek quickly averted his eyes and she laughed. Men could be so honourable and prudish sometimes. "I'll be down to the dining room in a minute."

"I'll leave you to get dressed and do your hair," Marek said politely as he turned around and walked back towards the door. "I'll serve up a bowl of stew and pour you a glass of wine. It will be waiting on the corner table for you." Marek closed the door and proceeded to walk down the hallway.

Taking a dress and some fresh underwear out of her

saddlebag, she slipped them on. She had stolen them from the prostitute's room after stealing her identity. Mishka had acquired an assortment of clothes over the years. They consisted of large and small sizes. Some were expensive and fashionable, while others were old, ragged and worn. She always disposed of her old clothes after changing identities.

Mishka walked over to a gold rimmed mirror hanging on the wall and admired herself. Her red dress was low cut, with slits up either side. Retrieving her dagger, she strapped it onto her thigh. It was concealed, but also within easy reach. Her hair hung wildly, a tangled mess. She snickered at the remark that the inn keeper had made. *Doing her hair, brushing it,* Mishka thought. It was a foreign concept to her, something she had never done before. All she had to do was think about her appearance. She pictured a long braid in her mind and her natural, mysterious ability activated. Her hair magically morphed, intertwining and forming a long, tight, perfect braid. Exiting the door, she walked down to the dining room. It was time to get to work, to complete her contract.

The stew was delicious and wholesome. It consisted of thick chunks of beef, along with vegetables and a thick red wine gravy. Mishka devoured it in no time, mopping up the remnants with a thick slice of bread and washing it down with the last of her wine. Looking over the rim of her glass, she noticed the vampire watching her. With a flick of her hood, the vampire nodded in her direction. Smiling and nodding in reply, she waved her empty glass in the air catching Marek's attention.

Wiping his hands on a rag, Marek hurried over. It was a quiet evening with only a few guests partaking in the evening meal. Others sat at the bar drinking. It was early though and the evening was still young. "I'll have two glasses of Dragon's Breath, thank you. One for me and one for my vampire friend," she said, sarcastically. As she pointed towards the table, she could almost swear that the vampire smiled at her. Distracted by a twang, she turned to see a man restringing his lute. *A fucking bard,* she thought, panicking. *And one from my homeland.*

"What are the chances?" Marek said, mischievously. "Dorian is an old friend who arrived shortly after you. He brought me some spices and rum from his desert homeland of Tarimisa, the capital city of the sandrigar." She looked down, avoiding eye contact. What if Dorian recognised her for who or what she was? "He is a man of many talents. As well as being a travelling merchant, he is also a renown bard. Unfortunately, he has come down with a case of tonsillitis and can't sing tonight. He is hoping that you would do the honours for him."

She had underestimated the inn keeper. It was obvious that he had numerous contacts. He would have to for the inn to thrive as it did. What was worth knowing was whether the inn keeper had orchestrated this or whether fate had dictated the circumstances and his friend had just happened to come by chance. Regardless, he had jumped at the opportunity and laid a carefully planned trap. It had provided him with an opportunity to test Mishka.

Smiling, she nodded. She knew most of the common songs and had even sung a fair few of them. The prostitute's voice was pleasant enough, but singing was an artform and only time would tell whether her voice would do the songs justice. With a scraping of her chair, she stood up. With a flick of his fingers, Marek sent a coin spinning through the air. Catching it with one hand, Mishka looked at the gold coin. "Your payment," he said, as he walked off to pour the drinks.

As she slowly walked towards Dorian, he began to strum the lute. It started off slow before speeding up. Dorian's fingers were a blur. She recognised the song instantly. She waited until Dorian played a series of low notes and opened her mouth. When the tempo quickened again, she began to sing.

'The king and queen sit on their thrones.
Drinking sweet, blood red wine.
The jester skips and prances gaily about.
Wearing bright, flamboyant clothes that are fine.
Maniacally, he pulls out a dagger and leaps up the steps.
And stabs the queen in the heart.
When interrogated and questioned by the king.
He said that he was only doing his part.

He insanely shouted the demons made me do it.
Before being locked away.
He rotted in the dungeon forgotten by the world.
Until he was executed in twelve months and a day.
Depressed, the king cried and mourned for his queen.
Blaming himself for being innocent and naïve.
Drawing a dagger and stabbing himself.
He followed his beloved to the grave.'

It was a sad, depressing ballad and even though her voice softened towards the end, it was still heard by all. There wasn't a dry eye in the inn. She received a loud round of applause. Even Marek clapped, giving a nod of approval. He had been testing her, watching her like a hawk, keeping her engaged and away from her contract. Even the vampire was watching her intently.

She continued to sing, while Dorian played the lute. The Elf Maiden was next, followed by The Midnight Thief, The Red Dragon and finally The Jolly Jester. Halfway through her performance of The Midnight Thief, she had noticed the Inn Keeper's wife carrying a large wooden tray. She could just make out the bowl of steaming stew and the glass of wine. Curtseying to the audience, she retreated to her table. She had sung five songs and her throat was parched. It was time for a well-earnt break.

Sitting down, she took a sip from the crystal glass. The Dragon's Breath burnt its way down her throat, but it was a pleasant sensation, easing her parchedness and leaving a lingering aftertaste. She twirled the amber liquid in the glass before taking another sip. She had heard about the Dragon's Breath, the infamous liqueur that the inn keeper had concocted. Intrigued, she had taken the rare opportunity to try it for herself. Although it was expensive, it was worth it.

Sipping the last of the amber liquid, she placed the crystal glass upon the table. Her chair scraped against the floor as she stood up. The inn keeper and the vampire were watching her every move. She casually walked past tables, excusing herself as she brushed past people and entered the toilets. Mishka whistled, surprised at how luxurious and modern it was. The porcelain tiles were decorated with roses and the wooden doors to the cubicles were polished and pristine.

Walking briskly, ignoring everything, Mishka went straight to the back wall. The window was partly open and let in a gentle breeze, cooling the bathroom and helping to air out any obnoxious smells. Trying to be as quiet as possible, she pried it open a little further. Grabbing the edges of the window frame, she hoisted herself up and gracefully slid through. The air was crisp and chilly. Even though it was the beginning of spring, the weather was inconsistent with warm days and cold nights.

Quietly, she navigated her way to the rear of the inn. Most inns kept their kitchen door open to help dissipate the heat.

Mishka was in luck. This inn was no different. She slowly eased the door open. The kitchen was empty. The inn keeper's wife hadn't returned yet. A large cast iron pot sat on the bench. Even with the lid on, the aroma of the stew wafted throughout the kitchen. The smell of fresh bread also drifted from the oven.

Mishka stepped carefully onto the polished wooden floorboards, her padded boots barely making a sound. Next to the door was a rack with freshly picked herbs hanging from it. Next to the rack were two shelves, stacked with an assortment of neatly labelled glass jars. Hanging on the wall above the shelves was a wooden plaque. Burnt into the wood, inscribing it with neat writing was the name 'Jenna'. As well as being an exceptional cook, Jenna also kept an organised and immaculately clean kitchen.

Lowering herself, Mishka crept forward and used the bench for cover. Concealed, she passed by the French doors leading to the dining room. As she neared the pantry, she heard a thick wooden door close, followed by the clicking of a lock. A keyring jingled as it was hung on a belt. Mishka looked around desperately. She had nowhere to go, nowhere to hide.

She quietly opened the pantry door with a soft creak "Who's there?" Jenna queried. Slowly, without making a sound, Mishka slid into the shadowy confines of the pantry. A mouse scurried out and she quietly eased the door closed.

She left it partly open, with a sliver of light creeping in. To close it fully would cause to much noise and alert the inn keeper's wife to her presence. Jenna approached cautiously, her light footfalls and nervous humming giving her away as she entered the kitchen. "I'm sure I closed the pantry," she muttered to herself. Mishka watched as Jenna's shadow loomed before the pantry door. Controlling her breathing, she held her dagger at the ready.

The woman's outline could be seen through the slit that the pantry door made. She was carrying an empty wooden tray, confirming what Mishka suspected. That they were hiding her target somewhere within the inn. Mishka leapt forward, the door swinging open and knocking the tray out of her hand. Smash! It clattered loudly onto the polished wooden floorboards. Her free hand shot out, grabbing Jenna by the wrist and pulling her into the pantry's confined space. In the blink of an eye, she had her dagger to the woman's throat. "Call for help and you're dead," she whispered threateningly.

A startled gasp was all that escaped Jenna's mouth. "You're going to have to kill me. I'm not about to betray our friend and let you assassinate her," she whispered, defiantly. It was a bluff. She didn't want to die. And she knew that if she raised her voice, she was as good as dead. Mishka tore her belt and ripped the brass key ring off. The assassin smiled wickedly as she jingled five keys in front of her. Jenna couldn't help but look into her eyes. She gulped, as she realised the assassin's eyes were devoid of emotion. She was a sociopath, the perfect assassin.

Jenna was about to die, have her throat slit and be left to bleed to death in her own pantry. She had to buy some time. "You may have my keys, but you don't know the secret knock," she smirked.

"What secret knock?" Mishka asked, puzzled.

"The one we use as a safety precaution, before opening the door." The pressure eased as the assassin contemplated this. The lie had worked. For now. Slowly, Mishka lowered the dagger. *Creak.* The noise was soft yet defined. A footstep upon the floorboards, as someone entered the kitchen. Letting go of her wrist, she covered Jenna's mouth with her free hand.

"Hunny. Was that you? Are you okay" Marek called out from the kitchen entrance. He had heard the tray clatter to the ground and was coming to check on his wife. The French doors closed behind him, as he slowly walked into Jenna's domain. "Garen, you're in charge of the bar for the moment." Cautiously, he approached the pantry. Kneeling, he picked up the tray and put it on the nearby bench. "Jenna," he shouted, beginning to worry.

With barely a sound, he unhooked the mace from his belt. Her dagger was razor-sharp, but it was no match against a mace. She desperately looked around for another weapon and spotted a large bulging sack. Mishka's brief distraction provided Jenna with the perfect opportunity. She clamped her teeth down on the side of Mishka's head and the assassin had to grit her teeth to keep from screaming.

"Marek..." Jenna cried out. It was all she managed to say before the hilt of the dagger smacked into the side of her head. Her legs became wobbly as she fought to retain her balance. Unable to do so, she collapsed to the floor next to the sack. Her arm flailed, knocking the sack and revealing its contents. Coconuts!

"I'm in the pantry getting some ingredients. I could use a hand," Mishka mumbled, mimicking Jenna's voice. It was far from perfect. Jenna tried to call out, to warn her husband, but her voice failed her. All she managed to do was moan, before slumping to the ground. The last thing she saw before her vision blurred and her eyes closed, was Mishka reaching for the sack of coconuts. As her head hit the floor, she embraced the darkness and fell unconscious.

Gingerly Marek opened the pantry door with the edge of his mace. Light flooded into the pantry revealing the unconscious form of his wife. It was all the distraction that Mishka needed. In that brief instant of momentary concern and worry for his wife, Marek let his guard down and lowered his mace. "Jenna," he said, apprehensively, as he knelt and gently shook her shoulder.

* * *

Mishka had positioned herself at the back of the pantry in between the small gap left by the right-hand side and the rear shelf. She'd opted for concealment, rather than proximity to her target. The space was less than ideal. It was confined and made her swing awkward. The sack emerged out of the darkness, swinging in a deadly arc and catching on the corner of the shelf with a loud crack. The shelf exploded into a pile of shards and with a loud rip the sack tore open, sending coconuts flying everywhere.

Instinctively Marek rose his mace. It had been ingrained into him from years of training. One of the coconuts smashed into it, cracking in half and spraying milk across his face. He was blinded momentarily and turning his face to the side, wiped his eyes with his free hand. The second coconut hit a bag of flour, sending it spraying everywhere. The last coconut ricocheted off the side of his head, hitting him just behind the ear.

Wobbly and disorientated, he collapsed to the ground. Improvising with the sack had been less than ideal, but the result spoke for itself. By chance and a stroke of luck, Mishka had succeeded. Now she needed to finish the job and kill them.

Walking into the light, Mishka prepared herself. She would start with the inn keeper. She knelt over him, her dagger poised. "Dad. Are you okay?" It was the son, Garen, checking up on his father.

* * *

"Fuck," she cursed. She was already wasting precious time and drawing too much attention. Normally, she would have taken her time killing them, making it agonisingly slow and relishing it. But she needed to hurry, to kill the assassin named Flow and be done with it. As she stepped out of the pantry, the inn keeper mumbled and grabbed her leg. Even concussed, he was trying to stop her. "Consider this your lucky day," she said, before kicking him in the face.

Mishka walked down the hallway and stopped at the first door. She chose a key and inserted the first one. Success! The door unlocked with a soft click. Grabbing the handle and holding her dagger poised, she opened it. Only to come face to face with a broom. It was a damn storage closet! She hurried to the next door and found it unlocked. Two nails poked out from the middle of the door. Something had obviously hung there at some point. She swung it open to find a small, single bed and a toy chest.

It was Garen's bedroom. Cursing, she went to the next room. Like their son's bedroom, it had two nails protruding from the middle of the door. A wooden plaque hung from it that read 'Marek and Jenna's bedroom.' She ignored it and proceeded to the last room. It was at the end of the hallway and was securely locked.

She had a choice of four keys. She looked at the lock, trying to deduce the type of key. Two of the keys were slightly smaller than the lock, which left two to choose from. She inserted one and turned it. The key turned fluidly and then stopped. There was no click, no releasing of the lock. Cursing, she fumbled with the key, trying to turn it back, trying to remove it. It wouldn't budge. The key was stuck. "FUCK!" she shouted, getting angry and frustrated. She kicked the door – once, twice, three times, venting her anger and putting force behind each kick. The door swung open, swinging on one hinge, the lock broken.

Mishka stood to the side, her form blurring as she changed her appearance. Her bones, muscles and skin changed, contorting and rearranging itself. Her hair and eyes changed colour and freckles, moles and scars formed. Strapping her dagger to the back of her belt, the Jenna clone stepped back into the entranceway. Darla stood at the bottom of the stairs, watching and waiting. She held a dagger, poised and ready to throw. Smiling, Mishka held up both hands and took a step down. She kept silent, refusing to talk due to her voice giving her away. Mishka had been unable to do the sacrifice, to eat Jenna's heart and take on her voice, knowledge and personality traits. She hoped that her appearance would be enough to enable her to get close to her target.

The wood creaked as Mishka slowly stepped onto the next stair. Darla merely stood there. Her cloaked hood turned slightly, as she sniffed the air. Sniffing her *scent* and determining *what* she was. Werewolves had been the only race that had been able to detect them. The other races had to rely on magic users. In a blur of speed, Darla hurtled her dagger towards Mishka. Her aim was perfect and precise. The dagger was aimed straight at her heart. Mishka's instinct and quick reflexes saved her though. Clenching her teeth, the faceless assassin grimaced in pain as the dagger embedded itself in her shoulder.

Frowning, she gripped the handle with her free hand and slowly pulled the bloodied dagger out. The woman was good. Hell, she was one of the best assassins in the world. "I am going to enjoy this. I'm going to be known as the assassin that killed the infamous Flow," she said arrogantly.

"Flow is an anadrome, the alias that I use. My real name is Darla."

"Why are you telling me this?" Mishka asked, confused.

"Because in a moment you are going to be dead and I wanted you to know my name, the name of the assassin that is about to kill you."

Cackling, Mishka threw the dagger back, splattering blood onto the wall. As the dagger left her hand, she bounded down the stairs two at a time. Her throw was precise, the dagger spiralling through the air as it rocketed towards its target. Darla just stood there calmly, as if she was accepting her fate. Mishka was shocked! In the blink of an eye, Darla pivoted and caught the dagger. Holding it backhanded, she advanced up the stairs and prepared to face the opposing assassin.

Mishka lunged, aiming for Darla's head, but she blocked it easily, deflecting to the side. A vicious side swipe and Darla blocked it again. With the scraping of metal against metal, their cross guards locked as they fought for dominance, an upper hand. While Mishka's blade was broader, Darla's was slightly longer. Darla was superiorly stronger, faster and better trained, but she was still recovering. She wasn't on top of her game. Because of this, they were evenly matched. The fight was the ultimate contest and could go either way.

Keeping their cross guards locked, Mishka moved their daggers to the side. Balancing on one leg, she brought her knee flying up towards Darla's stomach. Raising her other arm, Darla blocked the blow. Their daggers unlocked as the force of the blow sent her flying backwards. Like an acrobat, Darla tucked herself into a ball, somersaulted and landed in a crouch. Her cloak flung open slightly, revealing the short sword strapped to her belt. Darla could have used the short sword from the beginning, but she had decided against it. This was a battle between two assassins and Darla wanted to make it close and personal.

Mishka lunged forward and slashed high aiming for her head. Raising her dagger, Darla easily blocked it. Leaping forward, Mishka again went in with the knee. She had the upper ground and this time she raised her knee exceptionally high.

It was lightning quick, powerful and aimed straight at Darla's chest. This time though, Darla was ready for it. Her arm snaked around Mishka's calf, immobilising her leg and holding it firmly in place. In a blur of speed, she stabbed the assassin in the thigh, her blade slicing through muscle and bone. Mishka gritted her teeth. The pain was excruciating, but she refused to show this woman any emotion.

Retaliating, Mishka slashed again. Darla was now defenceless. Keeping a firm hold of the assassin's knee, she leant back slightly. She wobbled slightly and felt unsteady, but the manoeuvre saved her. Instead of a killing blow, the dagger sliced across her cheek and neck. Blood flowed in a steady stream, darkening her tunic with a red, blotchy stain. It was not serious though and given time her lycanthropy would heal the wound.

Pulling her dagger back, Mishka prepared to slash again but halted as she heard a noise. *A cranking sound*, coming from behind her. The distraction was all that Darla needed. Her hand shot up and grabbed hold of Mishka's wrist, immobilising it. Their muscles tensing, they both fought for control as the dagger moved between them. Utilising her height advantage, Mishka grunted, pushed down and eased the razor-sharp blade towards Darla's throat.

There was only one card left to play, one option left for Darla to do. She had refused to do it up to now, wanting the fight to be honourable and fair. Now she didn't have any choice. Tapping into her lycanthropy, harnessing its power, Darla made her bones denser and her muscles stronger. It was time to end this struggle, to show this assassin what she was truly capable of.

Slamming the assassin's hand against the wall, she heard bones crack as plaster and cement rained down upon them. Mishka's hand went limp as her dagger toppled onto the stairs before them. With the assassin's wrist broken, her leg injured and her dagger on the floor, she was less of a threat. Darla had learnt a long time ago, never to underestimate an opponent. Letting go of her wrist, the faceless assassin's arm slumped to her side.

Mishka's other arm jabbed forward with her fist clenched. The punch was fast, calculated and aimed at her jaw. Darla was prepared though. She was expecting it. Her own hand shot out lightning-quick and grabbed the assassin's wrist. She automatically felt the resistance, as Mishka tried to pull away. She twisted but had to let go as her grip failed and the assassin withdrew her arm. She didn't have the chance to break it, but she had managed to sprain her wrist. She would be in a great deal of pain and hesitant to try something like that again.

Grabbing the handle of her dagger firmly, she slowly and excruciatingly pulled it out. Letting go of Mishka's calf, she watched as the assassin hobbled on the step. It was time to finish this! That's when they both heard the twang. Turning her head, Mishka saw the kneeling form of Marek. In a steady grip he held a repeater crossbow and the bolt that he had fired was soaring straight towards them.

The bolt spun through the air. Mishka saw the tip and her expression changed. Panic set in. She cursed herself for her stupidity. She should have killed the inn keeper and his wife when she had the chance. All she had to do was slit their throats which would have taken no time at all. But their son calling out had stopped her. Mishka was an orphan herself. It had been a moment of weakness at the thought of taking the boy's parents away from him. Because of her mistake, Mishka now had a disintegration bolt soaring straight at her.

The bolt Marek had originally gone for was his anplam bolts, but he had decided against it. He had learnt his lesson when they had faced the lesser demon, Jaydrath. During that encounter he had almost burnt down the inn with his anplam bolts. Instead, he had chosen this one. His disintegration bolts. The bolts had a distinguishable white ceramic tip with blue runes intricately carved into it. It was nicknamed the 'disintegration' bolt because it was full of a corrosive acid that burnt away, disintegrating anything that it touched. It was also known as the shatter bolt and was protected by magical runes, stopping the acidic compound from burning through it.

When it hit a target though, the brittle ceramic casing was designed to shatter and spray its corrosive contents upon the target. The bolt came in two sizes – small and medium. From the size of the tip, Marek had opted for a medium bolt. He wasn't messing around. He was planning on causing the maximum amount of damage. He had aimed the bolt at the dead centre of her back. Darla would be shielded from the splash radius. The assassin would suffer a painful, excruciating death though. Timing it perfectly, gritting her teeth against the pain, Mishka somehow managed to pivot. Her arm shot out and with her sprained wrist she caught the bolt in mid-air.

Holding it by the shaft, she swung the bolt around in a deadly arc straight at Darla. Smirking, Mishka prepared to deliver the killing blow. She was honour bound. She would rather die than fail a contract. Even if it meant killing them both. They were engaged, committed to melee combat and there was nowhere either of them could go. Darla only had one option. Her hand darted forward and clamped around Mishka's wrist. It halted mid-swing, her hand holding it firm in a vice like grip. Smiling maniacally, an insane look in her eyes, Mishka let the bolt go. All Darla could do was watch the bolt spin end over end through the air, as it toppled towards the ground.

Bringing her dagger to bare, Darla slashed, slicing through the wooden shaft and sent the head of the disintegration bolt spinning through the railing. It passed through the two wooden balusters and started to topple. Switching her grip to a back-handed position, Darla raised her arm and prepared for the killing stroke. "Do you have any final words?" she asked, looking Mishka in the eyes. She didn't hold a grudge. It was a common courtesy from one professional to another. Mishka stood silently, defiant to the end. That's when Darla heard the faintest thud, as the head clipped on the edge of the staircase. The ceramic tip shattered and sprayed its deadly compound onto the underside of the stairs, the surrounding planks and one of the beams underneath.

Sizzling and cracking sounded as wood eroded and disintegrated. Five of the stairs exploded in a spray of wood as the beam and planks gave way. A jagged gap in the staircase was all that remained. Mishka was thrown backwards, landing awkwardly on the stairs above. She laughed, watching as Darla vanished, disappearing amongst the debris. And just like that the circumstances had changed.

Scrambling forward, Mishka retrieved her dagger. Marek was already cranking his repeater crossbow, preparing for another shot. Her throwing hand lay limp by her side, useless and broken. It didn't matter though. She was ambidextrous. Although slightly weaker, she was still more than capable of throwing the dagger with pinpoint accuracy. Marek finished cranking, the next bolt was locked and loaded. He raised the crossbow, as Mishka threw her arm back and aimed.

Only to feel an excruciating pain in her foot as she threw the dagger. Mishka released, her aim askew as the dagger spun through the air and embedded itself into Marek's shoulder.

"I'm not that easy to kill bitch," Darla smirked, as she clung to the jagged edge of a wooden plank. The plank jutted out slightly from the gap. As she fell, she had grabbed onto it and prevented herself from falling to the basement floor. Her quick reflexes had saved her.

Mishka grimaced as she bent down and grabbed the handle. The pain in her thigh was excruciating. "You just saved me from having to retrieve my dagger," she said, smirking. Clenching her teeth, she slowly began to pull it out. Releasing her grip with one of her hands, Darla fumbled at her belt. The short sword wasn't there. The scabbard had shifted during the fall, repositioning on her belt. She struggled to reach, to grab hold as her fingers brushed against the handle. Mishka pulled the dagger from her foot, dripping blood onto the staircase. "Now to finish the job," she said, looming above her.

Blood dripped in small droplets onto Darla's hand. The faceless assassin's arm swung back as she prepared to throw the dagger. Darla was at her mercy. The dagger was aimed directly at her chest. Her short sword swung as she fumbled to grasp the handle. Her fingers would brush the handle and then the sword would tease her, shifting position and dancing tantalisingly out of reach. All Darla could do was watch helplessly as Mishka's arm whipped forward. A glint of metal flashed by. A blur of speed as another dagger whistled expertly through the air and sliced through Mishka's forearm. Blood sprayed as her forearm spiralled through the air with her hand still clenching the dagger. Mishka screamed as she turned to face the new opponent.

The woman had been silent, like a wraith in the night, bypassing Marek without making a sound. Her timing had been impeccable, saving Darla's life. But why? It didn't matter, as it provided Darla with an opportunity. Stretching, her fingers brushing the handle, she finally managed to grab hold of it. With a hiss, Darla drew her short sword. Her muscles bulging and using her phenomenal, superhuman strength, she swung backwards, gaining momentum. Releasing her grip, she flipped, somersaulting through the air and landed like an acrobat in a crouched position on the jagged edge of the wooden beam.

Swinging the short sword in a deadly arc, she cleaved through the faceless assassin's knees. Mishka toppled forward like a fallen tree. She landed in a kneeling position with her thighs supporting her weight. Slowly, Mishka looked up and stared at the newcomer defiantly. A dagger in either hand, the woman crossed her arms. Swinging her arms back, she slashed Mishka across the throat with both daggers. The faceless assassin's head lolled back, hanging by a thread, almost decapitated. With a kick, the woman sent the corpse flying to the bottom of the basement.

Saved and glad to be alive, Darla looked at the woman before her, her mysterious saviour. Her outfit was pitch black, including her face mask. The mask covered her mouth and part of her nose but left her shimmering blue eyes exposed. Eyes that were captivating and stood out with her pale complexion. The vampire had discarded her cloak, leaving it draped over a chair in the dining room. It would have been cumbersome, hindering her effectiveness, her ability, her need to complete her mission. Her long black hair, with pink streaks dyed through it, was now tied back in a braided ponytail. Darla gasped. She recognised the woman, it was a past memory, clouded but there. She even remembered her name. "Thank you, Athelaine," she murmured.

Athelaine lowered her face mask and smiled. "You're welcome," she replied, her shimmering blue eyes glinting mischievously.

"Darla. Watch out! She's another assassin," Marek shouted. He was protective of Darla. She was like family. He was unable to fire his repeater crossbow with his injured shoulder, so he had left it on the staircase. Instead, he stood there stoically with his mace in his hand, ready to defend and protect her. Hell, he would die for her if he had to. Darla merely smiled and waved Marek over.

"It's okay, Marek. She is a friend. I don't know how I know…but I do."

Marek lowered the mace, keeping it by his side. It was a less threatening gesture, but it was there if he needed to use it. "One of your long-lost memories I take it," he asked, raising his eyebrows questioningly.

Darla nodded. "Something like that. Let me introduce you to Athelaine, an elite vampire assassin and leader of the Shadow Hand." Marek nodded in greeting, taken aback. She had saved Darla's life. If Darla trusted her and considered her a friend, then that was enough for Marek.

"My brother Rayze notified me. He recognised your dagger and informed me that the king had put a contract out on you." Rayze, of course. Pieces of the puzzle were slotting into place. It was all beginning to make sense now. But why hadn't Rayze said anything? Athelaine smiled, seeming to read her thoughts. "He asked me to apologise on his behalf. He wanted to reveal himself to you and tell you everything. But apparently there wasn't time." Darla nodded.

"But you said that you were here regarding the contract on Darla," Marek said, accusingly.

"That is correct Marek. I am here to protect her, as is my obligation."

Darla sighed. "The king wants my head. He won't stop until he gets it! If both of you could find me, then others will as well."

"Rayze also told me that according to the king, you killed his wife?" Darla nodded confirmation. "By the seven hells Darla. What were you thinking?"

"I made the mistake of accepting a contract to kill her. But as it turned out she was also a demon named Mavelyn."

Athelaine nodded, impressed. "That's your second demonic kill from what I've heard. Was she allied to Malgorath?"

"No, she had honour and morals. Part of me regretted killing her." A single tear streaked down her cheek. She was remorseful and still didn't know what to make of it. "She wasn't allied to Malgorath. We suspected that he is the one responsible for orchestrating the contract and manipulating me into killing her." Athelaine nodded, accepting her answer. "The king is also a demon. In his rage, his grief, he lost control and revealed himself. I saw the king for who and what he is," Darla continued, adding the information as an afterthought.

"So, Malgorath is either the king or one of the princes then? Rayze told me the king is distraught and angry, that he is grieving the loss of his wife. He doesn't believe the king is Malgorath though. I, on the other hand am not going to rule it out just yet." She scowled. "After all, my dear brother has been known to be wrong from time to time."

"The king has the resources and the power. He will keep sending assassins until one of them succeeds and delivers my head to him on a silver platter. There is only one way to resolve this." Darla sighed, feeling slightly overwhelmed.

Athelaine grimly nodded. "We ride to Sethanon, retrieve your dagger and kill a king."

"Except that it could be what Malgorath wants. We might be walking into a trap. Playing right into his hand," Darla said, contemplating the situation. She was anxious and didn't know what to do. She felt like a caged animal.

Athelaine smiled wickedly. Her shimmering blue eyes sparkled. "We will go regardless, even if it is a trap. And we will show Malgorath what a werewolf and a vampire assassin are truly capable of." The vampire turned to face Marek. "It looks like I will need to purchase a room for the night." Marek stared at her, slightly baffled. Athelaine chuckled. "We don't always sleep in coffins. Sometimes, we prefer to have a good night sleep in a bed." Darla roared with laughter. Retrieving his crossbow, Marek slung it over his shoulder and walked away muttering. Athelaine followed silently behind him. Smiling, she turned back to face Darla. "I suggest you get a good night sleep, little wolf. We set out early tomorrow."

Chapter 12

Darla lay on the bed with the blanket wrapped firmly around her. It was cold even though it was early spring. Her eyes were closed and her breathing was slow and laboured. For all intent and purposes, she was asleep. Throwing off part of the blanket, her arm shot up and grabbed the wrist looming before her. "Your reputation precedes you, Darla. Even when you're not on top of your game, you are still as alert as ever," Athelaine said, smiling. Throwing off the blanket, Darla let go of the vampire's wrist and sat up.

Athelaine was already dressed and ready to depart. She strapped her dagger and the short sword to her belt. Grabbing the pouch, she attached it next to the short sword. It contained the elven divinity stone. She had stumbled up to her room and retrieved it from the chest before going to bed. "Being alert has nothing to do with it," Darla replied dryly. "I could smell the stench of wine and blood from a mile away." The wine was one of Marek's sweeter ones, but the *blood!* Where the hell had she got hold of that? And for that matter, did she really want to know. Seeming to read her thoughts, the vampire smiled mischievously.

"Oh Darla! Don't worry. I didn't drain your friends or any of the guests. I drank from the faceless assassin's corpse."

Darla cringed. "If the blood tasted anything like her scent, it would have been foul and disgusting," she said, hiding her smirk.

Athelaine laughed. "The blood was disgusting, but I needed to feed and beggars can't be choosers." Clasping on her cloak, Darla followed her up the stairs. Marek and Jenna stood in the hallway with anxiety on their faces. Jenna stepped forward and handed Darla a basket of fruit, muffins and cheese and bacon rolls. It was enough to feed five people. "Thank you," Darla said, smiling and hugging her.

Jenna had been cooking up a storm, but that was her release when she was anxious.

"We know that this is something that you need to do. That the assassins will be relentless and keep coming unless you kill the king and negate this bounty on your head. Just promise me that you will be careful. I don't want to be forced to travel to Sethanon and rescue both of your arses," he said, laughing awkwardly with a tear in his eye. Stepping forward he embraced Darla, hugging her tightly, afraid that he would never see her again. Darla's eyes were moist, but she refused to cry. She needed to be strong and believe that she would return.

"I expect those renovations to be done by the time I get back," she said laughing. She turned around and followed Athelaine towards the front door. She didn't dare turn back, because they would see the tears streaming down her face if she did. Opening the door, they stepped out into darkness. The stars sparkled in the night sky and judging from the position of the moon, dawn was still a couple of hours away. Athelaine hadn't been joking when she'd said that they were leaving early!

Harnessing her lycanthropy, Darla's eyes turned a bestial yellow. The pitch blackness became as clear as day. Night vision was an attribute that the werewolves and vampires both shared. Leading the way, Darla proceeded down the steps towards the stables. Athelaine put her hand gently on her shoulder, stopping her. "There is no need to go to the stables. We're not travelling by horse," she said, stopping in the courtyard. "Don't worry. I've paid Marek and Jenna an ample amount to care for your horse. You might want to cover your ears though." Darla obliged, as pursing her lips, Athelaine let out a high-pitched whistle. Nothing happened. Darla took her hands away, lowering them to her side. They waited. Still nothing.

It was silent and fast, gliding downwards in the night-time sky. The only thing that gave it away was its scent. Darla glanced upwards and saw it outlined against the darkness. Even then, it was only the brief blotting out of the stars that distinguished its movement. Otherwise, the creature would be indistinguishable, almost invisible to the human eye. But Darla's bestial eyes could make out its majestic form. It was a nightwing! It explained why she didn't need Midnight. They would be flying to Sethanon.

The nightwings were midnight black, enabling them to camouflage themselves and blend into the star lit sky. Their body and tail had the similarity of a small dragon, hard and scaly, while its thick powerful legs and long arms were covered in thick dense fur. Instead of toes and finger, their bones elongated into strong razor-sharp claws. The nightwing's head was like that of a large bat, while its powerful wings were spider webbed with hollow bone and thick leathery membrane. Sharp bone shards protruded out of the wings, shards that could easily slice and impale its victims or prey. Darla had heard stories, that the nightwings were used as the primary mounts within the vampire nation of Nightingual.

An array of straps secured the saddle to the nightwing's body. Attached to the saddle were an assortment of saddlebags, a sword, a heavy crossbow and a quiver of bolts. A smaller make-shift saddle was strapped right behind hers. It was going to be uncomfortable, but Darla had endured worse. "Darla. I would like you to meet Dregga," Athelaine said, fondly patting the nightwing. Grabbing hold of the edge of the saddle, she nimbly mounted the nightwing and placed her booted feet in the stirrups. She then criss-crossed two other straps across her thighs, securing her to the saddle. Reaching out, she grabbed Darla's hand and hauled her up behind her. "That saddle isn't quite as secure," she laughed, as with two quick steps the nightwing launched itself into the air.

Flapping its powerful wings, the nightwing soared upwards. Darla had never been this high before and it was both exhilarating and scary. "Don't worry. I won't let you fall," Athelaine said, with a hint of a smile. They soared amongst the clouds. Everything was small, minute specks against the landscape. Darla couldn't help but stare, transfixed. It was spectacular, a breathtaking site to behold.

They took the quickest route, flying across the forests and rivers. From this height they looked like nothing more than a small clump of trees amongst a large puddle of water. The sky started to brighten as tints of yellow and orange started to show on the horizon. Dawn was approaching. "We need to go to ground and seek cover," Darla shouted, alarmed. Athelaine laughed and continued flying.

"Isn't it beautiful?" Athelaine said, spreading her arms wide and bathing in the sun's radiance. Darla watched in confusion. "Each member of my family is entitled to one of these rings," she said holding up her left hand. "Not only does it identify us as part of the royal family, but it is also engraved with ancient magical enchantments. It makes us immune to the harmful rays of the sun and enables us to mask our appearance if we need to."

Pulling on the reins, Athelaine angled Dregga slightly to the right. Streams of smoke could be seen in the distance, rising from a multitude of chimneys. As they neared, they could also make out the torches and lanterns flickering in the pre-dawn glow. It was their destination. The city of Sethanon, the beacon of the human empire.

Prince Jace woke with a start, throwing the covers off him. It was late morning and even though he wanted to stay in bed and hide away from the world, he didn't have that luxury. He was a prince and as such had his role and duties to do. Reluctantly he got out of bed and in his rush knocked over the empty glass vial that had been on his bed side table. It shattered on the floor. He cursed as he carefully walked past the shards of glass. It had been three days since they had been back, since his brother had been arrested and thrown into the dungeon. He had been having recurring nightmares. He would wake up screaming, sweating profusely with his sheets drenched. He was grieving for his mother. He was just glad that Varyn Kabel had provided him with a sleeping draught, enabling him one good night sleep.

Two days ago, their father had made a formal announcement that he would be courting and was in the search for a new queen. Women would be competing and flaunting themselves at his birthday. Jace was disgusted and appalled to think that he was already looking for someone to share his bed. To make matters worse, he planned to execute his traitorous son as part of his celebration.

It was an insult, a mockery of justice. The king's birthday was in a week. He had rushed to the dungeons immediately to inform Zane. The news was better coming from him. His brother had smiled while arguing defiantly about his innocence, but Jace knew Zane all too well. They had a bond that only brothers could have. It was a farce. Zane was scared, terrified because there was nothing that they could do.

Rylan had been supportive, a true and loyal friend. He had visited Zane as well and had even mediated, speaking to the king and defending Zane. Rylan had made some valid points, but the king was stubborn, pig headed and refused to listen. His mind was already made up and there was no persuading or deterring him from this course of action. The only person unable to visit Zane was Stryxen. The guards refused him entry due to his age. Jace planned on rectifying that. He was going to take him to visit their brother later in the day.

It would be a brief visit, because afterwards they needed to get ready for Stryxen's birthday celebration. An elaborate banquet consisting of all his favourite food, including a cake with thirteen candles. His younger brother was coming of age and becoming a man. First, Jace had some things to do, one of them being collecting his birthday present.

He flung open the curtains, letting in the sunlight. It was pleasantly warm. It was early spring and even though the mornings were still chilly, the weather was warm and the flowers were blooming. He threw off his bed clothes and proceeded to get dressed. Rummaging through his wardrobe, he quickly dressed himself in some black pants and a dark blue tunic. He finished off his ensemble with some padded boots and a blackish grey cloak. He fastened the cloaks clasp on the run, startling the guards as he swung his bedroom door open.

Rylan greeted him as he stepped into the hallway. "I'm glad I caught you," he said, stepping aside and walking down the corridor with the prince. "I was wondering if I could come with you and Stryxen when you visit Zane this afternoon."

"Sure. Zane would love to see you," Jace replied, smiling at his friend. Rylan stifled a yawn. He hadn't been sleeping well and looked exhausted. Putting up a mental barrier, he'd kept his emotions in check and supported the royal family. It had taken its toll though. He hadn't allowed the opportunity to grieve the queen and his mother. The queen had been like an aunty to him. Their families had been so close, he considered them part of his family structure.

As they stepped onto the staircase, the aroma of breakfast wafted up to greet them. Rylan had been awake since the crack of dawn. He had eaten hours ago. "I will see you after breakfast for weapons practice," Rylan said, smiling and bounding down the staircase. *Weapons practice. Fuck!* Jace cursed silently. He'd completely forgotten that weapons practice was today. It would have to wait; he had other things that required his attention. He knew he would reap the repercussions for it later.

Rylan had returned with them to Sethanon to become one of the King's Rangers. Due to the queen's death, he had also taken it upon himself to support the royal family. Because of the massacre there was now an opening in the King's Rangers and it had been Rylan's dream, something he had always wanted to do. The training was extensive, but Rylan was already well-versed in weapons and was a quick study. Jace was confident that his best friend would not only become a ranger but would excel at it. The king had automatically promoted Rylan to the rank of lieutenant due to his nobility, but the captain was aging and Jace had no doubt that he would be leading them in a year or so. Regardless, it was good to have his friend with him.

Knowing he could not eat yet because of his busy schedule, Jace grabbed a blueberry muffin from the kitchen. They were fresh out of the oven and still hot. Taking a large bite out of it, he mumbled a 'thank you' before dashing out the door. As he entered the courtyard, he quickly lowered his hood. The weapon master was getting the practice weapons out of the guard house storeroom. The reasoning behind it was that it was the only storeroom large enough to accommodate all of them. It was a lie, but he was sticking to that excuse. With him being the weapon master, no one dared to question him.

"Would you like a hand with those?" Rylan asked, offering his assistance. It was the perfect distraction. From within the confines of his hood, Jace mouthed a silent 'thank you'. A brief nod was all he got. Anything more and Rylan would have given himself away. Stuffing the last of the half-eaten muffin into his mouth, he sprinted towards the eastern gate.

"Shouldn't you be attending weapons practise?" one of the guards asked. His companion snickered, as he opened the gate with a creak. Both knew his routine, knew that he was shirking and avoiding the practice session.

* * *

"I have some errands that I need to do first," Jace replied curtly, stepping through the gate and entering the bustling city of Sethanon. He briskly walked along the main street, dodging the people walking through the busy thoroughfare. Horses trotted past, carrying wagons full of merchandise. Merchandise such as barrels of ale being carted to the taverns, cargo being transported from the docks and fresh food being sent to the markets. The thoroughfare was a hive of activity and the location of a multitude of thriving businesses. Businesses such as the Royal Blacksmith that Jace was making his way to see.

Jace quickly leapt out of the way of a steaming pile of horse dung, a present left for him from a passing horse. A present that just happened to be right in front of the blacksmith's workshop. The blacksmith was a tall, lanky, black-haired elf named Cazthalian, or Caz for short. Jace had learnt elvish through his studies and preferred to call the elf by his full name as a show of respect. The elf had moved from the elvish city of Garthanal about 10 years ago, commissioned by the king and establishing himself an extremely profitable business. His age was indiscernible. He had heard rumours that the elves had been granted the gift of longevity and could live for hundreds of years. Caz looked slightly older than Jace, but he had been told that the elf was even older than his grandfather.

The blacksmith smiled warmly at Jace as he walked out,

sweat glistening off his well-muscled body. His long black hair was tied into a ponytail with a leather thong and whipped back and forth behind him. In his hand he carried a broad bladed shovel, which he promptly used to scoop up the dung and throw it into the blazing inferno within. "The dung makes good fuel for the fire." he said, casually.

The elves were legendary blacksmiths, having learnt the trade from the dwarves and then refining it into their own unique art. Elven weapons and armour were outrageously expensive, but they were also second to none. Hence why Jace was paying a small fortune for this sword. It was being made using unique elvish techniques, techniques that Caz had not only learnt, but had also mastered.

The sword was light, but stronger than steel. It was made using a combination of obsidian and silver. It had resulted in a silver sword with black streaks, streaks that Caz had masterfully designed to resemble runes. Holding it up, he admired the craftmanship. The blade curved in and out from the guard, like jagged teeth, before elegantly straightening out. It would make an excellent present for his father's birthday. The king had promised the assassin's enchanted dagger to Stryxen. He planned on giving it to him on his birthday. Now he wanted his own magical weapon. Jace had obliged.

He gently ran the blade across his finger. The blade had cut through his thick leather glove as if it had been paper. "Have you got the ruby?" Caz asked, holding out his hand. The blacksmith still had some finishing touches to make to the handle, including inserting the ruby into pommel. Reaching into his pocket, Jace pulled out the ruby that he had bought from a travelling gem merchant. The blacksmith whistled, admiring the gem. "I'll have the sword ready in a couple of days." His father's birthday was still six days away though, giving him plenty of time to get things organised. He would collect the sword off Caz in a couple of days and then get it imbued with magical runes, powerful, devastating runes that would turn the weapon into a monster killer.

Checking up on the sword's progress was only part of the reason for visiting Caz. The main reason was to check on Stryxen's birthday present, a stunning silver and dark grey, purebred Majarelly battle horse. The elven plains of Majarelly were known for breeding the best battle horses in the world. The horse that Stryxen had been riding, had been on loan, belonging to Brenan, the captain of Zane's personal guards. Now Stryxen would have his own horse to ride and train. He would also learn the responsibility and money that went into owning a horse.

The horse had arrived yesterday and Jace had needed a place to hide it. Caz's stables were empty due to his assistant taking the horse and cart to get supplies from the dwarven lands. Because of this, he'd happily obliged, offering to stable the horse until Stryxen's birthday. Putting the ruby in his leather apron pocket, Caz led Jace back to the stable. The horse neighed as they entered and kicked the wooden gate, wanting to be let out. It was a feisty animal, stubborn and mean tempered. Training him would be a challenge and Jace could see his brother having his work cut out for him.

He approached the gate. The horse kicked it again, a warning to say, *"Don't come any closer."* Tentatively, Jace reached his hand out, ready to give the horse a gentle pat. He spoke softly, reassuring the horse and staring in its eyes. The horse lunged forward, nipping at his hand and grabbed hold of the tip of his leather glove. The glove came off and the horse casually began to chew on it. Snorting decisively and stamping its hooved foot, it dared him to come in and get it. Jace glared at the horse, cursing silently under his breath. Caz roared with laughter which didn't help his mood much either. Grumbling, he stormed out, Caz following and closing the stable door behind them.

"I don't think the horse likes you," Caz said playfully.

"Yeah, well the feeling's mutual," Jace replied angrily.

"If you want. I'll bring the horse to the castle later. I'll lock up early and deliver it before your banquet dinner."

"Thanks Caz," Jace replied meekly. "Won't that affect your work schedule though?"

* * *

The blacksmith shrugged. "I'll reopen early, while you're still snoring your pretty boy head off."

Jace muttered a farewell to the blacksmith who was still smirking and laughing at his own joke. He knew the prince hated being called a *pretty boy*. Slowly, the prince began his trek back down the thoroughfare. He quickly stopped in at a gaunter and acquired a new pair of leather gloves, expensive ones, fur lined and made from deer hide. The gloves were stiff, and needed to be worn in. He wouldn't wear them during summer, but during the cooler, mild weather of spring they were ideal. He turned off the thoroughfare and began his accent up the stone steps.

The steps led to the castle gate. During spring it made for a pleasant walk, being surrounded by apple trees and rose bushes. As Jace approached he could hear the clamour in the courtyard. Above it all, the weapon master's voice could be heard bellowing at the guards. Guards who were in the process of conducting weapon's practice and various drills. The two guards opened the gate with a loud creak, drawing everyone's attention. He entered the courtyard sheepishly. Steeling himself, he prepared for the onslaught of vigorous training and the snide remarks for being late.

The weapon master was a short, well-built man named Wesley. He had a thick, black moustache that merged into his coarse black beard. A beard that he wore with pride and had braided at either end with bright blue ribbons. His nine-year-old daughter braided his beard every morning, before kissing him goodbye. It was their special thing. The guards knew better than to say anything, wisely choosing to keep their mouths shut.

Rylan smiled as the prince approached. He had been practising for an hour but had barely broken a sweat. Six guards stood off to the side, nursing bruises, having already sparred against him. Wesley handed the prince a practise sword, which had its edges and tip blunted to avoid any injury. "Glad you decided to join us my prince", he said, with a slight undertone of sarcasm. Jace smiled, taking the jibe with a pinch of salt. He deserved it, he was late after all. "Your opponent is Rylan," he added with a smirk.

Jace stepped forward. "Just fucking great," he muttered. Rylan raised his sword to his forehead and Jace followed suit, demonstrating the formal salute, a show of respect to one's opponent. His sword felt clumsy in his gloved hand and he barely managed to deflect Rylan's first blow, his second or his third, all three consecutively, one after the other in a matter of seconds. Overhead, side, side, side, overhead, the blows were lightning quick, fluent and unrelenting.

Rylan suddenly went into a backswing, his movement graceful and timed perfectly. Jace was unprepared, not expecting it and the blunted blade hit his hand.

* * *

He winced with the pain and the sword flew from his grasp, landing in the dirt. He stood there shaking his injured hand as Rylan spun the other way, his leg extended and swept Jace's feet out from under him. The prince toppled backwards, landing with a soft thud. Wesley looked at the prince, concerned, not saying a word. "It's these damn new gloves," Jace complained, "they're stiff and need to be worn in. I can't expect to fight like this."

"What happened to your other gloves, my prince?", the weapon master asked.

"One of them got eaten."

Rylan roared with laughter. "Maybe I should send for the kitchen staff and get them to send down some more food for our prince. It might stop him from eating his gloves." Wesley couldn't help himself and started chuckling.

Jace glared at the two of them, but it was the weapon master that he took his wrath out on. "I'd be careful chuckles. Unless you want me to buy you a pretty little bonnet to go with your ribbons." It was a mistake and Jace knew it as soon as the words had left his mouth. He looked towards Rylan for support, but taking a step back, his friend could only look at him wide-eyed and in shock. He turned his gaze back towards the weapon master, looking at him pleadingly, asking for forgiveness.

* * *

Wesley's eyes were unforgiving, calm and calculating. In a voice flat and devoid of emotion he said, "Again little princess…and this time you face me!" Cringing, Jace grabbed his fallen sword and slowly stood up. This was going to be a long…and painful training session. Nobody commented on Wesley's ribbons. Nobody. Not even a prince!

Chapter 13

A few pebbles rained down from the cave ceiling as Dregga hung upside down, dozing. Darla and Athelaine lay on a thick fur rug, sleeping soundly nearby. They were holed up in a cave on the far side of the Hallow Mountains. Things hadn't gone as planned and they were lucky to be alive. They had heard an ear-piercing screech when they neared Sethanon. Scanning the skies, Darla had spotted them first.

Two gryphons reeling in from the west. They were large males hunting for food and had spotted the nightwing with their keen eyesight.

The nightwing could hold its own, in a one-on-one fight against a gryphon, but it would be ripped to shreds against a pair of large male gryphons. Athelaine pulled on the reins and Dregga swerved to the right, flapping his large wings and gaining speed. The nightwing needed no extra encouragement. It knew what kind of threat the gryphons were. Screeching loudly, the gryphons flapped their powerful wings and gave chase.

Darla scanned the landscape, searching. The gryphons were faster, but the nightwing was more agile. The screeching got louder and Darla started to panic as the gryphons closed in. "Over there," she shouted, pointing at a cave. Two more flaps and Dregga raced forward. Darla could smell the gryphons and sense their proximity. They were almost on top of them.

One of the gryphon's forelegs reached out, its razor-sharp claws ready to grab hold and pluck them out of the sky. Two sharp tugs on the rein. "Althune," Athelaine barked, a command in her native vampiric tongue. She reverted to common, the universal language used throughout the world of Aragoth. "Hold on tight," she said, smiling mischievously. With that Dregga retracted his wings and dove, plummeting like a rock.

* * *

Tucking in their wings, the gryphons chased after them. Dregga gained momentum and the distance between them increased slightly. Due to the nightwing's size and ability to retract its wings, it was more aerodynamic. The gryphon's features were a different matter. Their thick fur and feathers hindered them, providing Dregga with a distinct advantage. Spreading out his wings, the nightwing levelled out and soared along the mountain side.

Following suit, the gryphons extended their wings, clipping the mountainside and sending rocks and pebbles crashing to the trees below. Athelaine pulled the rein tugging on the right side. Dregga reacted immediately and turning, soared away from the mountain. The vampire had seen the cave entrance. She planned it perfectly, tugging the reins hard to the left. Swerving and tucking his wings in, the nightwing shot forward like a bullet. Then, finding purchase with his clawed feet, he bounded into the safety of the cave.

The cave was situated on the far side of the Hallow Mountains. It was man made, created by a team of dwarven engineers. The dwarves had been commissioned by the Brotherhood to dig out a cave entrance and a tunnel network with an exit to the northern wall of Sethanon. A section of the wall would then open, allowing Brotherhood operatives entrance into the city undetected. The section of the wall was activated in the same manner as the Brotherhood hideouts. A symbol would glow on the wall, activated by the operative's ring. A password would then be used to open the section. Darla knew the password since she had used it a few times to sneak into the city. How the Brotherhood had achieved this without anyone knowing was extraordinary.

The cave accommodated the trio perfectly. Athelaine and Darla watched the sun rise over Sethanon and the Kaspien Sea. It would have been a beautiful, picturesque view if it wasn't for the flapping and squawking gryphons hovering outside the cave. "They are wary, fearful of enclosed spaces. The cave will provide us a temporary sanctuary," Athelaine stated. Darla could hear the frustration in her voice.

"It is more than a temporary solution. The cave and tunnel network were commissioned by the Brotherhood. It will enable us to sneak into Sethanon," Darla replied smugly. They ate a muffin in silence. It was a fulfilling breakfast, full of nuts, blueberries and sweetened with honey. Finishing her muffin and licking the crumbs off her fingers, Athelaine unstrapped a thick, fur rug from her saddle. Flicking it out, she lay it across the stone floor. "We should try and get some sleep," the vampire said, yawning. Like Darla, she had barely got any sleep.

"I think I'll keep watch for a while," Darla replied, drawing her short sword. Even though the gryphons were hesitant, they were also unpredictable and she wanted to be prepared. As she contemplated their predicament, the sword radiated, glowing bright blue. Hovering, the gryphons leaned forward, lowering their heads in reverence and respect to the short sword. With a flap of their wings, they flew away. "What the hell?" Darla didn't know what to make of it. She was baffled, confused.

"Gryphons are intelligent creatures. They recognised the short sword for what it is," Athelaine said by way of explanation.

"What is it? I don't even know. All I know is that I was drawn to the weapon when I stole the divinity stone from Lord Dellavenor's castle."

"It is one of four divine weapons designed to defeat Malgorath," Athelaine replied as she struggled to keep her eyes open. The magic diminished and the blade returned to its usual silver colour. Darla sheathed the sword, her mind racing as several questions ran through her head. She turned to face Athelaine but saw that the vampire was fast asleep. The questions would have to wait. Curling up on the soft rug, Darla soon found her eyes closing as she joined Athelaine in a peaceful slumber.

Darla awoke to find the basket in tatters and its contents strewn about everywhere. "I'm so sorry," Athelaine said sheepishly. "Dregga didn't have an opportunity to hunt last night. He must have been hungry." The blueberries and peaches were gone and all that remained of the muffins were a scattering of crumbs. "He does have a sweet tooth," she added apologetically.

Darla shrugged, trying not to make a big deal of it. Then her stomach grumbled. "It's okay. Let's scavenge what we can," she replied, picking through the remains. Grabbing the two remaining cheese and bacon rolls, she handed one to Athelaine. The roll was fresh and mixed with the crispy bacon and half-melted cheese. It was delicious. There was one apple remaining which was slightly bruised from rolling on the hard rocky ground. It was still edible though. Cutting it in half, Darla shared it with Athelaine.

It was time to go, the trek through the tunnel would take them hours. Dregga would be safe until they returned. The surrounding countryside was full of deer, rabbits and other wildlife. Nightwings were nocturnal by nature. As long as Dregga hunted during the night and returned to the sanctuary of the cave by dawn, he would be safe from the gryphons. Giving Dregga an affectionate pat, Athelaine followed Darla into the darkness of the awaiting tunnel.

Darla drew the short sword with a soft hiss. It was unlikely that she would need it, but she had learnt a long time ago to be prepared for all eventualities. "You said before that the short sword is one of the divine weapons designed to defeat Malgorath."

Athelaine nodded beside her. "That is correct. My brother

wields another one of the divine weapons. Each of the weapons are inscribed with powerful runes and inserted with a special gem. The gem is connected to the runes. They work in harmony with each other and amplify the weapon's magic." Darla gazed at the purple gem inserted into the hilt of the short sword. A gem that had spoken to her, binding and linking her to the sword.

Darla gasped as the realisation came to her. "By the gods. It's a divinity stone." Smiling, Athelaine nodded.

"There are ten divinity stones in all. Each one is imbued with the soul of a fallen, a being that is an angel-demon hybrid. The fallen had immense power and were able to harness and draw upon both light and dark magic. The angels and demons considered them outcasts, abominations and a threat to their world. In their arrogance, they made a mistake, thinking that there were only ten hybrids." Darla listened intently, captivated by the tale as Athelaine told the story.

"They sealed the divinity stones away, silencing the hybrid souls for all eternity – or so they thought! They hadn't counted on two young adult female twins. The twin hybrids had managed to evade capture by hiding in plain sight and living amongst the angel and demon populace. The siblings stole the soul stones and escaped to our world. They hid the soul stones, keeping them safe and soon became goddesses amongst the five dominant races living in Aragoth."

* * *

"Don't you mean the ten main races living in Aragoth?" Darla stated, correcting the vampire. She received a stern look for her interruption. Taking a deep breath, Athelaine's expression softened and she continued.

"No. Back then there were only five major races living amongst each other upon Aragoth. The humans, elves, dwarves, goblins and sandrigar."

"The goblins?" Darla questioned.

Athelaine nodded, before continuing. "The goblins bioengineered the orc race using science and magic. Back then they were a very intelligent and sophisticated race. The orcs were bred to be warriors, the fighting force of the goblin army. It was their downfall. The brutish orcs rebelled, killing most of the goblin population and taking over the empire. The goblin royal family and some of their servants were the only goblins to survive the onslaught. They lived in servitude and became slaves to the orcs. Even the dim-witted ogres saw the power of the orc empire and joined their ranks. The Gorkin were a mutation, a by-product result from the raping between the orc queen and the goblin king and his sons. It was her main form of entertainment, while the orc king was off fighting and conquering."

"Prior to the downfall of the goblin empire, the two goddesses had slept with the five kings who ruled the five races. They bore twins with four of the races. Out of the twins, one was usually normal, while the other one would be mutated. The mutated children were the first of their race. Only one normal goblin child was birthed upon sleeping with the goblin king. It was as if they knew what was going to happen to the goblin race. Each child inherited divine powers. The goddesses controlled the amount of essence that was imbued into them, as they didn't want their offspring becoming too powerful."

They walked in silence for a little while. Darla pondered and reflected on this startling information. Athelaine waited patiently, knowing that questions would be forthcoming. "From what race did we originate from?" she asked, finally breaking the silence. Athelaine's lips curled slightly as she tried to hide her smile. It was a good question. It was the same question that she had asked when her father had told her all of this. Like Darla, she had also desired to know her heritage.

"Werewolves derived from the humans, while the vampires originated from the elves," Athelaine stated as Darla held up two fingers. "Gnomes came from the dwarves and the naga originated from the sandrigar." Darla now had four fingers held up. She looked perplexed.

"From what you said, the goblins inherited divine powers, as did the gorkin, through the consummation between the orc queen and the male goblins of the royal family. Does that mean that the orcs aren't linked to the divinity stones?"

Athelaine's smile said it all. "Oh, they are going to be pissed. And what about the ghouls? Where do they fit into all this?"

Athelaine refused to make eye contact as she looked straight ahead. Was she ashamed? Darla couldn't quite tell. She finally spoke after a moment of silence. "The ghouls are related to the vampire race. They were quite an intelligent subspecies and were primarily our servants and warriors. Then they rebelled and became outcasts. Now they are subterranean and feral from what I'm led to believe." There was something Athelaine was hiding and was refusing to tell her.

As they walked in silence, Darla's stomach grumbled reminding her of how hungry she was. They had been walking for hours and she estimated that it would be close to dinner time. "Hopefully Jocelyne has cooked a hearty dinner and there is enough for four people," Darla said wholeheartedly. "Roasted pheasant with all the trimmings, a nice thick peppered gravy and a bread roll to mop up the remains." She began salivating at the thought of it. Athelaine smiled as Darla's stomach grumbled once again.

"Don't you mean five people?" Athelaine replied sarcastically with a smirk. "With the way your stomach's been grumbling, I'd say you'll happily devour two portions." Darla's stomach grumbled for emphasis, driving home the point. They both burst into laughter.

* * *

"You're probably…" Darla stopped mid-sentence, distracted by a mark on the wall. It was a rune: V. It was faintly inscribed and covered in grains of stone and dirt, making it nearly invisible. It would be missed by most, but Darla recognised it instantly. It was Vexlan's rune. He had been planning on having a secret tunnel, connecting from the Brotherhood tunnel to his basement workshop. It was a safeguard, providing them with an emergency escape route. "This is Vexlan's symbol," she said excitedly.

"Who is Vexlan?" Athelaine asked, intrigued.

"Vexlan and his wife Jocelyne are good friends of mine," Darla replied with a beaming smile. It had been a long while since she had seen them and she was looking forward to it. She only wished that it was under better circumstances.

The password was a closely guarded secret that only Vexlan knew. But because of her closeness to the couple and considering that she stayed with them whenever she visited Sethanon, she knew exactly what password Vexlan would use. Or she hoped that she did. It was still a guess though and she hoped that her hunch was right. "I think I've just found us a short cut," she said with a wolfish grin. "Roxy." Nothing happened. Smirking, Athelaine was about to say something when a soft grinding sounded. And a section of the wall slid away to reveal a tunnel. A tunnel that lit up magically.

* * *

As they entered, the entrance slid shut behind them. "So, tell me about Vexlan and Jocelyne?" Athelaine asked.

"I have known them since the Brotherhood took me in," Darla replied, reminiscing. "It seems like forever. Jocelyne is the one that cast the deception spell on my ring." She held up her hand and gazed at the plain white gold ring. "I can't even remember what it used to look like. Apparently, the ring is linked to my lineage. I have dreams, vivid memories, but it is like piecing a puzzle together. It's all jumbled and I can't make any sense of it. I can't even remember my real name but for some reason Eve comes to mind."

Athelaine couldn't help but smile. "You are close. I'm sure you'll remember it soon."

"Why can't you tell me? You obviously know," Darla shouted. She was frustrated and angry. For most of her life, she hadn't even known her real name.

Athelaine sighed. She didn't take offense because she could understand Darla's frustration. "I have known you since you were an infant. Our families are the closest of friends. If I told you there could be serious ramifications. You need to remember on your own. It will come naturally. If you like I could teach you some meditation techniques?"

Darla smiled apologetically. "That would be nice. Thank you, Athelaine." They continued walking in silence and turned a corner. "Jocelyne is both a mage and an assassin." She smiled. "And a damn good cook. Vexlan is more like a rogue, a jack-of-all-trades. He is the one that created my identity, writing out my dossier and making sure I memorised it. He is also a bit of a tinkerer and spends most of his time in the basement – or his workshop as he likes to call it. They have a pet, a hybrid cross between a fox and a large dog. It spends most of its time down in the basement with Vexlan, keeping him company. The hybrid's name is Roxy or Foxy Roxy as Vexlan likes to call her."

"Hence the password," Athelaine stated. "And of course, only people that know about his devotion to their pet would guess it."

"Exactly," Darla replied as they proceeded down a small stone staircase. They came to a dead end, a cemented stone slab wall blocking their path. It was the entrance to Vexlan's workshop. Darla's Brotherhood ring glowed, radiating a bright blue glow and revealing the hidden rune. "Sneaky little Vexlan," Darla muttered. Vexlan had hidden the rune as an extra precaution. Anyone that had gotten this far and wasn't a Brotherhood member would be denied access and come to a dead end. The basement wall was extra thick, so unless you were a dwarven engineer, you would have one hell of a time trying to get through.

"Jocelyne," Darla said. There was a grinding sound and the thick wall swung inward to reveal a lantern-lit room. Vexlan's workshop. They stepped in cautiously, their booted feet barely making a sound. "Vex..." Darla was interrupted as a shadow flickered behind the hidden entrance. The person leapt forward with a small hammer, only to come to a screeching halt. Both assassins had instinctively drawn their daggers, with only the faintest hiss and now had them against either side of their attacker's throat.

"Darla! What in the seven hells. I haven't told you about the secret passage, let alone the passwords. You're lucky I didn't kill you," Vexlan said.

"Firstly Vexlan," Darla said calmly, holding her hand up with one finger extended. "I recognised your symbol. It stood out like a beacon."

"Maybe I need to cover it with a greater concentration of dirt. Obviously, the stone grains aren't covering it enough," Vexlan muttered. Darla laughed and held up a second finger.

"Two. I think I know you and Jocelyne well enough to guess what passwords you would use." Looking at her sheepishly under the rim of his thin framed glasses, he gave her a brief nod. It was the only acknowledgement that she was going to get. She smirked as she held up a third finger. "And lastly Vexlan, you must be delusional if you think you have a chance of taking either of us out." Athelaine giggled at the last comment. Both assassins lowered their daggers and Darla enveloped him in a hug. "It is good to see you, Vex."

* * *

"It's great to see you too, Darla," Vex replied. "Just let me get Jocelyne. It will make her day. She'll be over the moon. It has been so long since we've seen you." He ran part way up the stone stairs. "Jocelyne!" he shouted.

Roxy bounded towards the assassins excited, with her bushy tail wagging. Darla knelt and gave her an affectionate pat. "I'm curious. Why didn't he use Roxy's name for both passwords?" Athelaine whispered.

Darla laughed as she rubbed the crossbreed's ear. Roxy moaned contently. "Because if he didn't use Jocelyne's name for at least one of the passwords, she would have castrated him and fed his cock to Roxy."

Athelaine smiled wickedly. "I like this woman already."

Chapter 14

The guards thumped their chest plate as they saluted the princes. Grabbing the key ring off his belt, one of them fumbled as he tried to unlock the thick, wooden door. "Hurry up, you moronic oaf," Stryxen shouted impatiently.

"Be polite, little brother, otherwise the guards might ban you from visiting Zane," Jace reprimanded.

* * *

"I'd like to see them try," Stryxen muttered. Rylan tried to hide his amused chuckle behind a cough, which in turn earnt him a questioning look from both princes. The door unlocked with a click and swung open. Stryxen barged through the door knocking the guards aside.

"I apologise for my brother's behaviour," Jace said apologetically to the two guards. "He has taken Zane's condemnation badly and is struggling to deal with it." The guards nodded their understanding. Following Stryxen, they entered the confines of the dungeon. The dungeon was circular with four levels. The grey, dismal stone gave it a dark, eerie contrast and even though the torches flickered brightly they offered little comfort.

The dungeon was old and had been there for centuries. It was a marvel of dwarven architecture and had stood the test of time. Walking along the winding path, Rylan followed the princes. Their padded boots echoed on the stone steps and the flickering torches cast shadows. It was unnerving and put Rylan on edge. Unconsciously, his hand drifted to the hilt of his sword. It provided him with security, reassurance and comfort.

The dungeon accommodated one hundred cells. It was a bit of an overkill in Jace's opinion. He could only remember the dungeon ever only having twenty people in it. And that only eventuated due to some rioting during trade agreements. Ten guards would be stationed there whenever the dungeon was at full capacity. Two stationed at the main entrance, while two walked the perimeter on each level. Now there were only ten prisoners scattered amongst the dungeon cells. Because of this, the king had only stationed two guards at the entrance. Rylan and the princes continued walking in silence, the only sound being the occasional moan coming from one of the prisoners.

"I'm going to send my guards out into the city," Stryxen said, looking around the dungeon. "They can arrest people and fill up the rest of these empty cells." Rylan exchanged a concerned look with Jace.

The older prince just laughed. "Sorry to disappoint you, Stryxen, but even filling the dungeon to full capacity won't distract our father. Once he's got his mind set on something, he follows through with it. And he's determined to execute Zane on his birthday." He ruffled his younger brother's hair playfully. "Don't worry, leave it with me. I'll work out a way to free our brother and clear his name." As they continued walking, Rylan couldn't help but wonder if Stryxen's comment had a darker, more foreboding meaning behind it.

As they proceeded down the last set of steps, they heard a growl. The sound echoed throughout the dungeon. "What is that?" Stryxen asked inquisitively.

"Ghouls," Jace replied. "The dungeon connects to an

underground network of tunnels. The tunnels are infested with ghouls." Stryxen's eyes scanned the dungeon searching for the tunnels. Jace laughed. "Don't worry, Stryxen, we are protected by iron and magic." He pointed towards the end of the pathway. A row of thick iron poles embedded into the stone barred the way into the tunnel. In the centre, amongst the poles was a locked gate. Inscribed into the gate and the poles were magical runes that glowed bright blue, shielding the dungeon from the ghouls.

"Why didn't they just block the tunnel?" Stryxen asked.

"Because we have a dark history, one that I'm not proud of. Our great, great grandfather used to feed the prisoners to the ghouls. It was an atrocious practice. One that our grandfather abolished when his reign began," Jace replied, stopping in front of a cell.

"It is also rumoured that there is an underground city, lost and forgotten somewhere amongst the tunnel networks. Apparently, it is the home of the ghouls…and something else. After all my younger brother, who do you think controls the ghouls?" Zane chipped in, laughing.

"You are going to traumatise him and give him nightmares," Jace scolded him.

Zane merely shrugged. "I'm just giving him the complete picture and finishing the history lesson that you started."

* * *

Jace sighed, his expression softening. "How are you, brother?" Another shrug. It was to be expected. While he had the others fooled, Jace could see through the façade. His brother wasn't coping. He was afraid and clinging to a slim hope that Jace would be able to save him. Jace also felt guilty that he had put this burden upon his brother. He hadn't been strong enough to kill their mother. Their mother? The imposter that Zane had killed hadn't been their mother for a long time. Not since the demon corrupted her, took over her soul and manipulated her to its own agenda.

"Where's my present, Zane? It's my birthday today and I'm spending it visiting you in the dungeon. You don't have a present for me and you're not even attending my birthday banquet," Stryxen said with tears streaming down his face.

"Zane contributed to the present that we're both getting you," Jace replied diplomatically. "It'll be delivered just before the banquet." Even though Stryxen was sulking, Jace had piqued his interest.

"Really?"

"Yes. It's a present from both of us," Zane replied, going along with the lie.

"I managed to sneak this in for you," Jace said, reaching into his pocket and pulling out a large milky coloured orb. Zane recognised it immediately. It was his communication orb. He had given its twin to Kyrene, so that they could communicate over the vast distance between Sethanon and the dwarven lands. He stretched his arm through the bars and Jace calmly placed it in his open hand. "You're lucky that it was one of your guards on duty. They heard the musical ringing and fetched it from your room. They handed it to me and I said that I would take care of the matter."

"Thank you, brother," Zane replied, holding the orb to his face. "Kyrene." The orb turned blue and started chiming with a musical sound. A female face appeared on the orb with her long, black hair wavy and dishevelled. Zane considered her quite attractive for a dwarf.

"You've taken your sweet time," she said angrily.

"I'm currently indisposed," Zane replied diplomatically. He wasn't about to tell her of his predicament. "What can I do for you, Kyrene?"

"You can give us a chest full of gold for our troubles," she replied, her green eyes sparkling mischievously. Zane forced a smile, but Kyrene knew him all too well. She could see it in his eyes. "Are you okay?" Zane nodded.

"I'm just tired, Kyrene." Kyrene knew that there was more to it than that, but Zane wasn't willing to divulge anything. Not yet anyway.

* * *

Her face lit up, beaming excitedly. "We found it, Zane! We found the demonic half of the *Val'Markyl.*" Zane almost dropped the orb. He was speechless. He couldn't believe it. He had been hunting for the tome for what seemed like an eternity. Now the tome was complete. Now they would have the means for defeating Malgorath. "I wanted to give it to you for free, but Baron Gamel insisted on a chest of gold for compensation." Gamel was a self-righteous prick, deluded with visions of grandeur. He insisted that even his own wife call him by his title.

"What is the *Val'Markyl?*" Stryxen murmured to Jace inquisitively.

"It's a tome, an ancient book of magic. It will help us defeat Malgorath," Jace replied, whispering so that he didn't interrupt Zane. Stryxen shrugged, uninterested. Even though he was now of age, he showed no interest in magic.

"That's wonderful news, Kyrene. I will not only send a chest of gold, but also some crystal figurines for Lady Gwendyline and a white gold necklace embedded with rubies. A present for the baroness to match her beauty." Kyrene blushed. The baroness had a love for jewellery, hence why Zane thought he would butter up the deal by giving her something extravagant.

Gwendyline was their nine-year-old daughter. She was a

solitary child with few friends. Because of this she had developed a love for reading and collecting crystal figurines. Zane suspected that the reason Gwendyline isolated herself was because of her disabilities. The young dwarf was deaf and had also been born with a deformed leg and had to wear a metal brace to help her walk. She idolised Zane because whenever he visited, he always gave her the time of day and treated her as an equal. Like her mother, he had also taken the time to learn sign language.

Flustered, Kyrene quickly composed herself. His flattering had worked, but the baroness had also noticed his surroundings. "Are you okay, Zane? What's wrong?" she asked, concerned.

"I've got myself into a dire situation, Kyrene." The baroness gasped for breath. She was almost crying. "Don't worry Kyrene, I'll be fine. But I'm going to send Jace to deliver the gold and collect the tome."

"Don't forget the necklace and the figurines," Kyrene quickly added.

"I'll make sure Jace packs those as well."

"When will Jace arrive?" she asked. Kyrene was inquisitive, but she was also trying to be the gracious host. She was meticulously organised and would plan ahead of time, ensuring that Jace and his retinue were accommodated. His older brother would receive a banquet fit for a king. Zane felt envious.

"I won't be able to go until after dad's birthday," Jace whispered. Zane looked at him pleadingly. "Even if I leave now, I still wouldn't be able to make it back in time."

"I could cast a portal. That will make the trip quicker. You could be there and back in a day or two." Jace shook his head. He knew what was involved in casting a portal.

"You don't have the blood or the space to cast that type of portal." Before Zane could debate the point, he continued, driving the reality of the matter home. "You know full well that if I order your release, I will be joining you in the dungeon as well." Zane sighed, conceding defeat, knowing that his brother was right.

"My brother will leave after the king's birthday. Collecting the tome will have to wait," Zane said. "I will contact you closer to the time so that you can start organizing and planning." Kyrene smiled, Zane knew her all too well.

"I still wish that you were coming," she pouted. "Are you sure there isn't anything we can do?" Zane shook his head. He wanted to tell her, but he was afraid she would act rashly. It would start a war and fracture their alliance with the dwarves. But even if Kyrene was able to rally a large enough army, they wouldn't get here in time. A thought came to him, one that he quickly contemplated.

Mumbling an incantation, the words barely coherent, he cast a levitating spell. Letting go of the magical orb, the communication device floated, hovering in the air. His fingers and hands a blur, Zane started to communicate in sign language. He sent Kyrene a quick message that only she would understand. Kyrene even laughed, acting as if it was an amusing joke that they shared. Smiling, he ended the conversation and sent the orb floating through the bars towards his older brother. Before Jace could grab it though, Stryxen plucked it out of the air and shoved it in his pocket.

"Consider this my birthday present," he said, but before he could walk away Jace grabbed him forcibly around the shoulder. He was furious. Zane hadn't seen him that angry in a long time.

"THAT WAS RUDE!" he screamed.

"I DON'T CARE" Stryxen screamed back. "Get your hands off me, otherwise I'll have father throw you into the dungeon." Shoving him against the cell bars, Jace released his hold. He took a couple of deep breaths.

"Zane has entrusted me with the magical orb, so please hand it back, Stryxen," Jace said calmly, smiling and holding out his hand. He waited, trying to rein in his anger. His patience was thinning. "The orb, Stryxen!"

* * *

"No! The orb is mine." He pushed away from the bars. "I'm going to show father the bruises you've given me. Get used to this view because you'll soon be joining Zane."

"I don't care. Before they throw me in the dungeon though, I'll pummel you until you're black and blue." Stryxen paled.

"ENOUGH!" Zane shouted. "With me in here, both of you should be looking out for each other." He sighed, leaning on the bars. "Please, do this for me." He turned to Stryxen. "You are thirteen now, you've come of age and with that comes responsibility. You can look after the orb for now."

"No. Jace can have it." he said, sulking. He reluctantly handed it back to his older brother. His lip quivering, he ran back up the path crying. Jace looked at Rylan, who nodded briefly, before chasing after the younger prince.

"Thank you for giving me the opportunity to talk to Kyrene….and to say a final farewell," Zane said with a sigh, as he went and sat on the edge of his small bed. The mattress was indented with lumps. It was old, worn and very uncomfortable.

"Don't give up, Zane. There is still eleven days until dad's birthday. I will hound him every day if I must and try to talk him out of this idiocy and madness," Jace was defiant. He grabbed hold of the iron bars and shook it for emphasis. "I will get you out of here one way or another." Zane admired his brother's determination and persistence, but deep down they both knew it was futile, that their father wouldn't be swayed in his decision. The only way he was going to survive was through cunning, intellect and a little bit of luck. He had already set the wheels in motion, now he just had to wait.

"What in the seven hells is it now?" Jocelyne shouted, approaching the entranceway. "Hello Darla, Athelaine, welcome to our home. I have already set places at the dinner table for you both. Please come and join us." Vexlan led the way, ushering the two ladies upstairs.

"How did she know," Athelaine whispered to Darla, a little spooked and on edge by Jocelyne's reaction.

"Because sneaky little Jocelyne has cast a detection spell somewhere within Vexlan's tunnel," Darla replied, with a smirk.

Jocelyne smiled, her eyes twinkling mischievously. "Now, now Darla. Would I do something like that?"

"Yes, you would Jocelyne and you know it," Darla said, snickering as she embraced the woman in a fierce hug.

* * *

Athelaine laughed. "Like I said, I like this woman already." Taking the lead, Jocelyne escorted them to the dining room. A large oval shaped wooden table was set in the middle of the room. Four exquisitely carved wooden chairs were situated around the sides of the table. At the end of the table was a large wooden, cushioned stool. It was Roxy's special place at the table.

Jocelyne pulled out two chairs on one side of the table and nodding their thanks, Darla and Athelaine sat. "I hope you have made enough food. Darla is famished," Athelaine jibed. Opening her mouth, Darla started to protest but her stomach grumbled, giving her away. Closing her mouth, she looked down embarrassed, as Athelaine and Jocelyne roared with laughter.

As Jocelyne went back to the kitchen, Vexlan and Roxy took their seats. "We heard a rumour that you killed the queen?" Vexlan asked, going straight to the point. Darla nodded confirmation. "What in the seven hells were you thinking, Darla?"

"Firstly, I was contracted to do an extremely appealing and well-paid job and secondly the queen was a demon," Darla replied as Jocelyn carried two steaming bowls to the table and placed them in front of the two guests. The aromas wafting off the plate were tantalising. It was a large bowl of pheasant stew, with a thick sauce and lots of vegetables. Served on the side was a freshly cooked bun, lathered with butter.

"You managed to kill a demon. That's impressive. From the research that I have conducted, I have discovered that they are supernatural, not of this realm and that most of them are powerful, magical entities. How did you do it?" Vexlan asked, intrigued. He had always had a passion for creatures, science and magic.

"With the aid of this," Darla replied, standing and drawing the short sword. Vexlan gasped in awe.

"The gem is radiating as if it is infused with something. The runes along the blade are intricate. I have seen nothing like them before. The weapon is simply magnificent. I would love to study it sometime." Darla sheathed the short sword and screamed. Her legs went wobbly and she gripped the table to keep her balance. A voice resounded in her head, loud and authoritative. *"The Wolfsclaw is not a weapon to be studied!!"*

A memory came flooding back. *The Wolfsclaw hanging on an iron hook over the fireplace of her family manor. The weapon belonged to the king of the werewolf nation. Her father!* She was royalty, a princess. She could remember her surname, the name that depicted her as a royal - Lycanthorne. Their kingdom had even been named after them, except with slightly different spelling. Her given name still eluded her though. Vexlan looked at her worried.

"Another memory," Darla said, smiling and reassuring him. "Sorry Vexlan. The Wolfsclaw doesn't want to be studied."

Darla could see Vexlan's mind ticking, wanting to ask a hundred questions but Jocelyne returned, not giving him a chance. She juggled two bowls of pheasant stew, along with a large bowl of pheasant scraps. She placed the stew down for herself and Vexlan. Grabbing the large bowl of scraps, Vexlan reached across and placed the bowl in front of Roxy. With one soft bark, she leaned forward and began to gulp down large mouthfuls. Reaching out and grabbing Jocelyne's hand, Vexlan kissed it affectionately. Grabbing his spoon, he then began to devour his stew. He was devoted to her and appreciated everything that she did. It was all the thanks she needed.

Darla waited until her bulging cheeks subsided and she finished her mouthful. "The king is a demon as well. I briefly saw him reveal himself. I'm not sure about the princes though." The married couple continued eating, completely unphased by the news. Darla looked from one to the other, her eyebrows raised.

"We've suspected this for a while. We've questioned some of the maids and servants and have heard all kinds of stories. A young lady named Millie was especially distraught. She said that Prince Zane had apparently murdered one of his own guards," Jocelyne said.

* * *

"It's pure speculation. You surely can't believe the ravings of one maid. She has no credibility," Athelaine huffed, dismissing the notion.

Jocelyne nodded. "Normally I'd agree. There was something about Millie's demeanour though."

"It's not just Millie," Vexlan added. "Five other servants have told us similar things. The king has also thrown his son in the dungeon and made a public announcement that he is going to execute Prince Zane on his birthday."

"That could make Prince Zane our ally. We need to check it out and possibly rescue him," Darla said before shoving another mouthful of stew into her mouth. Athelaine gave her a look. "I said possibly. The sword will let me know whether he's a demon." Athelaine looked doubtful, but nodded, accepting Darla's lead.

"As well as the stories coming from the castle of demonic activity, there have also been monster sightings throughout the city. More so than normal," Vexlan said as he wiped up some sauce with his bun.

"Don't you mean the illusions?" Darla replied, amidst a mouthful of food. Ten years ago, the monster sightings started, but by the time the guards got there the monsters had vanished. There had been no attacks, just terrified people, traumatised by what they had seen. The guards started scoffing the citizens, ignoring the complaints, putting it down to fabrication and lies. Jocelyn had suspected that it had been illusionary magic. It made sense, it was the only rational explanation.

Jocelyne shook her head. "A week ago, the attacks started happening. No manifestations or illusions, this monster was substantial, real and very terrifying. First in was a young married couple, then a drunkard, a minor noble, a fisherman and last night a whore. All of them were ripped apart, their bodies mutilated and unrecognisable. People are afraid Darla, they are terrified. They are packing up and leaving town, moving to other cities. Our neighbour, the elderly candle maker and the baker down the street have closed their businesses."

"Is there anything I can do to help?" Darla asked, shoving another spoonful of pheasant stew in her mouth. Jocelyne and Vexlan had helped her change her identity and get her life back in order. They were family and she would do anything for them.

Athelaine was concerned though. "My heart goes out to your friends and their predicament Darla," she stated, bluntly. "But we need to kill the king, retrieve your dagger and clear your name first." Darla sighed and nodded in understanding. As harsh as it was to hear, Athelaine was stating the truth and she respected that.

* * *

"You are right," Darla said, conceding the point. "We will kill the king, clear my name and then hunt down this monster."

"We don't have time to go monster hunting," Athelaine shouted, thumping the table and cracking the wood. "After killing the king and clearing your name, we need to concentrate our efforts on taking out Malgorath." Jocelyne and Vexlan glared at her. Embarrassed, she lowered her eyes. "I'm sorry. I'm a guest and I was out of turn speaking like that. It's just that…. I'm honour bound to protect Darla. I don't want her putting herself at risk when she doesn't need to."

Jocelyne smiled warmly. "You didn't offend us. We all want what's best for Darla."

"You may feel honour bound to protect me," Darla said softly. "But I am also honour bound to protect my friends and the citizens of this city." Her tone was authoritative and left no room for argument.

"So be it," Athelaine replied, sighing and nodding her head in resignation. "We die together, fighting to our last breath."

Darla laughed. "Who said anything about dying? We play it smart and fight on our terms. Malgorath has taken things to the next level. He isn't resorting to illusions and trickery anymore. This creature is doing Malgorath's bidding. We kill it and we'll definitely get Malgorath's attention. We'll lure him out from the shadows and reveal him for who he is. And then end this once and for all."

"Side by side, we fight to the end," Athelaine replied. "First, we need to find a way to gain access to Everthorn Castle."

"I think I can help with that," Vexlan said with a smirk. "I suggest infiltrating the castle at King Erithen's birthday celebration. It's in just under two weeks. It will take me a few days to forge some official invitations and come up with aliases for you both. I can guarantee that I can get you into the celebration. The rest is up to you though."

The prince stumbled and almost fell. The hellhound had been drawn to something and was sending him a message telepathically. The link was something that he had with all his minions that were born from his essence. It enabled a direct and efficient line of communication. Malgorath had recognised the object immediately. It was a divinity stone! Not the one that had been lost to him, a different one. *Retrieve it for me my loyal hound.* The link broke off as the hellhound bounded towards its target. Failure was not an option. Malgorath would not let another divinity stone slip from his grasp.

"Thank…" Darla began to say, before being interrupted as Roxy began to bark. Suddenly, alarm bells sounded, high pitched and piercing. Darla and Athelaine winced, crying out in pain. Mumbling a few words, Jocelyne quickly silenced the alarm. Their supernatural lineage made their hearing sensitive, even at the best of times. "Thank you," Darla managed to say. Athelaine merely nodded. Although subsiding, their ears were still ringing. All eyes were on Jocelyne. Her expression said it all, something was wrong.

"Something has broken through the magical wards that protect and shield the shop," she said, rushing from the room. Vexlan was a step behind her, with Roxy barking and bounding after them.

"Fuck me! We can't even enjoy a meal in peace," Darla said, drawing her short sword. The blade glowed blue, the runes radiating intensely. It was warning her of the demonic creature that she was about to face. Athelaine smiled wickedly, baring her fangs. "Let's do this," Darla said, as they ran from the small dining area and followed Roxy's insistent barking.

Chapter 15

The magical fireworks illuminated the dining room with a myriad of colours. The lanterns were dimmed for the spectacular display, but also allowed the guests enough light to eat their appetisers. Smiling, Jace waved his hands as he muttered the last part of the incantation. It was an illusionary spell, designed for entertainment. A dragon soared above the children, guided by Jace's hand movements, only to explode into a dazzling array of colours.

Stryxen was only half watching, his attention captivated by the dagger sitting before him on the table. The dagger that his father had given to him as a birthday present. The enchanted dagger that had belonged to the assassin that had killed his mother. The dagger was his now, he didn't care about its history. It came with a simple dark brown leather sheath to protect it. His father was even true to his word and had polished it for him. It now looked as good as new.

The only thing that he wanted to change with the dagger were the magical runes. He wanted to make them powerful, dark and deadly. He wanted to personalize the dagger and make it his own. As he slid it back into the sheath, a quiet knock sounded at the door. With all the screams of exhilaration and joy, it remained indistinguishable and unheard. A dozen children were watching the firework display in awe. The children were Stryxen's friends, invited to join in his birthday celebration.

The children all belonged to rich, predominant families of Sethanon. Jace wouldn't even class them as Stryxen's friends. He could count on one hand the number of times that he had socialized and played with them. The children were pawns, enabling their parents to gain the king's favour. Their parents gained more standing and Stryxen received more presents. That's the only reason they were there. The person knocked a second time, louder and more insistent.

With the firework display finished, Jace excused himself from the table and walked over to open the door.

Millie stood there looking slightly embarrassed. Her apron was a mess. Normally working as a maid and a serving girl, her mother had brought her in to help cook for Stryxen's party. Jace hadn't seen her around much. Zane had informed him that he had finally bedded her and developed feelings for her. Soon afterwards something had traumatised her though. She had distanced herself from Zane, scared and wanting nothing to do with him. Jace had smirked, wanting to say that it was because of 'Zane's small cock', but had refrained seeing his brother's depressed state. Instead, he had simply said, "Perhaps it's for the best."

The woman had become a recluse, only working when she had to and even then, keeping to herself. "Excuse the intrusion, Prince Jace, but Caz the blacksmith is at the front door for you," she muttered, her head down and looking at the floor. Jace smiled, Stryxen's presents had arrived. Jace led them to the front door. Next to him was Stryxen and Rylan. Behind them followed Stryxen's twelve friends. They knew their place. They didn't dare walk in front of the young prince.

"Happy birthday, Prince Stryxen," Caz said, bowing gracefully.

"Where are my presents?" Stryxen asked, rudely. Jace

looked at him sternly and gave him a slap to the back of his head. "I would be careful brother unless you would like me to tell father about the way you treated me in the dungeon when we visited Zane." The threat was a mere whisper, spoken loud enough that only the two of them could hear.

"Please give my condolences to your brother, Prince Zane," Caz said politely. Jace tried to hide the smirk that crept onto his face, but his eyes gave it away as he nodded his thanks to the blacksmith. It was Caz's way of letting them know that his keen elven hearing had heard every word of Stryxen's threat.

"Zane is no longer a prince or our brother!" Stryxen shouted, irate at the blacksmith.

"Remember Prince Stryxen that Caz is delivering my present as well. If you continue this rude behaviour towards him, then you won't receive my present either," Rylan said calmly.

"I don't care!" Stryxen shouted turning his attention on Rylan.

"This is obviously a bad time. I will return the presents and lock them away in the forge. Good evening to you my princes," Caz said, bowing fluently and turning around. He proceeded to walk away and Jace started to close the door.

"NO!" Stryxen screamed. Caz stopped in mid stride and

turned to face the young prince. Jace swung the door back open. Tears were streaming down Stryxen's face. Choking back sobs, he took a deep breath and continued. "I am sorry Caz. I am taking my brother's imprisonment hard. We will pass on your condolences." He took another deep breath, choking back a sob. "Could I please have my birthday presents?"

"Certainly, my young prince," Caz replied, smiling. Stepping onto the gravel, Cazthalian eagerly led them to his wagon and the horses that were waiting there.

"When did your assistant arrive?" Jace asked, inquisitively, noticing that Caz had his wagon back.

"This afternoon after you left. I know how long the trip takes. I used to do it myself once upon a time, hence why I knew that she would be back this afternoon," Caz stated matter-of-factly. He had taken a gamble taking on a female assistant, but the young lady was his niece and he felt obliged. Dana had proven exceptionally capable, had absorbed everything that her uncle had taught her like a sponge. She was the only female apprentice in the land and by the looks of it would prove to be an exceptional blacksmith. "I wouldn't have offered to deliver everything otherwise," he added sarcastically.

"Smart arse elf," Jace muttered under his breath. Caz laughed heartily. He didn't take it as an insult, but merely as banter between two friends. The gravel crunching beneath his booted feet, Caz led them to his wagon. A stunning silver and dark grey horse was tied to the side. It reared, snorting and kicking out its two front hooves as they neared it. Cazthalian spoke soothingly in the elven dialect and the horse calmed, lowering its head. The elf beckoned the young prince forward to pat the battle horse. "Happy birthday, Stryxen. I got you your own purebred Majarelly battle horse," Jace said proudly knowing what the horse was like and keeping his distance. "I will let Brenan know that he can have his horse back now."

Tears streaming down his face, the birthday boy ran up and embraced Jace in a fierce hug. "Thank you, Jace. I promise I'll look after him. I'll groom him, feed him and love him to bits," Stryxen mumbled in between sobs. Jace was pleasantly surprised by the reaction. With the way his moods had been, it could have gone either way. Then again, both he and Zane had been the same at his age.

Jace held his brother close, enjoying the moment. "I love you too, Stryxen. Remember that as well as grooming, feeding and loving him, you will also need to train him. He is a very smart horse, the Majarelly are among the best battle horses in the world. You will need to be disciplined and strict with his training. If you ask nicely, I'm sure Rylan will help you with it. He is good with horses."

Rylan forced a smile. "Thanks a lot," he muttered, loud

enough that only Jace could hear. Laughing, Jace slapped him playfully on the back.

"Well, it's true, isn't it? You've always had an affinity to animals." Rylan couldn't argue with that, but still grumbled as he stepped forward. Caz lifted a dark leather saddle out of the wagon. The craftmanship was exceptional, with perfect, fine but durable stitching and hooks for saddlebags and weapons. It even came with some rope for tying down bedrolls, hunted game or equipment. It was the perfect present. An accessory that could be used with his new horse. But that was only part of his present.

Excitedly, Rylan ran over to help Caz lift out the second present. He had found it in a trinket store. The owner had inherited it and having no use for it, used it to hang and drape the trinkets. To him it was a piece of junk, a waste of space. He had been desperate and Rylan had bought it at a bargain price. It was called a Rocking Horse, a marvel of gnomish ingenuity. It was a mechanical horse that could be programmed to trot, canter and gallop. The saddle accustomed the rider to the steady, repetitive movement of the horse. The gentle rocking motion that the rider experiences is what earnt the mechanical horse its name.

The rocking horse was dented, scratched and rusted, but all the mechanics were in working order. The gnomes were renown for building things to last. It had taken them a while, but eventually they were able to perfect the rocking horse design. For a small fee, Caz had hammered out the dents, polished the scratches and removed the rust. The rocking horse now looked as good as new. Even though Stryxen had gone for short rides in the meadows with his brothers, he was yet to experience a long, arduous ride. The rocking horse would help prepare him for that. "Happy birthday, Stryxen," Rylan said, beaming with pride and happy with the presents he had chosen.

"What's this? A saddle and a piece of metal junk," Stryxen scoffed. Rylan was hurt, angry and embarrassed.

"It's called a rocking horse, Stryxen. It will help you prepare for long rides," Rylan tried to explain.

"A rocking horse. I'll rock it across my room, out my bedroom window and see if the piece of junk can fly," Stryxen sneered. This brought about raucous laughter from his friends. Suddenly, without any warning, he went face first into the dirt. Jace stood over his younger brother furious. "You're going to pay for that!" Stryxen threatened, then suddenly, unexpectedly he threw a handful of dirt at his older brother. Picking himself out of the dirt, he smiled and addressed Rylan. "Thank you, Lord Rylan, for the presents. I apologise for my ungracious behaviour and promise that I will put them to good use."

Rylan nodded. He didn't dare say a word, fearful that he might portray his true feelings regarding the matter. "Could you please take the horse to the stables, Caz? I'll have some guards carry the saddle and rocking horse up to Stryxen's room," Jace said, taking charge of the situation. Caz nodded. Saying some soothing words in the elvish tongue, he gave the Majarelly horse an affectionate pat. Grabbing it by the reins, he started walking it towards the royal stables.

"I'm bored. Let's go back to the banquet and eat," Stryxen said, leading the way. His friends followed obediently behind him like a flock of sheep. Jace and Rylan followed at the rear, talking quietly.

"I hope you have a wonderful birthday banquet, Stryxen. Unfortunately, I have duties that I need to do," Rylan said shrugging his shoulders apologetically. "It comes with being one of your father's rangers."

"What time do you expect me for horse training?" Stryxen asked. Rylan cursed under his breath. He had hoped that the young prince had forgotten.

"I'll be heading out on patrol," Rylan replied. It was the truth. He was leading a small group of six rangers out to patrol along the Blood Road and investigate the elven presence. When Brenan had informed him of the attack, the king had been furious. He was already irate due to the Zane situation and this just added to his foul mood. The king was on the verge of sending his general, rallying an army, invading the elvish lands and starting a war.

* * *

It took Rylan to reason with him and convince him to send the rangers. He would investigate and report back his findings. "But I could possibly teach you the basics and give you a few pointers before I leave." Stryxen beamed with excitement. "But it would have to be at dawn." And just like that Stryxen's heart sank, the disappointment showing on his face.

"To the seven hells with that," Stryxen cursed. "I'll train the damn horse myself. And by the time you get back I'll have the horse trained to be an absolute legend, a beast amongst horses."

Rylan bowed eloquently, trying to hide his amusement. "I'm sure you will, Prince Stryxen. Good luck with this endeavour and I hope you enjoy the rest of your birthday celebration." Jace cringed as he noticed the slight change in his younger brother's eyes. His mood and demeanour changed as if a switch inside his head had been flicked.

"I was going to send you up a large plate of food from the banquet, but now you can go and fuck yourself," Stryxen screamed, as Rylan turned around and began to walk back to the ranger barracks.

"So be it. It would probably leave a bitter taste in my mouth anyway," Rylan replied and continued walking. It would be a plain, simple meal tonight, but he didn't care. The company of his fellow rangers would be a welcome respite from the moody prince. Walking back down the corridor and escorting the group back to the dining room, Jace cursed Rylan. He was envious of his friend, wishing that he also had an excuse to exempt himself from Stryxen's birthday celebration.

Darla and Athelaine stood at the shop entrance and saw nothing. Roxy was barking furiously at something invisible. The shop was wrecked, a clutter of mess. Shelving and cabinets were broken, shattered and were nothing more than debris. Glass jars were smashed, their contents scattered amongst the shards on the floor. Darla's heart went out to Jocelyne. She had worked hard, accumulating and mixing a lot of elixirs. Her shop had always been neat and orderly. "Something is in the shop. Be careful," Jocelyne shouted, from behind the counter.

Vexlan was situated on the other side of the room, standing behind some broken cabinets. He glanced around nervously. He hadn't had the opportunity to get a weapon from the workshop, so he had improvised by picking up a broken piece of one of the cabinets. The piece was long and had two jagged nails sticking out of it. It would have to do. With a whistle, Roxy obediently ran to his side. They had managed to get to cover, Darla and Athelaine hadn't been so lucky.

* * *

"I can't smell anything. I can't pick up a scent," Darla said, stepping cautiously forward. She tapped into her lycanthropy and her eyes changed colour to a bestial yellow. The eyes of a werewolf. Her eyes scanned the room, searching and saw nothing. Roxy darted from cover, growling, her heckles raised. "Good girl," Darla whispered, scanning the immediate area in front of Roxy. Then she noticed it, some debris move ever so slightly, crunching under the weight of something heavy. Crunching sounded in multiple locations, as the thing moved, running straight towards her.

"When I say move, dive to the left," Darla instructed, her voice only slightly louder than a whisper. She waited until the last minute. "Now!" Darla dived to the right as Athelaine dived in the opposite direction. As Darla dived, her arm struck out, slashing with the short sword. It was uncontrolled, driven, guided by the sword. Black blood sprayed across the floor. A giant, demonic dog, materialised where she had been only moments before. Turning its head, it glared at her with its ruby-red eyes and snarled at her menacingly.

To call the creature a dog was an understatement. It was the size of a small horse, broad and muscly. Its head resembled a dragon's. Its skin was leathery with its body covered in thick, black fur. It was a predator, a creature out of nightmares. Its left foreleg was sliced open. Black blood flowed down it, pooling on the floor. She had wounded it, but in so doing, all she'd done was piss it off.

Turning quickly, it charged at her, hitting her with the force of a battering ram. It had surprised her that an animal so big and bulky could move so quick. She crashed through a cabinet and lay there winded amongst a pile of debris. Lunging at her, the hellhound prepared to tear her to shreds. Darla spun, rolling backwards and narrowly missed its snapping maw.

Athelaine darted in from the side in a blur of speed, distracting the hellhound as her daggers sliced across its side. "It's hide is too tough," she shouted. "My daggers aren't penetrating. Hell, they're barely scratching the surface." She somersaulted backwards as the hellhound swiped at her with one of its massive, clawed paws. Darla flipped into a standing position, leapt forward and swung the short sword. The blue blade swished across in a deadly arc. And hit nothing. The hellhound just vanished.

Darla swivelled, scanning the area nervously. *Crunch,crunch.* She back-stepped cautiously, her boots crushing debris. Her bestial eyes caught the movement. A jar shattering into tiny shards. She swung the short sword, a blaze of blue light. Again nothing! She continued to step back, watching for any sign. She felt like she was playing a deadly game of cat-and-mouse. And she was the mouse!

"Simply amazing," Jocelyne said in awe. "The creature has a

phasing ability. That's why you can't hit it, even with your mystical sword. When the creature phases out, it's physical form transfers to another dimension. It is still present in this world, but only in a spirit form. That's how it's managed to hunt, to kill and still evade the guards."

"That's just great, Jocelyne. But how do we fucking kill it?" Darla barked.

"Leave that to me. A stasis spell should be able to temporarily trap it in this world, but you'll have to kill it quickly."

"Really? And here I was thinking you wanted me to tame it to become a new play mate for Roxy?" Darla replied sarcastically.

"And what a marvellous pet it would be." Darla rolled her eyes. Jocelyne's scientific and magical curiosity is what had attracted Vexlan. They were like two peas in a pod. "I'll need you to draw the creature back into our dimension before I can cast the spell though."

"And how exactly do I do that?" Darla asked.

"Use your sword as bait," Jocelyne explained. Darla looked at her sceptically. "It makes perfect sense when you think about it. Vexlan and I were here before you, but the creature remained stationary. It didn't move, make a sound or attack either of us. As soon as you and Athelaine came though, it targeted you. Only you! Look at your sword." Darla glanced at the blue blade. It radiated and hummed. "I think your sword is acting like a beacon to the creature. The two are somehow linked." Darla nodded, processing and strategizing a plan of action.

She couldn't think of anything. "Fuck it. I'll improvise." She took a step forward, holding the short sword in front of her. "You want this, Fluffy," she shouted, waving the weapon back and forth. "Then come and get it." She saw movement to her left. A piece of debris shattered as the hellhound stepped on it. It was manoeuvring, moving into a position ready to attack. Darla continued to taunt the creature, baiting it, while watching its every movement. With a shimmer, the hellhound materialised leaping in mid-air straight towards her.

Darla dived out of the way, rolling to the side and landing in a crouch. Leaping up, she swung the short sword, slicing upwards. Black blood sprayed across the floor. It was a deep gash, but the hellhound seemed unphased. As it turned to face her a bright green light encircled the creature, wrapping itself around it, before fading to a faint glow. The hellhound tried to phase and couldn't. Darla could read the confusion in its eyes. She smiled wickedly. "You're mine now, Fluffy."

Turning, facing Darla, the hellhound pounced. She slashed at its underside the cut diagonal and deep. Its fore-claws tore into her shoulders, digging in and drawing blood. The sheer force and weight of the hellhound bowled her over, toppling her onto her back amongst a pile of shattered glass and wooden shelving. Some nails stabbed her lower back, but she ignored the pain because they were the least of her problems.

The hellhound had pinned her to the ground with its fore-claws and now stood over her, growling menacingly. As it glared at her with its ruby-red eyes, the hellhound's powerful jaw opened wide and revealed its razor-sharp teeth. It was about to tear her head off. It lunged forward as Darla's arm shot up in a deadly arc. The blue blade was a blur. It stabbed the hellhound through the side of the head, puncturing its brain and killing it instantly.

The faint glow subsided as the spell dissipated. Grunting, Darla rolled the hellhound corpse off her. "I'm sorry that I've brought this into your home."

Jocelyne looked around, taking in everything one last time. She briskly walked over and gave Darla a hug. "It is only a house. Our home is where we live and what we make of it." Releasing the hug, she became all business. "You have ten minutes Vexlan to grab what you need. We're leaving."

"Why? The creature is dead," he asked, confused.

"Because it's my fault," Darla answered, her words softly

spoken, barely louder than a whisper. She felt guilty and was on the verge of tears. This had been like a second home to her.

"Because the hellhound was drawn to this location by Darla's short sword. It acted like a beacon to the creature and being one of Malgorath's minions it would have broadcast this information to the demon prince," Jocelyne stated.

"Fuck!" Vexlan cursed. "So, we've been compromised?" Jocelyne nodded. With Roxy bounding by his side, Vexlan ran to his workshop and began to pack. Jocelyne quickly did a mental list and began packing elixirs that weren't broken.

"Follow me. I'll need you to carry my books and tomes," she said, barging past them. The jars clanking, she ran upstairs with the satchel hanging by her side. She dashed over to the bookshelf and like a mad woman, started grabbing books and throwing them at Athelaine and Darla. They caught most of them, dropping only a couple and then hurried back down the stairs.

Waiting at the top of the staircase to the workshop, Vexlan beckoned to them. "Hurry up. We need to go," he shouted. Juggling the books and tomes, they hurried down the staircase and into the awaiting tunnel. Holding her husband's hand, she had a last look around, picturing everything, taking it in and storing it to memory. They didn't know whether they would ever see their house again. The Brotherhood would compensate them, but that wasn't the point. This was their home and they had dedicated part of their lives into making it what it was.

Squeezing her hand, Vexlan led her down the stairs. Slinging a large satchel over his shoulder, he began to drag a sack of equipment and items. Things that he deemed important and irreplaceable. He looked at a large chest sitting on the floor. It contained an assortment of wealth but was too hefty and would have to be left behind. "Carry these," Darla said, placing her share of the books and tomes in his outstretched hands.

Tapping into her lycanthropy, her arms and back broadened as the muscles and bones became denser and stronger. She hefted the large chest onto her shoulder and held it in place with her hands. It was awkward and uncomfortable, but she refused to leave it behind. She knew how hard her friends had worked. She didn't want them to suffer and would do anything for them.

Smiling, Athelaine placed her share on top of Darla's and grabbing the sack, swung it easily over her shoulder. Like Darla, she was willing to help. Roxy barked from within the confines of the tunnel, running back and forth, beckoning them to follow. Darla and Athelaine entered first, taking the lead with Roxy. With a sigh, Vexlan mumbled his wife's name. With a steady grinding, the section closed and sealed them in darkness. The instant the grinding stopped, Jocelyne started mumbling and tracing something on the secret entrance with her finger. Darla recognised the smell instantly. Blood! Jocelyne was using powerful and deadly blood magic.

"An explosive ward," Athelaine gasped. Even in the dark, she could see Darla's questioning look. "I've studied all kinds of magic over the years. It has always been an interest of mine. I recognised the rune and the incantation."

"How old are you?" Vexlan asked, intrigued. The vampire's age was indiscernible. She looked like she was in her late twenties. Jocelyne whacked him on the back of his head and rolled her eyes. Athelaine gave them a wicked smile and laughed.

"Don't you know that it's rude to ask a woman's age? That's especially true for vampires," she replied.

"The explosive ward will stop Malgorath or any of his minions from following us," Jocelyne said smugly. "When activated it will explode and collapse this section of the tunnel. Lead the way. Because we don't want to be anywhere near the entrance when it explodes."

Nodding, Darla and Athelaine led the way back to Dregga and their camp. They walked in silence, deep in their own thoughts Things hadn't gone as planned. They rarely did. But they were one step closer to killing the king and clearing Darla's name.

<u>Chapter 16</u>

"The king sat at the table eating cherry pie," Malgorath sang, eating his breakfast and tapping the table in tune with the song. "He started to choke and thought he would die." He had already devoured one slice and was about to start the second. As he picked up the thick slice of bread, a dollop of the raspberry jam drizzled onto his finger. The bread was freshly baked and still warm from the oven. He licked it off and took a large bite. Chewing, his cheeks bulging, he hummed the rest of the song.

Even though his hellhound had been dispatched by one of the divine weapons, Malgorath found himself in a joyful mood. An opportunity had presented itself, one that he had quickly taken advantage of. Changing his appearance to one of the guards, he had started a rumour claiming a confirmed sighting of the assassin. The gossip had spread like wildfire. Hearing it from multiple sources, the king had ridden out with a dozen guards to investigate. Prior to the king's departure, Malgorath had masked his appearance, changing it into that of the king. He had written a letter, forging the king's writing perfectly and stamped it with the king's wax seal. Smiling, he had then handed it to General Iryss.

Malgorath had contemplated creating other hellhounds but had refrained. Transferring his essence and creating lesser demons and demonic creatures was a temporary solution, a means to an end. It was an ability that only the greater demons had, but infusing his essence also drained his power. It was a gambit, because if he left himself in a weakened state, he would be vulnerable. He needed to maintain his authority. Once he had five divinity stones, he would be able to create a portal large enough to transport a small demonic army to this world. With all ten he would be able to maintain a permanent portal between the two worlds and terraform this one to his liking.

* * *

As he shoved the last bit of his breakfast into his mouth, he wondered how King Erithen was doing. He suspected that his enemies would have laid a trap. It is what he would have done if he had been in their shoes. The king would die, saving him from having to do the deed. It would be a step closer towards his kingship and the ultimate ruling of this world.

Erithen's horse trotted, as nodding, he waved to the citizens. He had a dozen guards surrounding him and protecting him from harm. It was like a royal procession, something that his family hadn't done for a long while. He made a mental note to take his family out more, to socialize with the populace. He wanted the citizens to be happy. He wanted to demonstrate that his family cared. He wanted them to be safe and to ease their fears. That was impossible though. To do that, they needed to kill Malgorath and the demon lurking within him was scared. As much as he blamed the assassin, he knew Malgorath was the puppet master, the one that had orchestrated the demise of his wife. He had to follow Malgorath's orders though, at least for now, until an opportunity presented itself.

He had been angry, grieving and had acted rashly. Now that he had calmed down and had a chance to contemplate, he was willing to remove the bounty on the assassin. Instead, he would hire her to kill Malgorath. Then he could rule the

Hiberathian Kingdom in peace. Not all demons were evil. He had considered both him and his wife among those and hoped to prove that to this assassin. If all went well, she would become his ally, not his enemy.

As the horses reigned in outside the shop, one of the merchandisers came running over. "My liege," she said, bowing. Erithen beckoned for her to rise, with a wave of her hand. "I'm a seamstress. My shop is next door." The woman pointed to a quaint little shop next door with dresses on wooden mannequins displayed in the windows. "I was working last night when I heard a dreadful commotion coming from Roxy's." The king looked at the elaborate sign hanging on the wall next to the door. It was written in intricate writing with a detailed picture of a hybrid dog.

"Why didn't you inform the guards straight away?" Erithen asked.

"Because I was too scared to leave the shop my liege," the woman mumbled, apologetically. Nodding in understanding, the king motioned the guards to the entrance. The door was locked so the guards would have to break it down.

"Don't worry. We're here now. We'll deal with the situation," Erithen said, dismissing the seamstress. Two guards holding huge two-handed war hammers stood on either side of the door. They swung, their hammers hitting the door simultaneously and shattering it. The powerful blow even ripped the hinges off, leaving a cracked door frame and a pile of debris. The debris crunched under the king's booted feet as he entered the shop, flanked by his guards.

With a nod of his head, all but two of the guards dispersed, fanning out and searching for the occupants and the assassin.

The two guards remaining shadowed the king and walked on either side of him. Their job was to protect the king at all costs, even at the expense of their own lives. The shop was a mess, full of debris and shattered glass. Various liquids decorated the floor, splattered amongst the glass and giving off a mixture of aromas. One of the guards ran back into the shop. "There's a pot of left-over food on a bench, the remains of last night's dinner, I think. Their unfinished bowls are still on the table. I think they left in a hurry," he reported.

The king nodded curtly, only half listening as he noticed the pile of black dust. His nose crinkled at the smell of the dust. The dog had been transformed into a demonic monstrosity. It had been Malgorath's doing. He left the shop and proceeded down the small hallway that led to the dining area. The three guards followed close behind. With a loud clatter, four guards hurried down the staircase. "There is no sign of anyone," one of them reported. The king merely nodded and continued through the dining room. They had escaped, disappeared into the night.

Another guard's booted feet clanked on the stone stairs as

he hurried up from Vexlan's workshop. They could be heard from a mile away. Frustrated from their wasted efforts, Erithen proceeded to the entrance. "My liege," the guard said excitedly. "We have found what appears to be a secret entrance. Tyris noticed some stone dust and some oil along a section of the wall. Tyris, his ranger captain. It made sense. Even in his fifties, his eyesight was as keen as an eagle. Erithen beamed from ear to ear, his mood suddenly brightened.

He proceeded down the stairs and slapped the guard on the shoulder. "Well done. Have you got the entrance open?" Noticing the guards despondent look, he realised that they hadn't. "Four of you have war hammers. Stop sitting around like morons. Have some fucking initiative and use them. I want you to turn that entrance into a pile of rubble." The entrance would be magically sealed and it was futile to try and look for a password. It would be like looking for a needle in a haystack.

As he walked down the last of the stone stairs, the four hammermen positioned themselves. Their two-handed war hammers were solid, deadly weapons and even as thick as the stone wall was, they would make short work of it. The four hammers smashed into the wall simultaneously, cracking it and sending rock shards and dust flying in all directions.

Swinging their mighty war hammers back, their muscles bulging, the four guards smashed the wall again. A spiderweb of large cracks appeared. Large, jagged chunks of rock toppled to the ground revealing a hole in the wall. The hammers swung back in tandem. "Halt!" Erithen screamed, stepping forward. Something had caught his attention. A glow radiating from the other side of the wall, a glow that intensified. "It's some kind of magical …" His last word was cut off as the wall exploded.

As exhausted as they were, they had slept restlessly. The hellhound had rattled all of them. Roxy and Dregga instantly became best friends. Dregga would flick his tail and Roxy would chase it playfully. Exhausted, Roxy curled up at Vexlan's feet and fell asleep while her new best friend flew off to hunt. The following morning, they woke to find Roxy curled up next to the nightwing. "My own best friend has forsaken me," Vexlan joked, shoving the last of his blueberries into his mouth.

It was a light breakfast, gathered from nearby bushes. "I'm going hunting. I will try and get us some food," Darla said, standing up. "Unless they have cleared the campsite, there should be a bow and a quiver of arrows there."

"I've heard that there is an abundance of rabbits around this area," Vexlan stated. "Ever since the king's guards did a culling and got rid of most of the wolves, the rabbits have been breeding like…well you know… rabbits." Darla laughed, but as she walked to the cave entrance Jocelyne screamed in alarm.

"It's my detection spell. Something has triggered it," she said, alarmed. She mumbled an incantation and her eyes glazed over, turning pure white. Darla felt goosebumps. She'd seen Jocelyne do it countless times before, but no matter how many times she saw it, she always had the same reaction. It freaked her out!

"Darla. Go!" Vexlan ordered. "Don't worry about Jocelyne. She'll be fine." Nodding, Darla left. She nimbly climbed down the mountain and walked along the riverbank to the campsite. The campsite stood out. It was hard to miss with the destroyed carriage and corpses from the queen's retinue. The bodies were unrecognisable, having been torn apart by wolves, pecked at by carrion birds and eaten by insects. All that was left was their armour, torn clothing and skeletal remains. It was the natural cycle; all living creatures, humanoid or animal returned to the earth eventually.

Looking around, she soon found what she was looking for. The bow lay discarded next to a tree trunk, but Darla had to climb the tree to recover the quiver of arrows. It took her the better part of an hour, but Darla managed to snare half a dozen plump rabbits. Roasted over the fire, it would make a substantial lunch. She had no idea what they were going to do for dinner. Pleased with herself, she whistled a merry tune as she walked back and began the climb up the mountain slope.

Having climbed castle walls using her claws, she found the mountain slope a piece of cake. She still took her time though. To rush a mountain climb could result in certain death. Hauling herself up into the cave entrance, she untied the string of rabbits and smiling, proudly showed them her prized catch. "Lunch is..." Darla said before realising that something was dreadfully wrong. "What is it?" she asked, panicking as she looked at their grim expressions.

"Let's just say that you don't have to worry about this bounty on your head anymore," Athelaine said, laughing nervously.

"Jocelyn's explosive trap was set off. It killed a dozen guards and..." Vexlan explained. He was unable to finish as Darla interrupted.

"Malgorath?" she asked, excited and hopeful. Just the thought of it felt like a giant weight had been lifted off her shoulders.

"No Darla," Jocelyne said despondently. "Malgorath is still alive. I killed the guards and..." Jocelyne started to sob and Vexlan hugged her tightly, holding her close. Composing herself and choking back a sob, she continued. "I killed the king."

Malgorath climbed the last few steps to the royal rookery. He had morphed his appearance, changing it to resemble that of Prince Zane. It was his favourite and taking on his identity ensured that there wasn't any chance of a reprieve. He had struggled, fighting for dominance over his hosts soul, battling continually for supremacy. The soul had been sweet, naïve and innocent. It had attracted him. He thought it was easy pickings, but he was wrong.

The soul had been stronger than he thought. The body was his now, he had devoured the soul. He could feel his power manifesting. He grew stronger and stronger each day. "Soon," he said to himself as he opened the rookery door. His human host would die during the transformation, but he would have his true demonic form. The form would be substantial, of flesh and blood and attuned to this world. He would be a demon prince and he would be unrivalled.

"What's that my prince?" the rookery master asked. Malgorath was amazed that he'd managed to hear anything over all the squawking. The rookery master was methodical and organised, having set out the cages into different regions. In total there was usually around one hundred ravens housed within the rookery.

"Nothing. I was talking to myself," Zane said.

* * *

"I heard from my apprentice that you were locked up in the dungeon?" The rookery master looked a little nervous. He glanced at a nearby knife, contemplating whether to go for it. Malgorath needed to defuse this situation quickly.

He laughed. "It was a complete misunderstanding. It's been cleared up and I've been released." The rookery master relaxed, feeling more at ease. The Zane imposter lowered the sack that he had been carrying to the floor. "I have grave news. My father is dead. I need these sent out." Tears streamed silently down his face.

He opened the sack revealing one hundred rolled and tied pieces of parchment. Each one was also stamped with the royal seal in a red wax circle. One hundred invitations, each delivered by one of the ravens to all the kings, queens, nobles and generals. Even the high lord of the Brotherhood and the Emperor of the Orc Empire were receiving invitations.

"All the leaders are invited to pay their condolences at my father's funeral in two weeks' time. After the funeral, my brother will have his coronation and be sworn in as king." The rockery master nodded and sighed.

My condolences, my prince," he said, lowering his head. "Your father was a great man and will be sorely missed." He whistled loudly, summoning his apprentice. "We'll send these out immediately." They would have to carefully tie the sealed parchment to each of the raven's legs. "It was one hell of a job! Nodding his thanks, Prince Zane turned around and walked back down the stairs into the castle interior. As he entered the staircase, a dark shadow enveloped him as he morphed back to his normal host. Nobody noticed that the tears had stopped, now replaced by the evil smirk that lit up his face.

Chapter 17

They had arrived at the meadow the day before. Rylan had been present when Brenan informed the king, but being at the battleground, he could now see the carnage and devastation himself. The entire meadow was littered with rotting corpses. It was the first time any of them had encountered the aftermath of a battle and it was unnerving. They proceeded east to the Black Raven Inn. Brenan had recommended it and the king had given Rylan a pouch of gold coins for accommodation, supplies and other expenses.

Rylan's keen eyesight observed that the dead bodies were missing various things. Armour, jewellery and weapons that the elves had already plundered. The spoils of war. Flocks of birds took flight as they trotted across the meadow. Carrion eaters, feeding off the dead. It was nature taking its course, yet they gagged at the smell despite the face masks they had on. The odour was motivation enough for them as nudging his horse's side, Rylan put his horse into a gallop. His companions followed suit, right behind him.

The horses got into a regular, steady rhythm and arrived at the inn an hour later. "Wow. Are you king's rangers?" a young lad asked as they entered the courtyard.

Dismounting, Rylan nodded and smiled. "Yes. My name's Rylan and these are my companions." He reached into the coin pouch and pulling out one of the gold coins, flicked it to the stableboy. "This is for looking after our horses. They have had a hard ride and need brushing, some oats and water."

Garen looked at the gold coin in astonishment. "How long will you be staying?"

"We'll be leaving first thing in the morning," Rylan replied.

* * *

"I'll have them saddled and ready for you. You've overpaid me though," Garen muttered.

Rylan smiled again and laughed, but the stableboy still seemed apprehensive. "Give the horses a treat. They deserve it."

"All I can offer is to mix some blueberries in with their oats. But even after that, you have overpaid me," he replied, contemplating things. Coming up with a solution, he yelled out to one of the men working on the second story of the inn. "Dad. The king's rangers have overpaid me. Could you give them a meal and a round of ale on the house?"

The man nodded and after briefly speaking to the other workmen, he carefully climbed down a long, sturdy wooden ladder. "That's my dad Marek. He's the innkeeper of this fine establishment. Jenna, my step-mum, is the best cook in the Hiberathian Kingdom," Garen said beaming, his satisfaction at the compromise evident.

Marek met the rangers at the entrance to the inn. "Greetings, inn keeper. My name is Rylan. My fellow rangers and I would like to book one of your merchant rooms for the night," the ranger leader said, glancing at the creaking sign swinging above Marek's head. The hook had been secured and the sign now swung on two even chains. Marek hadn't got around to painting it though and the raven was now a dull grey colour.

* * *

"I should probably get around to repainting that one of these days," Marek said, embarrassed.

Rylan shrugged nonchalantly. "Personally, I wouldn't bother. It adds character to the inn. I take it that you are doing some renovations?" he asked casually, fishing for information.

"The inn got damaged. I'm making the most of the situation by modernizing it and doing some renovations," Marek replied offhandedly.

"Damaged? Did the elves do this?"

Marek laughed. "No, no, they were caught up in it, but they didn't cause the damage. A lesser demon did."

"A lesser demon?" Rylan replied disbelievingly.

"Yes. The demon and the elves were after the divinity stone that Darla had acquired." Rylan laughed. *Acquired* was just a polite way of saying stolen. "The elves and some of the king's men fought the demon. A man named Rayze also joined the fight, but it was eventually Darla who killed it," the inn keeper said proudly. Escorting the rangers inside, Marek went behind the counter. Opening a drawer, he pulled out a large brass key. "That will be four gold coins," Marek said handing the key to the leader of the rangers.

* * *

Reaching into the pouch, Rylan handed Marek five gold coins. "Put the extra gold coin towards the cost of your renovations," he said, smiling. Marek nodded his thanks and quickly pocketed the coins. Opening the side door, the innkeeper then led the rangers into the dining room.

Marek pointed to the staircase. "Go to the end of the hallway and turn right. Your room is the last on the right. Dinner will be served in about an hour. Would you like it brought to your room?"

"No, thank you. We'll freshen up and come back down in an hour," Rylan said, leading the rangers up the stairs. The room was spacious and the beds were comfortable. It was a luxury, compared to the hard ground they had been sleeping on. Gnomish plumbing had also been incorporated, allowing for a bath and a toilet to be situated in a small alcove area. The bath also had a heating system allowing for the luxury of both hot and cold water. Refreshed and clean, the rangers went down for dinner.

Dinner consisted of a chicken and vegetable casserole with a slice of freshly baked bread on the side. They wiped up the rich and flavoursome sauce with the bread leaving the bowl empty and relatively clean. Afterwards, the rangers washed it down with a large mug of ale. They returned to their room, deciding to have an early night and get a good night sleep.

Rylan had separated them into three pairs. Harold and

Gwethren would travel to Balgleen, look after the horses and restock their supplies. Their orders were simple. If Rylan and the three rangers with him failed to return within two days, they were to gallop back to Sethanon and inform the king. Rylan was planning for every eventuality.

A day had passed and the four rangers had just entered the Glenonenal Forest. All had been quiet. There had been no sign of an elven presence. They had been about to return to Balgleen when they heard the faint neighing of horses. Rylan took the lead and darted to the next tree. Ezran, the rookie of the group followed silently behind him. He was a shadow, following his every move. Even though inexperienced, he had demonstrated intelligence, initiative and had proven himself to be a capable fighter. Rylan was proud to have him on his team.

They were trespassing and even though they were representing their king, stealth was called for. Their padded boots barely made a sound and only left the slightest of indentations in the damp earth. With the series of buttons done up on the waist area of their mottled cloaks, it tightened and wrapped the fabric tightly around them. It still allowed the flexibility of movement while providing them with the perfect camouflage. He motioned the other group forward using a silent hand signal.

A faint crunch sounded as Hylan and Frey stepped on a pile of twigs hidden amongst some leaves. "Fuck," Rylan cursed, drawing his sword. Alarmed, Ezran unhooked his pair of wickedly curved war axes, as with a spray of leaves, their two companions shot into the air entangled in a giant net. Then without any warning, Rylan felt the cold steel of a blade against his throat.

Other elves appeared, materializing out of thin air without a sound. Lowering his sword, Rylan waved for Ezran to lower his war axes. The rookie who was eager and determined to prove himself obeyed reluctantly. The last thing Rylan wanted to do was escalate the situation. "What is your business here?" an elf asked, stepping forward. He was obviously the captain of the squad.

"We are here to seek an audience with King Therondal," Rylan replied calmly.

"You will see him soon enough," the elven captain sneered, nodding to the guard behind him. In a blur of speed, the guard lowered the dagger. Whipping it up, he smashed the ranger in the back of the head with the pommel. Rylan's knees buckled and he toppled like a fallen tree. The last thing he saw was Ezran fall next to him before his eyes rolled up into the back of his head and he fell unconscious.

Rylan woke up groaning. His head was pounding and felt like the size of a watermelon. He sat up and felt a steady, rhythmic rocking. Slowly and carefully, he opened his eyes and took in their surroundings. "Fuck," he cursed as the brightness of the sun increased the pounding in his head. Lurching forward, he vomited between two wooden poles. They were in a cage, trapped like animals. They were prisoners of war.

The cage was being transported in a large wagon. It was made from a unique wood only grown in the elven lands. Nedlewood. A wood that was light and malleable but became stronger than steel when imbued with magic. Rylan's keen eyesight had automatically distinguished the intricately carved runes engraved into the wood. Escape was impossible.

He pulled his hood up, shielding his eyes from the glare of the sun. Slowly turning his head, his eyes roamed and took everything in. They were travelling along the Blood Road in the middle of a convoy. A line of supply wagons travelled behind them laden with resources, tools, food, crates of weapons and barrels of whisky, wine and ale. They were numerous, going back as far as the eye could see. Elven warriors rode on either side of the wagons, protecting their precious cargo. His worst fears had been confirmed. It was an elven army. King Therondal was declaring war.

As they rode over a large rock in the road, the cage was jolted violently. A groan caught his attention. It was Ezran slowly regaining consciousness. Raff and Frey were in the cage as well, lying face down. Whether they were unconscious or dead, he didn't know. Rylan only hoped that

Harold and Gwethren were okay. Hopefully they had left Balgleen and were enroute to Sethanon to inform the king.

"I see that you are finally awake. Would you like some water?" an elf said, as he rode up next to the wagon. He handed Rylan a canteen through the bars. Even though the elf had his hood up, Rylan noticed the faint sparkle of the crown underneath.

"Thank you, Therondal," Rylan replied, grabbing the canteen. Laughing, the elf threw back his hood. He had long, silvery hair that mostly hung down to his lower back. A small, tightly woven braid hung over each shoulder. On his head he wore a simple, yet elegant crown made from white gold. The crown was embedded with sparkling diamonds. Therondal's green eyes sparkled mischievously.

"Well spotted, ranger. With keen eyesight like that you should be an elf."

"If you already know that we are part of the king's rangers, then why capture us and lock us in a cage. It is a declaration of war," Rylan said as calmly as he could.

"Were you invited? No! You were trespassing in elven territory. Yet you speak about the elves declaring war." Therondal huffed at the notion. The elven king was getting angry. Rylan needed to be diplomatic.

* * *

"Your elves crossed the border, unprovoked and attacked. We were only investigating your intent. We were trying to avoid a war," Rylan stated.

"My elves were trying to retrieve our divinity stone. A stone that was stolen from us and is now in your king's hands," Therondal spat. This was not going well.

"Erithen won't stand for this. Release us now and avoid any bloodshed," Rylan said. Therondal laughed.

"Erithen is dead. We are on our way to attend his funeral and Prince Jace's coronation. Your fate rests on whether they return our divinity stone. If they don't, you and your fellow rangers will die. The human princes will be publicly executed and Sethanon will burn. There will officially be war between our kingdoms." With that Therondal rode off, leaving Rylan with the canteen.

Jace sat on the throne exhausted. For the last couple of nights, his sleep had been restless. He'd opted not to take the sleeping elixirs since they dulled his mind and left him feeling sleepy. He had been stressed ever since his father and a dozen guards had disappeared. Guards had reported an explosion so catastrophic that it was rumoured that the ground trembled throughout the city. Jace naturally feared the worst.

* * *

Houses had been damaged and the guards had been dealing with complaints from irate citizens. It had taken a day before they found the ruined remains of the townhouse shop that the king had been investigating. Half the guards had been dispatched to dig through the rubble and debris. That had been two days ago. They had made significant progress and had recovered the bodies of eight of the soldiers, but there was still no sign of the king.

Jace looked at the sword resting by the throne. Caz had delivered it to the castle when Jace did not pick it up. He had apologised profusely, but Caz had merely smiled, waving away the apology, understanding that Jace was stressed and had a lot on his mind. Caz had inserted the ruby into the pommel, wrapped the hilt, binding it in dark leather strips and shaped each side of the guard to resemble screeching gryphon heads. The blacksmith had truly outdone himself. The sword was magnificent.

General Iryss and Varyn Kabel stood to his side, resolute statues, silent and watchful. Stryxen was quietly playing with his blocks behind them while humming a song that Jace didn't recognise. The young prince's tutor was sick, so the responsibility of his education fell upon Kabel. The varyn had tasked him to build a castle, claiming that he was educating his young pupil in various mathematical concepts. When Jace had pointed out that neither he nor Zane had received fun educational activities such as this, the varyn had merely shrugged.

The varyn and general were there to give guidance and counsel. The doors banged open, echoing in the hall. A guard burst through, running forward and kneeling before the prince. "My liege, I bring news from the dig site," he said, panting for breath. Jace was still getting accustomed to being called 'liege'. It was a term only used to address his father, the king. His role had become that of a regent though, a temporary king until his father was found or he was sworn in. Even though he had been groomed for the role, he was anxious and stressed, feeling that he was far from ready to be king.

"We have recovered the guard's remains but found no trace of your father. We did find some black dust scattered amongst the remains like the dust that was found at the queen's resting place." Well, that confirmed it. The king was dead. The demonic dust: the same that his mother had. He was sure that neither of them had been Malgorath though. The demon prince was still lurking amongst them. Malgorath could secretly be residing in him, his brothers, the guards or even the peasants? They were no closer to knowing his identity.

Jace thumped the armrest out of unbridled anger and frustration, knocking the sword and sending it crashing to the floor. "My father is dead." Tears streamed down his eyes. Even though he was a demon, Jace had loved him, nonetheless.

"We can continue the search, my liege," stated the guard, looking up.

Jace halted him. "To continue searching is pointless. It is futile to search for something we'll never find," he said, wiping away the tears. He needed to be strong.

"The king is lost to us. Until he returns, Prince Jace is your new king," Iryss commanded. "Inform the guards to cease the search and return to the castle." The guard nodded.

"Your highness," he said, nodding and saluting Jace with a thump of his breastplate. Turning around, he left to relay the message.

"I'll organise for the king's funeral to be organised in two weeks' time," Kabel said, contemplating a schedule. "Your coronation can be afterwards. With your consent my liege, I will draft a letter, magically reproduce it and send them via raven." Jace gave him a brief nod. He walked over to a large desk with a quill, ink pot and a stack of parchment. Jace remembered his father being annoyed at Kabel for going to his room to draft letters. Irritated, he had ordered a wooden desk be made for him and set up in the throne room. All the king's business was now done there.

The wooden chair creaked as he sat down. Dipping the quill,

he began writing. Jace and Iryss watched silently, allowing him to concentrate. Jace couldn't help but smirk. The varyn had a quirk of humming while he wrote. The prince had always found it amusing. "Your father gave me this before he left. He wanted me to safeguard it. It was almost like he knew that he was about to die," Iryss said, handing him a document. It had been sealed in wax with the king's stamp, which was now neatly cut in half. The general had read the contents of the document before handing it to the prince. He knew what it said and was making sure Jace abided by it.

Jace opened the document and read it. *'Upon my unforeseen death, Zane Everthorn is to be beheaded at Jace's coronation.'* He paled unable to believe what he was reading. It was even signed *Erithen Everthorn.* Shocked, Jace reread it. He couldn't believe it. Even in death, his father had ensured Zane's execution. Jace nodded, teary eyed and handed back the document. Jace had thought that he could somehow save his brother, but it was impossible. There was nothing he could do. Their father had sealed his fate.

"I have finished, my liege," Kabel said proudly. He read it to Jace who nodded his approval.

His mind was numb and he had only been half listening. Satisfied, the varyn began to mumble an incantation. Magical ink from the pot sprayed onto the pile of parchment, copying the original invitation word for word, the printing perfect and precise. "I will summon the rook master, my liege." Kabel beckoned to one of the guards standing at the door.

The guard ran over and Kabel gave him his instructions. "How many invitations will you be sending out?" Jace mumbled, coming out of his stupor and looking at the varyn.

"Fifty, my liege. We will send them to the kings, queens and nobles of the elvish, dwarven, gnomish, sandrigar, werewolf and vampire nations. Even though we are technically at peace, I would still recommend excluding the gorkin, orcs and the naga." Both Jace and Iryss nodded their agreement. He didn't know how long it was before the guard arrived with the rook master. His mind was still reeling from the news of his brother's execution. The only solution that he could think of was to delay the funeral or postpone his coronation.

Jace looked up, startled as the thick wooden door burst open and the guard entered, escorting the flustered rook master. "Why have you summoned me, my liege? I have sent the documents regarding the king's funeral and your coronation as requested. All the ravens are enroute now."

"All the ravens?" Jace asked, confused.

"Yes. All the ravens to the kings, queens, nobles and generals. Even the high lord of the Brotherhood and the Emperor of the Orc Empire are receiving invitations. Prince

Zane delivered the invitations yesterday afternoon and we worked all night and sent the ravens off on their errand." The raven master looked perplexed and confused.

"I've only just written out the invitations," Kabel screamed. "What do you mean Zane delivered them to you yesterday?"

"Exactly that!" the rook master screamed back. "Prince Zane informed me of the king's death. He said that his imprisonment had been a misunderstanding. That he had been pardoned." Jace gripped the armrest of the throne. This was an absolute nightmare.

"Guards!" Iryss yelled. "Check on Zane's whereabouts. If he has escaped, hunt him down and bring him here in shackles. I will behead him myself." He turned on Jace, his eyes wild and full of anger, daring Jace to question his authority. Jace's eyes blazed golden, lighting up the throne room. The magic surged through him in a torrent, but he controlled it. He had learnt calming techniques, how to control it and rein it in. But at the moment he didn't care, so he left it raging through him, unbridled.

"I will talk to my brother personally," he said, his words a threat, his voice as quiet as a whisper. The guards looked fearfully between their regent and the general. Jace's eyes returned to their normal colour and he addressed the guards with a smile. "Could you please escort my brother to me immediately, so that we can address this matter." The guards nodded and briskly walked out the door.

Jace could hear the rattling even before they entered the throne room. They still insisted on Zane wearing manacles; still thought that he posed a threat. He briefly turned to the general but refrained from saying anything, because he already knew the answer. He knew exactly what the general would say. The guards entered, walking on either side of Zane as the condemned prince walked with his shoulders slumped and looking towards the ground. Jace almost didn't recognise his brother. His normally well groomed, brushed hair was unkempt and hanging down his face. His posture was that of a broken man. What the hell had happened to him?

Then Zane looked up and in a startling revelation Jace realised why. His face was bleeding and swollen. He was battered and bruised. The king's regent leapt to his feet, outraged. "Who did this to my brother?" Jace screamed.

"I ordered the guards to interrogate Zane. He was responsible for your mother's death and I have no doubt that he is responsible for your father's," Iryss stated calmly. Wild magic surging through him, Jace clenched his fist tightly and swung his arm in a back handed blow. The wild magic glowed, making his fist as hard as iron. The general's face crumpled as bones shattered and blood sprayed everywhere. The blow knocked the general back a step and he wobbled on his feet, but he refused to fall and show any sign of weakness. Glaring at Jace and spitting out a mouthful of blood, Iryss went for his sword.

"Are you going to draw a weapon on your future king?" Jace asked. The two guards started advancing, their own gauntleted hands resting on the hilts of their swords. Kabel was mumbling an incantation, a precautionary measure in case the regent didn't have the situation under control. The general's eyes darted nervously, taking all this in. Dripping blood, his hand rested on the sword hilt, gripping it tightly.

"No, my liege. I would never draw a weapon against my king," he replied finally, spitting out another mouthful of blood. Stryxen quietly stood and handed the general a handkerchief. In his heightened magical state, Jace thought the handkerchief was mottled with black dots. Blinking to clear his head, Jace watched as the general nodded his thanks to the young prince. Bringing it to his face, he wiped away the blood. Within seconds the handkerchief was saturated and the black dots were gone, as if they were a figment of Jace's imagination.

"How long has this treatment been going on?" Jace asked calmly.

"For two days. Ever since the king disappeared," Iryss replied, confused by the question.

"Prince Zane didn't look like this when he came to me," the

rook master stammered.

"Exactly," Jace said smugly, making his point. "The person who sent out the invitations was an imposter. It was Malgorath in disguise. Which means my brother is innocent!"

"Your brother is still going to be beheaded. It was the king's last command before his death. He has it in writing. It is law!" Iryss stated, getting out the king's letter once again. Kabel calmly grabbed it off the general and adjusting his glasses, unfolded the parchment and read it.

"The evidence is there to prove Zane's innocence," Jace shouted, frustrated.

"Maybe, my liege. But this is the last documented command by the king. We need to abide by it, it is law. To deny and disregard it is treason," Kabel explained, as he folded the parchment back up and handed it to the general. Kabel had always been fair and loyal, he was the voice of reason. Jace ground his teeth, a bad habit that he did whenever he was anxious. He had tried diplomacy, arguing and reasoning with them. It was futile, it hadn't worked. He was left with only one option.

Dregga gracefully landed, tucking his wings in and bounding into the cave. The nightwing almost bowled over Roxy, who bounded forward with her tail wagging. For the most part, the two had been inseparable. Athelaine dismounted gracefully while Darla sat in her saddle grinning as she waved something at them. "You actually got it," Vexlan said in disbelief. Darla didn't say a word. She dismounted, ran over to Vexlan and handed him the prized parchment.

The parchment was highly detailed and had a broken, red wax seal. It was an invitation to the king's funeral and Prince Jace's coronation. When one of Vexlan's contacts had notified him about the invitations and its contents, Darla and Athelaine had mounted Dregga and taken flight for Crystril. The Lady Roselyn had automatically received an invitation, being one of the king's vassals. Darla had immediately taken advantage of the situation, calling in the favour that Lady Roselyn owed her.

They had organised to meet at a dress shop and secretly return Lady Roselyn's invitation. The tailor who owned the shop catered for the nobility and upper-class citizens, designing modern and very expensive dresses and lingerie. Jocelyne and Vexlan had lent the two assassins a considerable sum. The two women had spent hours in the shop, trying on various styles. The dresses they eventually chose were both stylish and practical for their purposes. They needed to be altered and adjusted, so they had organised to pick them up on the day of the event.

Darla had cut the top of a small boulder with the short

sword. The mystical weapon sliced through it, creating a smooth, flat surface. It made for an ideal desk for Vexlan to work at. Reaching into his pack, he got out a variety of ink, a quill, parchment, a used red candle and a wooden block that was already engraved with the king's seal. Vexlan had forged the king's documents before and was well prepared. Placing everything in a neat orderly pile, he adjusted his glasses and got to work.

Vexlan excitedly started writing on the parchment, singing a song. *'The naga slithered and snuck, like a quacking duck'*. Athelaine placed her hand across her mouth to muffle her giggle. It wasn't any known song or well-known ballad. It was whatever Vexlan thought of and to make matters worse, he couldn't sing so it was out of tune.

Chapter 18

Raiff stood upon the main deck of his warship, looking through the spyglass and grumbling. His ship was named after the majestic, predatory bird on his figurehead. The Seahawk. His ship was smaller than other warships and didn't have the armour or the firepower that other warships consisted of, but it was sleeker. It was more manoeuvrable and was the fastest ship in the fleet.

* * *

He looked again watching and anticipating. There was definitely something out there. The ripples in the water gave it away. Whatever it was, it was large, fast and moving towards the fleet. The general's command ship in the centre of the fleet was a behemoth of a warship, making Raiff's look like a child's toy. The general had named it the Juggernaut, an appropriate name compared to its size and its immense firepower.

Two other warships were sailing at the front. While two other warships took up the rear position along with a large cargo ship which followed slowly behind the generals. The nimble Seahawk was tagging along as a scout, a spotter for any potential dangers they may come across. The general had informed him that when they arrived, the other four warships would wait out in the open sea and only be called upon if needed. Raiff didn't buy it. He wondered whether the emperor was just using the opportunity to secure the capital city and start another invasion.

He felt a massive hand on his shoulder and turned to face Jarl. The big, well-muscled orc was his second-in-command. He was the quartermaster, a close friend and could tell Raiff was worried. "What is it, Capt'n?" he asked, concerned.

"I'm not sure," Raiff replied, as the ripples got closer. "Prepare the boom guns." Jarl nodded and turning around, walked down the steps to the main deck. He didn't want to raise the alarm because there would be consequences if he was wrong. A fellow captain had made that mistake once, thinking there was some kind of sea monster about to attack and it had turned out to be a large underwater rock. The general had sliced open the captain's jaw and demoted him. It had never healed properly and left the orc with a speech impediment. Raiff didn't want to make the same mistake. There was only one thing to do. Spinning the wheel, he turned the Seahawk and put it onto a course straight towards the ripples.

"Prepare the boom guns on the port side," Jarl bellowed, relaying the command. The boom guns were a gnomish invention. The large barrel was made from a combination of bronze and iron and could be loaded with a hollow iron ball filled with an explosive liquid. The balls had to be loaded carefully. Although robust and solid, there had been instances where drunken orcs had been clumsy, dropping the iron ball, causing an explosion and sinking their own ship.

Through a series of magical runes engraved in the barrel, the iron ball was then propelled at the target at a high velocity, exploding on impact. This was the reason why they had been cautious and not loaded the starboard boom guns. There had been an incident a few years ago when a warship misaimed their boom gun and accidently sunk an orc fishing boat. The orc captain and his entire crew had been executed. It was publicly demonstrated and declared by the emperor as orcish law.

* * *

Although the barrels could be manoeuvred using a mechanical gear system, it was a timely process. Spinning the wheel, Raiff turned the ship towards the port side. The sleek warship turned easily, gliding through the water and positioning the boom guns directly at the ripples. He could hear the crew grunting as they loaded the iron balls into the six barrels. The ripples were fast, speeding up and heading straight towards the general's massive command ship. "Goblin crap," he cursed, adjusting his course. There was too much of a risk of hitting the general's ship.

He veered the sleek ship and headed towards the nearest ripples. Raiff had an inkling of what was causing the ripples, but he needed to confirm it. The ship glided harmlessly through the ripples. There was no collision, no attack. There was nothing.

The ripples dispersed just like that, into gentle waves lapping against the hulls of the ships. Then without any warning, fountains of water sprayed into the air around them, spraying onto the deck and rocking the ship as it glided through the sea. Giant tentacles erupted out of the water, snaking into the air. The tentacles were a deep purple with a greyish underside that were lined with black knobs and suckers. "Kraken," Raiff yelled in warning. Reacting to the warning, the helmsmen aboard the other ships began evasive manoeuvres.

* * *

He spun the wheel to the right and then to the left, skimming across the water. Tentacles were erupting all around him. He looked for the ripples, the signs that gave away the tentacles' position. The two warships at the rear had already been obliterated. One minute they were there and then they were gone, wiped from existence, sunk into the deep dark abyss of the ocean. Whether it was the result of the tentacles or the ships colliding with each other, nobody knew. Raiff had prewarned the general that having the fleet in formation and so close together was dangerous, but all it had earned him was a reprimand. The warning had been given but had gone on deaf ears. And now, there was utter chaos because of that decision.

Being closed into a tight formation had proven to be disastrous. Raiff cringed as he watched the Juggernaut slowly turn and scrape against the hull of one of the warships. Some of the crewmen were thrown overboard as the warship tipped sideways, before righting itself. The skilled helmsman had avoided near disaster. He tried to turn the warship away, only for a massive spray of water to slam it back against the command ship. Erupting out of the water, the tentacle smashed down. The warship had nowhere to go. Wood shattered as the ship was torn in half. Orc crewmen could be seen floundering in the water, screaming for help. They were as good as dead. No ship would risk stopping and trying to save them. To do so would be certain death for the captain and his crew.

* * *

The tentacle slammed into the Juggernaut, cracking the wood and putting a hole in its hull. The warship had shielded the command vessel, protecting it from further damage. Another tentacle emerged joining the first and stretched up to the sky. They looked like giant tree trunks, toppling as they both came slamming down. The command ship's boom guns roared in unison. A deafening roar that sent their payload of explosive iron balls rocketing towards the tentacles.

The iron balls exploded on impact, the first one causing a chain reaction and detonating the others. The tentacles were close, impossible to miss. The massive explosion tore the tenacles apart, raining fleshy globs into the ocean. Water cascaded around them as the kraken's head emerged out of the water. Its eyes roamed, taking in the scene, before glaring at the command ship. The Seahawk hadn't warranted the kraken's attention yet. Raiff was about to change that. "By the gods, the kraken is even uglier than you Jarl and that's saying something," he said, teasing his friend. Jarl merely laughed, a deep rumbling chuckle.

Spraying up water, the Seahawk skimmed across the ocean heading straight towards the Juggernaut and the cargo ship. With a spray of water, a tentacle rose in front of them. Spinning the wheel, the Seahawk glided, cutting through a wave and tilting to the side. It dodged nimbly, avoiding the tentacle as it flicked, slapping the position where the ship had been only moments before.

* * *

Two more tentacles rose, erupting from the depths. Instead of rising high into the air though, they slithered, weaving across the ocean and wrapped themselves around the large, slow moving cargo ship. It lifted the massive ship into the air as if it were a toy and weighed nothing. From the vantage point of the Juggernaut's poop deck, the general and the emperor watched the scene unfold. "Fire," Jarl yelled.

"Delay that order," Raiff shouted. The boom guns remained silent. His quartermaster looked at him questioningly, concerned. "I will take full responsibility," he said, turning the wheel and positioning the Seahawk. Flinging its tentacles forward, the kraken threw the cargo ship straight at the Juggernaut. Orcs flew from the ship screaming as the ship spun end over end, before crashing into the centre of the Juggernaut. Wood shattered as the deck and hull were obliterated and the ship was torn in half like some child's broken toy. Both halves bobbed in the ocean as water flooded into the hull and they began to sink.

"Fire," Raiff screamed as a tentacle erupted out of the water on the starboard side, spraying the deck and rocking the boat. The half a dozen boom guns on the port side roared to life, sending their explosive payload straight towards the kraken's head. Raiff cursed. The rocking had caused the shots to go askew. The giant tentacle rose into the air and was about to come crashing down.

* * *

Two of the iron balls fell short and two soared over the kraken. The tentacle began its deadly decent. The remaining two hit the kraken in the lower part of its head. Severely injured, the kraken submerged and the tentacle waved askew, smashing through the forward mast. The mast toppled overboard, taking the crewman in the crow's nest with it. Jarl was at the railing in an instant throwing a rope overboard. Unlike the other warships, it was Raiff's motto that none of his crew got left behind. Whether the kraken was dead he didn't know. Grunting, he steered the Seahawk towards the sinking Juggernaut, ready to rescue the survivors and face his punishment.

He pulled alongside the bottom end of the Juggernaut. Most of it was sunk, with only the masts and the poop deck visible. The orc and the naga leaders and their delegations were grouped tightly together. Jarl let out a low chuckle. It was almost comical. Even though the orcs and naga were allies, they barely tolerated each other at the best of times. A brutish orc and his ogre companion were the only thing separating the two delegations. Stepping forward, the orc stepped on the naga queen's swishing tail. The queen wailed in pain. "Watch where you step, you orcish oaf. Otherwise, my royal guards will dice you up and feed you to the fish," she hissed.

"You will address me as General Chalgar, you worthless half breed snake," the orc spat. His hand went to his sword as the two royal guards flanking their queen reared, their broad, barbed spears pointed threateningly at the orc general. The spears glistened with naga venom. The venom was deadly, causing excruciating pain and was considered lethal to most of the races on Aragoth. The general remained unphased, ignoring the eminent threat. A huge shadow loomed before them all. The ogre quartermaster was nine feet tall and very imposing. Chalgar's tusks curved inward as he smiled wickedly. "I'd be careful with your threats, snake queen. Ugrin hasn't eaten yet and he likes eating snakes."

Jarl carefully lowered the plank onto the edge of the poop deck. He secured his end to the hull of the Seahawk. "Snakes yummy. Ugrin wants to eat snake," the ogre roared, brandishing his huge, spiked club. "Ugrin smash snakes, make them all gooey and mushy. Then Ugrin spread it on bread and eat it." The ogre looked around confused. "Where bread Chalgar. Ugrin need bread if he going to eat snake." The emperor laughed, amused and began walking up the plank with his bung foot clanking as he walked. It was a deformity that he had been born with. When asked if it impeded his fighting he had simply replied *"I am the brains of the empire, I leave the fighting to my general and his army."*

"Why Emperor Ferek laugh?" Ugrin asked.

"Because Ugrin can't eat snake. He's going to have to catch fish to eat," Chalgar replied, annoyed.

* * *

"But Ugrin sick of fish. He had fish yesterday," the ogre complained. Chalgar ignored the ogre's whining and proceeded up the plank after the emperor. He had made Ugrin his quartermaster because of the fact that he was a stupid thug. He was all brawn and very little brains, which is the way Chalgar liked it. The ogre would intimidate and keep the crew in line, but never question orders. Raiff on the other hand preferred having someone that was his equal as a quartermaster.

The general stormed up the plank behind the emperor. "You will be executed for allowing the Juggernaut to be sunk," he accused, glaring at Raiff with his one good eye. Chalgar had lost his eye and received a nasty scar from a slash from his opponents battle axe. A drunken orc had sliced his hand open and slammed it down on the large wooden table, smearing it with blood. It was a challenge, a one-on-one fight for the leadership, the honour of being bestowed the rank of general. Chalgar had sliced his hand open and placed it on top of the smear accepting the challenge.

Even with one eye, he had killed the challenger, cutting off both of his arms and then his head. It was brutal, an example of what would happen to anyone that dared challenge him. He now wore an eyepatch with twin axes crossing over each other engraved onto it. It was the royal insignia of the orcs, made especially for him by the emperor. Chalgar wore it with pride. After all, he was the emperor's general, his right-hand and cousin.

* * *

"Why? I'm just following orcish law. If I had fired on the orc cargo ship, it would have warranted the execution of me and my crew," Raiff replied, shrugging. Jarl chuckled next to him, amused by the exchange. The emperor laughed as well, but the look he gave Raiff was far from pleasant. Raiff had outsmarted the emperor, used his own laws against him. The emperor had been humiliated and there was going to be consequences.

"Even though you didn't personally destroy the Juggernaut. You were still involved in its destruction. You could have saved the ship, but you chose not to," Ferek stated, pondering the situation. "Your crew shall live, but you will be executed.

"Emperor Ferek," Jarl mumbled, conflicted and partly regretting getting involved. He was loyal though and had to defend his captain.

The emperor looked at the quartermaster, his eyebrows raised. He wasn't used to being questioned. "Do you want to join your captain in death. Do you?"

"No sire. I'm just questioning his punishment. Captain Hargl's warship fled the battle when they could also have offered assistance. Captain Raiff however attacked the kraken which posed a greater threat. He then came to your immediate rescue." The emperor reflected on this new information. The quartermaster had proven to be insightful and loyal, qualities that he respected and admired.

"You are lucky to have such an honourable and loyal quartermaster," Ferek said. "Chase down and sink the fleeing warship. I won't have cowards in my general's army." Raiff nodded in agreement, not daring to say anything. "Taking what your quartermaster said into account, your punishment will be the loss of a hand. You may choose which one." Raiff instantly held out his left hand. Grinning sadistically, the general drew his broad sword. With a single swipe, he lopped off the captain's hand.

Dark purple blood sprayed onto the deck amidst Raiff's severed hand. Ripping off his black tunic, he quickly wrapped it around the stump. "I'm going below decks to cauterise the wound. The cabin is yours, my emperor," he said bowing low. He turned to the naga queen. "You may sleep in my quartermaster's room. The mattress is bigger and it should accommodate…. your physique." It was the most diplomatic thing he could come up with.

Queen Shylar was the youngest naga queen in history. Like the orcs, the naga challenged for supremacy. She had trained young, practicing night and day. When it came time to challenge her mother, she had honed her skills, speed, strength and stamina to extraordinary levels. She had not only taken the throne but defended her right to be queen on six different occasions. Shylar smiled and nodded politely to the captain, her long red hair dancing as if it had a life of its own.

As he ran down the stairs two at a time, Jarl turned the wheel. The Seahawk veered gracefully, skimming across the water and chased down the other warship. Opening the hatch, Raiff quickly ran down the stairs. He was already starting to feel lightheaded. He had only a matter of moments before he would bleed out. As he quietly passed the hammocks, he heard a deep, rumbling snore. The orc had been on the night shift, but Raiff marvelled at how he had managed to sleep through the entire kraken attack. The other nineteen orcs that had also been on the sleep shift, were scattered around the hull sleeping in their hammocks.

The orc captain grumbled as he made his way to the door at the back of the hull. It had been a while since he'd had to sleep in a hammock, but due to the circumstances, he and Jarl would be sleeping in the hull tonight. His quartermaster would not be happy. Ever since his promotion, he'd got use to his large, comfy bed. Navigating his way past the hammocks, his vision started to blur and his legs felt wobbly. Even though he was trying to stem the flow of blood, he was leaving a steady trail along the floor. He was losing blood fast. He couldn't help it. His legs gave out and he started to fall.

A strong hand grabbed him, hauling him back to his feet. "Let's get you to Bungle and get that stump cauterised," Jarl said, smiling as he wrapped his captain's arm around his shoulder. Supported by his friend, they made their way to the door. "Who knows, maybe Bungle might have some kind of mechanical gadget that he could attach to your stump." He knocked loudly on the door. "Maybe a giant metal claw. We can call you Captain Crabby." He laughed at his own joke.

The giant crabs, local to the northern part of the Jardoshian Empire, were a delicacy and his favourite food. Smaller crabs could be caught in the Yavel and Kaspien Seas, but Jarl hadn't had the opportunity to drop his large rectangular crab pot. The door opened and a small red, orange and purple haired gnome stood in the doorway. His hair was spiky as if he had been electrocuted, making him look like some kind of eccentric scientist. Apparently, it had resulted from one of his failed experiments. The gnome was an outcast they had stumbled upon during one of their raids. The orc protocol was to kill without question, but Raiff had taken a liking to the little fellow.

He had proven his worth and become a valued crew member. He was a tinkerer, scientist and the ship's medic. Raiff had created this little section of the ship, out of the way and hidden from prying eyes. If the emperor found out about him, there would be consequences. Even though Bungle was isolated though, he was happy. "Good to see you, captain. Looks like you have gotten yourself into quite a predicament," he said, looking over his wire-rimmed glasses.

* * *

The gnome moved aside as Jarl led the captain into his room. The room was perfectly square and attached to the hull. Raiff had spent a small fortune having it specially made. Surprisingly though, he found that the gnome's little hideaway actually reinforced the integrity of the hull. In the centre of the room was a large wooden workbench, which Bungle was quickly clearing. Along three of the walls were rows upon rows of shelves. Some of the shelves consisted of contraptions and inventions while others consisted of books, vials, jars and various building resources. The remaining wall consisted of a wardrobe and a small bed, table and chair.

His muscles bulging, Jarl lifted the captain up, cradling him like a child and carried him across to the gnome's workbench. The large workbench was the only thing sturdy enough to accommodate the orc's bulk and size. "I do apologise, captain, but this is going to hurt like the seven hells," Bungle said, pulling down a small contraption from a shelf. The contraption was compact, made of various metals and had a glass cylinder filled with a red liquid. The liquid was similar to the liquid that they used in the iron balls, explosive and highly flammable.

The result was what the gnome called his 'Little Flamer.' Pulling a lever, he ignited a small orange flame. He waited patiently until the bright flame turned blue, growing in heat and intensity. Gently, turning the flamer as if he were cooking, he cauterised the wound. His eyes bulging from intense pain, Raiff ground his teeth together refusing to scream. If the emperor heard him scream, it would demonstrate a sign of weakness. Raiff dreaded to think what the repercussions would be for that. The pain was excruciating. He opened his mouth as if to scream, but before any sound could come out, his eyes rolled back in his head. His body limp, the captain fell unconscious.

Raiff woke up with a start, to the deafening sound of the boom guns. Even without a mast, the Seahawk had managed to get within shooting range. The sound resided to be replaced by a faint whistling, the sound of the iron balls shooting through the air. Then there was a loud explosion. Wood cracked and screams could be heard as the crew were either burnt alive or left to drown. The emperor had made good on his promise. The warship was destroyed.

The captain sat up on the workbench, wincing as he knocked the stump. It was bandaged tightly but the end was discoloured a bright yellow. "I spread an antiseptic paste on the wound to keep away infection," Bungle said walking over.

Raiff nodded and standing up, gently patted the gnome on the shoulder. "Thank you, Bungle. You saved my life."

"You're welcome, captain, but please take it easy for a few days and allow the wound time to heal."

* * *

The Seahawk captain laughed as he opened the door. "I can't promise you that Bungle, but I'll try." He ran towards the captain holding out a vial of greenish-blue liquid.

"Take this. It will numb the pain and help you sleep." Raiff nodded his thanks and smiling, the gnome added excitedly. "I've also been working on a gadget that you can attach to the stump on your wrist. I got the idea while you were sleeping captain. I still need to tweak the automatic loader and adjust the gears and the spring loading mechanism, but I think you'll like it." The captain looked confused. It was beyond his comprehension and completely baffled him. "When it's finished, it will help you with your whomping, smashing and killing." Raiff smiled. Now the gnome was speaking his language.

Raiff bid the gnome goodnight and closing the door went to his hammock. It took him three attempts, but he finally managed to get into the damn thing. Adjusting his pillow, he tried to get comfortable and closing his eyes, readied himself for a restless night's sleep. A few minutes later, he heard the opening of the hatch and the clanking of the footsteps that followed. He opened his eyes to see Emperor Ferek standing by his hammock. "Your quartermaster has informed me that the kraken attack and the broken mast is going to delay our time of arrival. I need you to send a raven to the human Prince Jace to inform him of our predicament and notify him that we are going to be late."

* * *

Grumbling, Raiff sat up. "I'll need access to my cabin so that I can get the parchment, ink and sit at my desk to scribe it." Smirking, the emperor handed him a piece of parchment, an ink pot and a quill.

"You're resourceful, captain. Do it down here and bring it up when you have finished." With that, he left. Raiff waited until the clanking subsided and the hatch closed. Then climbing out of the hammock, he got a lantern, lay on the floor and got to work. The message was short and stated the facts. Climbing up the stairs, he opened the hatch and walked to the cage behind his cabin. Getting some twine, he rolled the message tightly and tied it to the raven's leg. "Safe travels, my friend," he said releasing the raven into the air. Flapping its wings, the raven flew away into the night.

As the captain walked back around the side of his cabin, he peeked through the slits of the shutters on his window. The emperor was already curled up in his bed, softly snoring and fast asleep. Grumbling, Raiff opened the hatch and went back to his hammock. Climbing into it he heard a slight clank. Reaching into his pocket, he pulled out the glass vial. He had forgotten all about it. Unstoppering it, he gulped it down. He didn't even have time to adjust his pillow and get comfortable before he was fast asleep.

Chapter 19

Darla and Athelaine walked along the cobblestone road giggling, with their arms linked. Their hoods were up, covering most of their features and hiding them in shadow. Two guards nodded politely in greeting as they walked by on patrol. "Morning," Darla replied as she casually glanced at them.

* * *

"You're so flirtatious," Athelaine chided, nudging her friend playfully before giggling. Darla was still a wanted woman, still had a bounty on her head. It made the perfect disguise and gave them free reign of the city. They overlooked her because of Athelaine. They were on the lookout for a solitary woman that was armed and dangerous, not a pair of women giggling in the street.

"Darla darling. It's been forever since we've seen you," a third woman said jovially as she ran up and embraced Darla. It was Lady Roselyn. Her face beaming, Darla couldn't help but notice the horrific scar. Even after countless healing sessions, her jaw had never set properly. It was a constant reminder of what she had endured. A young five-year-old boy stood next to her; his blonde hair neatly combed.

The boy was tall for his age due to his heritage. His father had been a bandit leader that was nicknamed the 'Troll.' He had been about eight feet tall. Whether he truly was a half-breed troll, or just a freak of nature, Darla didn't know. His genetics had obviously passed onto Lady Roselyn's son though. Beaming from ear to ear, he embraced Darla in a hug. "Hello Aunty Darla. It is good to finally meet you. Thank you for rescuing my mum all those years ago."

"You're very welcome," she replied, feeling slightly awkward and not quite knowing what to say.

"I hope you don't mind. Considering everything that we've

been through, I considered you an aunty to Kerin," Roselyn replied, embarrassed.

"I'm honoured," Darla said, smiling as Kerin released her and took a step back. As well as tall and well-built, the boy was also extremely polite. Roselyn had done well, grooming and raising him by herself. He already had the beginnings of becoming a fine lord. Darla nodded her approval, impressed. "Athelaine, I would like to introduce you to Lady Roselyn." To the untrained eye, it appeared as if Darla had merely pointed towards Roselyn with her hand, while gently brushing her cloak. The movement was both quick and fluid, flawlessly executed.

Reaching into her cloak pocket, Roselyn withdrew the invitation that had appeared only moments before. "I take it you ladies are also attending the king's memorial and Prince Jace's coronation?" she asked excitedly.

"Definitely," Darla and Athelaine replied in unison, pulling out their own invitations and giggling.

"Then let's go and buy some new outfits for the occasion," Roselyn said, pirouetting and leading the way. The whole encounter was a performance, scripted and played out to perfection. It provided them with a way of returning Roselyn's invitation without attracting any unwanted attention.

* * *

A short stroll around the corner and they were standing out the front of an elaborate two-storey building. The building had large windows of panelled glass with wooden mannequins dressed in expensive, fashionable dresses displayed for all to see. A painted wooden sign with intricate gold writing was fastened above the doorway. *Flessangerie,* short and abbreviated for Flamboyant Dresses and Lingerie. The name was catchy and suited the upper-class shop.

"I'm going to have a look in the toy store, mum," Kerin said, smiling and jiggling his money pouch. Roselyn gave him a hug. Waving, the young lord ran across the street, eager to spend his savings.

As they opened the door, a little brass bell chimed, announcing their presence. Roselyn stepped forward, leading the way. Dashing forward, the owner bowed gracefully. "Welcome to Flessangerie. My name is Lana and I am the owner of this fine establishment. What may I interest you ladies in today?" she asked politely. Darla couldn't help herself. She giggled as she threw back her hood.

"So polite, posh and formal," Darla teased. Both assassins knew Lana quite well. As well as being the owner of the predominant boutique store, she was also a Brotherhood operative.

"I wasn't addressing you or Athelaine. I was talking to the beautiful Lady Roselyn," Lana replied, as she fussed with

Roselyn's blondie brown coloured hair. Rushing off, she returned with three dresses draped over her arm. "These colours will look gorgeous on you." She handed her a dark blue, low-cut dress and guided her to an alcove to try it on. She then neatly draped a dark purple and maroon dress over a nearby chair. "Mira, could you please get Darla and Athelaine's bags from the cupboard behind the counter?" The young assistant rushed off as Darla and Athelaine proceeded towards the change room area.

Grabbing her bag, Darla nodded her thanks to the assistant. "Mira could you also please make our guests a cup of coffee?" Smiling, the assistant nodded.

"What? No cream buns to go with our coffee?" Darla jibed, with a wicked grin.

Lana rolled her eyes. "And could you also please get our guests a cream bun to go with their coffee?" Darla giggled as she opened her bag. Her aqua coloured dress was low cut with slits up the side. A dark brown leather belt accompanied it to accommodate for the pouch. The pouch contained the elven divinity stone and the wyvern's tooth. Both were important in their own right. It was too dangerous leaving them behind. Now she carried them everywhere she went.

Athelaine raised her eyebrows and smirked as she pulled out her sexy black lace lingerie. It was the perfect accessory to the sleek black dress that she was going to wear. Unlike her friend's sexy lingerie, Darla wore an elastic, gnomish-designed undergarment. It was practical and would apparently withstand her transformation. Even though it was a new upgraded design, it was yet to be tested. The number of outfits that she had to discard and burn due to them getting shredded with her transformation was astronomical. Darla clung to the slim sliver of hope that this one would withstand it, but she was sceptical.

All three women left the boutique in their new dresses. Lana had even sprayed Darla with some strong, exotic perfume. She claimed that it would mask her scent. The store owner then bagged their old clothes and stored them safely in the cupboard under lock and key.

The assassins wore their weapons strapped to their thighs. They felt naked without them and had a niggling feeling that they were going to need them before the end of the night. Kerin ran out beaming and waving around his new purchase. The toy sword was of the highest quality. It was carved from wood, had exquisite detail and came with a leather sheath. Running back and forth, he swished and swiped.

"When my busy schedule permits, I'll visit Crystril and give you some weapons training," Darla said, smiling. When things settled, she'd treat herself to a holiday. She deserved it. Unfortunately, she couldn't see it happening anytime soon.

* * *

"That would be great, Aunty Darla," Kerin screeched.

"You've committed yourself now," Athelaine said giggling. Darla nudged her friend playfully. Their jovial mood quickly vanished though as they found themselves outside the gate to the castle. His boots clanking on the cobblestones, one of the guards approached them. It was time to see if their counterfeit invitations worked.

A knock at the door startled him awake. Jace's sheets were a dishevelled heap. He yawned from exhaustion. His sleep had been restless and plagued with nightmares. It was the day of his father's funeral and his coronation. The day his brother would be executed. Climbing out of bed, he put on his robe and opened the door. "Good morning, Millie," he said pleasantly. Although subdued, his brother's ex-lover was back on household duties and was here to fill his bath.

"Could you please give this to Zane?" she said, handing him a handwritten note with trembling hands. "I love your brother Prince Jace, but I freaked out. He's not Malgorath, he didn't do those horrible things. Please! Don't let him be executed." She quickly ushered past him to fill up the bath. Jace couldn't help but notice the tears streaming down her face. Bending over, she carefully removed the half a dozen heat rocks from the fire using a pair of iron tongs. Carrying the red-hot heat rocks, she placed them in the compartment under the bath.

Jace's bath was different to his brothers. Even though it was slightly smaller, the plumbing was connected to piping that led to a freshwater lake. The result was water coming straight from the large tap. Fresh, clear sparkling water. The servants marvelled at how much easier it was, especially considering they didn't have to fill up a bucket. "Zane loves you too," he said smiling. "I will do what I can. But you can give this to him yourself." He smiled as he handed the note back. It was both the truth and a lie. He loved his brother and would do anything for him, including sacrificing himself but Zane's fate was sealed. There was no chance of a reprieve, or of getting him out of it. Jace had only one choice.

"Thank you," Millie replied, forcing a smile, as she turned on the tap. She threw in two round balls. One was an aromatic soap and the other consisted of relaxing herbs. The bath quickly filled as the water gushed out of the tap. When it was two-thirds full, she quickly turned the tap off. "Enjoy your bath, Prince Jace." She nodded and quietly left his room. Left to his solitude, Jace de-robed and slid into the warm soapy water. The bath was warm, just the way he liked it. Closing his eyes, Jace soaked and briefly forgot his troubles.

He got out and dressed in black pants, a dark blue shirt and a black jacket with gold stitching and gold buttons. The ensemble had been specially made for his coronation. The clothes were practical and suited the purpose, so Jace decided to wear them to the funeral as well. He refused to come back and get changed for his coronation.

He strapped the scabbard to his belt and hooked on a pouch. The pouch contained Zane's communication orb. He planned on giving it back to his brother. Looking in the mirror, he adjusted the position of the sword. It was the sword that he had planned on giving to his father, a sword that was fit for a king. It was his now and he was wearing it in homage of his father.

Shouting, cracking and thumping sounded. Jace glanced out the bedroom window, to see what the commotion was. It was a beautiful spring day and the rookies were having weapons practice. Wooden swords and shields smashed against each other as the rookies went through the progressive, arduous drills. All the while, Wesley stood to the side barking commands. Jace sighed, wishing he could be down there partaking in the drills instead of having to deal with the problems, dramas and responsibilities that he now faced.

His gaze wandered to the harbour and took in the ships that were moored there. The smaller ones were local fishing trawlers, who had already brought in their catch of the day. Some of the larger, uniquely designed ones were foreign. They belonged to the delegations from the various nations, who were here to attend the funeral and coronation. The dwarves had reluctantly opted to stay at the castle, but they insisted on stationing their own guards at the door. A heavy guard detail consisting of four dwarves guarding one door. They were taking every precaution.

The guards had reported that the elves had arrived with an army. They made the guards nervous and Jace couldn't blame them. Refusing to announce themselves at the castle, they had arrogantly walked past and booked accommodation at the Fox and Goose. It was a renown upper class inn near the castle, that if rumours were true was accommodating some of the other delegations as well. Had things become that strained between them? Were they on the brink of war?

Rylan and the scouts hadn't returned either. This worried him greatly. He just hoped that he could resolve the situation. Opening the bedroom door, he was immediately greeted by General Iryss and the two guards on duty. In tandem, the three of them thumped their breastplates in salute. "Good morning, my liege," Iryss said, with a brief nod.

Iryss had been to an expensive healer, a retired battle priest who had a little, cozy shop in the upper, richer part of Sethanon. Recognising Iryss for who he was, he automatically gave him a substantial discount. Paying the battle priest and lying down, Iryss had let the man get to work. The finished job had been less than satisfactory. Irate, the castle guards had to be called to escort their general out.

* * *

His face was fully healed, but also disfigured. The battle priest had tried to explain that the damage had been to extensive, but Iryss had refused to believe him. His jaw had widened and his nose had flattened, resembling that of a pig. There was a darkness in him now, a voice in his head, whispering and plotting revenge against the king. Smiling, the general walked beside his king, biding his time.

"Good morning, general," Jace replied, locking the door. He started walking at a brisk pace, heading for the church situated next to the western wall. The western gate was left open and manned continually. It allowed the populace entry for the Sunday service and to commune with the priests about their troubles and sins. The services were usually done by the priests, but today's service warranted High Cleric Navrik because it involved the death of a king.

Navrik was a well-built bald man with a black goatee. Jace hadn't seen him in twelve years, not since their grandfather's death. He had avoided the church and whatever laid underneath it. The catacombs were a place that had haunted his childhood. The catacombs were massive, the lower levels apparently connecting to the ghoulish tunnels. They had been sealed off and forgotten about. The royal catacombs where his ancestors were buried, was in a different section. A section that only Navrik had access to. They had placed an urn with the black dust gathered from the site there for their mother. Soon another urn would be placed beside it. That of their father.

The General walked next to him, his plate armour clanking on the wooden steps. The two guards walked behind them, like silent shadows. At the bottom of the stairs, Stryxen almost bowled them over as he ran up to them. "Don't leave without me," he said, wiping the remnants of his breakfast off his chin.

"We wouldn't dream of it," Jace replied, smiling and ruffling his younger brother's hair. Two more guards took position in front of them, stalwart, ready to protect. His stomach grumbled as they passed the kitchen. The aromas of the feast that they were cooking for his coronation, filled the hallway and made his mouth water. He hadn't felt like breakfast this morning, opting just to have a mug of coffee. He now regretted his choice.

As they entered the courtyard, a horse galloped to them. Jace and his retinue stopped as one of the rangers gracefully dismounted and knelt in front of him ready to report. The ranger's name was Gwethren and he was one of the six rangers that had been sent out to investigate the elven threat. Looking up at his regent, the young ranger's green eyes said it all. The news was grave! "The elven army are massed outside the northern gate. Rylan and my companions are alive and appear to be unharmed. They are locked inside a cage though. Would you like me and Harold to mount a rescue attempt?"

* * *

"Your offer is commendable, but also suicidal," Jace replied. "I will not lose more rangers this day." Gwethren and Harold had arrived back late the day before. They had been delayed due to the elven army. The pair had backtracked to the Black Raven Inn, cut south and entered through the eastern gate of Sethanon. "How many elves are there?" Jace had to ask, even though deep down he already knew the answer.

"Too many, my liege. We would be lucky to hold out for a day, two at the most." Jace grimly looked at the general.

"Are the guards in place?" The general nodded. It was his only option. He needed to confront the elves and try and reason with King Therondal. He would try diplomacy and if that failed, he would arrest Therondal and throw him in the dungeon. The elves wouldn't dare attack if their king was imprisoned. Or so he hoped. "Thank you, Gwethren. You're dismissed." The ranger stood up and thumped his fist against his light armoured chest. Jace was deep in thought as he continued towards the church. He wasn't even a king yet and he was already beginning to feel the burden of leadership.

The large wooden doors of the church opened, causing the multitude of candles to flicker. "My liege," Navrik said, bowing respectfully. He led them to some seats reserved for the royal family at the front of the church. At his grandfather's funeral, all five of them had sat here. Now there was only the two of them. Clutching hold of Jace, wrapping his arms tightly around him, Stryxen started to cry. As he buried his head into Jace's shoulder, Jace spoke soft, reassuring words and stroked his hair soothingly. Tears streamed down his own face for the father that they had lost. The general and the guards stood respectfully to the side as they let the brothers grieve.

The wooden door was flung open as a messenger rushed in. Jace stood, as panting, the messenger handed him the note. He looked at the black wax seal and the insignia engraved into it. He was intrigued. It wasn't an insignia that he recognised. Carefully he cut through the wax seal and opened the parchment. The writing wasn't neat and the grammar, punctuation and spelling were poorly. It was written in the common, universal tongue though and even though it took a little while, Jace was able to decipher it. It was from an orc. "The orcs won't be here in time," he mumbled.

"Why?" Stryxen asked annoyed. Jace knew how much he had been looking forward to meeting the orcs. Jace read the message. *'Humee Prince Jace, we the orcs are transporting the orc and naga groupies to the humee city of Sethanon. Gotted attacked by a kraken. Sunk lotsa ships. My ship de fastest. Broka mast and escaped. Now delayed. Captain Raiff Grudgen of the Seahawk.'*

* * *

"They are still coming. It just looks like they have been delayed," he said, resting his hand reassuringly on his brother's shoulder. "Thank you. You're dismissed," he said, addressing the guard. "And leave the church door open. The delegations should be arriving soon." The guard nodded and left. As soon as the door jamb had been inserted, the first delegation arrived as if on cue.

A white haired, stout dwarf entered. His white gold crown embedded with rubies, depicted that he was royalty and even though his long white hair and beard showed his age, his bright blue eyes, gleamed mischievously with cunning and intelligence. "Welcome, King Lionel," Jace said, nodding to the dwarf in greeting.

"My condolences, Prince Jace," Lionel said, sighing. "Your father was a great man. He will be missed." A hooded delegation entered and without announcing themselves, automatically took a row of seats at the back. With a wave of dismissal, the six guards took position in the aisle, silent and watchful. Pulling back their hoods, they revealed their fine features, their long hair and their pointed ears. The elven delegation had arrived.

Hiding his clenched fists behind his back, he forced a smile and nodded to King Therondal. He returned his attention back to the dwarven king as he introduced the rest of his delegation. "This is my son Prince Wryndar, his wife Princess Jirleve, my general Afren, one of his captains Rygar and I believe you already know my niece Kyrene."

He nodded respectfully to each of them. "By brother Zane knows the baroness quite well. Unfortunately, he is indisposed. I'm sure he would love to talk to you later though," Jace said softly, addressing the baroness. A guard stepped forward and led them to their seats. The remaining six dwarven warriors stood to the side in the aisle, opposite their delegation.

The dark skinned, tattooed Sandrigar were the next to arrive, followed by the delegations of the gnomes, werewolves, vampires and gorkin. Jace had never met the royalty of these races before, but nodded to each of them respectfully as they were ushered to their seats. There would be time for introductions and small talk later at the coronation. Taking his seat, he nodded to the high cleric. Stepping onto the raised platform Navrik began the ceremony.

Darla kept her cloak wrapped around her with the hood up. The guard escorted her, Roselyn and Kerin to three seats before dismissing himself. As she sat down, she sniffed, catching a scent familiar to her but unable to remember who it belonged to. Before she could investigate this further, Athelaine leaned forward and caught her attention. Luck had it that she was only two seats down. The man sitting in between them smiled.

"Darla, I would like to introduce you to my father, King Vlathmire." The man had jet black hair with streaks of grey running through it. His neatly trimmed goatee was the same. He looked like he was in his fifties, but Darla knew for a fact that he was much, much older. Like the elves the vampires had the gene for longevity. Darla had insisted on keeping a low profile and pretending that she was with the human delegation. There were so many human nobles that it was hard to keep track of them. The perfume would also mask her scent from the other werewolves, adding to the ruse.

"I love the perfume that you are wearing. What is it called... Deception?" Vlathmire said with a slight smirk.

"No, it is a new fragrance called Stake in the Heart," she replied with her own smirk. The vampire king roared with laughter. It was common knowledge that a normal stake wouldn't kill a vampire. The stake had to be blessed and soaked in holy water. Roselyn patted her knee, gaining her attention. "It's good to see you, Vlathmire," she said, giving his hand a gentle squeeze.

"You too, child," he replied affectionately. Darla turned her attention to Roselyn.

"Sandrik, I would like you to meet my cousin Darla," she said by way of introduction. The baron was crying openly, mourning the loss of the king. He nodded politely in greeting before turning his head away.

Darla sniffed again. "What's wrong?" Roselyn asked, concerned. The scent was stronger now. It belonged to a werewolf. One from her past.

"Nothing. It's just allergies," Darla replied casually. It was a blatant lie but if her suspicions were right, it was not only personal but also something that she didn't want to get her friend involved in. Reaching into her pocket, Roselyn pulled out a handkerchief and handed it to her.

"The Baron Sandrik is struggling; he's an emotional mess," she whispered in her friend's ear. Darla was only half listening as she focused on the scent. "Recently his wife was murdered and now his best friend King Erithen. He is mourning both of their losses. On top of that, his son Rylan has gone missing. He was on a mission…"

Darla tuned out completely, refusing to listen to the gossip. Her head was lowered and to the casual observer it looked like she was either crying or praying. Either way it would be seen as a sign of respect to the dead. Secretly, her eyes were glancing toward the representatives of the werewolf delegation. She gasped and quickly turned away. Tears streamed down her face as a mixture of emotions surged through her. Sadness, confusion and anger. Her suspicions had been right. Sitting a couple of seats away, representing the werewolf delegation and wearing her father's crown was Lance.

He had once been her best friend and they had been inseparable. A surge of childhood memories flooded her mind, almost overwhelming her. *Her and Lance swimming in the river, running through the forest, playing tag, playing pranks on other children and laughing until they almost wet themselves.* One dream stuck out from the others. *The look in Lance's eyes as he said that he was going to marry her and become king of the werewolves.* And here he was acting the role.

He had always planned to be king, whether she wanted it or not. Then just like that she remembered her name. Her true name. "My name is Evelyn Lycanthorne," she whispered with a gasp. She looked down at her solid white gold band. It had changed. The red rubies and the engraved wolf heads had reappeared. She felt teary. It felt like an eternity since she'd seen the true ring, the ring that depicted her lineage. She had reclaimed her identity.

Her stomach was a tangle of knots and she felt physically sick. She had been saving to buy Lance's freedom along with his families. Yet here they were representing her race and laughing as they joked with the Gorkin delegation sitting next to them. Evelyn couldn't help but wonder whether they had ever been prisoners or whether they had been free for all of this time? It had been a scam, a ruse. The money that she had been saving would only fund Lance's reign. She had been foolish and naïve to allow herself to be betrayed like this, but she planned to rectify it soon. Taking a deep breath, she listened to the high cleric as he gave his service.

"We are here today to honour, respect and pay tribute to a man, father and king. King Erithen now rests for all eternity…" Jace tuned out from what the high cleric was saying, focusing on what was to come next. He and Stryxen had already said their personal goodbyes. The funeral was just a formality that the prince was taking advantage of. "Prince Jace has a few words to say. Then each delegation will have an opportunity to pay their respects and say their farewells," Navrik said, nodding to Jace and stepping off the raised platform.

It was time. Sighing, he stepped onto the platform. "Welcome everyone. Gathered here today are family, close friends, acquaintances and even strangers. Although deeply saddened, I am also extremely honoured that my father has received such a turnout. Even though he is dead, there is at least some comfort knowing that he is not here to feel the betrayal of one of the races that we called one of our closest friends and allies."

He cleared his throat before continuing. "Before his demise, my father sent out half a dozen scouts to investigate the rumour of an elven attack on the border of the Hiberathian Kingdom. Two of the scouts made it back, reporting the capture and imprisonment of their four comrades. If that isn't a declaration of war, then surely the elven army that you brought along with your delegation is. They are camped outside the front gates of Sethanon besieging the city." General Iryss whistled as he drew his sword. From behind two hidden alcoves, a dozen guards charged out with their weapons drawn.

The other delegations were in an uproar of murmurs. Weapons were drawn in response to the armed guards. Kabel was mumbling, preparing to cast a spell. Whether it was a protection spell or one of mass destruction, Jace couldn't tell. "To draw blood in the church is sacrilege," Navrik roared, fearful, racing forward. Jace had devised the plan with the general. He thought the ruse was a masterstroke. It enabled them to reveal what the elves had done and catch them unprepared. The guards were there as a precaution to ensure that things went smoothly. It was a mistake. The whole plan had gone pear-shaped. It had caused confusion and chaos. King Therondal sat there amidst it all, roaring with laughter.

"Enough!" Jace shouted, his eyes glowing as the wild magic surged to the surface. Deathly silence ensued. With soft scraping, weapons were sheathed. All eyes were fixated on him, fearful and attentive. His laughter abruptly silenced, even King Therondal sat there pale and fearful. Controlling the magic, Prince Jace's eyes returned to their normal colour. "Now, what do you have to say for yourself, King Therondal?" Smirking, Kabel nodded approvingly. The young prince had managed to restore order. He was proving to be a fine king.

King Therondal stood up. His composure restored, he addressed Jace and those assembled. "Your rangers are safe for the moment, but their fate depends on your actions." The threat was left hanging there. Jace nodded his understanding. "It has come to our attention that the Everthorn royalty of Sethanon has stolen our divinity stone. Or do you deny these allegations, Prince Jace?"

It was Jace's turn to laugh. "Do you mean the divinity stone that was stolen by one of your own elven lords? The divinity stone that was going to be given to the demon prince, Malgorath. The divinity stone that a squad of my brother's guards fought a lesser demon for. They vanquished it and recovered the sacred artifact."

"Recovered or stole?" Therondal accused.

"It is locked away in a magical vault in my brother's room. Let us depart and go and retrieve it for you. We can resolve this grave misunderstanding and restore the unity of our alliance." King Therondal nodded and rose, along with his delegation.

* * *

Jace turned to Navrik. "I will take my leave and escort King Therondal to the divinity stone. Please let the other delegations pay their respects to my father." Turning, he addressed the assembled royalty of Aragoth. "I will join you all in the throne room shortly for my coronation." With Stryxen, Kabel and the general by his side, he exited the church. Guards walked silently, flanking them on both sides with their weapons drawn, ready for any trouble. King Therondal and the elven delegation followed closely behind.

"How are you going to get Zane's magical vault open?" the young prince asked, curiously.

"Zane told me his password," Jace replied, shrugging.

"What!!" Stryxen screamed. "How come he didn't tell me the password?"

"Because he was too busy getting arrested and thrown in the dungeon. He only had enough time to tell one person. And that was me!" Jace shouted, quickening his pace. He wasn't in the mood for Stryxen's antics and him feeling slighted and left out. Hurrying up the staircase, he startled the guards as he rounded the corner. "Open the door to my brother's bedroom," he ordered. The senior guard's key ring rattled as he fumbled for the correct key. The door swung open and Jace and Stryxen barged in, leading the way with the elven delegation and a cohort of guards following close behind.

* * *

Walking over to the secret compartment's location he mumbled the words *Targeth Bownd Ven Fanal End Glurie*. The incantation was a password in the elvish language. A password which would unlock the secret compartment and disarm the magical runes within. In the common tongue the password translated to *Brothers Bound in Honour and Glory*. It was a motto that he and Zane shared. Blinking back tears, Jace reached into the compartment and retrieved the satchel.

"Here is your damn divinity stone," he said throwing the satchel at King Therondal. Opening the satchel, he tipped the large, green, diamond shaped emerald into his hand. "Now release my rangers!" Mumbling the incantation, he closed the secret compartment. As he slowly stood up, he watched the confliction of emotions flicker onto the king's face. His emotions changed abruptly from happiness to bafflement and finally anger.

"What's wrong?" Archbishop Lazoreen asked, concerned. The archbishop was also the king's younger brother and Prince Jerrick's father. He was nobility but had also relinquished any right to the throne. Irate, Therondal handed the archbishop the green emerald. The archbishop gasped, his eyes going wide.

"What kind of fool do you take me for?" Therondal shouted. Irrationally he drew his sword. Jace responded and drew his own. The sword was heavier than normal, well-balanced and as sharp as a razors edge. Multiple hisses sounded as other swords were drawn from their scabbards. The Sethanon guards outnumbered the elves, but there would be casualties on both sides. His sword swung, becoming a barrier as Jace protectively pushed Stryxen behind him. He was blinded momentarily and looking down saw the gem inserted in the pommel. It was sparkling in the light.

It was like a slap in the face, reminding him of his father, of who he was, of the honour that the Everthorn's had in respecting their alliance with the elves and the dwarves. "Stop!" he yelled. "I am not a fool Therondal. If I was, I would cut you down where you stand and disregard the alliance that we have. I have returned your divinity stone in the hope that we could resolve this."

"This isn't our divinity stone," Lazoreen said meekly. "It is nothing but a giant, diamond shaped emerald."

Stryxen laughed. "I told you it was nothing but a giant emerald."

"This is what was given to us," Jace screamed, frustrated.

"The divinity stones have a magical link to the nobility of each race. There is no magical link with this," Lazoreen explained, holding out the emerald.

"That's because it's a fake," Therondal screamed, swiping it off his hand in a fit of rage. The emerald spiralled for what seemed an eternity, before shattering on the floor. A multitude of tiny emeralds sparkled in the light.

"You didn't know. Did you?" Lazoreen asked. "Haven't you ever sensed the magic in your own divinity stone?"

"No!" Jace shouted. "How could we? Our divinity stone was inserted into my father's crown. He only wore it on special occasions. For the most part, he wore a replica, opting to keep the crown locked away in a secured vault.

"I believe Prince Jace," Lazoreen said after considerable contemplation. "They don't have our divinity stone. Their only crime is being naïve and foolish."

"You're the fool if you believe their lies Lazoreen," Therondal spat. The king was beyond reasoning with. He had heard the rumours about how the elven Prince Velander had been psychopathic and unstable. Jace began to suspect that it ran in the family. Lazoreen appeared to be the only rational one. "You will give us back our divinity stone, Prince Jace, otherwise you will die and Sethanon will burn." Raising his sword, screaming maniacally, he swung wildly at Jace.

With a ringing of steel, Jace blocked the blow and deflected the sword to the side. Therondal swung again, pressing the attack. Jace easily blocked it. Another swing and Jace's sword moved to intercept. He realised his mistake instantly.

The king had feinted the swing, pulling back and thrusting his sword forward. Jace had left himself open, fully exposed. He was about to be impaled and there was nothing that he could do. "No!" Lazoreen screamed, dashing forward in between them.

Therondal's sword stabbed through the archbishop's light armour, as easily as butter. With a spray of blood, it erupted through his back. "No!" Therondal screamed, his eyes wide and his lip quivering. He let go of his sword and watched in shock as his brother's corpse fell to the ground amidst a pool of blood. Lazoreen looked at his brother and tried to speak, but all he could do was cough up blood. With a final wheeze, his head lolled to the side and he died. "This is your fault," Therondal screamed, staring at Jace. Fuelled by grief and hatred, tears streamed down his face as he rushed forward and grabbed the hilt of his sword.

As he pulled it out of his brother's corpse, Jace slashed across. The blade whistled, glistening in the lamp light. The stroke was both fluid and graceful as the blade sliced through the elven king's gauntleted wrist. Blood sprayed onto the floor as the sword dropped to the ground. The elven guards screamed, their swords hissing as they were drawn from the sheaths. General Iryss cut two of the guards down with a wicked slash before they had time to react. The clashing and scraping of metal sounded as the guards took to battle.

* * *

One of the elves managed to slice a Sethanon guard brutally across the neck before being cut down by two of the guard's companions. Jace watched as two of the elves got swarmed, the Sethanon guards stabbing them repeatedly in a frenzy. There were three elven guards left. The floor was littered with bodies and blood.

"Drop your weapons," Jace said calmly. The three elves obliged, their weapons clunking to the floor. Wiping blood off the blade, he sheathed the sword, before turning to address the general. "Take Therondal to a healer and then throw the elves into the dungeon. I'm going to attend my coronation." Exiting his brother's bedroom, he walked back down the hall. His thoughts were sombre. He had failed with his diplomacy. They were now at war with the elves and to top it off, they didn't even have the elven divinity stone to aide them in their battle against Malgorath.

Chapter 20

Jace sat on the throne as Kabel gently placed the crown onto his head. Applause sounded, echoing throughout the throne room. Kabel had taken the opportunity to retrieve the crown, while the guards had seated the various delegations. He was now officially a king. The crown fit perfectly, with the blue divinity stone inserted in the front and tiny sapphires surrounding it. The divinity stone radiated, pulsating and bonded to him, while the sapphires sparkled in the torchlight.

The sound of crystal shattering caught everybody's attention. Millie stood there embarrassed, almost in tears. She had dropped one of the crystal glasses. Dinner was about to be served. The feast was bountiful and smelled divine. The cooks had outdone themselves. Stepping forward next to his newly appointed king, General Iryss scowled before making an announcement.

"The elves have been arrested for their betrayal against the alliance and thrown in the dungeon. Before dinner is served King Jace needs to fulfill the last written order documented by his father, King Erithen. He is to execute his brother Zane for his treasonous acts against his family and Sethanon. The condemned prince is being escorted to the throne room as we speak," he said, raising his voice so all could hear. Jace's eyes glowed brightly with wild magic, fuelled by his emotions. He was furious.

"What do you think you are doing, General? Under whose authority were you given permission to make such an announcement?" he said rising to his feet.

As he leaned in close, Iryss's eyes briefly turned as black as midnight. "Under Malgorath's authorisation," Iryss whispered. Turning around, he walked away and mingled with some nearby guards. His brother was innocent. Deep down Jace had always known it. Any chance of saving him had just dissipated into a pile of ash. Malgorath had played him and ensured his brother's death.

"Our condolences on Prince Zane's soon-to-be death and this unfortunate burden that you have to bare," The High Councillor said diplomatically. His face was hidden under his hood, but everyone in the throne room could hear him as clear as day. Jace politely nodded to the mysterious Brotherhood leader. He rarely attended events, which made Jace nervous, wondering why he was attending his coronation. What made this event so special?

"Zane isn't a prince anymore. He lost that title when he was disowned from the family. Now he is a nobody. Hell, I'm ashamed to even call him my brother," Stryxen yelled, standing up from his seat. The two men sitting next to the high councillor tensed, leaning forward, their muscles bulging. Calmly the high councillor put out a reassuring hand and shook his head. The two men looked at the high councillor and leaned back, accepting his decision. Stryxen merely sat there flicking his bottom lip, goading them to react.

The two men sitting next to the high councillor were behemoths. They were his personal bodyguards and the only delegation that he needed. Being tall, well built and rugged looking, they made the high councillor look like a dwarf sitting between them. Yet they were like little puppies eating out of the high councillor's hand. It made Jace wonder how powerful the mysterious Brotherhood leader was.

* * *

The thick, double wooden doors opened and a dozen guards escorted Zane in. Half of them were Zane's own personal guards while the other half were the king's personal guards, loyal to General Iryss. His manacles clanked as he slowly shuffled forward. The powerful runes inscribed in them were linked between the manacles and the chain, nullifying Zane's magic. "Don't worry, brother. Do what you have to do," Zane said, giving him a weak smile. He knelt in front of his brother and hung his head as Jace drew his sword.

The six guards belonging to the king saluted Jace and then the general. Without a word, they walked back into the castle interior. "Captain, you and your squad may leave as well," Iryss ordered, glaring at Brenan. All six of the guards stood there resolute and defiant.

"No general. Zane's guards can stay," Jace stated. The general nodded, but he was clearly not happy.

"I'm sorry for pushing you away. I love you, Zane," a hysterical woman cried. It was Millie! Jace halted as the servant ran forward weeping. Collapsing on the ground, kneeling next to him, she embraced the man whom she whole heartedly loved. She unfolded the letter with trembling hands and read it to him. "Please forgive me," she cried.

"There is nothing to forgive," Zane said, stroking her hair.

Leaning forward, he kissed her, his lips briefly brushing against hers. "Even in death, I will still love you."

"Please reconsider. Don't do this Jace," she wailed as Bear and Beast gently lifted her up and led her away. Reaching towards his pouch, the king pulled out his brother's communication orb. Zane shook his head.

"Keep it brother, in remembrance of me," he said, with tears in his eyes. It was a last ditch effort, the gamble could go either way. Jace raised his sword and imbued it with his wild magic. The blade began to glow with fiery blue flames dancing and flickering as if they had lives of their own. Concentrating, tapping into his emotions, his grief came surging forth like a tidal wave. He had lost his mother, father and now he was about to lose his brother. The blade turned from blue, to white. The magic was powerful, fuelled by his emotions. Screaming, Jace swung with all his might and cleaved the chain in two. The link was severed and with-it Zane's magic returned.

Smiling, Zane stood up and mumbling an incantation, disintegrated the manacles. "I will not execute my brother for a crime that he did not commit," Jace said, as he turned his fury on the general. "The fact that you admitted to following Malgorath's orders, proves my brother's innocence." The general didn't argue or deny it, he merely laughed. "I don't care if it was my father's wishes, his last written order. I am king now. I make the rulings. I make the decisions," Jace said with authority. He had to take command of the situation. He had to lay down the law and let everyone bare witness.

"Thank you, my brother," Zane said, gingerly standing up and grabbing Jace's shoulder affectionately. He was still recovering from the torture. His gambit had relied solely on his brother's actions. They had grown up together and had been inseparable. He knew his brother well and had risked everything, gambling on the fact that Jace wouldn't kill him. Stumbling, he almost fell. Matthias and Larin were there in an instant, supporting him on either side.

Brenan and Rayze joined them with their weapons drawn, ensuring that there wasn't any trouble. Together, they slowly proceeded towards Millie. "Death cannot keep us apart. I love you, Millie and will never leave you." Embracing her, holding her close, he kissed her passionately. Beast, Bear, Matthias and Larin drew their weapons and the six guards formed a wall, a barrier, in front of their prince. They were expecting trouble.

"You are weak. A disgrace to the Sethanon royal bloodline. If you won't kill Zane, then I will," Iryss screamed, as his body began to transform. His eyes were pitch black and devoid of emotion. He started grunting as his jaw reformed, broadening and growing longer. Two tusks grew, protruding upwards. His teeth grew longer and razor sharp. Teeth that would tear through the flesh, muscle and bone of his victims. Thick dark brown fur covered his face. He drew his sword.

The weapon had been given to him years ago by the king. It had been symbolic having a screeching gryphon head attached to the pommel. Now the blade danced with red flames and the head had reshaped itself into some demonic monster. "Then after I kill your brother, I will kill you. I will pave the way for Malgorath's reign. I will be his general and lead the demonic hordes. I will be known as General....."

"I don't care what your demonic name is," Stryxen said blatantly. He stood transfixed as the demonic general approached. The young prince was even smiling. "From now on I will call you General Boarface." The young prince wasn't even afraid. Jace dashed forward and grabbed him by the arm. A moment later, six guards were there by his side, joined in battle.

"You and your squad should be protecting Zane, Captain," Jace said, watching as Rayze swung his obsidian-bladed sword. He was graceful, a master swordsman. Stepping back, the demon dodged the stroke. It was fearful, recognising the weapon for what it was.

"Prince Zane asked us to assist you, my king," Brenan replied, as he swung with one sword and then followed through with the other. Jace nodded, appreciating the help.

"Finally. A challenge," Boarface said with a laugh, as holding up his gauntlet it transformed into a demonic clawed hand. The claws extended. They were already wickedly sharp, but now they were also the length of large daggers. "This is what is going to happen to the Everthorn reign," he said, as he swung his mighty sword. The throne shattered into a pile of debris. The general laughed, the sound deep and rumbling. His intent was clear. He was going to eliminate the royal Everthorn bloodline.

Suddenly, a small fireball flew over Jace's head and hit Boarface square in the face. It did nothing, except piss him off. Kabel had been administering Zane, putting salves on his wounds and giving elixirs to help heal him. He now stood mumbling, preparing to cast another spell. A black ball of energy soared from his hand. It was powerful, ancient dark magic. The ball expanded, hitting the demon in the head. It engulfed the demon and then dissipated as Boarface absorbed it. "Is that the best you can do?" he goaded.

Lightning quick, in a blur of movement the demon swiped at Rayze. Rayze was motionless, then waiting to the last moment he pirouetted out of the way and swung his sword. The sword easily sliced through the demon's wrist, severing the claw and dropping it to the ground. Within moments it evaporated into a pile of black dust. Holding up his stump, Boarface laughed as the clawed hand grew back. The demon's regenerative powers were phenomenal and would make it almost impossible to kill.

The demon swung his mighty sword. The strike was perfectly timed with power and precision. Brenan easily dodged, the flaming blade swinging harmlessly over him. Jace raised his sword by pure instinct, the manoeuvre ingrained into him through years of practice. Instantly, the blade was engulfed with blue flames. His wild magic had reacted and saved him. Sparks flew as both swords clashed. Turning his sword and adjusting the blade, the king deflected the general's sword harmlessly away.

Chaos erupted as booted feet thudded on the floor. "For Blackrock!" King Lionel shouted, leading the charge. Kyrene hurried over towards Zane and Millie, leading Jirleve by the hand. "Have you got the blood, Kyrene?" Zane asked urgently. Smiling, she held up a flask. Zane gave her a hug. "Thank you." He grabbed the flask of goat's blood and started drawing symbols on the ground.

Zane's voice was barely a whisper. Energy emitted from the runes, sizzling, joining together to form a small sizzling blue portal. Looking across, Jace realized that this had been Zane's strategy. He had planned for this eventuality. It hadn't taken Zane long, but he still needed to hurry. "I'll be back in a minute," he said, before stepping into the portal and disappearing. Even though he was only gone a couple of minutes, it seemed like an eternity. Exiting the portal, he carried a large tome. It was a book of ancient magic. It was his half of the Val'Markyl – the angelic tome.

Placing the tome on the ground, Zane grabbed the flask of blood and dipping his fingers in began to draw more runes.

These runes were elaborate and more complicated. They needed to be because he was not only casting a larger portal, but one that spanned over a greater distance. The portal would take them to Holguard. It was where he had first met Kyrene. Now, that seemed like a lifetime ago. It is where they would make their stand.

Darla turned towards Roselyn. The Lady of Crystril could see the urgency in her eyes. "I want you to take Kerin back to the inn. Go to your room and lock the door. If you don't hear from me by the end of the night, you both grab your horses and leave. Ride back to Crystril. You'll be safe there," Evelyn said, as she stood up and drew her short sword. Athelaine and Vlathmire stood up, their fangs bared menacingly as they drew their weapons. The three of them ran forward to battle the demon.

Roselyn, Sandrik and Kerin stood up and raced towards the double doors. Their chairs crashed behind them. The Sandrigar and Gnomish delegations were already there, having the same idea as them. Escaping and surviving. Grabbing the handle with his gauntleted hand the Sandrigar general screamed and started convulsing. Grabbing him forcibly around the waist, Roselyn pulled him off the handle. His gauntlet was charred, his hand ruined. It was then that Roselyn saw the shimmer. "Magic," she said softly. There was no escape.

The stocky dwarves ran in either side of Jace and began

hacking at the demonic general. His armour and body were imbued with demonic energy though. Like Brenan and his squad, the dwarven weapons weren't magical. They were useless against him. It was futile. Lionel turned his head slightly. "Get the princeling to safety," he said, as he swung his broad bladed sword.

"Thank you, King Lionel," Jace replied as he dragged the reluctant prince away. He was confused, he couldn't understand his younger brother's morbid fascination with the demon. Then it dawned on him. He was a role model, Stryxen had always looked up to him. Did he want to fight the demon? Was he trying to prove himself? "This is for your own protection," he said, forcibly pushing his younger brother behind him. "You don't need to prove anything to me, Stryxen." He turned back to face the battle, back-stepping and using himself as a shield.

All he could do was watch helplessly as the demonic general swung. The dwarven king tried to block, but the flaming sword shattered the broad blade and sent it tumbling to the ground. It then sliced through the dwarven king's armour and into his chest. Lionel toppled backwards screaming. His hand went to his chest to desperately try and stem the flow of blood. It was useless, the wound was fatal. "You will never get our divinity stone demon," Lionel yelled, coughing up blood. "It is safely back at Holguard." Laughing, he coughed up more blood. His eyes staring blankly at the ceiling, he went limp and died.

* * *

The runes radiated, emitting energy as they joined together and began to glow. A small portal formed, which rapidly began to expand. "Jace, Brenan, Wryndar. We are leaving now," Zane shouted. Wryndar dived under the flaming sword, tucking, rolling and gracefully landing back on his feet. Being engaged in battle, he had what the dwarves called 'battle lust'. Even though he had seen his father die, he was caught up in it. He was unresponsive, focusing on the battle at hand. There would be time to grieve and mourn later.

"Jace, Brenan, Wryndar. We are leaving now," Kyrene shouted, repeating the order to retreat. Three more dwarven guards fell, victims to the demon's mighty claw and sword. Their weapons were useless. The demon seemed invincible. Snapping out of the battle lust, Wryndar came to his senses. Looking around, he saw the carnage and death. Taking charge, he ordered the retreat.

"The portal," Evelyn shouted, pointing and dodging a thrust from the demonic general. Roselyn nodded and herded the group around the chairs. Huddled together, they ran past the shattered throne. The dwarves plated greaves smashed against the wooden floor as they ran towards the portal. Roselyn and her group were right behind them. They would be cold in the dwarven lands, but at least they would be alive.

* * *

With the dwarves retreating, Zane's guards were the only thing standing between Jace and the demon. Two of them had already fallen. Matthias had been cut in half, the demon's sword slicing through his armour, flesh, muscle and bone. Both halves had been cauterised by the flaming blade, leaving a smouldering corpse in its wake. Larin's corpse lay between Bear and Rayze. The demon had raked his chest and head in one vicious swipe. The claws had sliced through his armour like tissue paper. He now lay in a pool of blood, shredded and unrecognisable.

Slowly the four of them were forced to retreat as the demonic general swung tirelessly at them with his sword and claw. Jace could only watch as they got closer and closer. The dwarves had already entered the portal, yet Zane remained, holding it open for them. "You're my brother, Stryxen and I love you. I am trying to protect you. We're trying to save you. Why are you behaving like this?" Jace asked, frustrated.

"Because you are a coward. You should be fighting the demon," Stryxen screamed.

"They are protecting us. Sacrificing themselves so that we can escape," Jace replied calmly. "Don't let their sacrifice go in vain."

"Their weapons are useless against it. You are the only one that can stop it!"

* * *

"No, I'm not. Rayze seems to be holding his own." Jace looked up. The guards and the demon were almost upon them. Stryxen glared at the mysterious guard. There was more to him than what he was making out. Loud banging sounded at the double doors as the Sethanon guards tried to enter and rescue those within. The guards were level with them, along with the demon. Then three newcomers joined the fray, assisting the guards and reinforcing their ranks.

"Fight the demon and help Rayze kill it."

"All of us will die, Stryxen. We need to go now!"

"Since you won't die by the general's hand, then you will die by mine." Jace was shocked as Stryxen lunged forward. He felt a burning, excruciating pain. Looking down he saw Stryxen's dagger sticking out of his stomach. Blood was covering his tunic. The enchanted blade was buried to the hilt. He pulled the blade out slowly. Even though the blade was covered in his blood, Jace could see that Stryxen had changed the runes. He didn't recognise them, but he could sense their dark, foreboding power. Stryxen laughed and it was then as Jace raised his head that he saw his midnight black eyes.

"Jace!" Zane screamed as Roselyn and her group entered the portal. "Stryxen! What have you done?" Stryxen's skin tore apart, shedding like that of a snake. His clothes were ripped to shreds as Malgorath's body emerged and continued to grow. Six, seven, eight. Finally at nine feet his body stopped growing. It was pure muscle and bone. His black skin consisted of rough, spiky scales. His red eyes shone with intelligence and cunning as he took everybody in. Laughing, he revealed his long, razor-sharp teeth.

Malgorath smirked. "Stryxen's soul put up a fight Zane. But his sweet, innocent soul has been devoured. Now only I remain. Malgorath, Prince of demons." It all made sense. Stryxen's mood swings had been torture for him. It had been an ongoing battle for his soul. Jace and Zane felt like fools. "Up until now I have only manipulated events by planting thoughts, casting illusions and creating minor demons with my essence. I've even impersonated the both of you over the years. Our mother and father were easy prey. The demons that I had infused them with rebelled, so I had to kill them. Part of their humanity had infused with their demonic host. Somehow the two of you managed to reject my essence. I suspect that it was your magic protecting you and thwarting my plans. No matter. Instead of possessing you, I'll just have to kill you." He laughed heartily, the deep, rumbling sound, resonating throughout the throne room.

"Now that Stryxen is of age, I am at full power. I can begin my reign and conquer this world. All I need are five divinity stones to summon a portal and bring a small army through. We will lay waste to this world. Once I have all ten divinity stones, I will be unrivalled! I'll have enough power to oppose the angels. I will be the ultimate ruler of both realms. Those of you that don't pledge your loyalty to me will either become slaves… or die."

Evelyn, Athelaine, Rayze and Vlathmire cautiously took a few steps backwards. Brenan gave a silent order and the guards followed Evelyn's example. They were all cautious and hesitant, wary of what was about to happen. "Hello Darla. It has been a while." Evelyn turned to see the high councillor. His two bodyguards stood on either side of him. They were brothers and fellow lycanthropes. Their names were Trivlen and Granthen. They had their weapons out, prepared for battle. Trivlen was armed with two wickedly curved swords, while his brother had a whip with a scythe blade attached to it. Focusing on the demons, Evelyn didn't even hear them approach.

"My name is no longer Darla. It is Evelyn Lycanthorne," she replied. She could sense the high councillor's smile from under his hood.

"I'm glad that you have reclaimed your identity. Let us know when you want to retake your kingdom. We will aide you in this. I think the best course for now is to retreat and regroup." Evelyn nodded in agreement.

"Close the portal Zane," Jace shouted. "It's up to you to find a way to kill Malgorath. Don't let our sacrifice be for nothing." Tears streaming down his face, Zane nodded as he stepped through and closed the portal.

Malgorath laughed. "The only thing that you have done is delay me. I will travel to the frozen tundra of the dwarven lands and lay waste to it. From the ruins and ashes of Holguard I will take the dwarven, gnomish and sandrigaren divinity stones." The demon prince snatched the crown off Jace's head.

Jace's hand snaked out and grabbed it. "This is the royal crown of Sethanon and rightfully belongs to me," he said defiantly, as the wild magic ignited his hand and arm in blazing blue fire.

The demon prince winced, surprised. He was immune to the elemental magic of this world. Yet somehow Jace's magic affected him. Daintily, Malgorath plucked the divinity stone from the crown. "You can keep your pretty, little trinket," he said, letting go of the crown. "This is all I want." He held up the sparkling divinity stone, admiring it. Then his free hand lashed out in a blur of speed. The force of the blow was phenomenal and would have killed most people, but Jace's wild magic protected and shielded him. Lifted off his feet he was sent hurtling backwards. Darting across, Evelyn caught him and carefully lowered him to the ground.

"He needs a healer," she said. Varyn Kabel was there in an instant. Slicing open his tunic with a short, bladed dagger, Kabel analysed the wound. Black lines spider webbed around the cut. Gingerly, he reached out to touch one of the lines, then pulled back instantly.

"This is caused by dark magic. It is beyond my capability. Even a cleric or battle priest wouldn't be able to heal him. The best that we can do is ease his passing" He pulled out a vial. "It will put him to sleep and allow him to die peacefully."

"That is right Kabel," Malgorath said in a booming voice. "The runes on my dagger consist of powerful dark magic. Magic that is currently spreading and infecting him as we speak. There is no cure. He is going to die an excruciating death."

"No! There is another way. Evelyn can save him. You know what you must do?" the High Councillor said. Evelyn looked mortified. She had never turned anyone before. The High Councillor sighed. "I'm sorry Evelyn, but it is the only way King Jace will survive." Tapping into her lycanthropy, Evelyn's eyes became yellow and bestial. Her teeth sharpened and grew slightly. With her hood up, no-one even noticed. Evelyn wasn't ready to reveal herself, not yet. Sliding her arms under his armpits, she lifted him up to a sitting position. Her head darted forward, biting into the soft skin of his neck.

Withdrawing, she pulled back with the king's blood dripping off her teeth. She had done it. She had given Jace lycanthropy and the regenerative powers that went with it.

Malgorath hadn't even noticed. He looked at the delegations remaining. "Now give me your divinity stones and bow before me. Declare your allegiance."

The gorkin and werewolf delegations scrambled forward, knocking their seats over in the process. They had been waiting for this opportunity, biding their time until Malgorath emerged. Dropping to their knees, they bowed low to the demon prince, pledging their loyalty. The gorkin placed their divinity stone obediently at the demon's feet.

Picking up the gorkin's turquoise divinity stone, Malgorath held it next to it's counterpart. Mumbling words of power in his ancient demonic language, he pushed the two divinity stones together. Red light blazed forth as the two divinity stones fused. The divinity stone grew as it transformed and changed colour. It still resembled its diamond shape, but it was shiny and black, with bright purple lights flickering within.

Lance looked nervously at the demon before him. "I apologise my liege, but our divinity stone was stolen by some fanatics." Malgorath's free arm swung across in a blur. His claws were the size of small daggers and just as sharp. In the blink of an eye, half of Lance's face was ripped off. It was far from lethal, but even with his regenerative powers, it would leave a scar.

"I can sense them. I am bonded to the divinity stones, linked to them for all of eternity. The vampire's, werewolves and elven divinity stones are here. Retrieve them and prove your undying loyalty to me." Lance smiled, determined to prove himself. As he turned to face the rebellious group, Rayze was there slamming into him and knocking him to the ground. The werewolf crown clattered to the ground and rolled half-way towards the group, before spinning and dropping to the ground with a high-pitched clink.

Frantic, Lance bounded towards it on all fours. Rayze pivoted and in a blur of speed, brought Nightbringer around in a deadly arc. It sliced through Malgorath's wrist and sent it spiralling through the air. Black smoke slithered like a snake from the stump, twisting, turning and then evaporating. In its place was another black clawed hand. The demon prince had regenerated instantaneously. The decapitated hand landed on the ground and turned into a pile of black dust. Rayze paled in shock and started to back away. Malgorath laughed. "I will forgive this transgression vampire, if you hand over the divinity stone and swear allegiance."

"Never," Rayze replied, defiantly. Red, pink and purple fire burst forth from Malgorath's hands. Demonic fire. Fire that engulfed Rayze's cloak, burning him. Flinging the cloak off him, it soon became a pile of ash. The vampire staggered, even through the cloak he had been severely burned. The demon prince's hands flared up again. Rayze was dead to rights, a sitting duck. Again, demonic fire shot forth.

* * *

Vlathmire ran forward so quickly that he seemed to vanish. Throwing himself in front of Rayze, he looked his son in the eyes and smiled. The demonic fire slammed into his back and engulfed him. "Nooo...," Rayze cried, as his legs gave way. Sprinting forward Athelaine caught him and carried him to safety.

"Cast a portal," Evelyn said. "We need to escape while we can." The High Councillor nodded and slicing his palm, used the blood to draw the runes. He did it quickly his hands a blur. Complex spells like this were second nature to him. "Granthen, I need you to use your whip to retrieve my crown for me."

"Your wish is my command your highness," Granthen replied. With a crack he sent the whip shooting forward. As it snaked through the air, Lance picked up the white gold crown. He had reclaimed it. It was his. The scythe blade sliced down severing four of Lance's fingers, before wrapping around the crown. With a yank, Granthen pulled it out of the traitor's hand. The crown skipped and skidded along the ground as the bodyguard retrieved his whip.

The runes ignited, flaring to life as the High Councillor finished the incantation. A glowing blue portal swirled with energy. "We are retreating," Evelyn shouted. "Everyone into the portal." Malgorath's hands flared up again and demonic fire started raining down on them.

* * *

Sheathing his swords, Trivlen approached Evelyn. "I will carry King Jace for you my queen," he said, kneeling before her. His muscles bulging, he scooped up and cradled Jace's body and beckoning to Brenan and the guards, led the way to the portal. Kabel walked forward mumbling an incantation. Looping his whip, Granthen carefully unravelled the end and retrieved the crown. Lance's eyes glowed yellow as he approached. His muscles and bone structure were elongating and becoming denser and stronger. His fur was already starting to manifest, growing at an alarming rate.

"I thought I could smell the stench of two traitorous werewolves. Return my crown and bow before me and I may accept you back into the pack," Lance said furiously. "Refuse and I will tear you apart limb by limb and then eat your organs." Unlike Evelyn and Lance, Trivlen and Granthen were restricted like most werewolves and could only transform on a full moon. Granthen stood resolute and defiant. "Well, if you're planning to be king you need to declare Tarath'Doin."

In the werewolf language it meant 'mortal combat'. The rules dictated that once announced, the challenger had to fight the ruler in one-on-one combat to the death. No weapons were allowed, both combatants had to transform and fight as werewolves. The winner became king or queen of the werewolf nation. From memory, it had only happened once in Evelyn's lifetime, when her father successfully defended his rulership as king of the werewolves.

* * *

"I would rather give it to the true heir of Lycanthaw," Granthen replied as he pulled back Evelyn's hood and placed the crown on her head. Lance initially looked confused and then it dawned on him.

"Evelyn," he whispered. "I thought you were dead."

"No traitor. You only wish I was. I have the crown, Wolfsclaw and the moonstone." She pulled out the moonstone dangling from the white gold necklace. She was so used to wearing it, she had forgotten about it until now. Up until remembering her identity, she had merely thought of it as a trinket. It was more than a trinket though, it was her family heirloom and depicted her as a royal, as a Lycanthorne. "I am the true heir of Lycanthaw and I plan on taking back my kingdom. I declare Tarath'Doin," Evelyn said, her voice carrying throughout the throne room.

"So be it. I will kill you now bitch and retake my crown," he screamed, finishing his transformation and bounding towards her on all fours. Shards of wood were torn up by his claws. He pounced high into the air with his mouth open wide and his claws outstretched.

Just as Kabel finished his incantation. The shield shimmered as Lance slammed into it, revealing itself momentarily. He bounced off and landed on all fours again as two balls of demonic fire slammed into the shield. Kabel stood their defiantly, maintaining the spell, the protective dome shaped shield that encircled the group. Another two balls of demonic fire, followed by another four in rapid succession. All of them slammed into the shield and dissipated. Kabel stumbled as the barrage began to take its toll.

Malgorath brought his hands together, focusing his demonic energy. Lance stood up, growling. He was frustrated and angry. "You still need to fight me bitch before you become queen. I'll be waiting for you in Lycanthaw." The demonic energy sizzled, blazed and grew. The demonic fireball was huge. Evelyn nodded, turned around and walked back towards the portal. Everyone had gathered before it, waiting for her and Kabel. Malgorath released it, hurtling it spinning towards the group. The demonic fire hit the shield with the force of a battering ram, shattering it and propelling through.

The force of the impact had deflected it slightly, sending the blazing demonic energy hurtling above their heads. It slammed into the portal. The blue energy changed colour as it absorbed the demonic fire. "What happened?" Bear asked, concerned.

"The demonic energy has possibly changed the destination of the portal," the High Councillor replied.

"Everybody! Enter the portal," Evelyn ordered. "Any place is better than here." Brenan nodded and led the way, with his twin swords drawn. Everyone entered one after the other.

The entire shield dissipated and Kabel collapsed exhausted. "High Councillor, Varyn. We need to go now." The three of them were the only one's remaining. Kabel stood up on wobbly legs and began to stumble towards the portal. The next fireball hit Kabel in the back, engulfing him in demonic fire. His scream echoed throughout the throne room. There was nothing they could do. Evelyn and the High Councillor entered the portal.

They were in an underground cavern on the outskirts of an ancient city. The outer wall had cracked and crumbled, leaving gaping holes entering the city. A multitude of buildings loomed before them, but one stood out. A small castle emitting an eerie, green glow. "Where in the seven hells are we?" Beast asked, looking around. The blue light of the portal cast an eerie light, illuminating a portion of the cavern. Then as Darla and the High Councillor came through, it dissipated completely. They were cast into complete darkness. A growl sounded, far off in the distance.

"What was that?" Bear asked, alarmed. The High Councillor mumbled softly and a glowing white orb appeared, hovering above his hand. The growl sounded again, closer this time. Another five echoed in response. "You have got to be fucking kidding me," Darla cursed. She recognised the growls. She had encountered the creatures before. They were dangerous and deadly.

* * *

Bear swung his sword about, looking out into the darkness. "Do you mind telling us?" Beast asked, sarcastically. "You obviously know where we are."

"I don't know where we are," Darla replied. "I know that growl though. There are ghouls nearby and I'm assuming that this ancient city is their home."

I would like to give a heartfelt thank you to my family and friends. Without their love and support, this endeavour would not have eventuated. Janet-Marie, you have encouraged me, supported me and been a shining star, guiding and helping me throughout this venture. My editor, Emmanuel thank you for all your hard work, guidance and feedback that you provided. My cover designer Thea, you're awesome, you never cease to amaze me with the magical, artistic talent that you provide. Your covers help to bring my manuscript to life. Thank you, Rachel Sanderson for being both a fan and a colleague. You have inspired and kept me motivated. I am honoured and privileged to have a friend like you.

My cats also should get a special mention for all the snuggle breaks that they provided me (even if it was just meowing for attention half the time). Bands like Shinedown, Godsmack, Def Leppard, Pop Evil, Falling In Reverse and Papa Roach (just to name a few) also deserve a mention for their awesome music, which I spent countless hours listening to and getting inspiration while I write my novels. Lastly, I would like to thank my fans. I hope you enjoyed reading the novel as much as I enjoyed writing it!

Born and raised in Perth, Western Australia, this is Steven Wombell's second fantasy novel - *The Werewolf Assassin*, which is Book 2 to his Divinity Stone series. Holding a Bachelor of Education, he is a passionate primary school teacher, who loves inspiring and passing on his knowledge to his students (especially when it comes to teaching narrative writing).

An enthusiastic lover of both fantasy and science-fiction, he always enjoyed writing this kind of material. Passionate about these genres he often gets inspiration through novels, movies, music and computer games. His other interests include cooking, Lego, cycling, travelling and volleyball. When he isn't writing or partaking in one of his interests, he can be found catching up with friends and family. They are extremely important to him, because without their love and support this novel would have never eventuated.